between shades of gray

of gray

THE GRAPHIC NOVEL

PHILOMEL BOOKS
An imprint of Penguin Random House LLC, New York

First published in the United States of America by Philomel Books,
an imprint of Penguin Random House LLC, 2021

Adapted from *Between Shades of Gray* by Ruta Sepetys, published by Philomel Books in 2011

Library of Congress Cataloging-in-Publication Data is available.

Manufactured in Canada

Hardcover ISBN 9780593204160
1 3 5 7 9 10 8 6 4 2

Paperback ISBN 9780593404850
1 3 5 7 9 10 8 6 4 2

TC

Graphic novel edited by Liza Kaplan. Original novel edited by Tamra Tuller.
Design by Ellice M. Lee.
Text set in CCMEANWHILE, CCYadaYadaYada, CCExtraExtra, Bell MT Pro

#1 *NEW YORK TIMES* BESTSELLING AUTHOR

RUTA SEPETYS

between shades of gray

THE GRAPHIC NOVEL

ADAPTED BY Andrew Donkin
ART BY Dave Kopka

COLOR BY Brann Livesay
LETTERING BY Chris Dickey

PHILOMEL

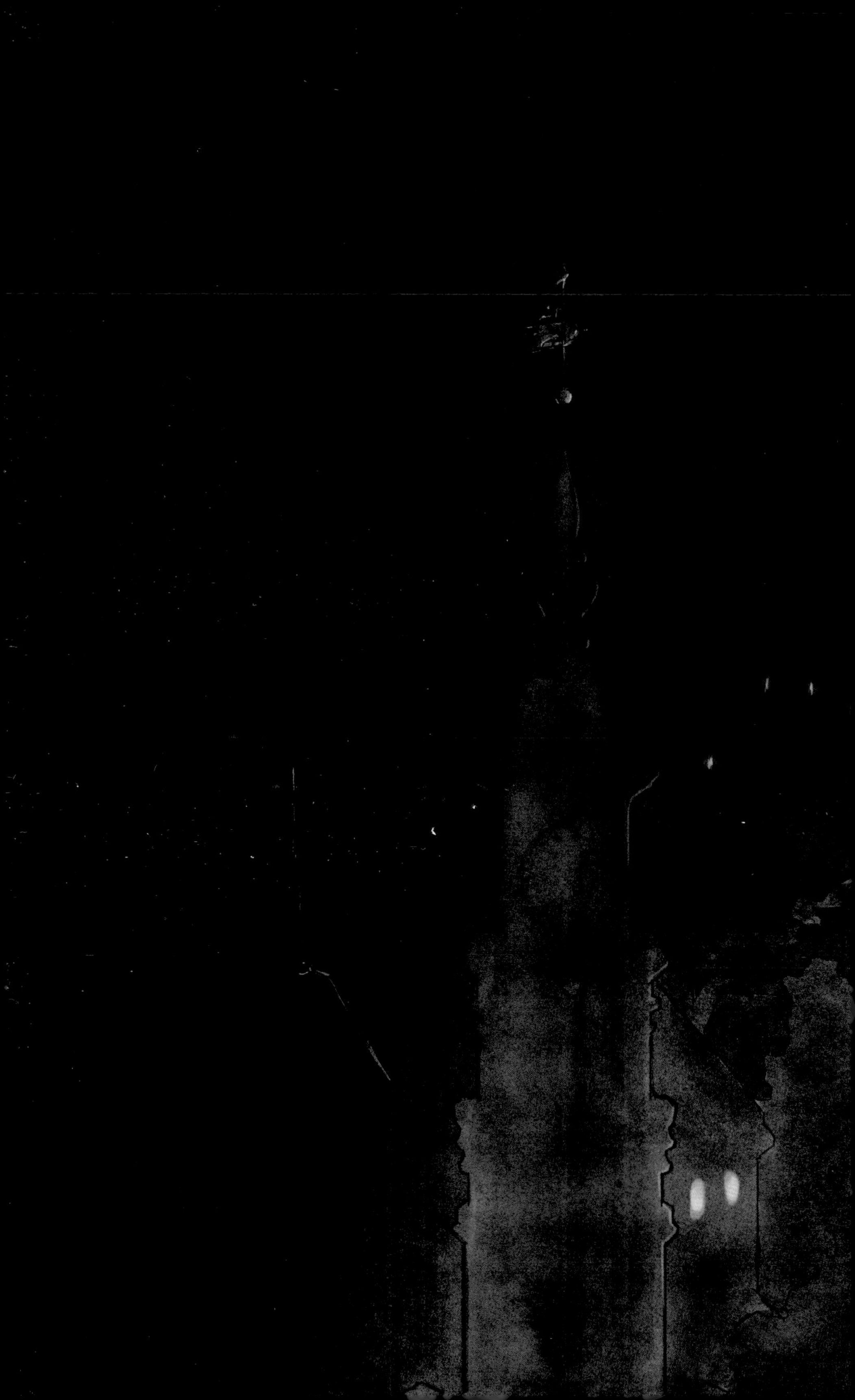

Thieves & Prostitutes

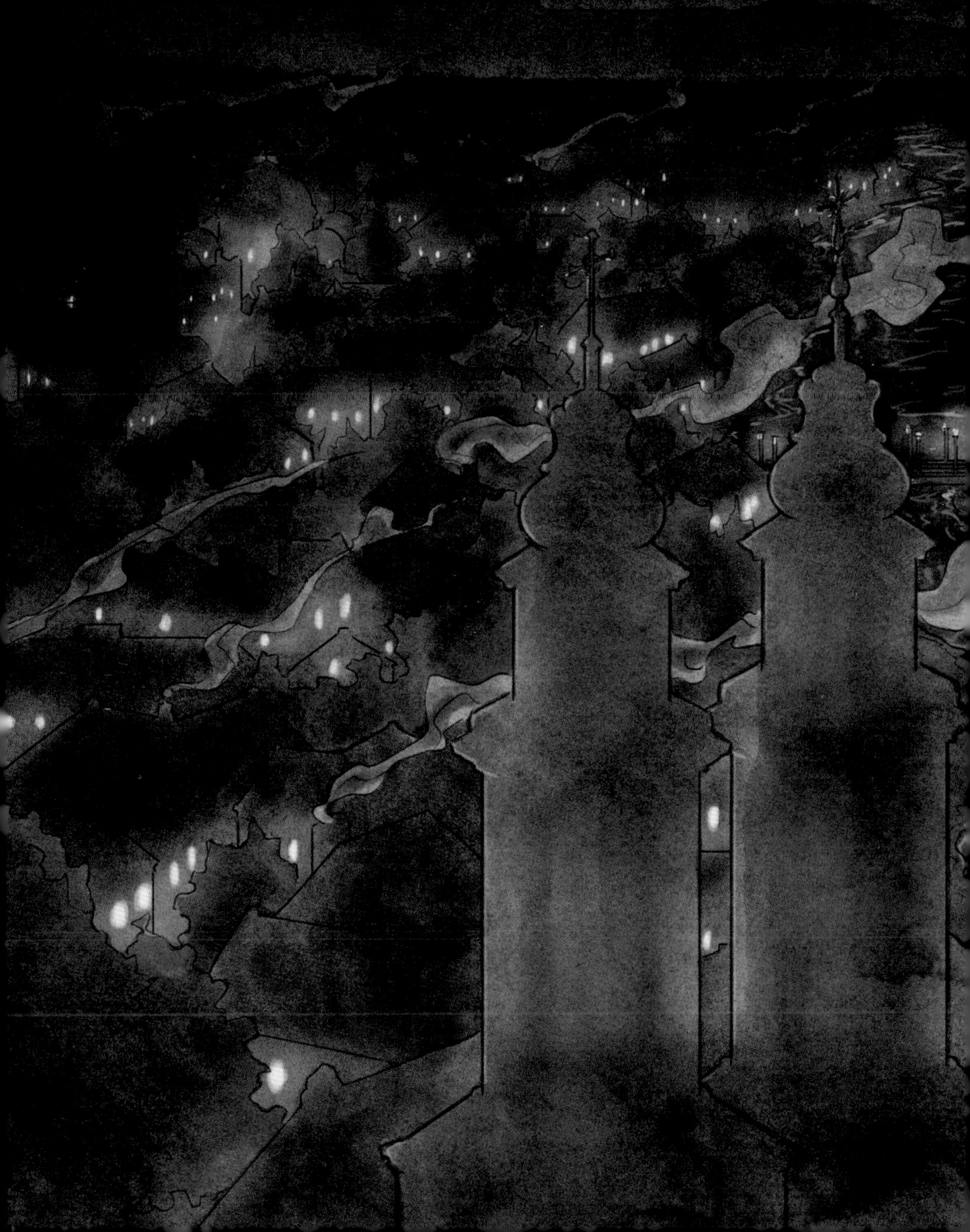

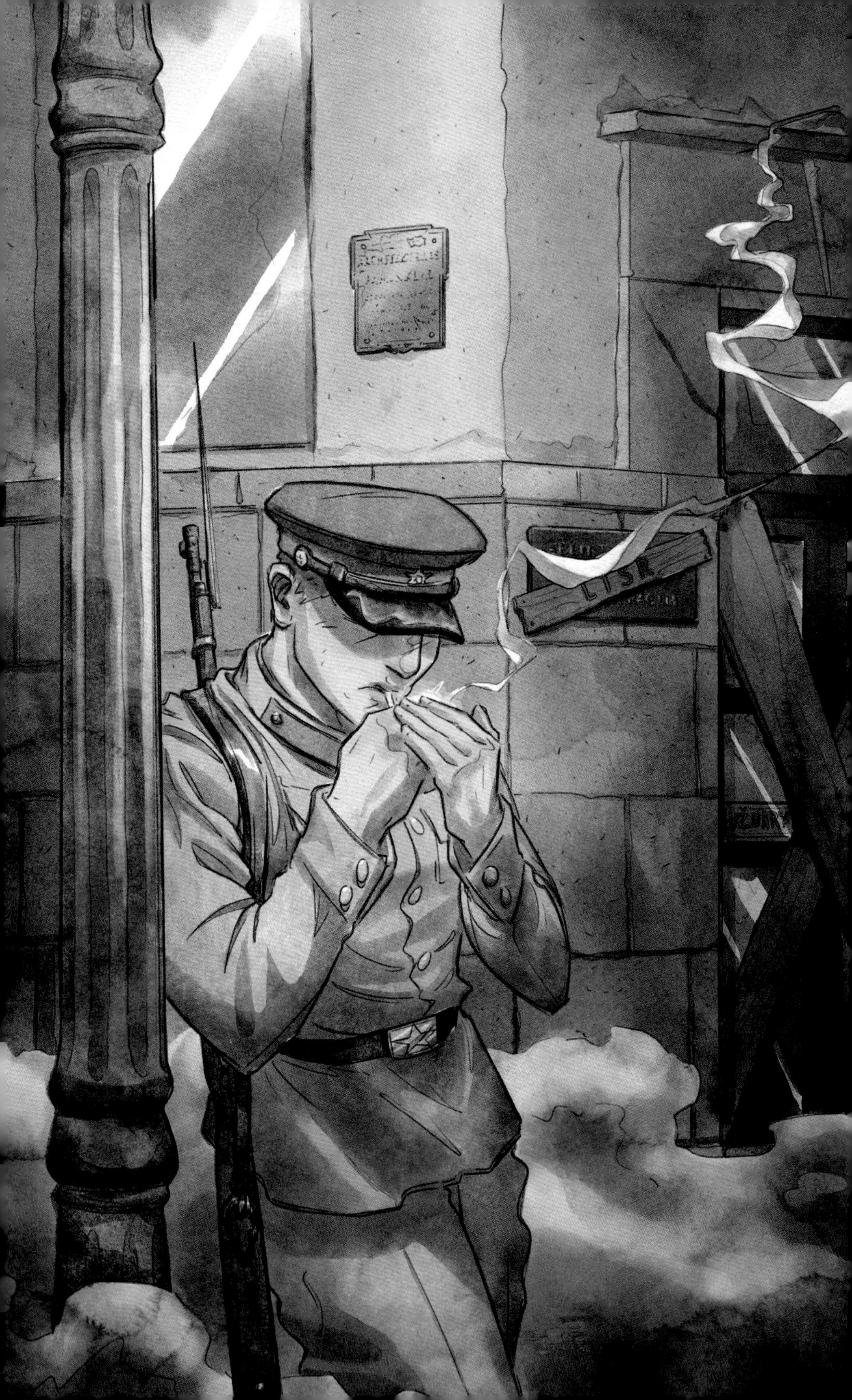

LISR

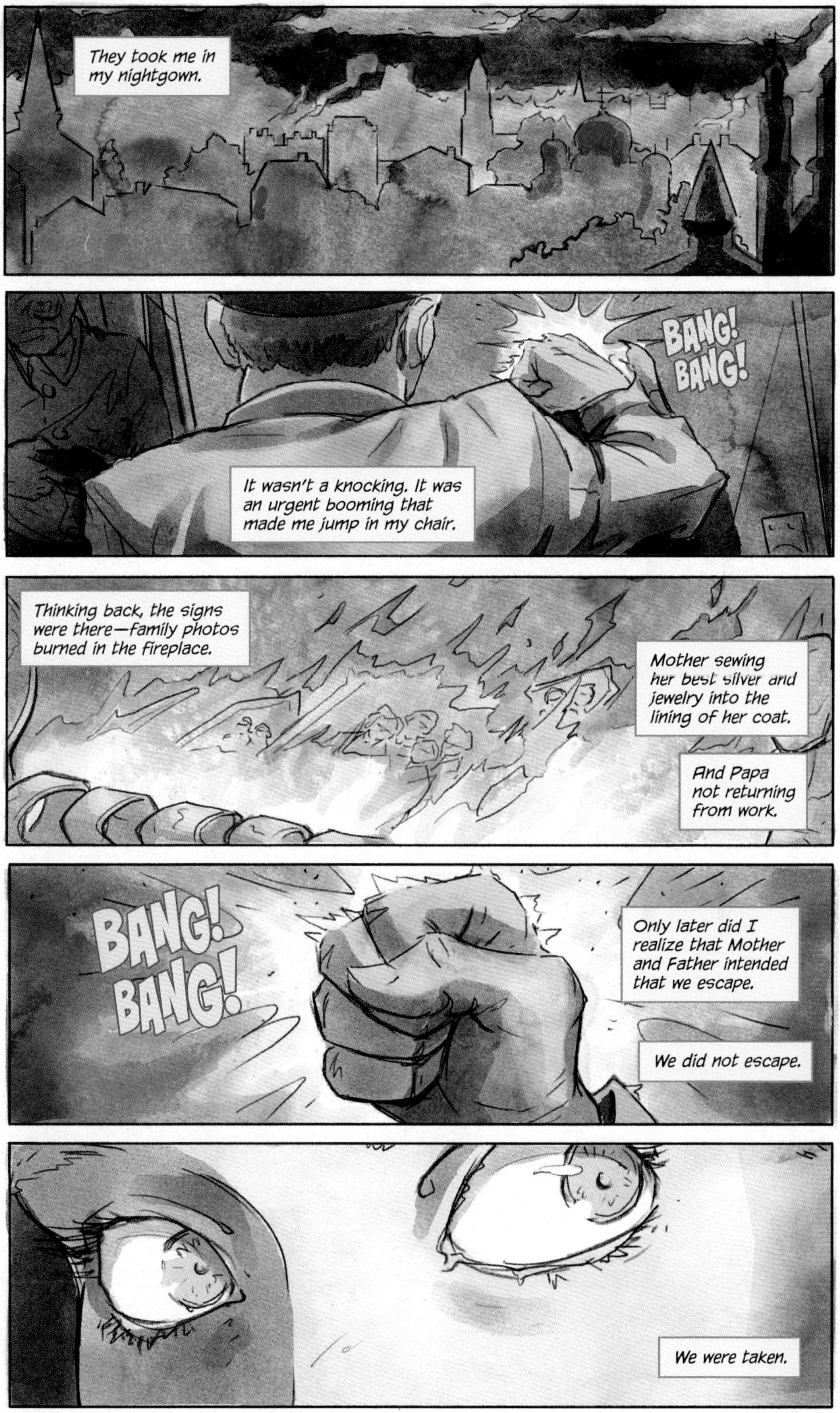
They took me in my nightgown.
BANG! BANG!
It wasn't a knocking. It was an urgent booming that made me jump in my chair.
Thinking back, the signs were there—family photos burned in the fireplace.
Mother sewing her best silver and jewelry into the lining of her coat.
And Papa not returning from work.
BANG! BANG!
Only later did I realize that Mother and Father intended that we escape.
We did not escape.
We were taken.

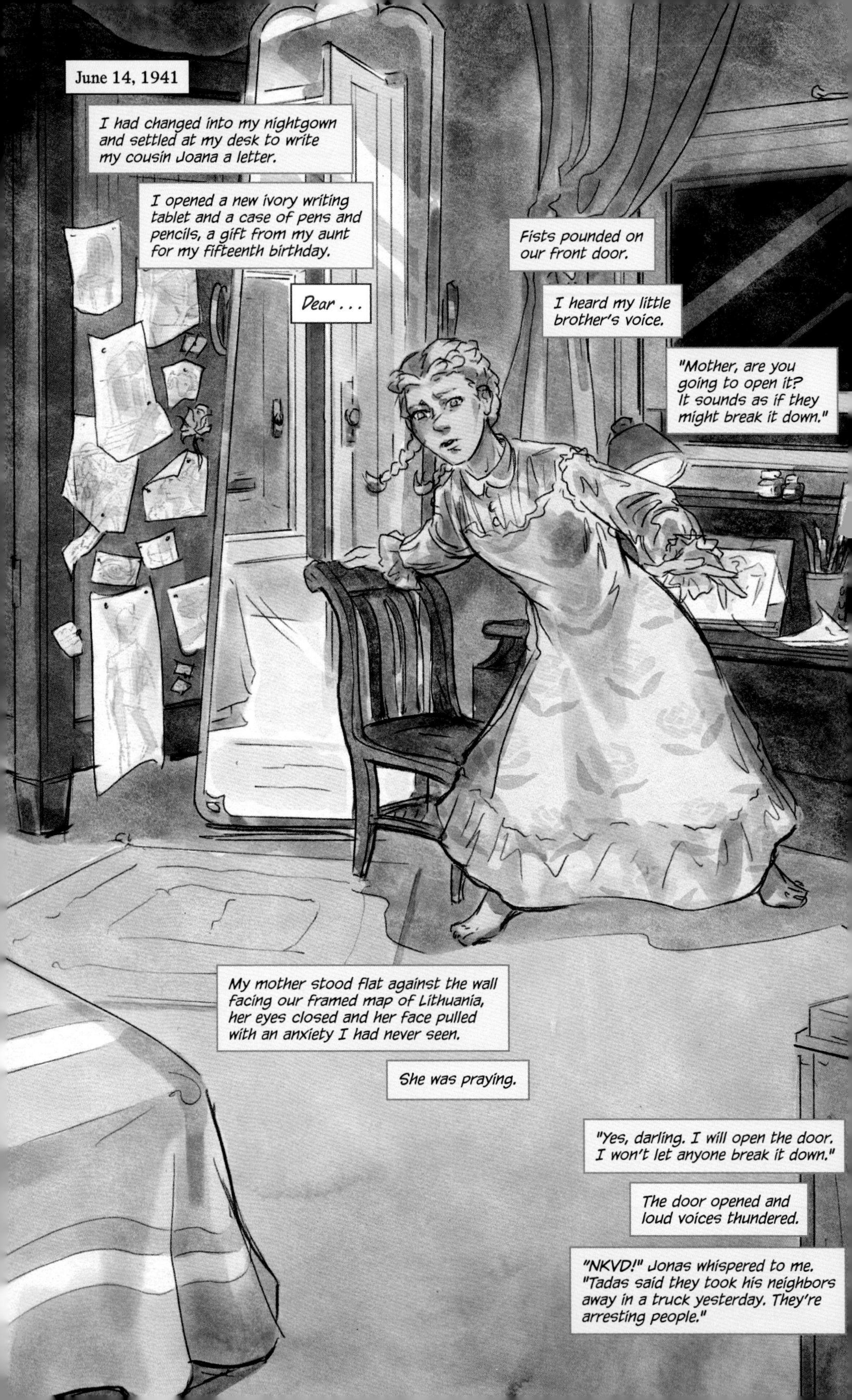
June 14, 1941
I had changed into my nightgown and settled at my desk to write my cousin Joana a letter.
I opened a new ivory writing tablet and a case of pens and pencils, a gift from my aunt for my fifteenth birthday.
Dear . . .
Fists pounded on our front door.
I heard my little brother's voice.
"Mother, are you going to open it? It sounds as if they might break it down."
My mother stood flat against the wall facing our framed map of Lithuania, her eyes closed and her face pulled with an anxiety I had never seen.
She was praying.
"Yes, darling. I will open the door. I won't let anyone break it down."
The door opened and loud voices thundered.
"NKVD!" Jonas whispered to me. "Tadas said they took his neighbors away in a truck yesterday. They're arresting people."

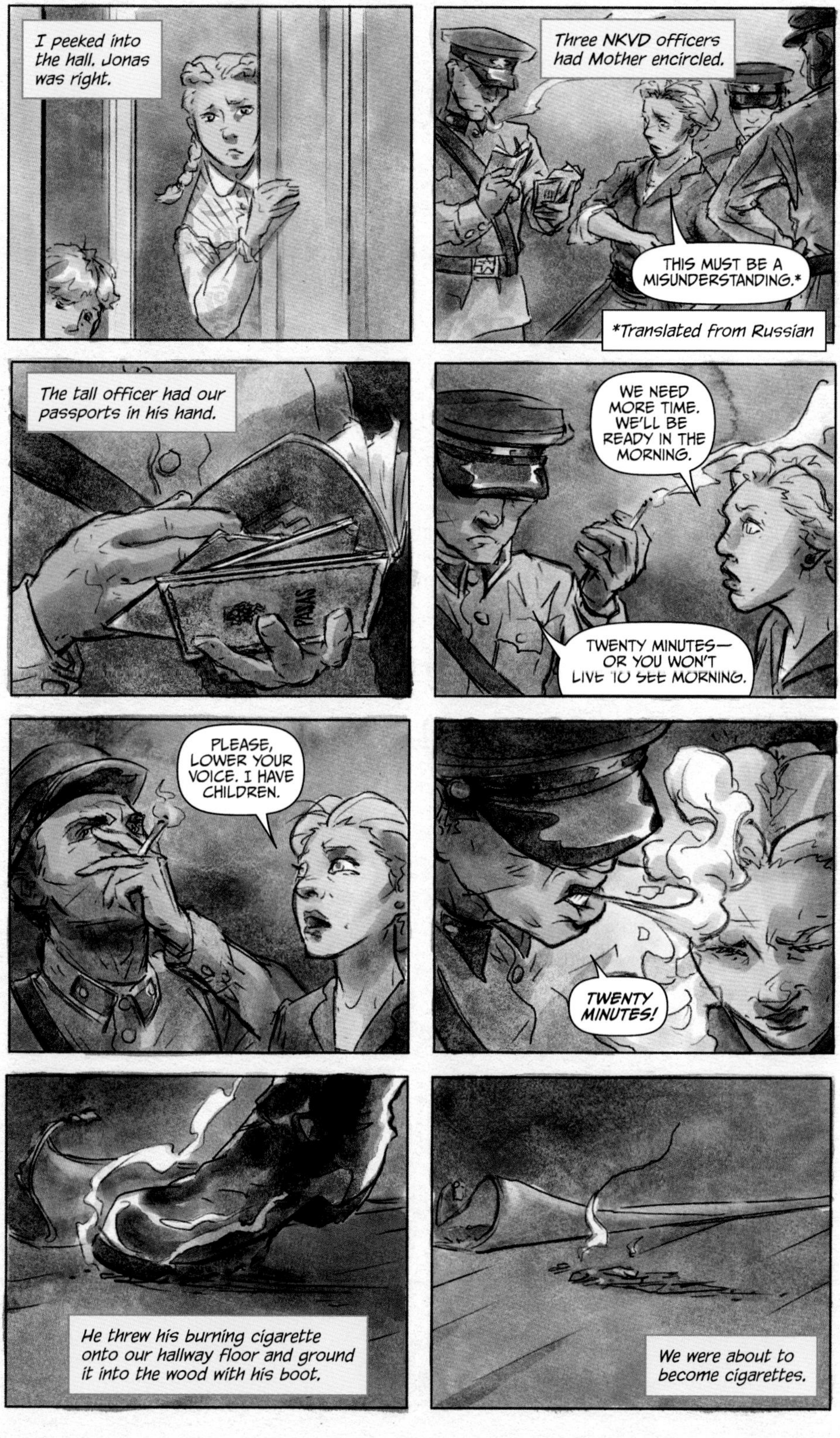
I peeked into the hall. Jonas was right.
Three NKVD officers had Mother encircled.
THIS MUST BE A MISUNDERSTANDING.*
*Translated from Russian
The tall officer had our passports in his hand.
PASAS
WE NEED MORE TIME. WE'LL BE READY IN THE MORNING.
TWENTY MINUTES— OR YOU WON'T LIVE TO SEE MORNING.
PLEASE, LOWER YOUR VOICE. I HAVE CHILDREN.
TWENTY MINUTES!
He threw his burning cigarette onto our hallway floor and ground it into the wood with his boot.
We were about to become cigarettes.

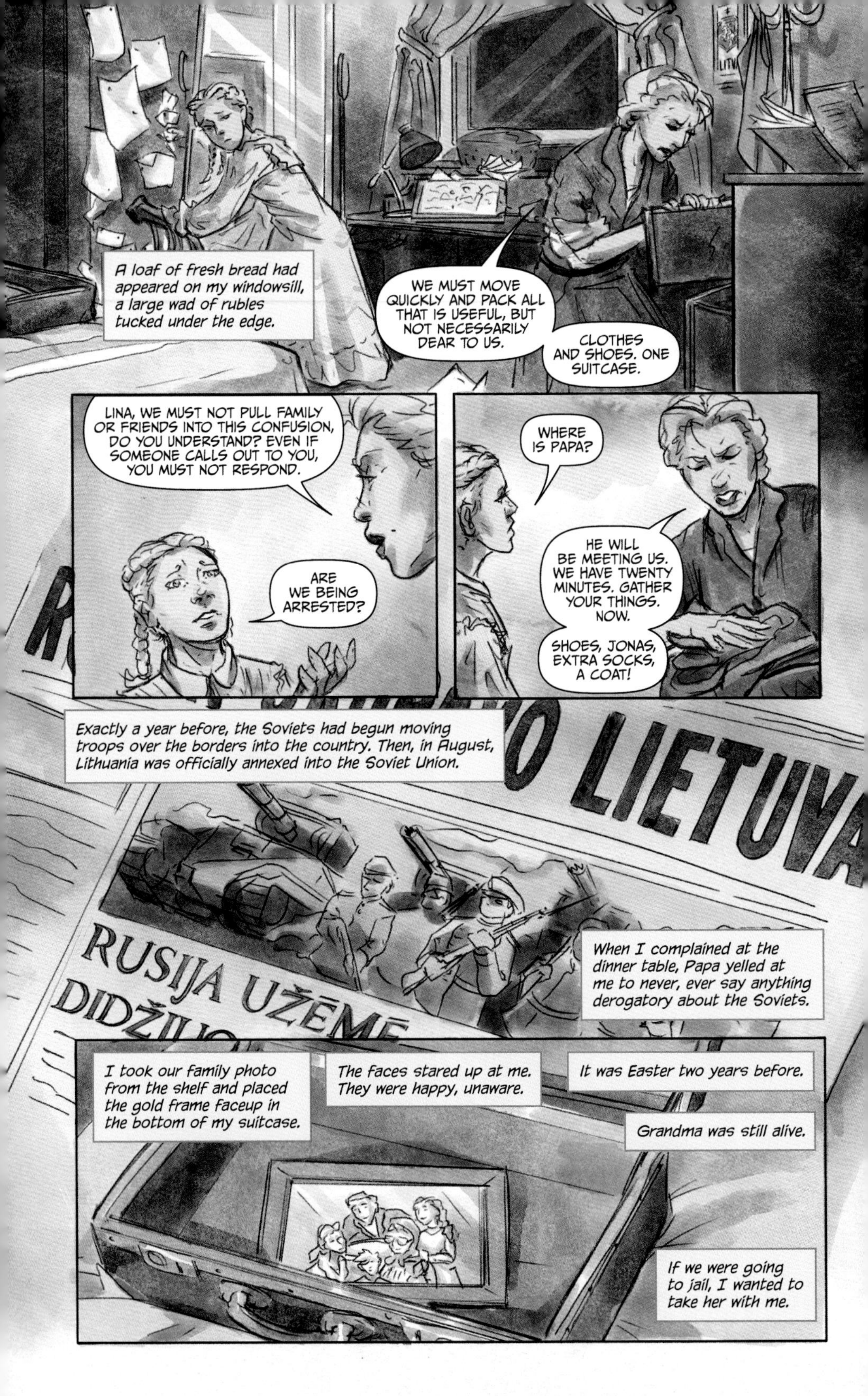
A loaf of fresh bread had appeared on my windowsill, a large wad of rubles tucked under the edge.
WE MUST MOVE QUICKLY AND PACK ALL THAT IS USEFUL, BUT NOT NECESSARILY DEAR TO US.
CLOTHES AND SHOES. ONE SUITCASE.
LINA, WE MUST NOT PULL FAMILY OR FRIENDS INTO THIS CONFUSION, DO YOU UNDERSTAND? EVEN IF SOMEONE CALLS OUT TO YOU, YOU MUST NOT RESPOND.
ARE WE BEING ARRESTED?
WHERE IS PAPA?
HE WILL BE MEETING US. WE HAVE TWENTY MINUTES. GATHER YOUR THINGS. NOW.
SHOES, JONAS, EXTRA SOCKS, A COAT!
Exactly a year before, the Soviets had begun moving troops over the borders into the country. Then, in August, Lithuania was officially annexed into the Soviet Union.
LIETUVA
RUSIJA UŽEME
When I complained at the dinner table, Papa yelled at me to never, ever say anything derogatory about the Soviets.
I took our family photo from the shelf and placed the gold frame faceup in the bottom of my suitcase.
The faces stared up at me. They were happy, unaware.
It was Easter two years before.
Grandma was still alive.
If we were going to jail, I wanted to take her with me.

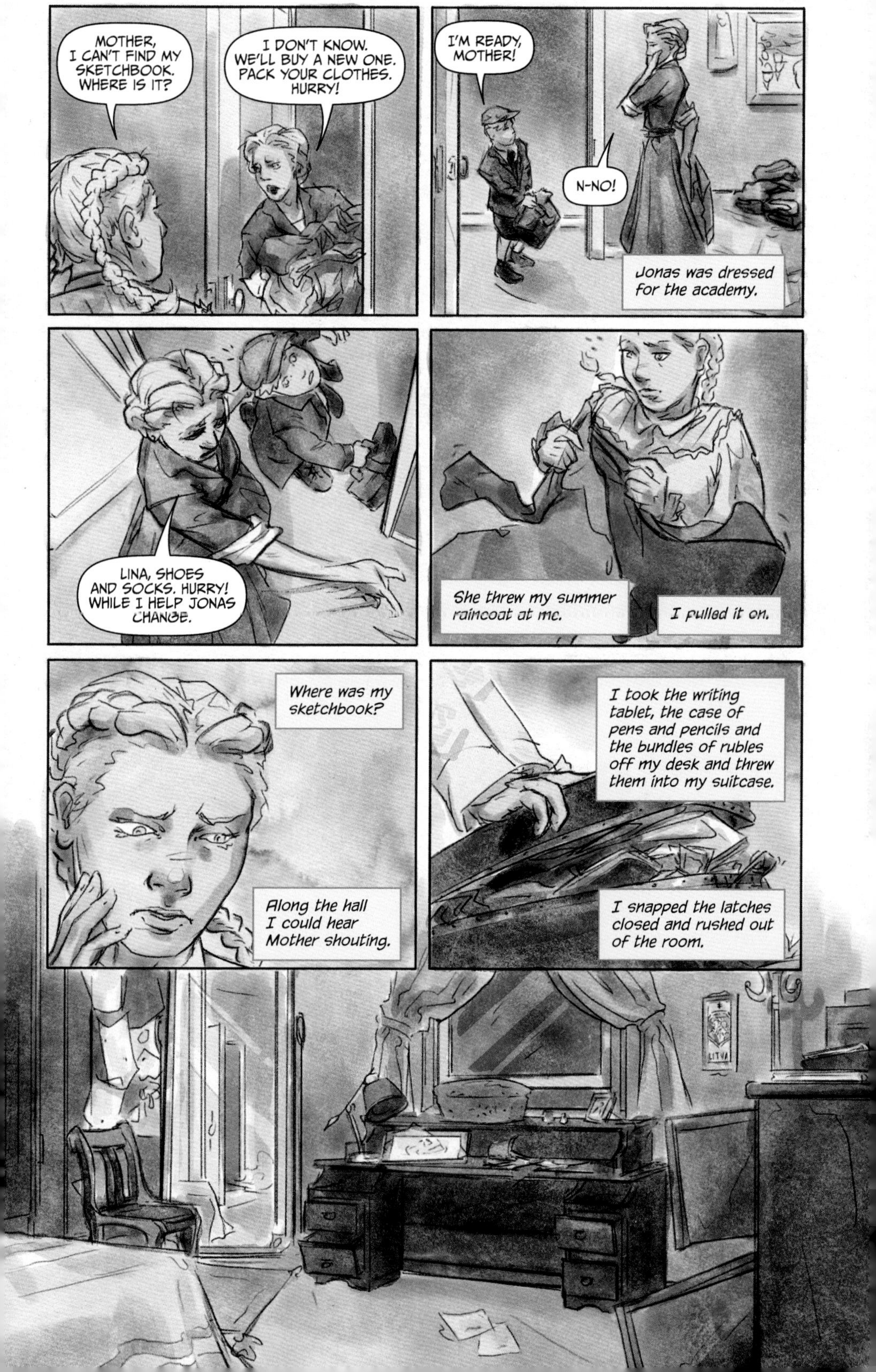
MOTHER, I CAN'T FIND MY SKETCHBOOK. WHERE IS IT?
I DON'T KNOW. WE'LL BUY A NEW ONE. PACK YOUR CLOTHES. HURRY!
I'M READY, MOTHER!
N-NO!
Jonas was dressed for the academy.
LINA, SHOES AND SOCKS. HURRY! WHILE I HELP JONAS CHANGE.
She threw my summer raincoat at me.
I pulled it on.
Where was my sketchbook?
Along the hall I could hear Mother shouting.
I took the writing tablet, the case of pens and pencils and the bundles of rubles off my desk and threw them into my suitcase.
I snapped the latches closed and rushed out of the room.
LITVA

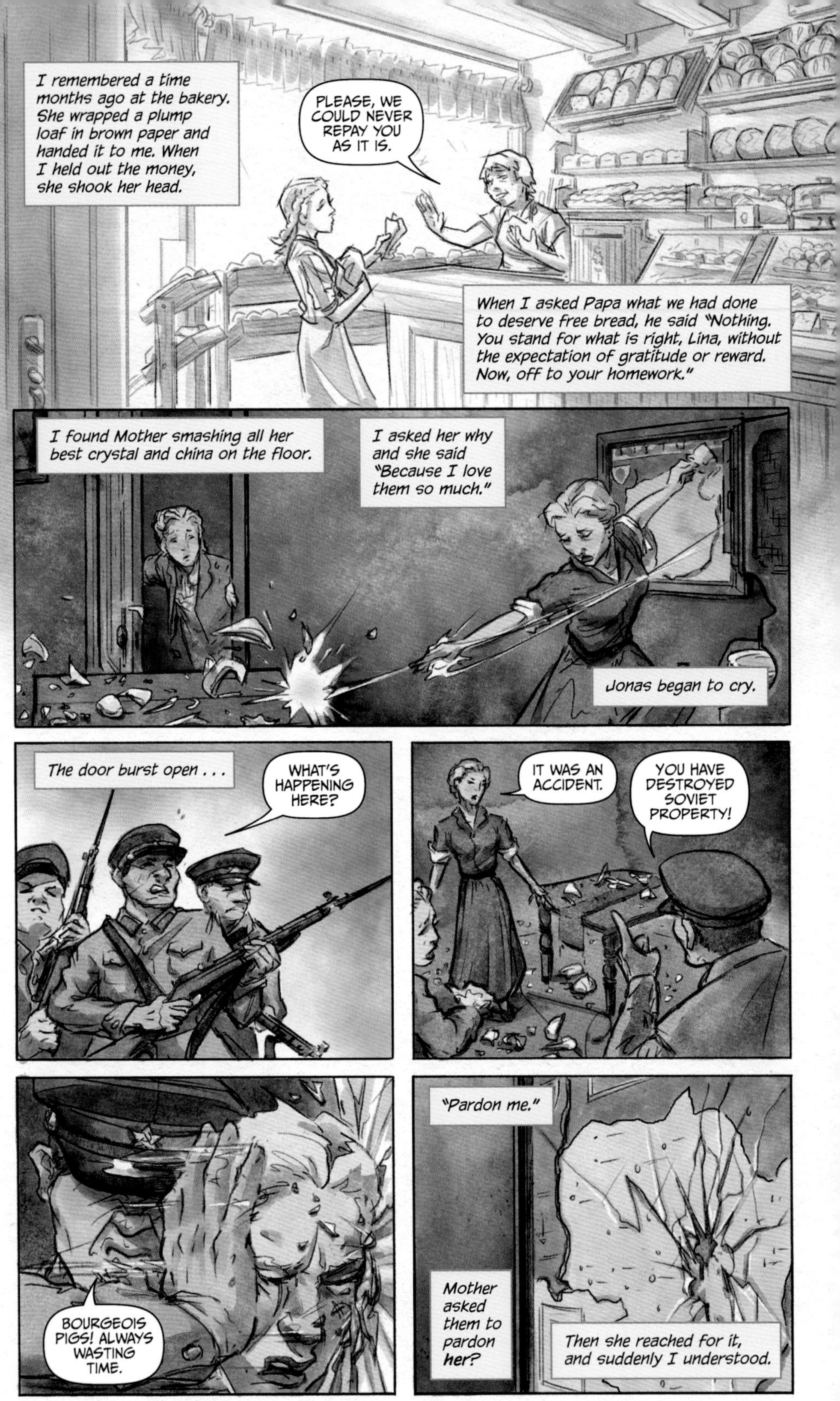
I remembered a time months ago at the bakery. She wrapped a plump loaf in brown paper and handed it to me. When I held out the money, she shook her head.
PLEASE, WE COULD NEVER REPAY YOU AS IT IS.
When I asked Papa what we had done to deserve free bread, he said "Nothing. You stand for what is right, Lina, without the expectation of gratitude or reward. Now, off to your homework."
I found Mother smashing all her best crystal and china on the floor.
I asked her why and she said "Because I love them so much."
Jonas began to cry.
The door burst open . . .
WHAT'S HAPPENING HERE?
IT WAS AN ACCIDENT.
YOU HAVE DESTROYED SOVIET PROPERTY!
BOURGEOIS PIGS! ALWAYS WASTING TIME.
"Pardon me."
Mother asked them to pardon **her**?
Then she reached for it, and suddenly I understood.

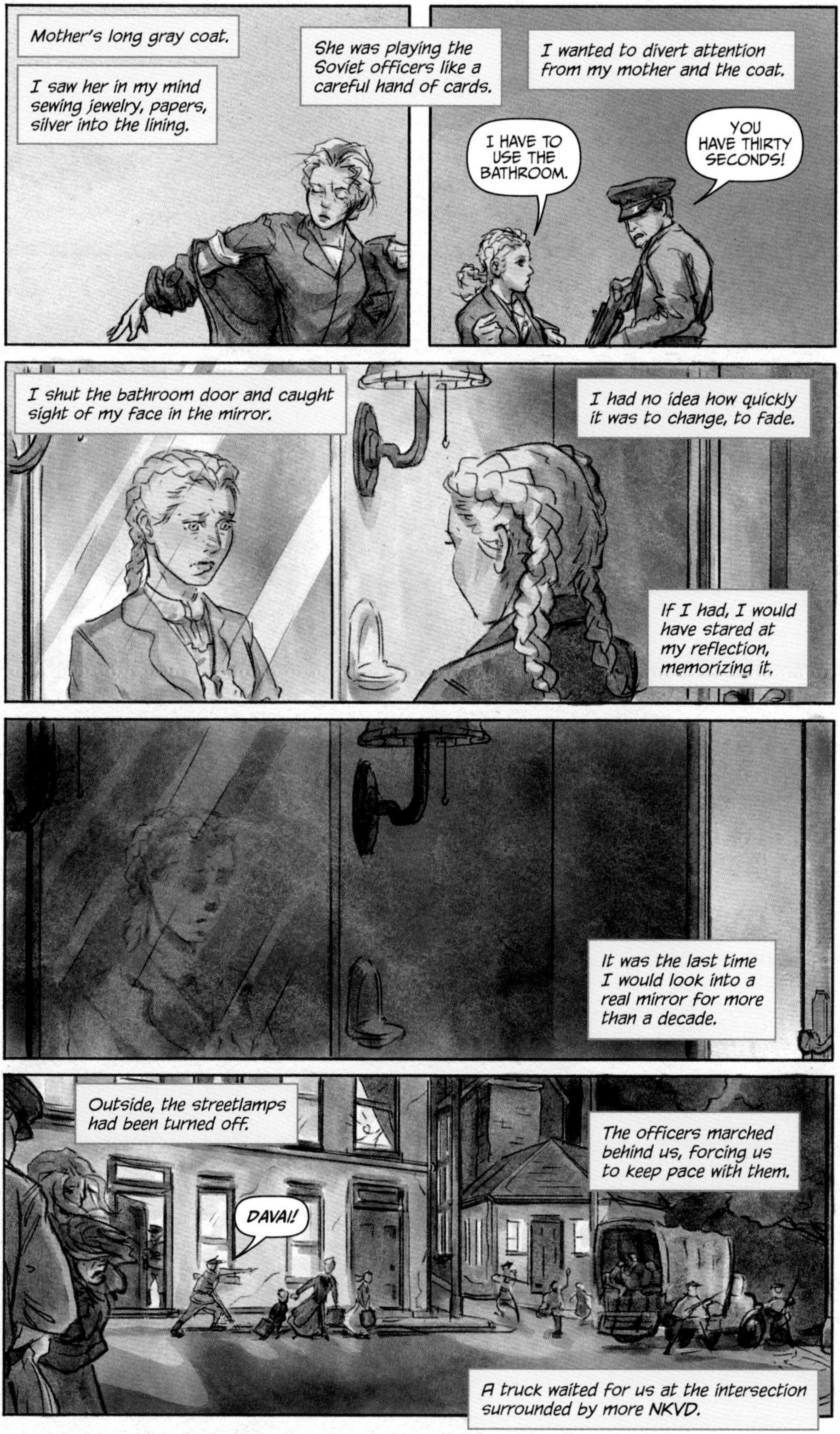
Mother's long gray coat.
I saw her in my mind sewing jewelry, papers, silver into the lining.
She was playing the Soviet officers like a careful hand of cards.
I wanted to divert attention from my mother and the coat.
I HAVE TO USE THE BATHROOM.
YOU HAVE THIRTY SECONDS!
I shut the bathroom door and caught sight of my face in the mirror.
I had no idea how quickly it was to change, to fade.
If I had, I would have stared at my reflection, memorizing it.
It was the last time I would look into a real mirror for more than a decade.
Outside, the streetlamps had been turned off.
The officers marched behind us, forcing us to keep pace with them.
DAVAI!
A truck waited for us at the intersection surrounded by more NKVD.

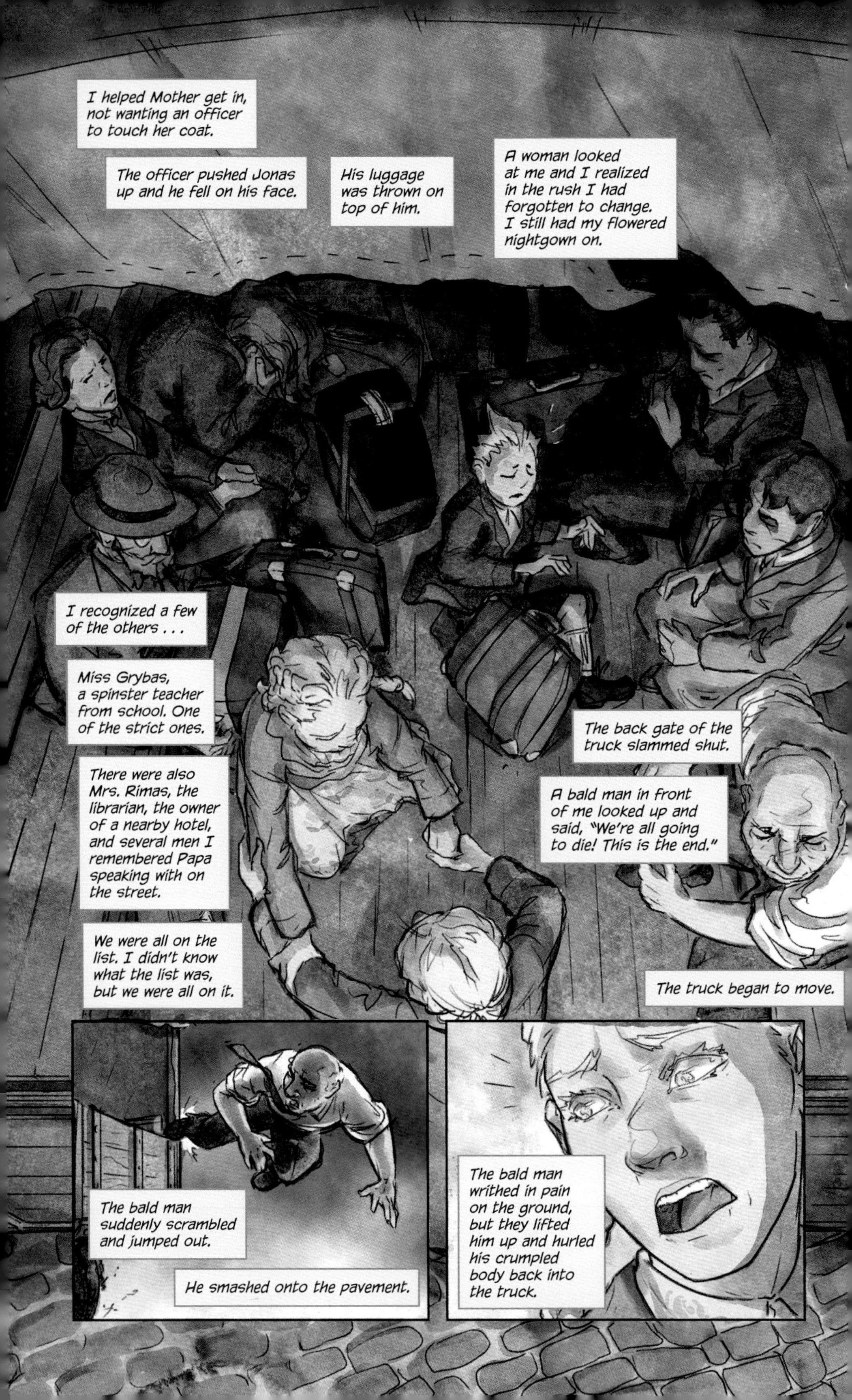
I helped Mother get in, not wanting an officer to touch her coat.
The officer pushed Jonas up and he fell on his face.
His luggage was thrown on top of him.
A woman looked at me and I realized in the rush I had forgotten to change. I still had my flowered nightgown on.
I recognized a few of the others . . .
Miss Grybas, a spinster teacher from school. One of the strict ones.
There were also Mrs. Rimas, the librarian, the owner of a nearby hotel, and several men I remembered Papa speaking with on the street.
We were all on the list. I didn't know what the list was, but we were all on it.
The back gate of the truck slammed shut.
A bald man in front of me looked up and said, "We're all going to die! This is the end."
The truck began to move.
The bald man suddenly scrambled and jumped out.
He smashed onto the pavement.
The bald man writhed in pain on the ground, but they lifted him up and hurled his crumpled body back into the truck.

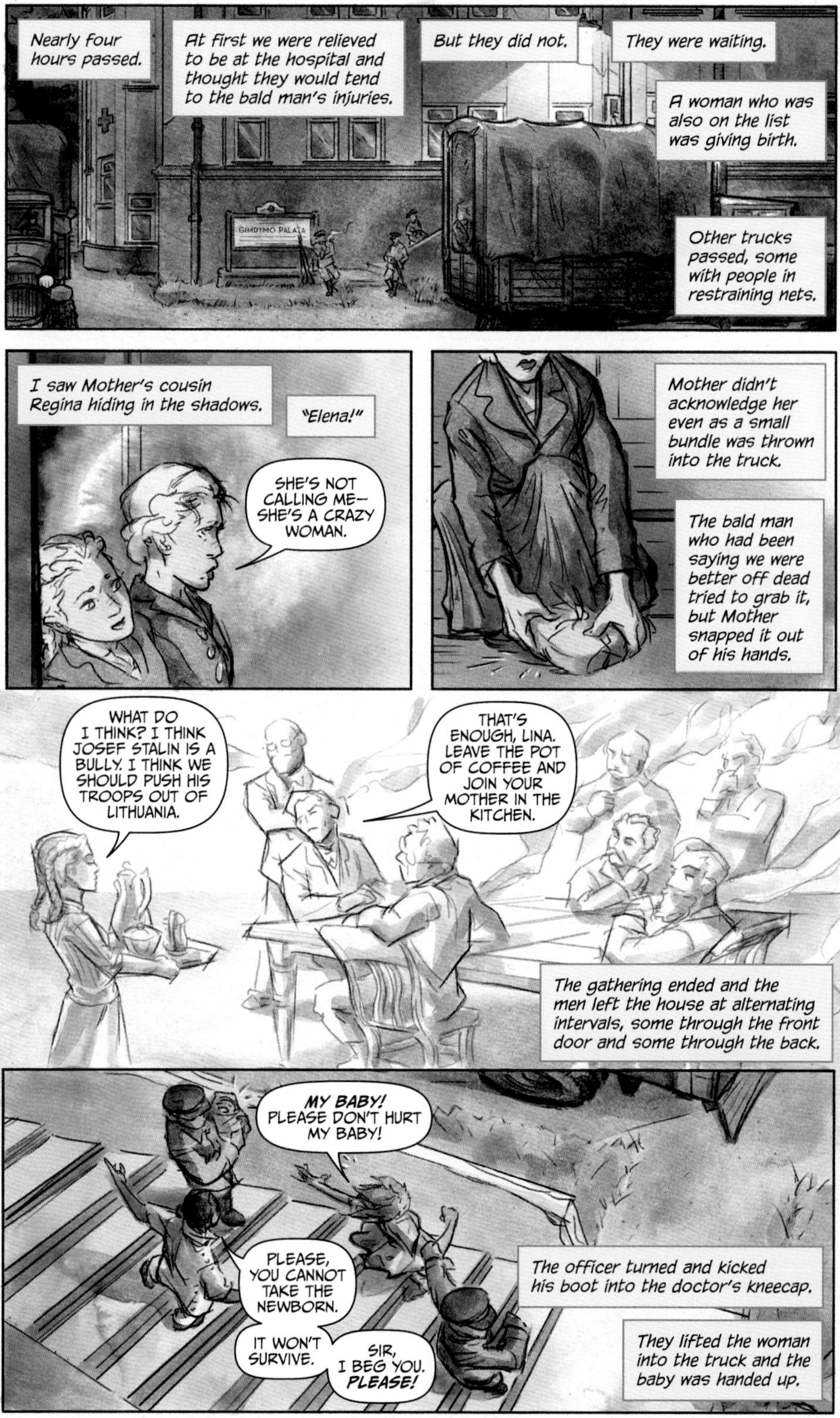
Nearly four hours passed.
At first we were relieved to be at the hospital and thought they would tend to the bald man's injuries.
But they did not.
They were waiting.
A woman who was also on the list was giving birth.
GIMDYMO PALATA
Other trucks passed, some with people in restraining nets.
I saw Mother's cousin Regina hiding in the shadows.
"Elena!"
SHE'S NOT CALLING ME— SHE'S A CRAZY WOMAN.
Mother didn't acknowledge her even as a small bundle was thrown into the truck.
The bald man who had been saying we were better off dead tried to grab it, but Mother snapped it out of his hands.
WHAT DO I THINK? I THINK JOSEF STALIN IS A BULLY. I THINK WE SHOULD PUSH HIS TROOPS OUT OF LITHUANIA.
THAT'S ENOUGH, LINA. LEAVE THE POT OF COFFEE AND JOIN YOUR MOTHER IN THE KITCHEN.
The gathering ended and the men left the house at alternating intervals, some through the front door and some through the back.
MY BABY! PLEASE DON'T HURT MY BABY!
PLEASE, YOU CANNOT TAKE THE NEWBORN.
IT WON'T SURVIVE.
SIR, I BEG YOU. PLEASE!
The officer turned and kicked his boot into the doctor's kneecap.
They lifted the woman into the truck and the baby was handed up.

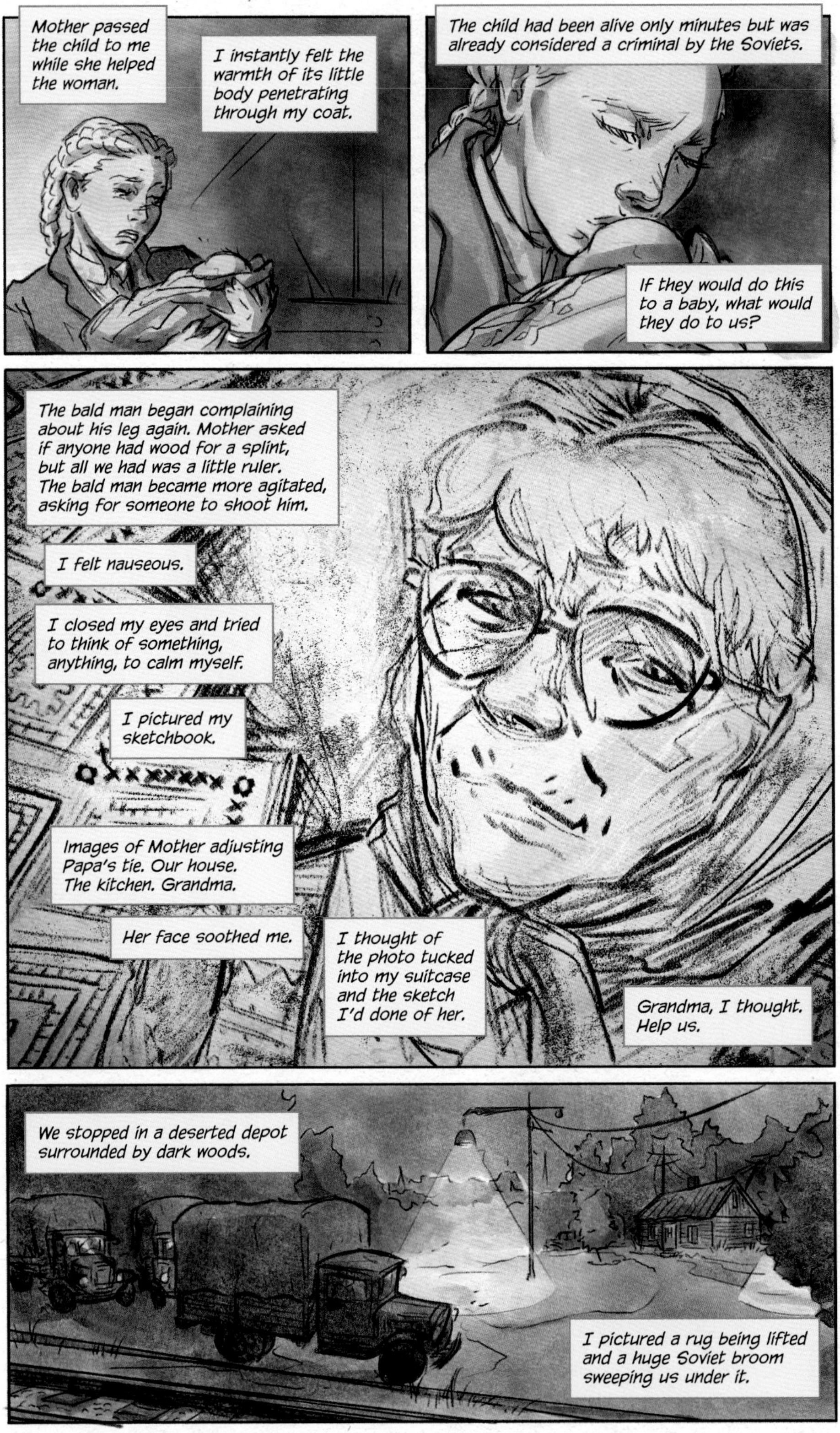
Mother passed the child to me while she helped the woman.
I instantly felt the warmth of its little body penetrating through my coat.
The child had been alive only minutes but was already considered a criminal by the Soviets.
If they would do this to a baby, what would they do to us?
The bald man began complaining about his leg again. Mother asked if anyone had wood for a splint, but all we had was a little ruler. The bald man became more agitated, asking for someone to shoot him.
I felt nauseous.
I closed my eyes and tried to think of something, anything, to calm myself.
I pictured my sketchbook.
Images of Mother adjusting Papa's tie. Our house. The kitchen. Grandma.
Her face soothed me.
I thought of the photo tucked into my suitcase and the sketch I'd done of her.
Grandma, I thought. Help us.
We stopped in a deserted depot surrounded by dark woods.
I pictured a rug being lifted and a huge Soviet broom sweeping us under it.

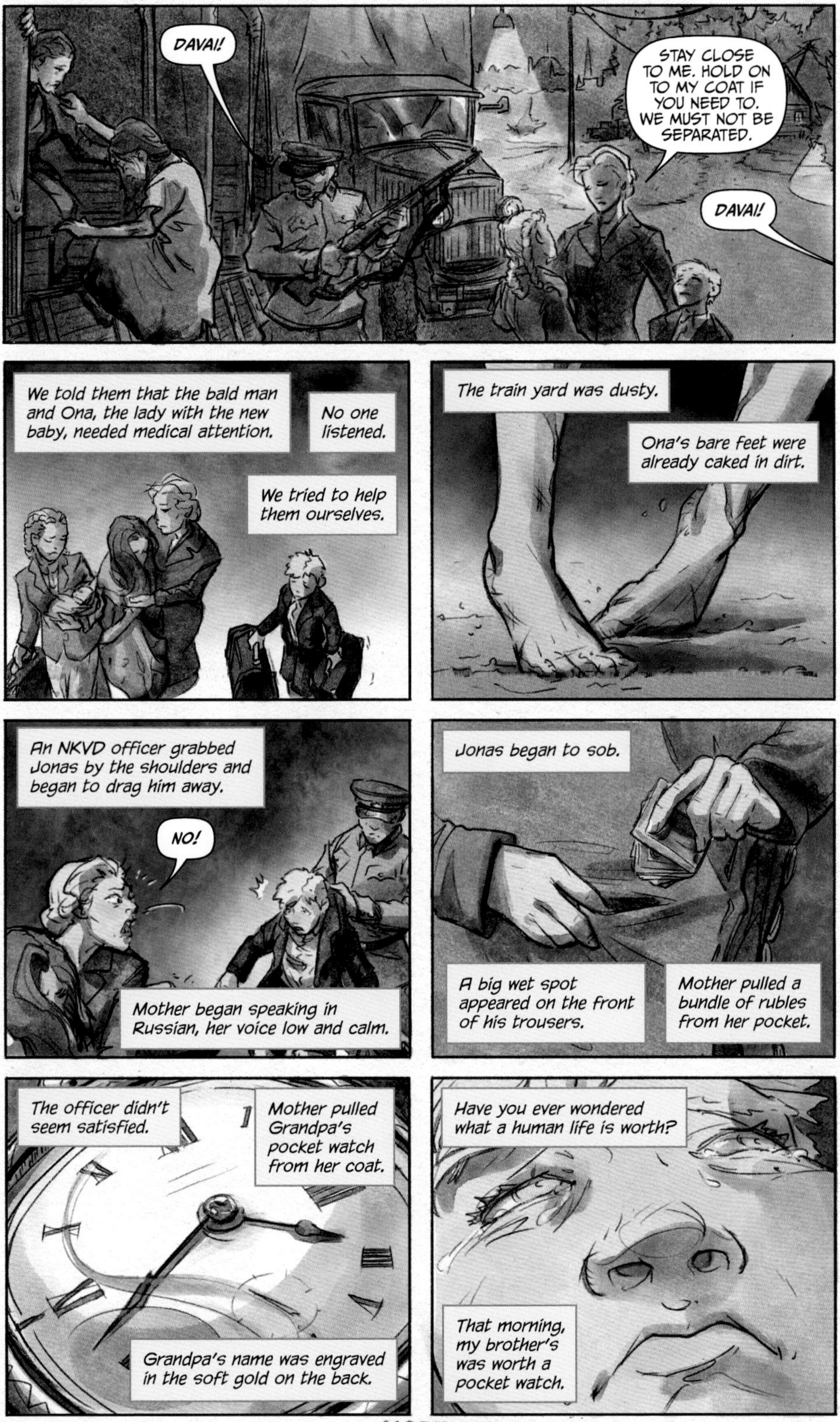
DAVAI!
STAY CLOSE TO ME. HOLD ON TO MY COAT IF YOU NEED TO. WE MUST NOT BE SEPARATED.
DAVAI!
We told them that the bald man and Ona, the lady with the new baby, needed medical attention.
No one listened.
We tried to help them ourselves.
The train yard was dusty.
Ona's bare feet were already caked in dirt.
An NKVD officer grabbed Jonas by the shoulders and began to drag him away.
NO!
Mother began speaking in Russian, her voice low and calm.
Jonas began to sob.
A big wet spot appeared on the front of his trousers.
Mother pulled a bundle of rubles from her pocket.
The officer didn't seem satisfied.
Mother pulled Grandpa's pocket watch from her coat.
Grandpa's name was engraved in the soft gold on the back.
Have you ever wondered what a human life is worth?
That morning, my brother's was worth a pocket watch.

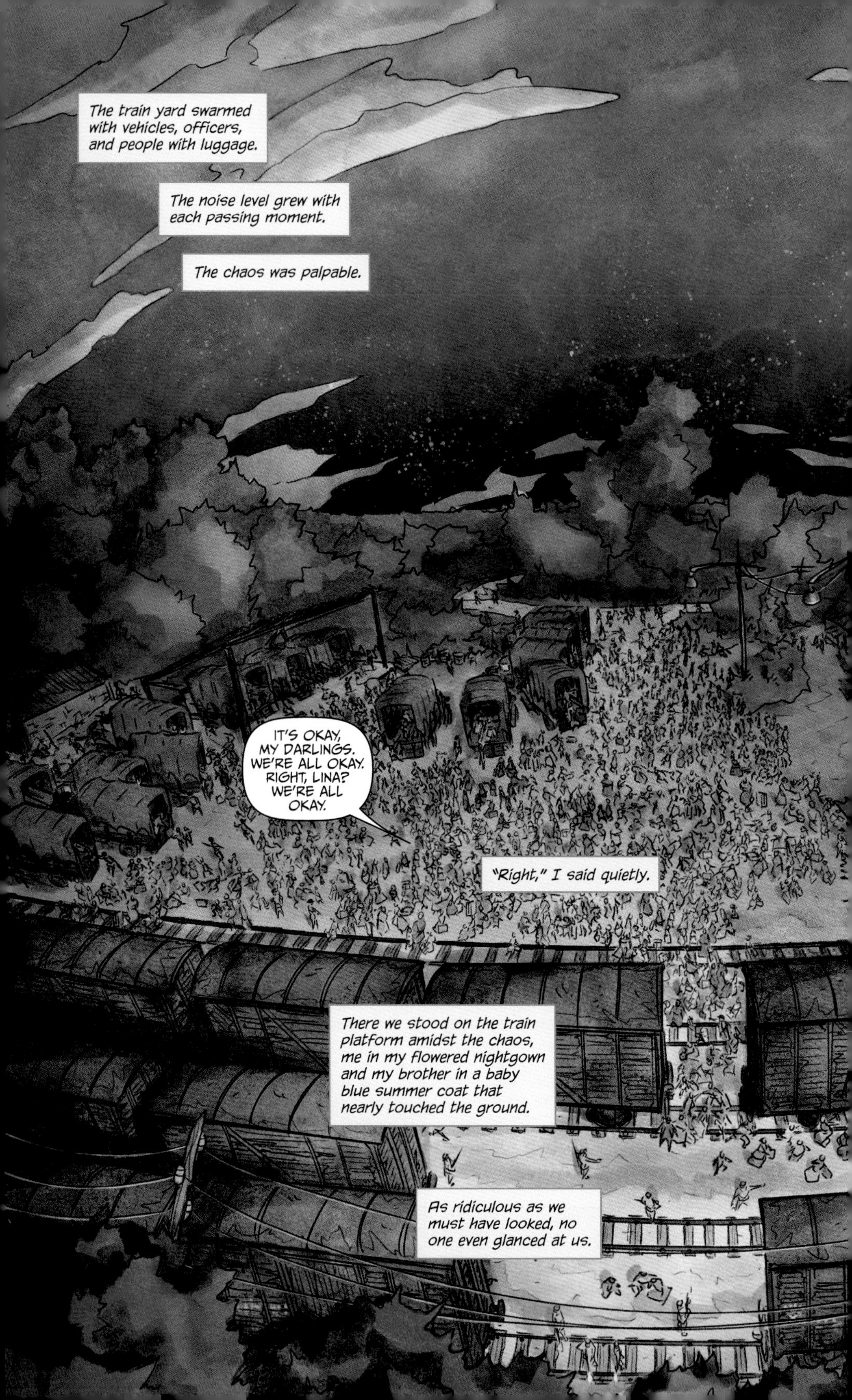
The train yard swarmed with vehicles, officers, and people with luggage.
The noise level grew with each passing moment.
The chaos was palpable.
IT'S OKAY, MY DARLINGS. WE'RE ALL OKAY. RIGHT, LINA? WE'RE ALL OKAY.
"Right," I said quietly.
There we stood on the train platform amidst the chaos, me in my flowered nightgown and my brother in a baby blue summer coat that nearly touched the ground.
As ridiculous as we must have looked, no one even glanced at us.

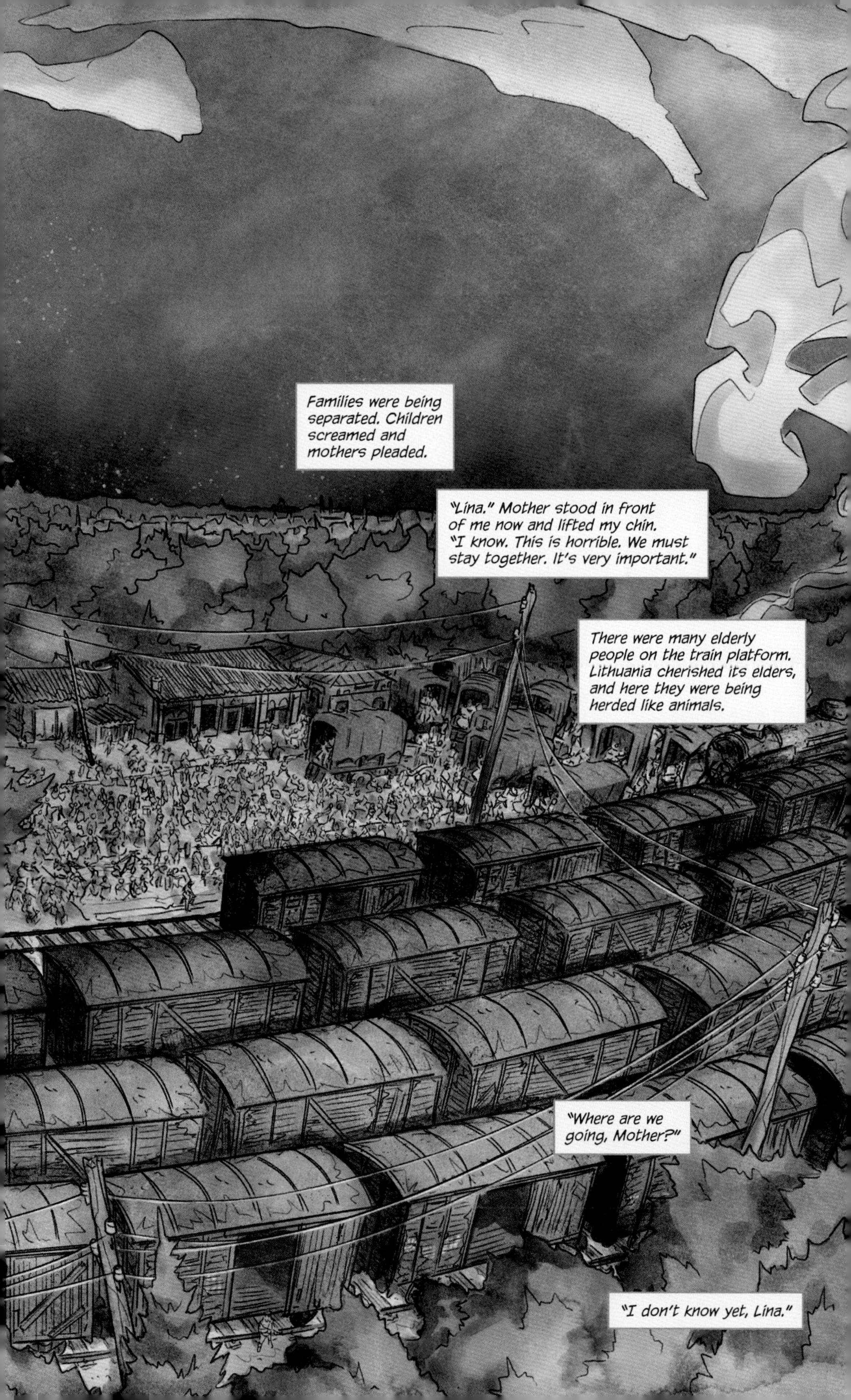
Families were being separated. Children screamed and mothers pleaded.
"Lina." Mother stood in front of me now and lifted my chin. "I know. This is horrible. We must stay together. It's very important."
There were many elderly people on the train platform. Lithuania cherished its elders, and here they were being herded like animals.
"Where are we going, Mother?"
"I don't know yet, Lina."

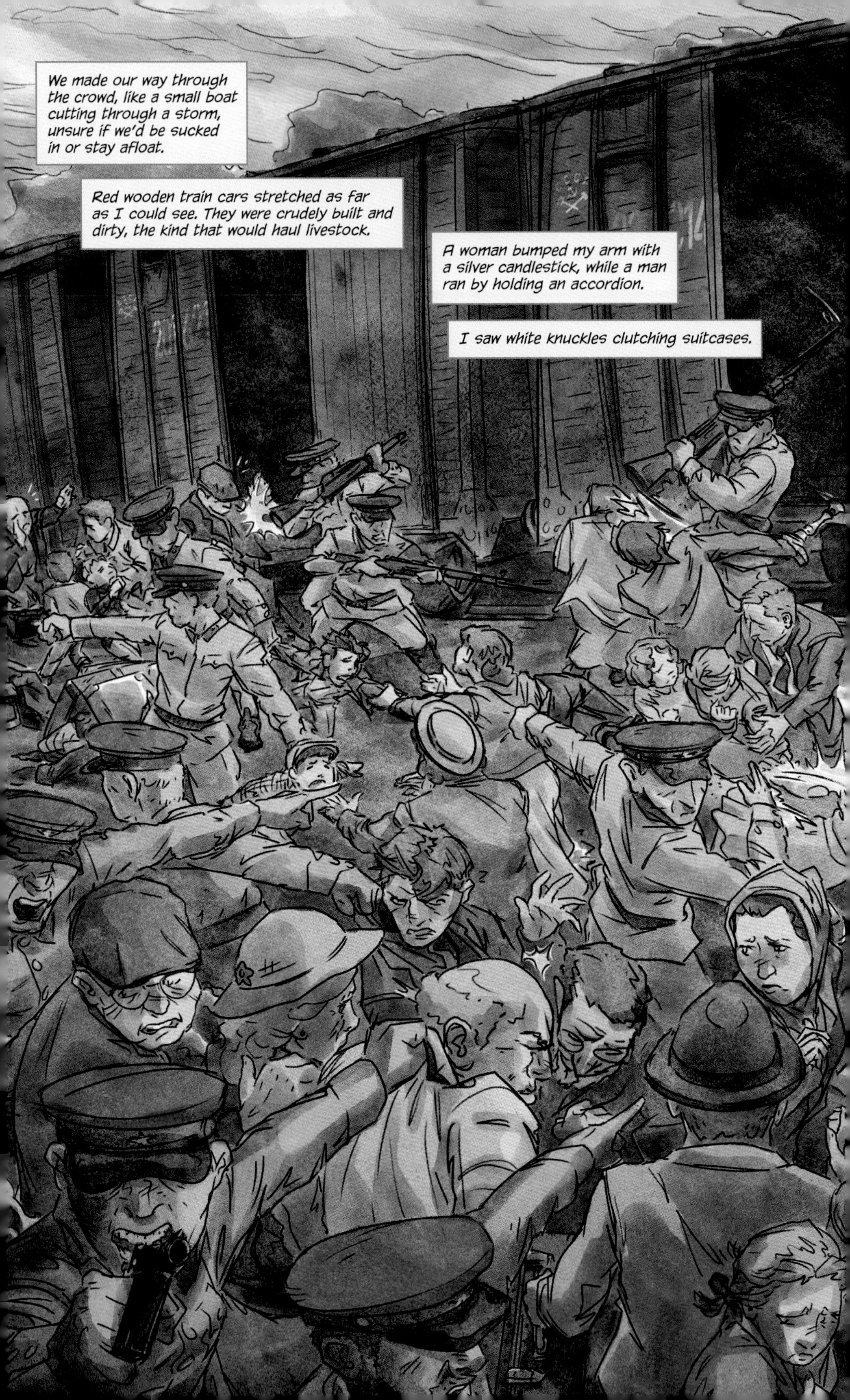
We made our way through the crowd, like a small boat cutting through a storm, unsure if we'd be sucked in or stay afloat.
Red wooden train cars stretched as far as I could see. They were crudely built and dirty, the kind that would haul livestock.
A woman bumped my arm with a silver candlestick, while a man ran by holding an accordion.
I saw white knuckles clutching suitcases.

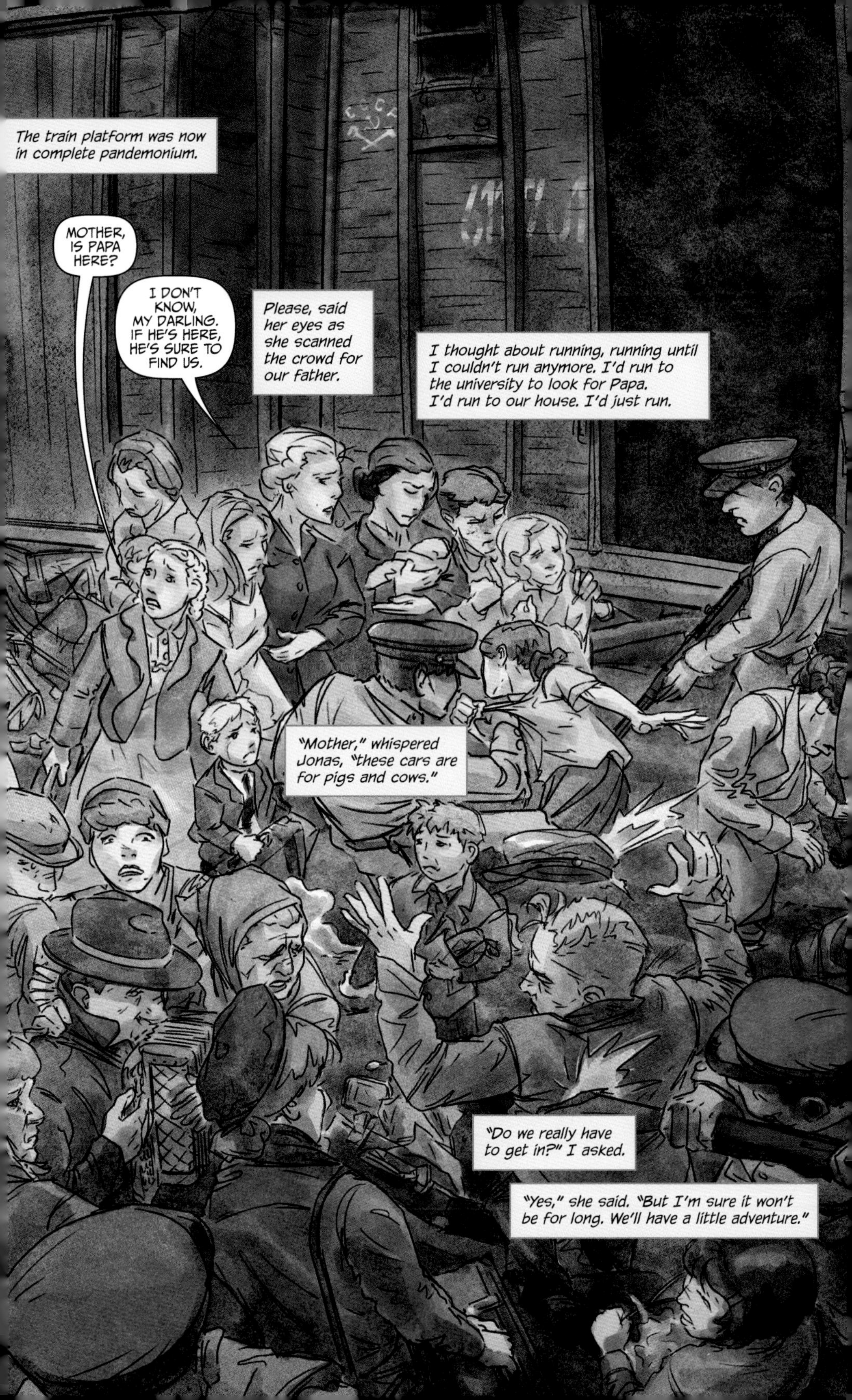
The train platform was now in complete pandemonium.
MOTHER, IS PAPA HERE?
I DON'T KNOW, MY DARLING. IF HE'S HERE, HE'S SURE TO FIND US.
Please, said her eyes as she scanned the crowd for our father.
I thought about running, running until I couldn't run anymore. I'd run to the university to look for Papa. I'd run to our house. I'd just run.
"Mother," whispered Jonas, "these cars are for pigs and cows."
"Do we really have to get in?" I asked.
"Yes," she said. "But I'm sure it won't be for long. We'll have a little adventure."

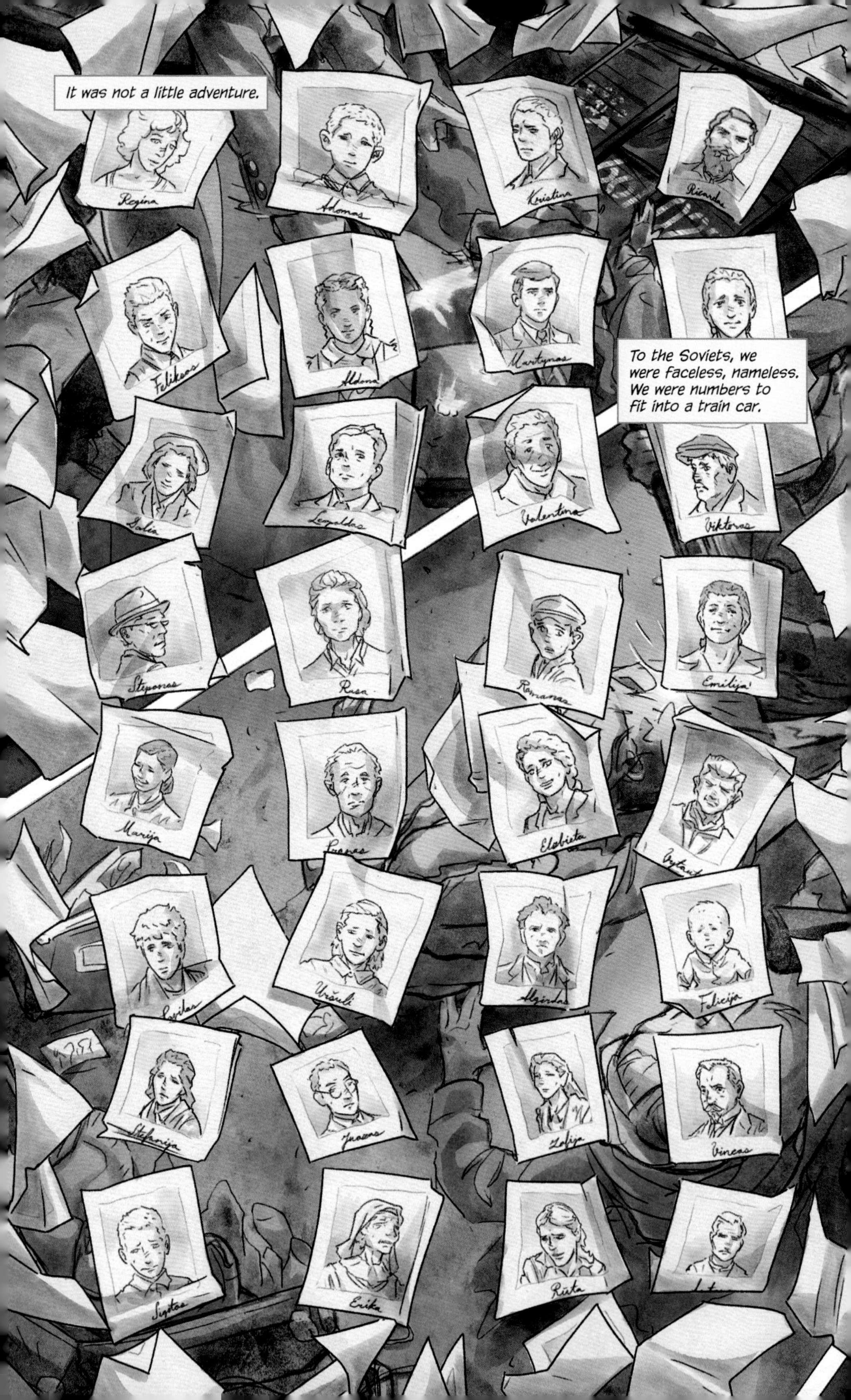
It was not a little adventure.
Regina
Adomas
Kristina
Feliksas
Aldona
Martynas
To the Soviets, we were faceless, nameless. We were numbers to fit into a train car.
Galia
Leopoldas
Valentina
Viktoras
Steponas
Rasa
Romanas
Emilija
Marija
Felicija
Stefanija
Juozas
Zofija
Vincas
Erika
Rūta

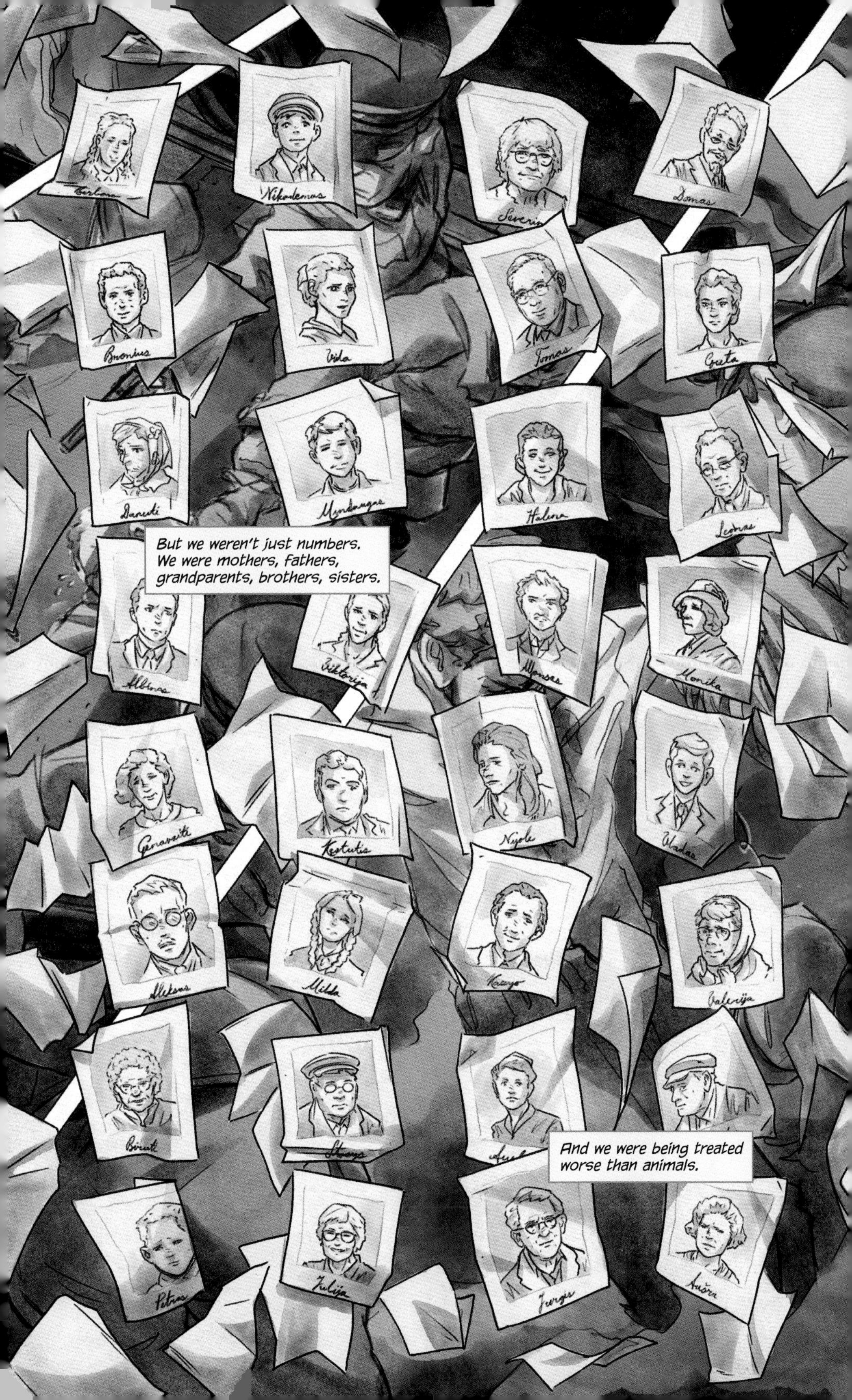
But we weren't just numbers. We were mothers, fathers, grandparents, brothers, sisters.
And we were being treated worse than animals.

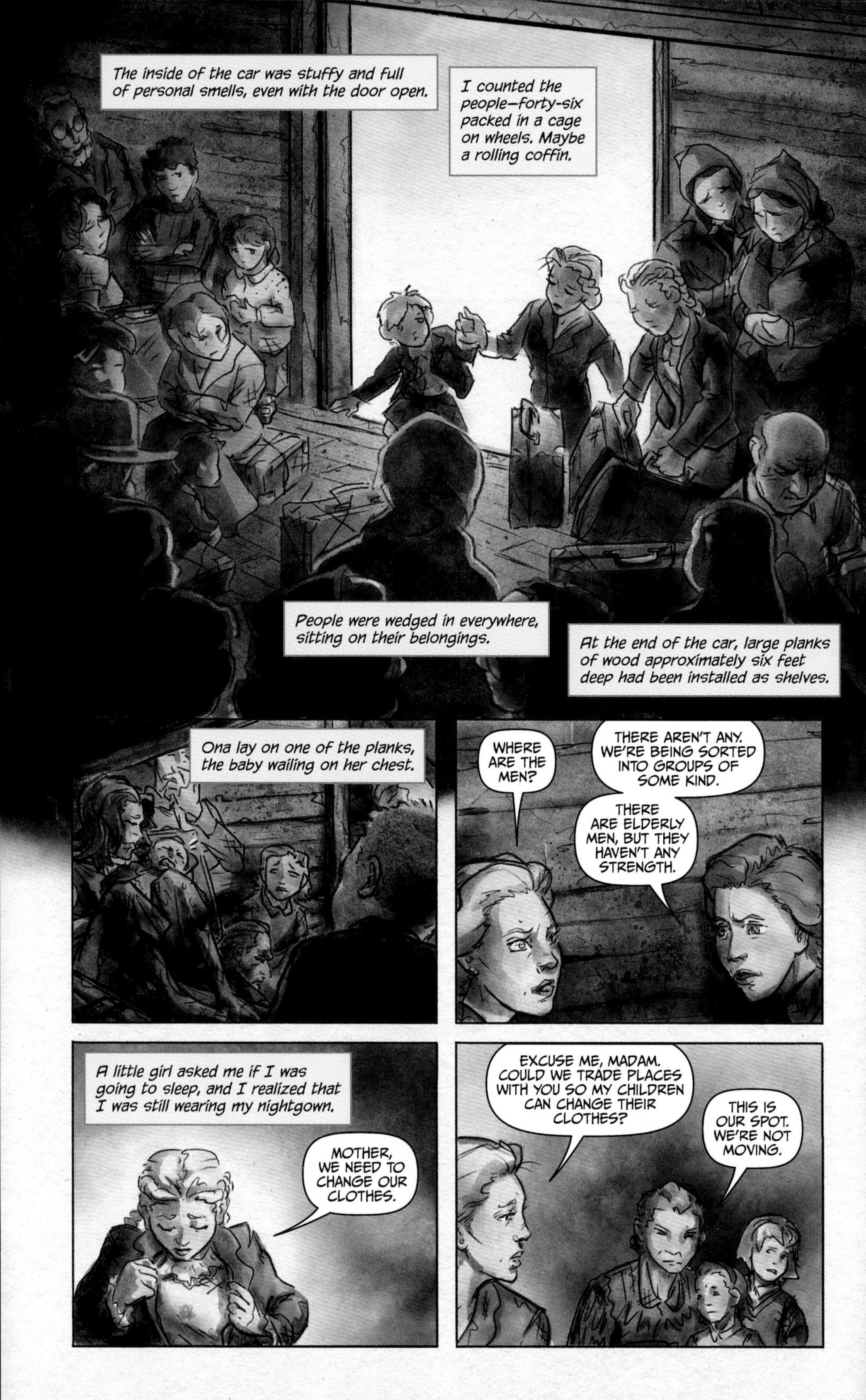
The inside of the car was stuffy and full of personal smells, even with the door open.
I counted the people—forty-six packed in a cage on wheels. Maybe a rolling coffin.
People were wedged in everywhere, sitting on their belongings.
At the end of the car, large planks of wood approximately six feet deep had been installed as shelves.
Ona lay on one of the planks, the baby wailing on her chest.
WHERE ARE THE MEN?
THERE AREN'T ANY. WE'RE BEING SORTED INTO GROUPS OF SOME KIND.
THERE ARE ELDERLY MEN, BUT THEY HAVEN'T ANY STRENGTH.
A little girl asked me if I was going to sleep, and I realized that I was still wearing my nightgown.
MOTHER, WE NEED TO CHANGE OUR CLOTHES.
EXCUSE ME, MADAM. COULD WE TRADE PLACES WITH YOU SO MY CHILDREN CAN CHANGE THEIR CLOTHES?
THIS IS OUR SPOT. WE'RE NOT MOVING.

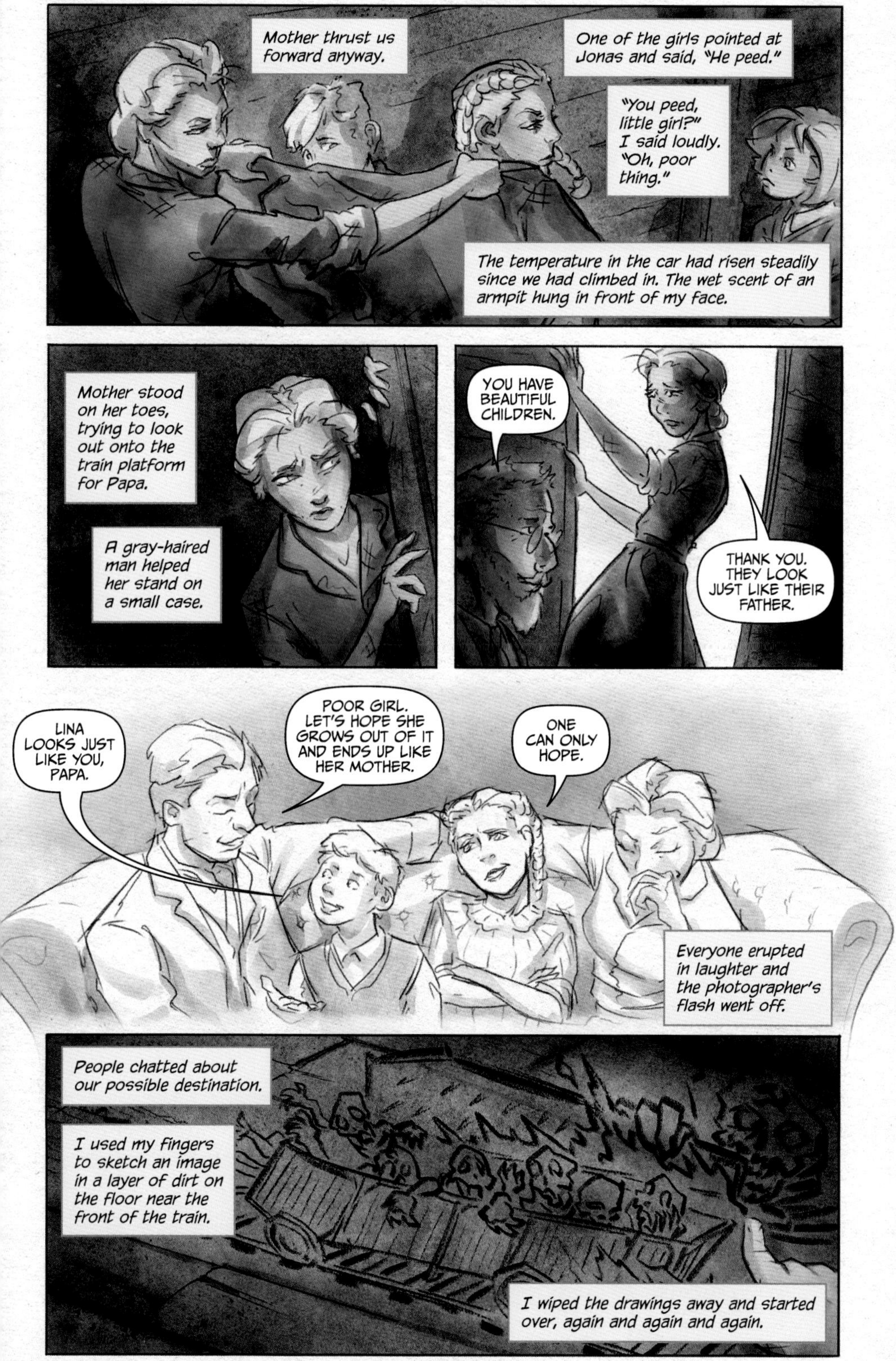
Mother thrust us forward anyway.
One of the girls pointed at Jonas and said, "He peed."
"You peed, little girl?" I said loudly. "Oh, poor thing."
The temperature in the car had risen steadily since we had climbed in. The wet scent of an armpit hung in front of my face.
Mother stood on her toes, trying to look out onto the train platform for Papa.
A gray-haired man helped her stand on a small case.
YOU HAVE BEAUTIFUL CHILDREN.
THANK YOU. THEY LOOK JUST LIKE THEIR FATHER.
LINA LOOKS JUST LIKE YOU, PAPA.
POOR GIRL. LET'S HOPE SHE GROWS OUT OF IT AND ENDS UP LIKE HER MOTHER.
ONE CAN ONLY HOPE.
Everyone erupted in laughter and the photographer's flash went off.
People chatted about our possible destination.
I used my fingers to sketch an image in a layer of dirt on the floor near the front of the train.
I wiped the drawings away and started over, again and again and again.

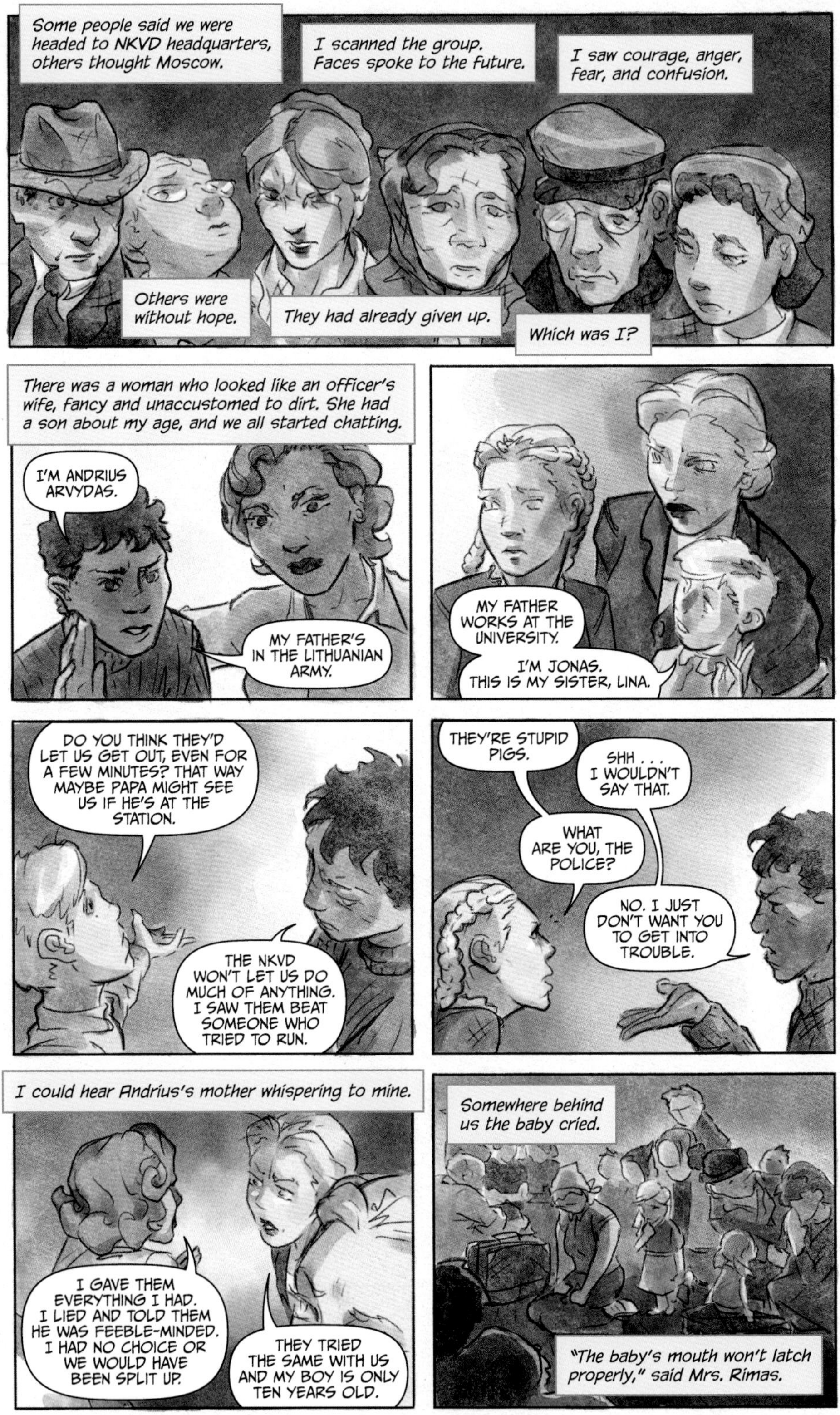

Some people said we were headed to NKVD headquarters, others thought Moscow.
I scanned the group. Faces spoke to the future.
I saw courage, anger, fear, and confusion.
Others were without hope.
They had already given up.
Which was I?
There was a woman who looked like an officer's wife, fancy and unaccustomed to dirt. She had a son about my age, and we all started chatting.
I'M ANDRIUS ARVYDAS.
MY FATHER'S IN THE LITHUANIAN ARMY.
MY FATHER WORKS AT THE UNIVERSITY.
I'M JONAS. THIS IS MY SISTER, LINA.
DO YOU THINK THEY'D LET US GET OUT, EVEN FOR A FEW MINUTES? THAT WAY MAYBE PAPA MIGHT SEE US IF HE'S AT THE STATION.
THE NKVD WON'T LET US DO MUCH OF ANYTHING. I SAW THEM BEAT SOMEONE WHO TRIED TO RUN.
THEY'RE STUPID PIGS.
SHH . . . I WOULDN'T SAY THAT.
WHAT ARE YOU, THE POLICE?
NO. I JUST DON'T WANT YOU TO GET INTO TROUBLE.
I could hear Andrius's mother whispering to mine.
I GAVE THEM EVERYTHING I HAD. I LIED AND TOLD THEM HE WAS FEEBLE-MINDED. I HAD NO CHOICE OR WE WOULD HAVE BEEN SPLIT UP.
THEY TRIED THE SAME WITH US AND MY BOY IS ONLY TEN YEARS OLD.
Somewhere behind us the baby cried.
"The baby's mouth won't latch properly," said Mrs. Rimas.

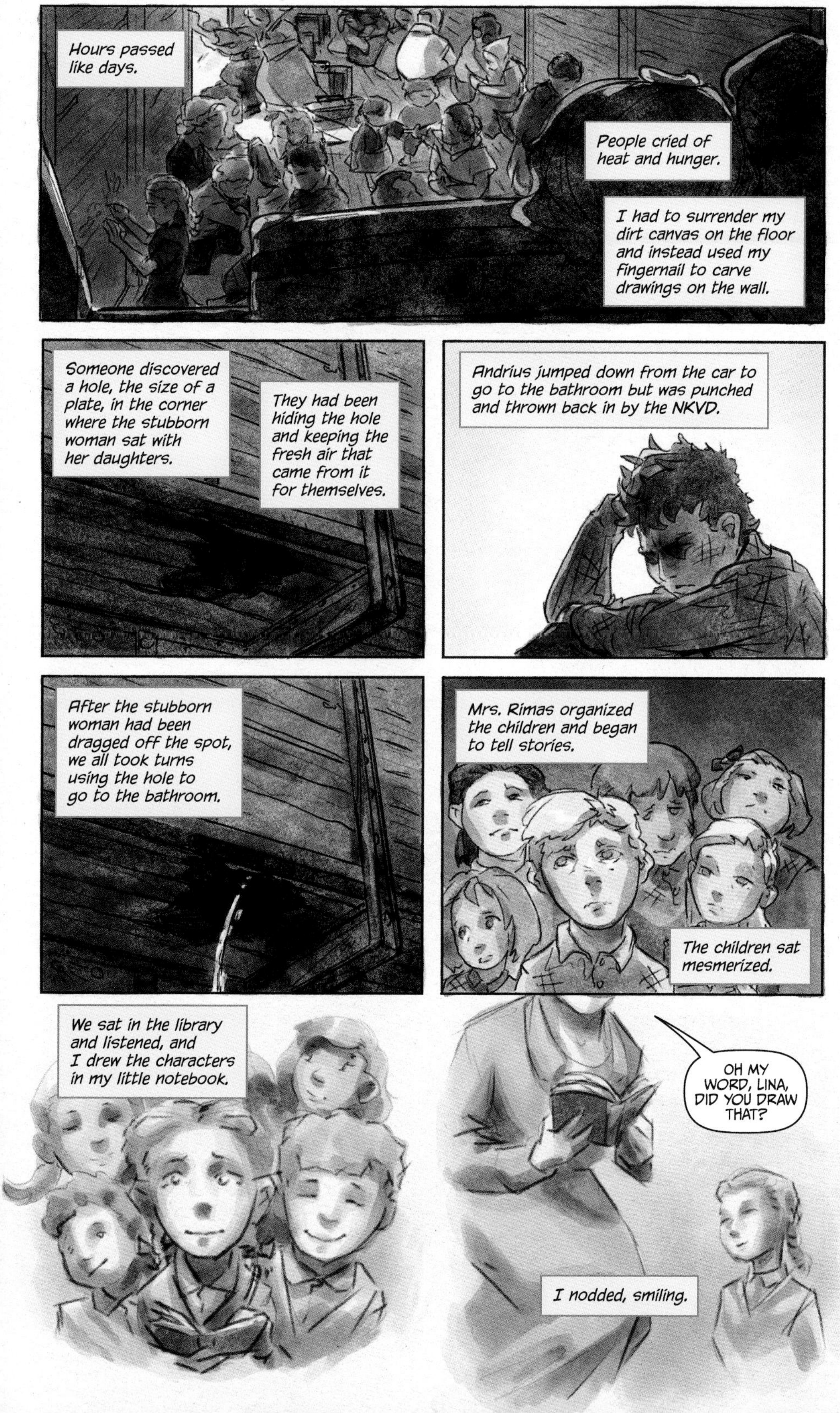
Hours passed like days.
People cried of heat and hunger.
I had to surrender my dirt canvas on the floor and instead used my fingernail to carve drawings on the wall.
Someone discovered a hole, the size of a plate, in the corner where the stubborn woman sat with her daughters.
They had been hiding the hole and keeping the fresh air that came from it for themselves.
Andrius jumped down from the car to go to the bathroom but was punched and thrown back in by the NKVD.
After the stubborn woman had been dragged off the spot, we all took turns using the hole to go to the bathroom.
Mrs. Rimas organized the children and began to tell stories.
The children sat mesmerized.
We sat in the library and listened, and I drew the characters in my little notebook.
OH MY WORD, LINA, DID YOU DRAW THAT?
I nodded, smiling.

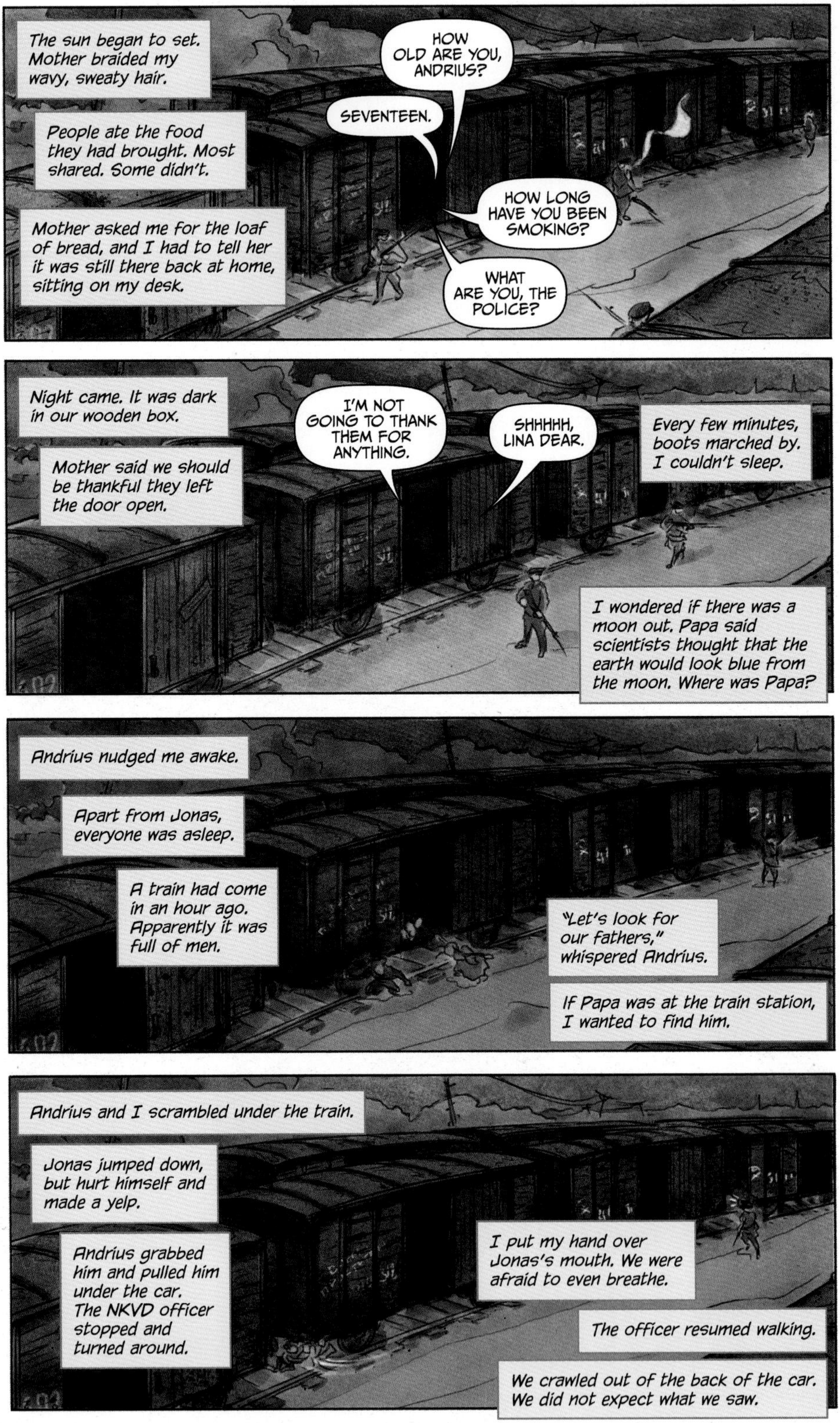
The sun began to set. Mother braided my wavy, sweaty hair.
People ate the food they had brought. Most shared. Some didn't.
Mother asked me for the loaf of bread, and I had to tell her it was still there back at home, sitting on my desk.
HOW OLD ARE YOU, ANDRIUS?
SEVENTEEN.
HOW LONG HAVE YOU BEEN SMOKING?
WHAT ARE YOU, THE POLICE?
Night came. It was dark in our wooden box.
Mother said we should be thankful they left the door open.
I'M NOT GOING TO THANK THEM FOR ANYTHING.
SHHHHH, LINA DEAR.
Every few minutes, boots marched by. I couldn't sleep.
I wondered if there was a moon out. Papa said scientists thought that the earth would look blue from the moon. Where was Papa?
Andrius nudged me awake.
Apart from Jonas, everyone was asleep.
A train had come in an hour ago. Apparently it was full of men.
"Let's look for our fathers," whispered Andrius.
If Papa was at the train station, I wanted to find him.
Andrius and I scrambled under the train.
Jonas jumped down, but hurt himself and made a yelp.
Andrius grabbed him and pulled him under the car. The NKVD officer stopped and turned around.
I put my hand over Jonas's mouth. We were afraid to even breathe.
The officer resumed walking.
We crawled out of the back of the car. We did not expect what we saw.

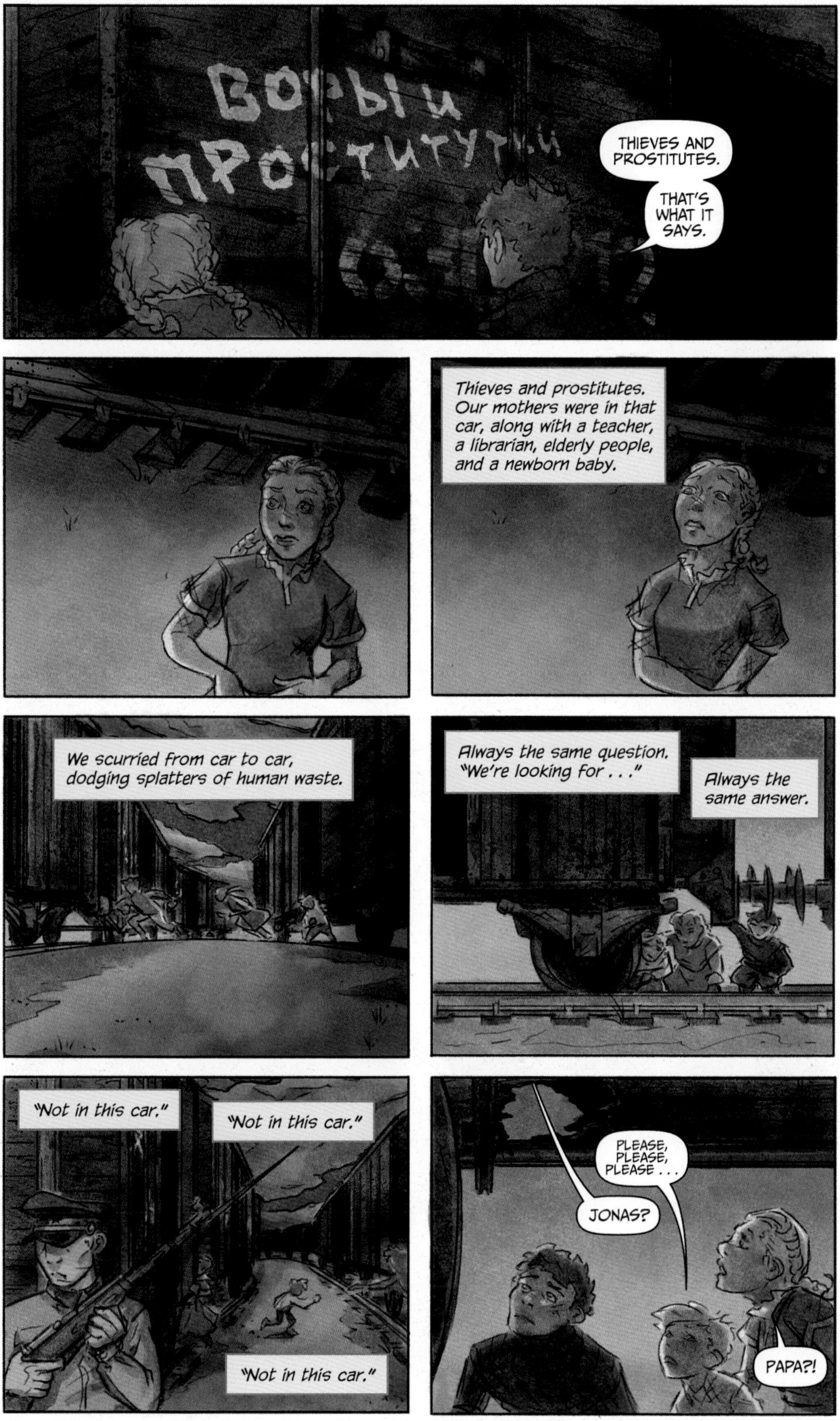
THIEVES AND PROSTITUTES.
THAT'S WHAT IT SAYS.
Thieves and prostitutes. Our mothers were in that car, along with a teacher, a librarian, elderly people, and a newborn baby.
We scurried from car to car, dodging splatters of human waste.
Always the same question. "We're looking for . . ."
Always the same answer.
"Not in this car."
"Not in this car."
"Not in this car."
JONAS?
PLEASE, PLEASE, PLEASE . . .
PAPA?!

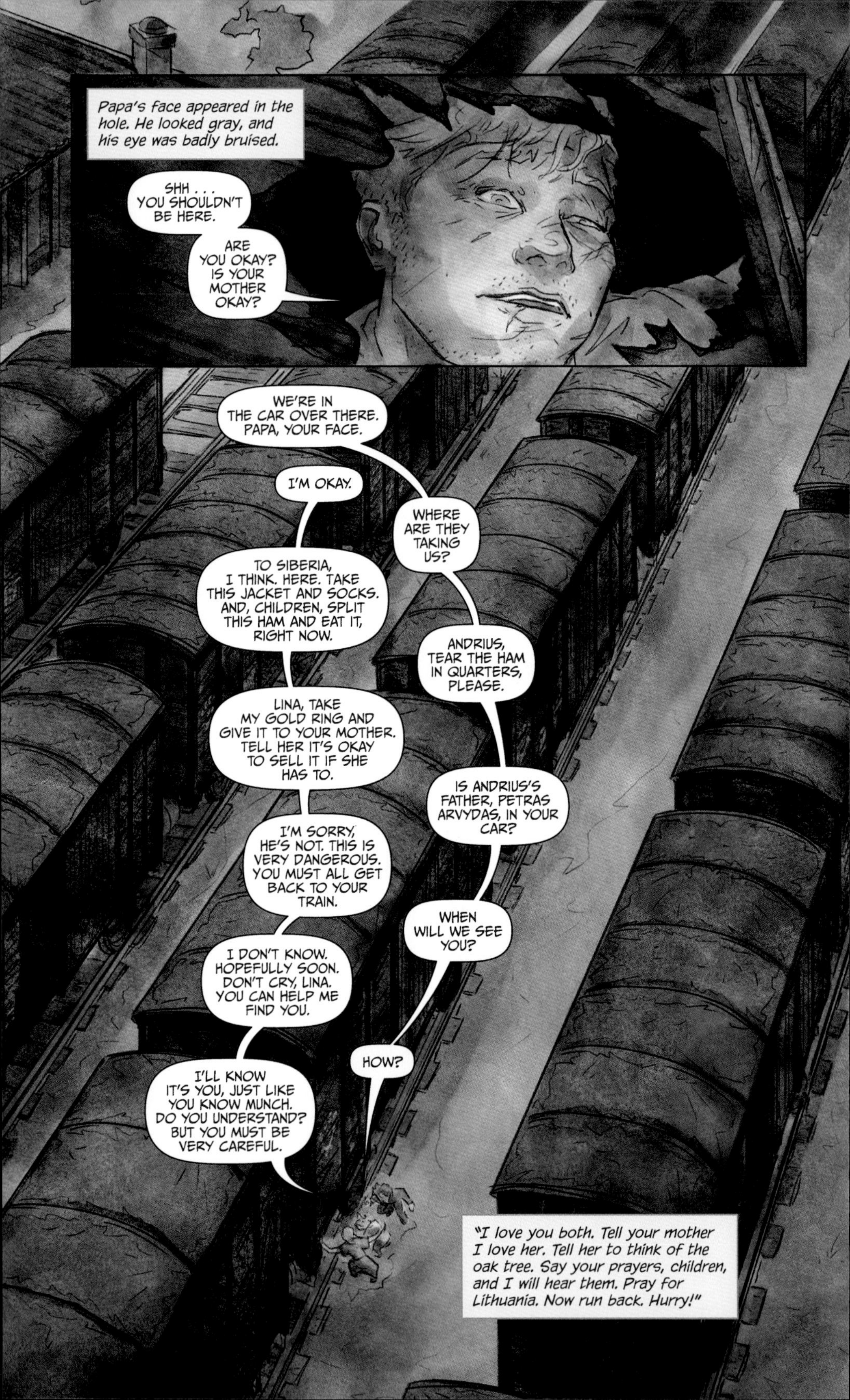
Papa's face appeared in the hole. He looked gray, and his eye was badly bruised.
SHH . . . YOU SHOULDN'T BE HERE.
ARE YOU OKAY? IS YOUR MOTHER OKAY?
WE'RE IN THE CAR OVER THERE. PAPA, YOUR FACE.
I'M OKAY.
WHERE ARE THEY TAKING US?
TO SIBERIA, I THINK. HERE. TAKE THIS JACKET AND SOCKS. AND, CHILDREN, SPLIT THIS HAM AND EAT IT, RIGHT NOW.
ANDRIUS, TEAR THE HAM IN QUARTERS, PLEASE.
LINA, TAKE MY GOLD RING AND GIVE IT TO YOUR MOTHER. TELL HER IT'S OKAY TO SELL IT IF SHE HAS TO.
IS ANDRIUS'S FATHER, PETRAS ARVYDAS, IN YOUR CAR?
I'M SORRY, HE'S NOT. THIS IS VERY DANGEROUS. YOU MUST ALL GET BACK TO YOUR TRAIN.
WHEN WILL WE SEE YOU?
I DON'T KNOW. HOPEFULLY SOON. DON'T CRY, LINA. YOU CAN HELP ME FIND YOU.
HOW?
I'LL KNOW IT'S YOU, JUST LIKE YOU KNOW MUNCH. DO YOU UNDERSTAND? BUT YOU MUST BE VERY CAREFUL.
"I love you both. Tell your mother I love her. Tell her to think of the oak tree. Say your prayers, children, and I will hear them. Pray for Lithuania. Now run back. Hurry!"

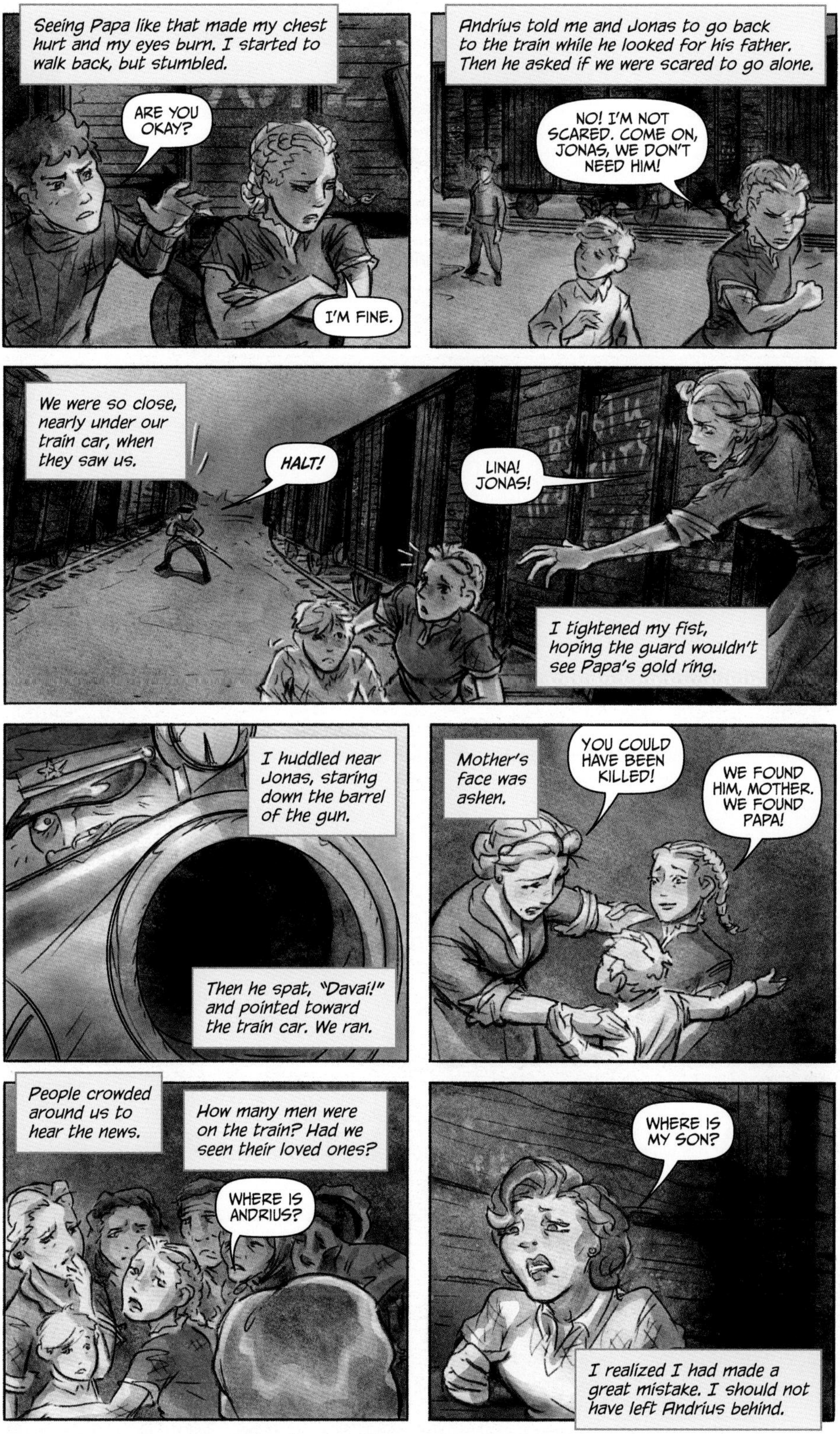
Seeing Papa like that made my chest hurt and my eyes burn. I started to walk back, but stumbled.
ARE YOU OKAY?
I'M FINE.
Andrius told me and Jonas to go back to the train while he looked for his father. Then he asked if we were scared to go alone.
NO! I'M NOT SCARED. COME ON, JONAS, WE DON'T NEED HIM!
We were so close, nearly under our train car, when they saw us.
HALT!
LINA! JONAS!
I tightened my fist, hoping the guard wouldn't see Papa's gold ring.
I huddled near Jonas, staring down the barrel of the gun.
Then he spat, "Davai!" and pointed toward the train car. We ran.
Mother's face was ashen.
YOU COULD HAVE BEEN KILLED!
WE FOUND HIM, MOTHER. WE FOUND PAPA!
People crowded around us to hear the news.
How many men were on the train? Had we seen their loved ones?
WHERE IS ANDRIUS?
WHERE IS MY SON?
I realized I had made a great mistake. I should not have left Andrius behind.

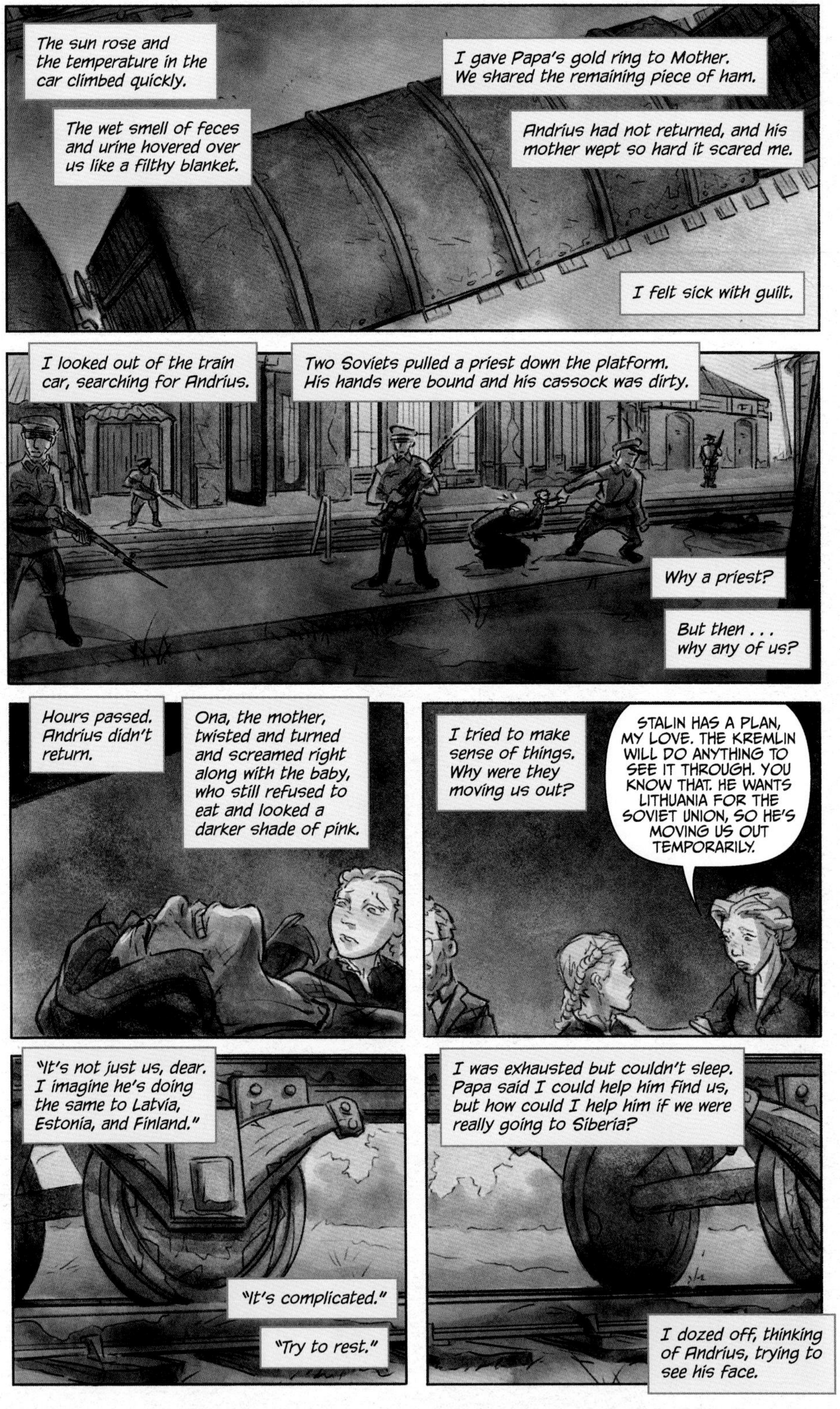
The sun rose and the temperature in the car climbed quickly.
The wet smell of feces and urine hovered over us like a filthy blanket.
I gave Papa's gold ring to Mother. We shared the remaining piece of ham.
Andrius had not returned, and his mother wept so hard it scared me.
I felt sick with guilt.
I looked out of the train car, searching for Andrius.
Two Soviets pulled a priest down the platform. His hands were bound and his cassock was dirty.
Why a priest?
But then . . . why any of us?
Hours passed. Andrius didn't return.
Ona, the mother, twisted and turned and screamed right along with the baby, who still refused to eat and looked a darker shade of pink.
I tried to make sense of things. Why were they moving us out?
STALIN HAS A PLAN, MY LOVE. THE KREMLIN WILL DO ANYTHING TO SEE IT THROUGH. YOU KNOW THAT. HE WANTS LITHUANIA FOR THE SOVIET UNION, SO HE'S MOVING US OUT TEMPORARILY.
"It's not just us, dear. I imagine he's doing the same to Latvia, Estonia, and Finland."
"It's complicated."
"Try to rest."
I was exhausted but couldn't sleep. Papa said I could help him find us, but how could I help him if we were really going to Siberia?
I dozed off, thinking of Andrius, trying to see his face.

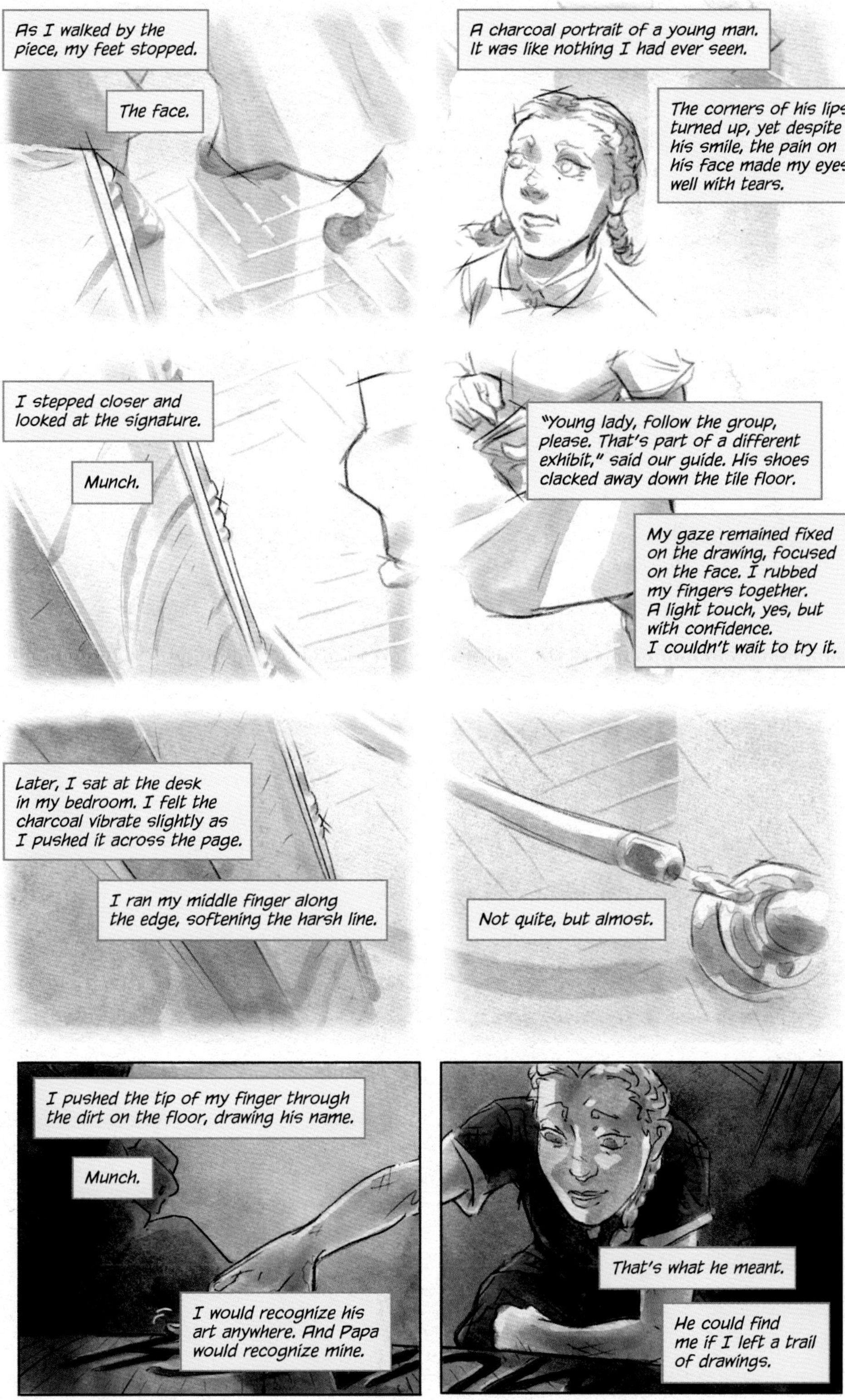
As I walked by the piece, my feet stopped.
The face.
A charcoal portrait of a young man. It was like nothing I had ever seen.
The corners of his lips turned up, yet despite his smile, the pain on his face made my eyes well with tears.
I stepped closer and looked at the signature.
Munch.
"Young lady, follow the group, please. That's part of a different exhibit," said our guide. His shoes clacked away down the tile floor.
My gaze remained fixed on the drawing, focused on the face. I rubbed my fingers together. A light touch, yes, but with confidence. I couldn't wait to try it.
Later, I sat at the desk in my bedroom. I felt the charcoal vibrate slightly as I pushed it across the page.
I ran my middle finger along the edge, softening the harsh line.
Not quite, but almost.
I pushed the tip of my finger through the dirt on the floor, drawing his name.
Munch.
I would recognize his art anywhere. And Papa would recognize mine.
That's what he meant.
He could find me if I left a trail of drawings.

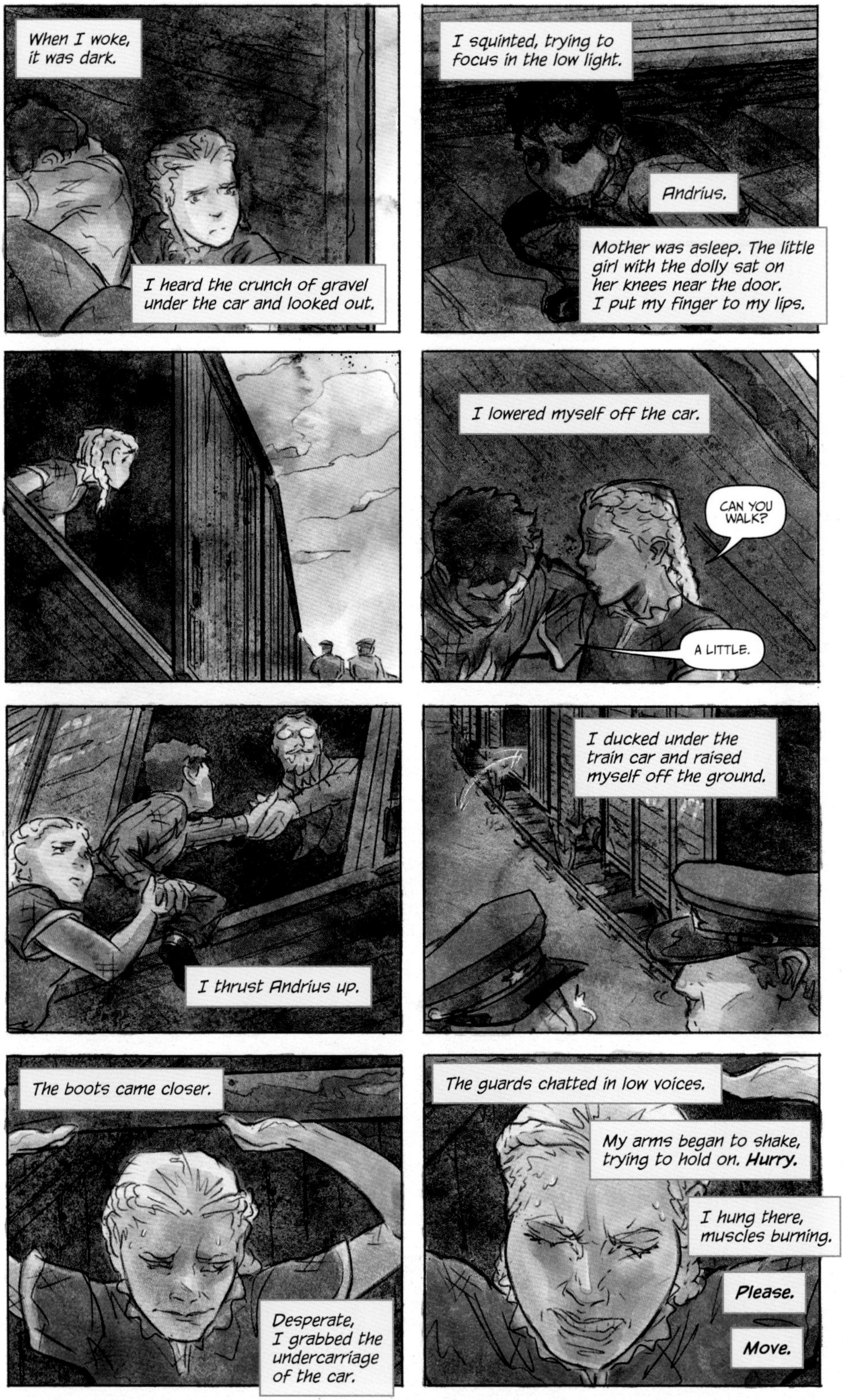
When I woke, it was dark.
I heard the crunch of gravel under the car and looked out.
I squinted, trying to focus in the low light.
Andrius.
Mother was asleep. The little girl with the dolly sat on her knees near the door. I put my finger to my lips.
I lowered myself off the car.
CAN YOU WALK?
A LITTLE.
I thrust Andrius up.
I ducked under the train car and raised myself off the ground.
The boots came closer.
Desperate, I grabbed the undercarriage of the car.
The guards chatted in low voices.
My arms began to shake, trying to hold on. **Hurry.**
I hung there, muscles burning.
Please.
Move.

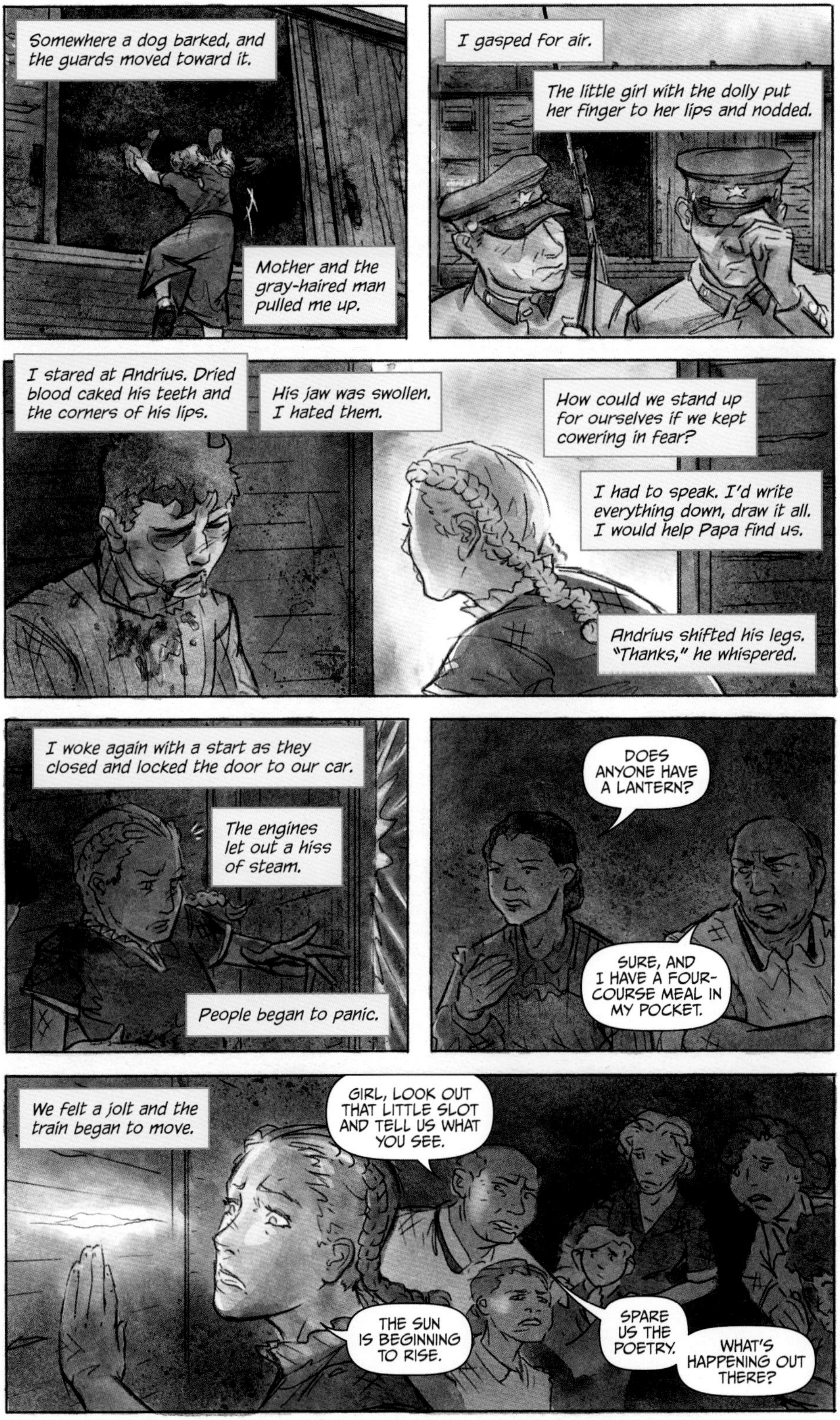
Somewhere a dog barked, and the guards moved toward it.
Mother and the gray-haired man pulled me up.
I gasped for air.
The little girl with the dolly put her finger to her lips and nodded.
I stared at Andrius. Dried blood caked his teeth and the corners of his lips.
His jaw was swollen. I hated them.
How could we stand up for ourselves if we kept cowering in fear?
I had to speak. I'd write everything down, draw it all. I would help Papa find us.
Andrius shifted his legs. "Thanks," he whispered.
I woke again with a start as they closed and locked the door to our car.
The engines let out a hiss of steam.
People began to panic.
DOES ANYONE HAVE A LANTERN?
SURE, AND I HAVE A FOUR-COURSE MEAL IN MY POCKET.
We felt a jolt and the train began to move.
GIRL, LOOK OUT THAT LITTLE SLOT AND TELL US WHAT YOU SEE.
THE SUN IS BEGINNING TO RISE.
SPARE US THE POETRY.
WHAT'S HAPPENING OUT THERE?

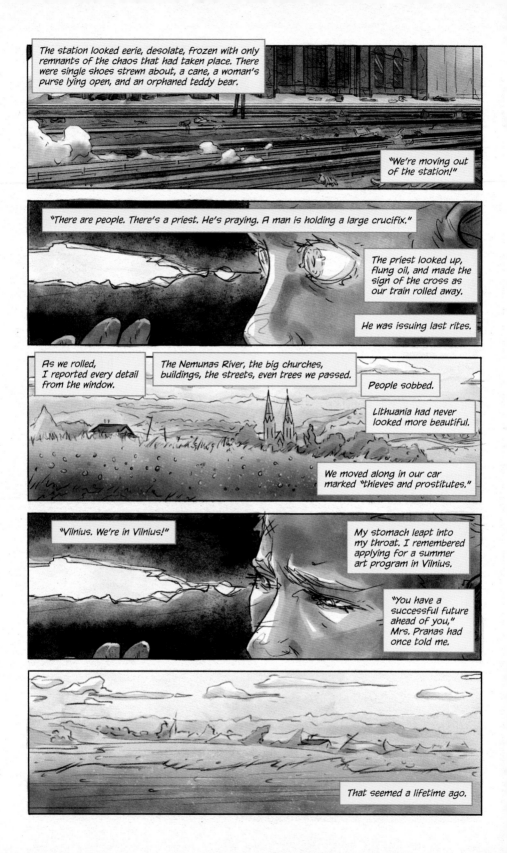

The station looked eerie, desolate, frozen with only remnants of the chaos that had taken place. There were single shoes strewn about, a cane, a woman's purse lying open, and an orphaned teddy bear.

"We're moving out of the station!"

"There are people. There's a priest. He's praying. A man is holding a large crucifix."

The priest looked up, flung oil, and made the sign of the cross as our train rolled away.

He was issuing last rites.

As we rolled, I reported every detail from the window.

The Nemunas River, the big churches, buildings, the streets, even trees we passed.

People sobbed.

Lithuania had never looked more beautiful.

We moved along in our car marked "thieves and prostitutes."

"Vilnius. We're in Vilnius!"

My stomach leapt into my throat. I remembered applying for a summer art program in Vilnius.

"You have a successful future ahead of you," Mrs. Pranas had once told me.

That seemed a lifetime ago.

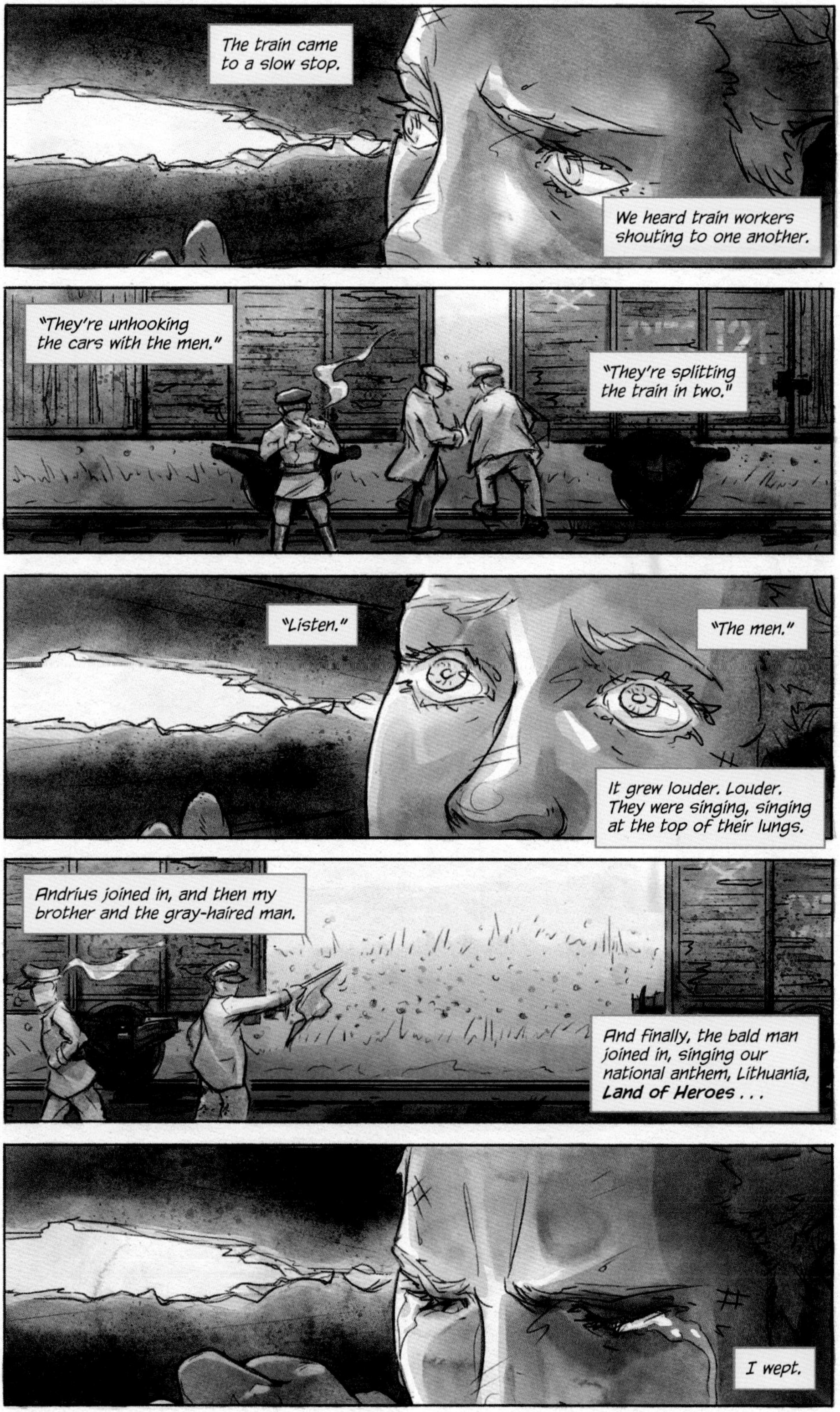
The train came to a slow stop.
We heard train workers shouting to one another.
"They're unhooking the cars with the men."
"They're splitting the train in two."
"Listen."
"The men."
It grew louder. Louder. They were singing, singing at the top of their lungs.
Andrius joined in, and then my brother and the gray-haired man.
And finally, the bald man joined in, singing our national anthem, Lithuania, **Land of Heroes . . .**
I wept.

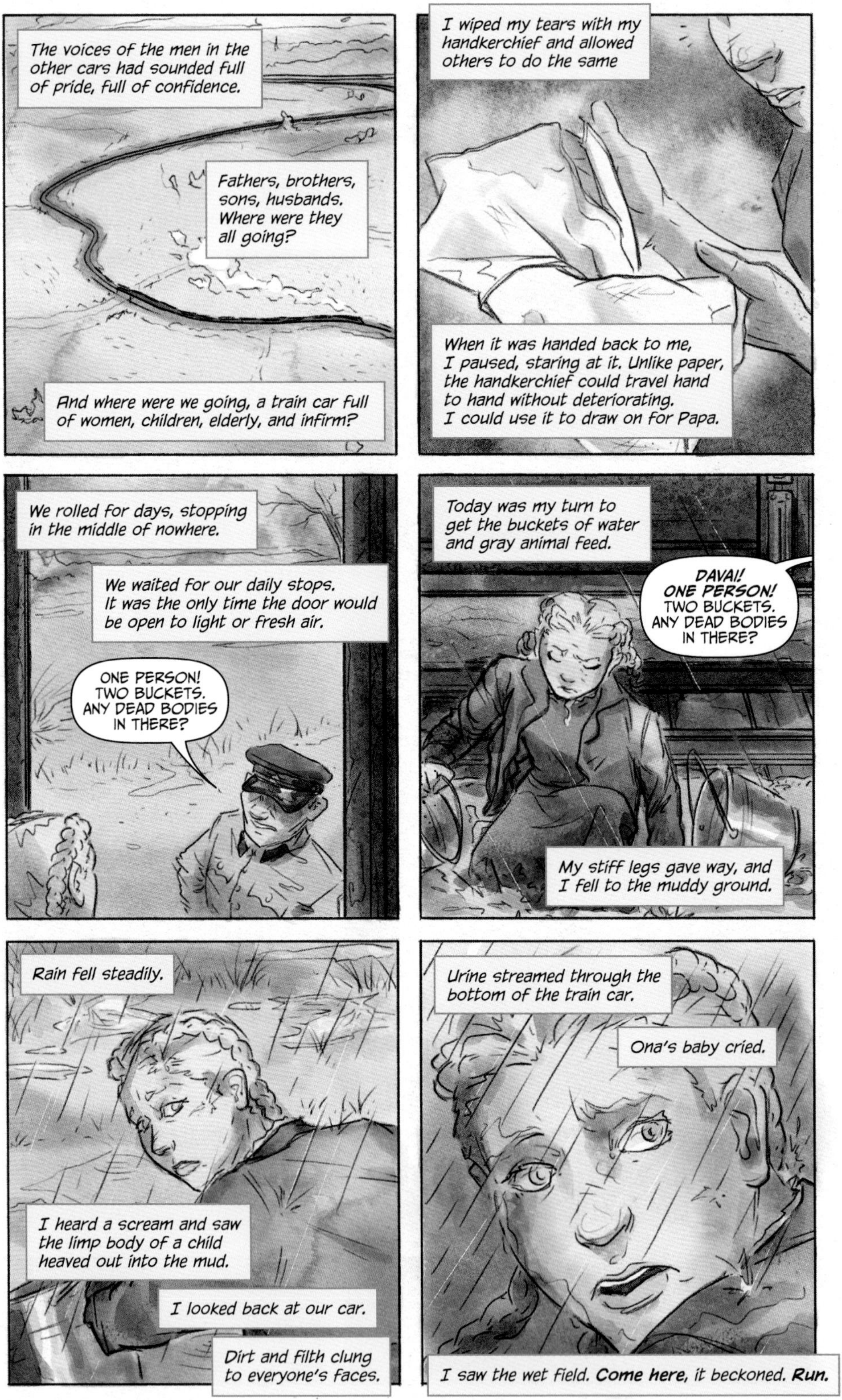
The voices of the men in the other cars had sounded full of pride, full of confidence.
Fathers, brothers, sons, husbands. Where were they all going?
And where were we going, a train car full of women, children, elderly, and infirm?
I wiped my tears with my handkerchief and allowed others to do the same
When it was handed back to me, I paused, staring at it. Unlike paper, the handkerchief could travel hand to hand without deteriorating. I could use it to draw on for Papa.
We rolled for days, stopping in the middle of nowhere.
We waited for our daily stops. It was the only time the door would be open to light or fresh air.
ONE PERSON! TWO BUCKETS. ANY DEAD BODIES IN THERE?
Today was my turn to get the buckets of water and gray animal feed.
DAVAI! ONE PERSON! TWO BUCKETS. ANY DEAD BODIES IN THERE?
My stiff legs gave way, and I fell to the muddy ground.
Rain fell steadily.
I heard a scream and saw the limp body of a child heaved out into the mud.
I looked back at our car.
Dirt and filth clung to everyone's faces.
Urine streamed through the bottom of the train car.
Ona's baby cried.
I saw the wet field. Come here, it beckoned. Run.

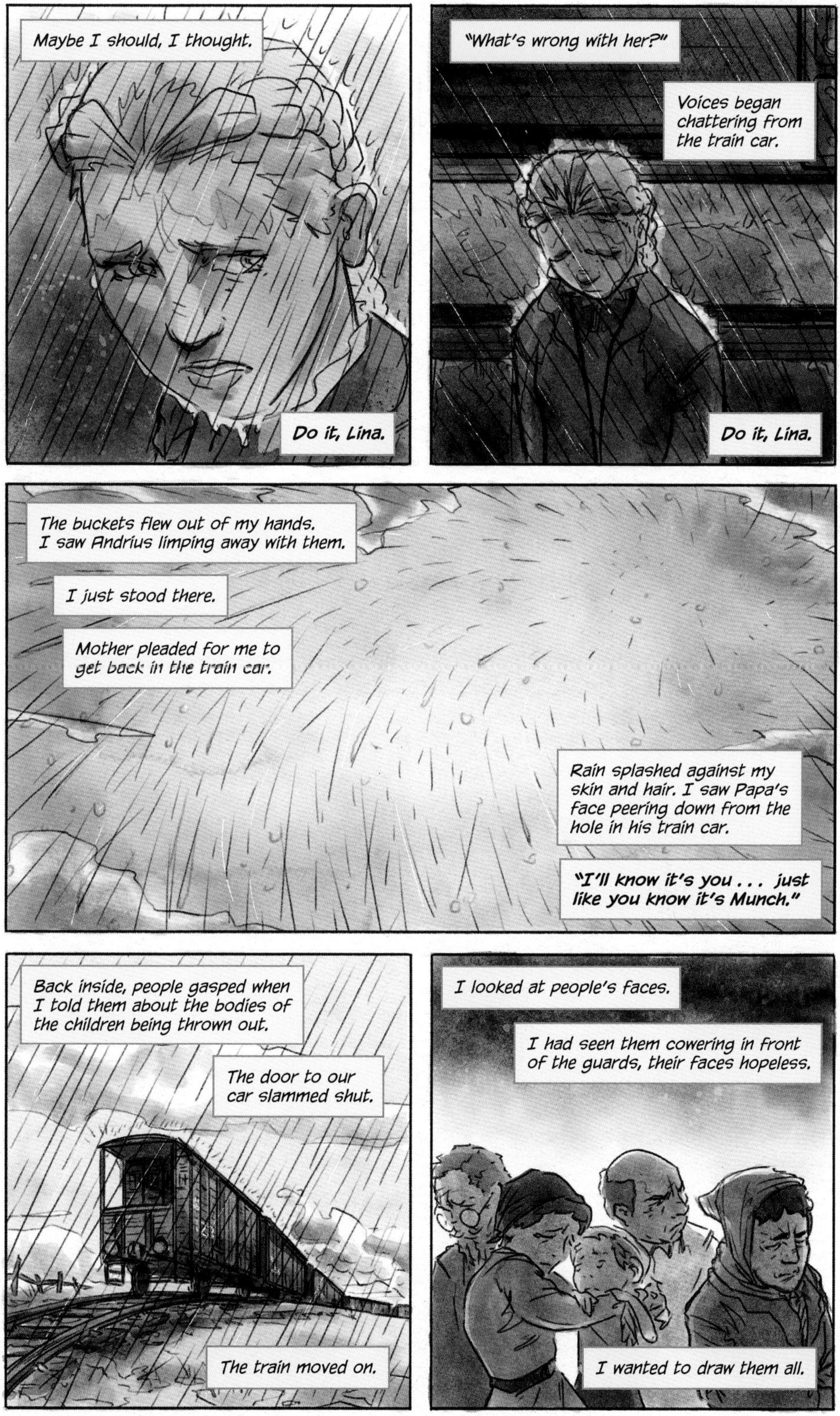
Maybe I should, I thought.
Do it, Lina.
"What's wrong with her?"
Voices began chattering from the train car.
Do it, Lina.
The buckets flew out of my hands. I saw Andrius limping away with them.
I just stood there.
Mother pleaded for me to get back in the train car.
Rain splashed against my skin and hair. I saw Papa's face peering down from the hole in his train car.
"I'll know it's you . . . just like you know it's Munch."
Back inside, people gasped when I told them about the bodies of the children being thrown out.
The door to our car slammed shut.
The train moved on.
I looked at people's faces.
I had seen them cowering in front of the guards, their faces hopeless.
I wanted to draw them all.

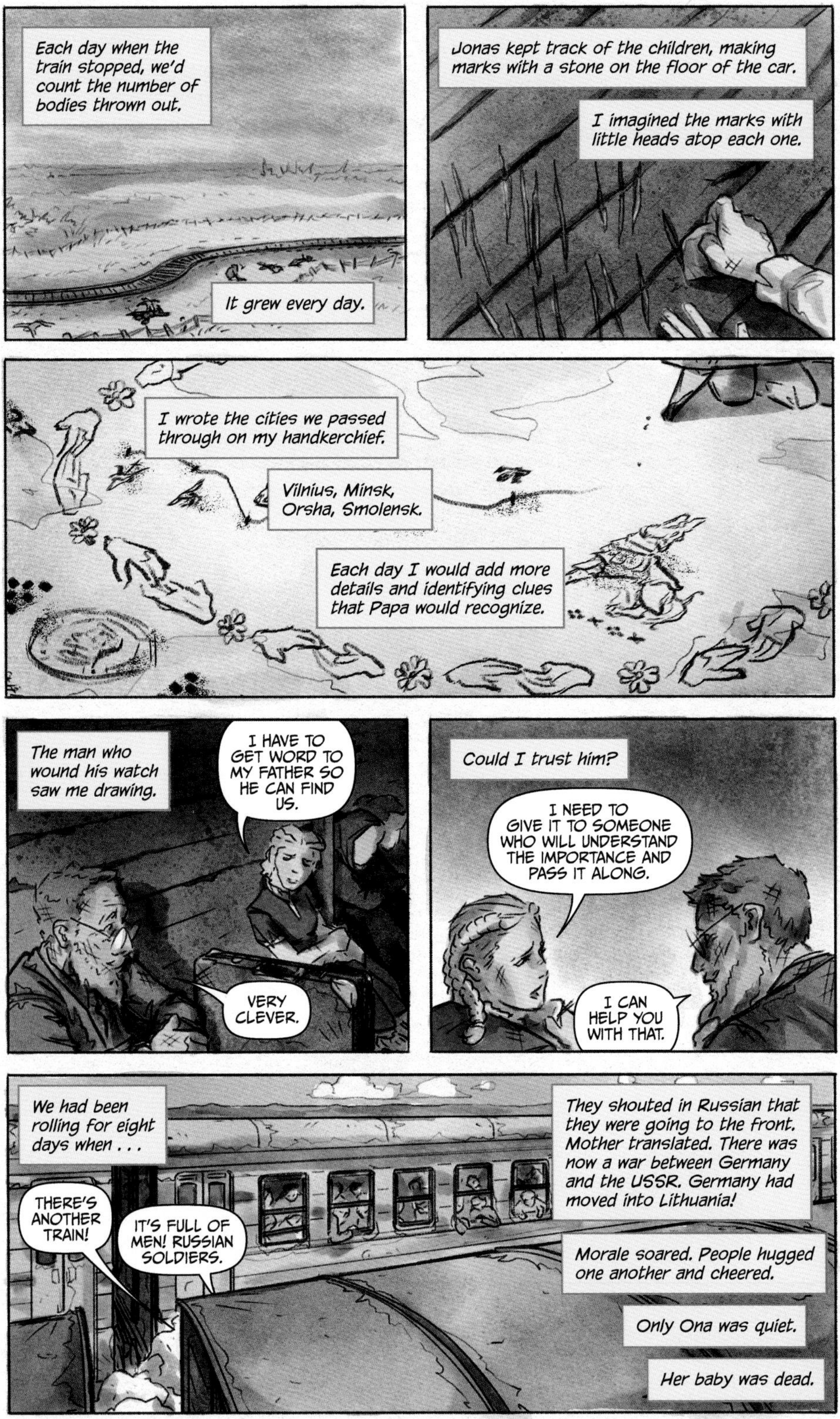

Each day when the train stopped, we'd count the number of bodies thrown out.
It grew every day.
Jonas kept track of the children, making marks with a stone on the floor of the car.
I imagined the marks with little heads atop each one.
I wrote the cities we passed through on my handkerchief.
Vilnius, Minsk, Orsha, Smolensk.
Each day I would add more details and identifying clues that Papa would recognize.
The man who wound his watch saw me drawing.
I HAVE TO GET WORD TO MY FATHER SO HE CAN FIND US.
VERY CLEVER.
Could I trust him?
I NEED TO GIVE IT TO SOMEONE WHO WILL UNDERSTAND THE IMPORTANCE AND PASS IT ALONG.
I CAN HELP YOU WITH THAT.
We had been rolling for eight days when . . .
THERE'S ANOTHER TRAIN!
IT'S FULL OF MEN! RUSSIAN SOLDIERS.
They shouted in Russian that they were going to the front. Mother translated. There was now a war between Germany and the USSR. Germany had moved into Lithuania!
Morale soared. People hugged one another and cheered.
Only Ona was quiet.
Her baby was dead.

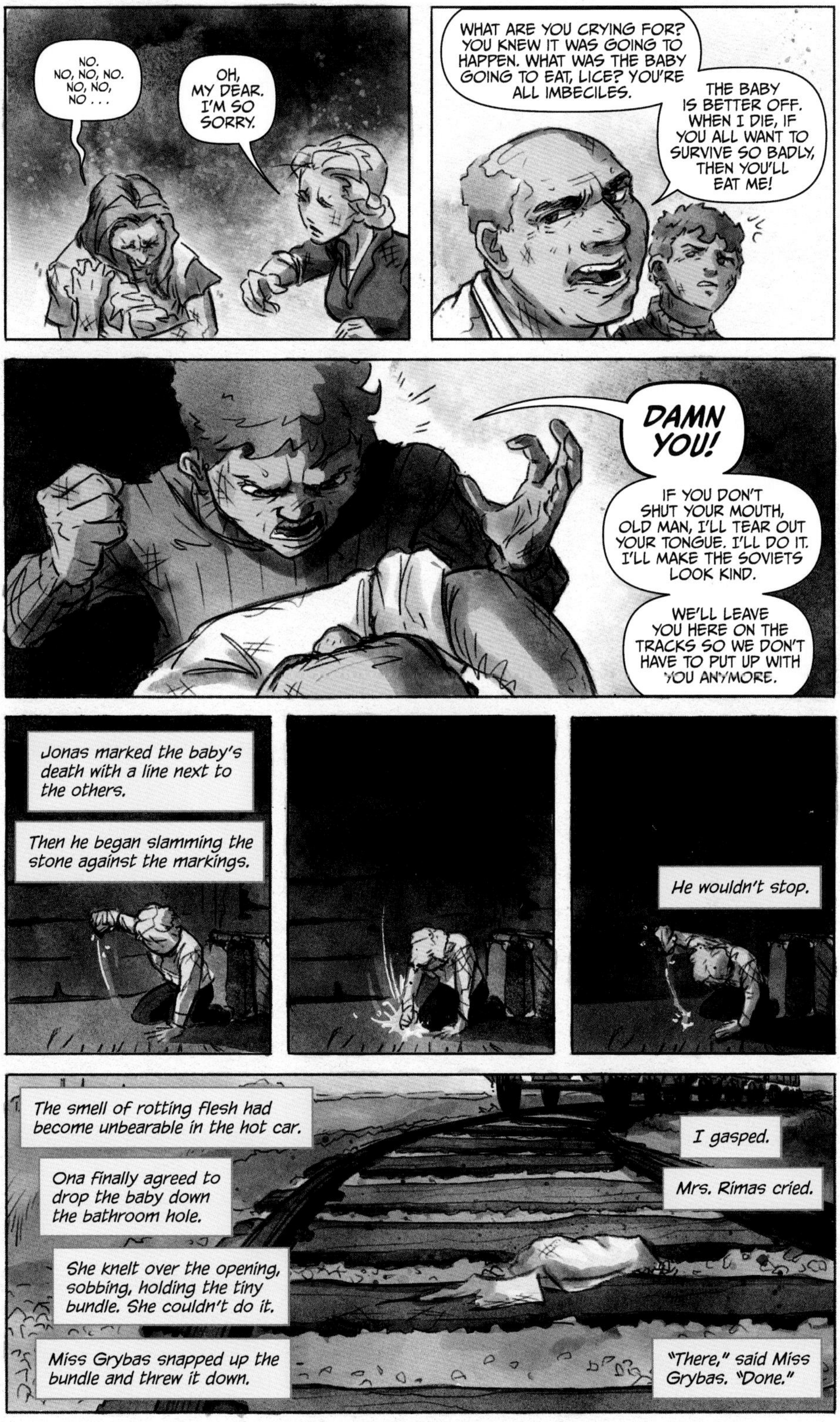

NO. NO, NO, NO. NO, NO, NO . . .
OH, MY DEAR. I'M SO SORRY.
WHAT ARE YOU CRYING FOR? YOU KNEW IT WAS GOING TO HAPPEN. WHAT WAS THE BABY GOING TO EAT, LICE? YOU'RE ALL IMBECILES.
THE BABY IS BETTER OFF. WHEN I DIE, IF YOU ALL WANT TO SURVIVE SO BADLY, THEN YOU'LL EAT ME!
DAMN YOU!
IF YOU DON'T SHUT YOUR MOUTH, OLD MAN, I'LL TEAR OUT YOUR TONGUE. I'LL DO IT. I'LL MAKE THE SOVIETS LOOK KIND.
WE'LL LEAVE YOU HERE ON THE TRACKS SO WE DON'T HAVE TO PUT UP WITH YOU ANYMORE.
Jonas marked the baby's death with a line next to the others.
Then he began slamming the stone against the markings.
He wouldn't stop.
The smell of rotting flesh had become unbearable in the hot car.
Ona finally agreed to drop the baby down the bathroom hole.
She knelt over the opening, sobbing, holding the tiny bundle. She couldn't do it.
Miss Grybas snapped up the bundle and threw it down.
I gasped.
Mrs. Rimas cried.
"There," said Miss Grybas. "Done."

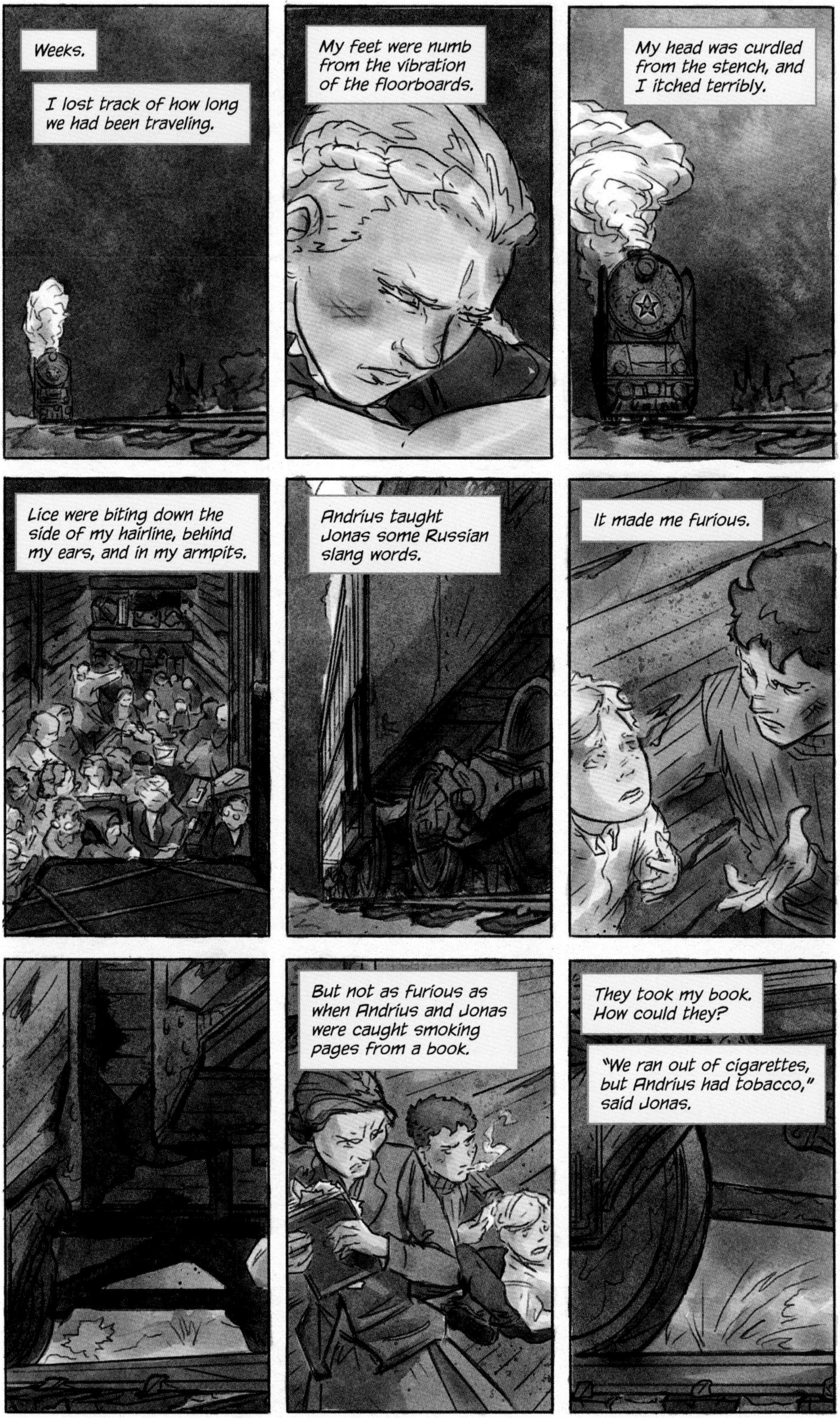
Weeks.
I lost track of how long we had been traveling.
My feet were numb from the vibration of the floorboards.
My head was curdled from the stench, and I itched terribly.
Lice were biting down the side of my hairline, behind my ears, and in my armpits.
Andrius taught Jonas some Russian slang words.
It made me furious.
But not as furious as when Andrius and Jonas were caught smoking pages from a book.
They took my book. How could they?
"We ran out of cigarettes, but Andrius had tobacco," said Jonas.

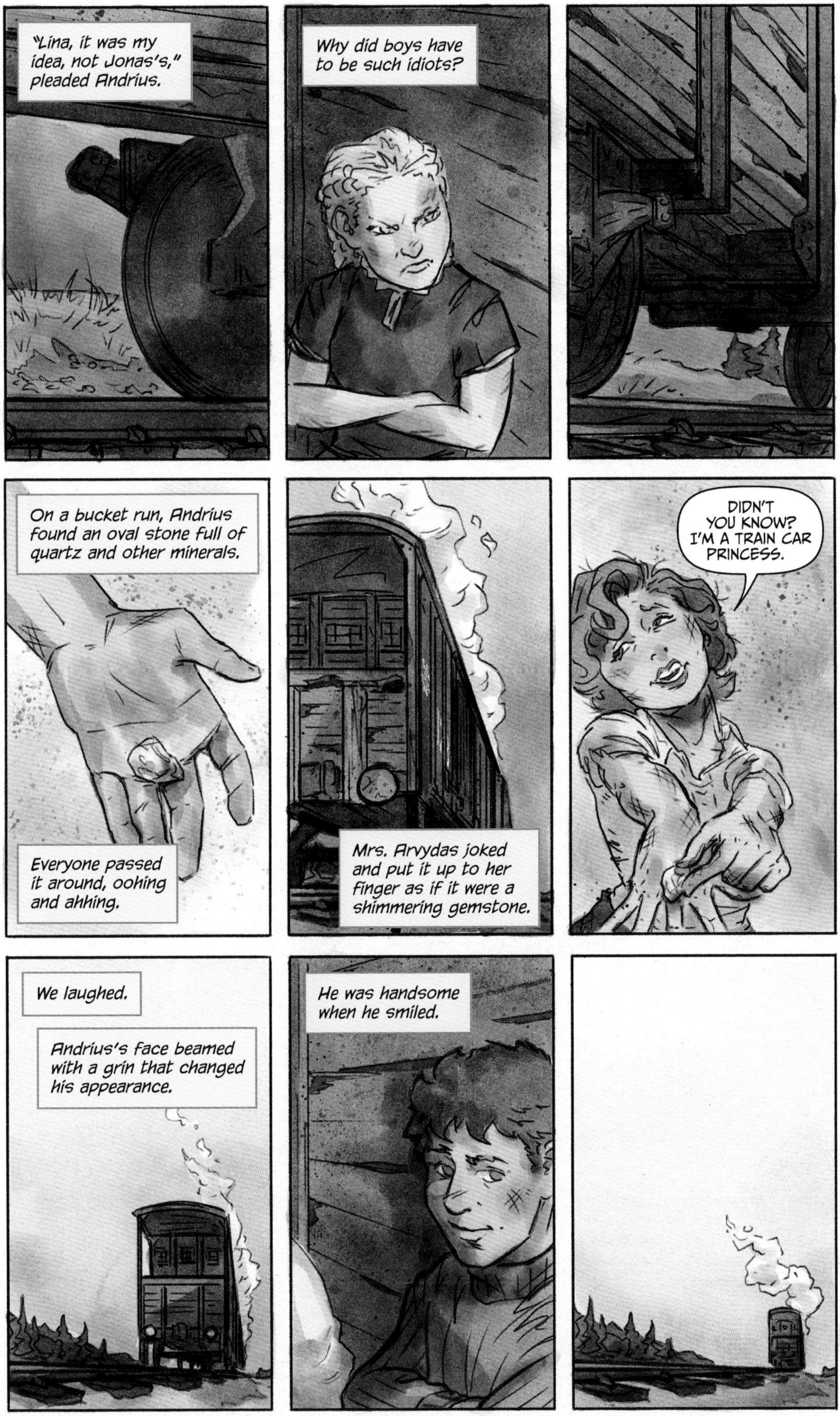
"Lina, it was my idea, not Jonas's," pleaded Andrius.
Why did boys have to be such idiots?
On a bucket run, Andrius found an oval stone full of quartz and other minerals.
Everyone passed it around, oohing and ahhing.
Mrs. Arvydas joked and put it up to her finger as if it were a shimmering gemstone.
DIDN'T YOU KNOW? I'M A TRAIN CAR PRINCESS.
We laughed.
Andrius's face beamed with a grin that changed his appearance.
He was handsome when he smiled.

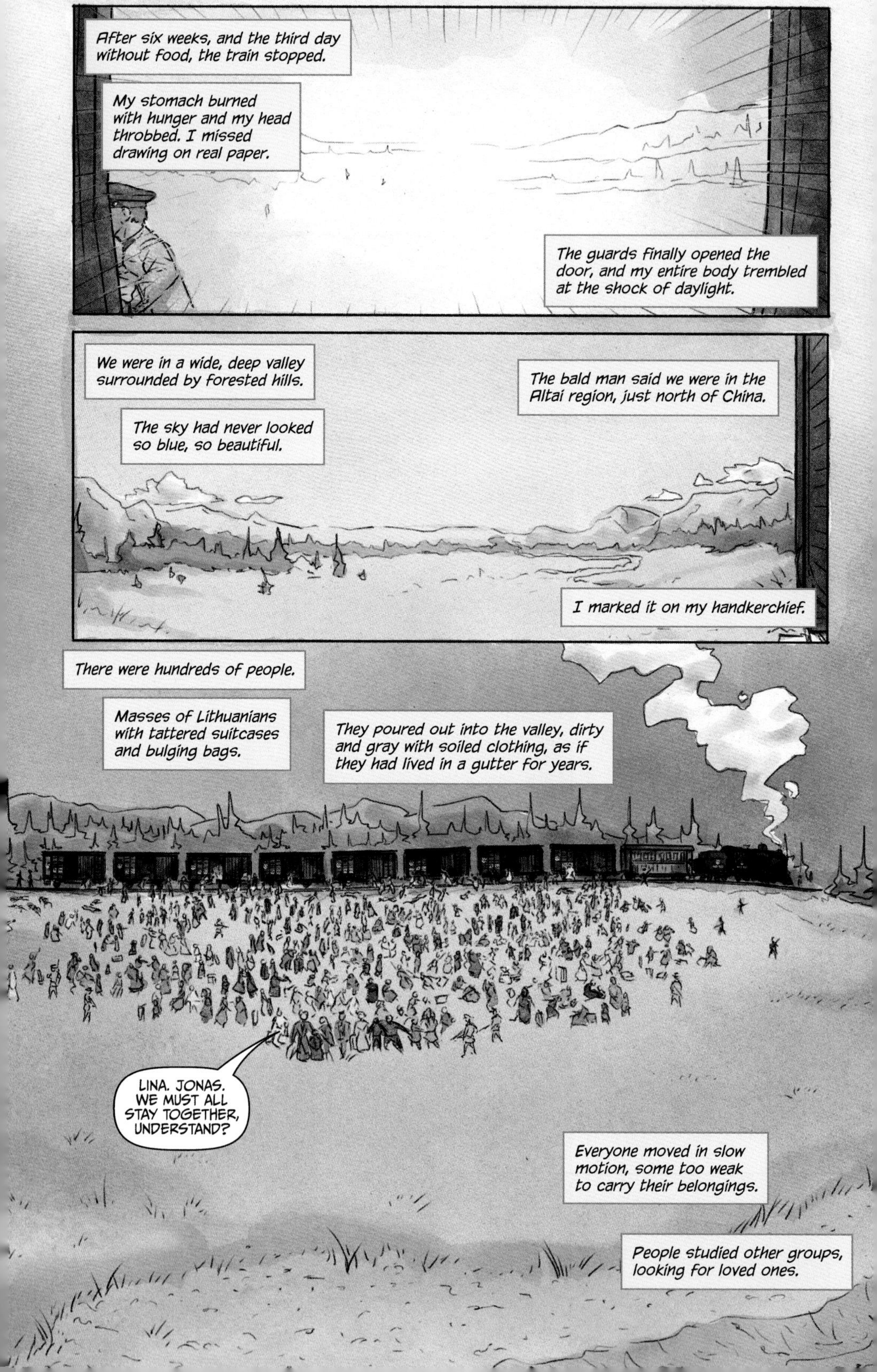
After six weeks, and the third day without food, the train stopped.
My stomach burned with hunger and my head throbbed. I missed drawing on real paper.
The guards finally opened the door, and my entire body trembled at the shock of daylight.
We were in a wide, deep valley surrounded by forested hills.
The sky had never looked so blue, so beautiful.
The bald man said we were in the Altai region, just north of China.
I marked it on my handkerchief.
There were hundreds of people.
Masses of Lithuanians with tattered suitcases and bulging bags.
They poured out into the valley, dirty and gray with soiled clothing, as if they had lived in a gutter for years.
LINA. JONAS. WE MUST ALL STAY TOGETHER, UNDERSTAND?
Everyone moved in slow motion, some too weak to carry their belongings.
People studied other groups, looking for loved ones.

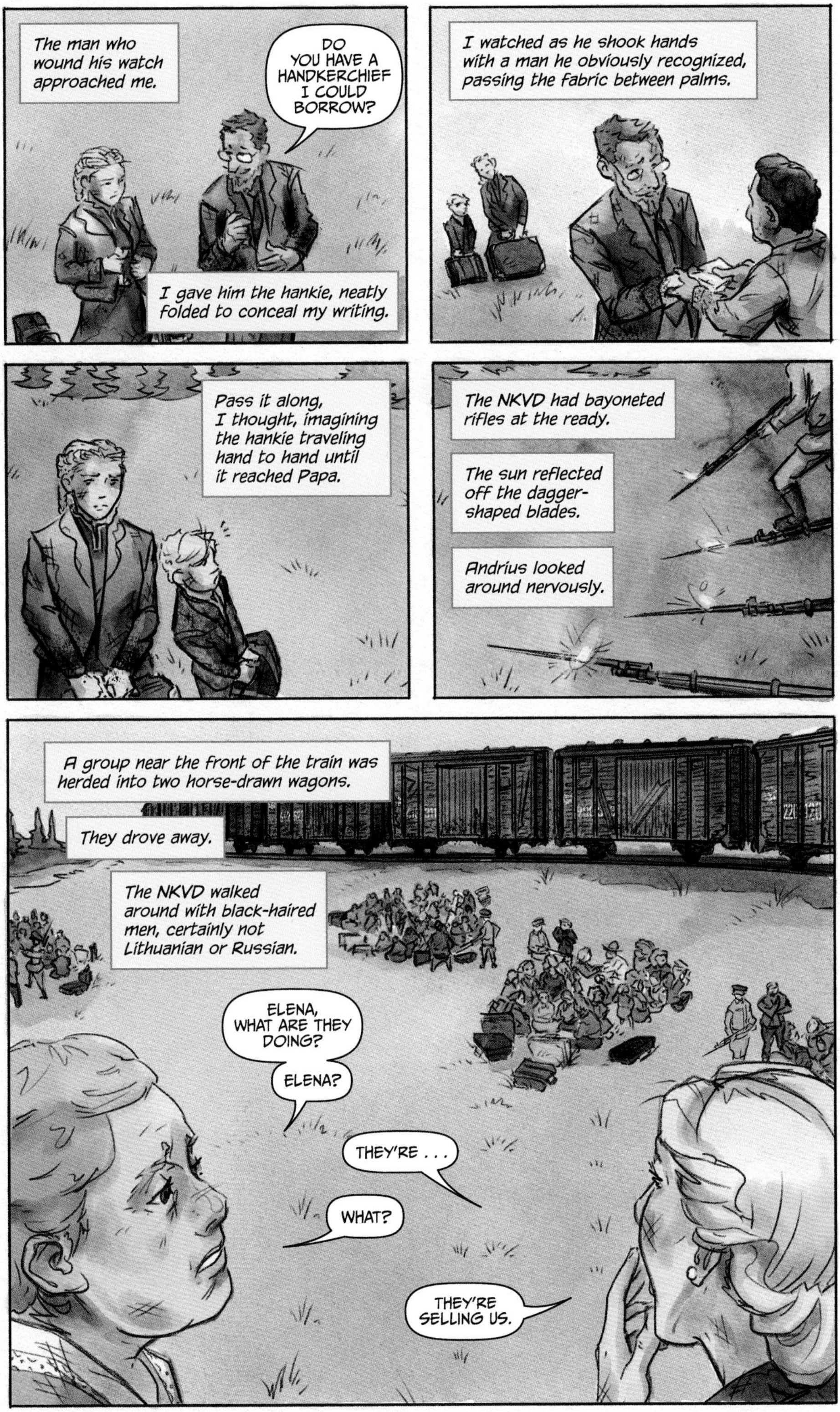

The man who wound his watch approached me.
DO YOU HAVE A HANDKERCHIEF I COULD BORROW?
I gave him the hankie, neatly folded to conceal my writing.
I watched as he shook hands with a man he obviously recognized, passing the fabric between palms.
Pass it along, I thought, imagining the hankie traveling hand to hand until it reached Papa.
The NKVD had bayoneted rifles at the ready.
The sun reflected off the dagger-shaped blades.
Andrius looked around nervously.
A group near the front of the train was herded into two horse-drawn wagons.
They drove away.
The NKVD walked around with black-haired men, certainly not Lithuanian or Russian.
ELENA, WHAT ARE THEY DOING?
ELENA?
THEY'RE . . .
WHAT?
THEY'RE SELLING US.

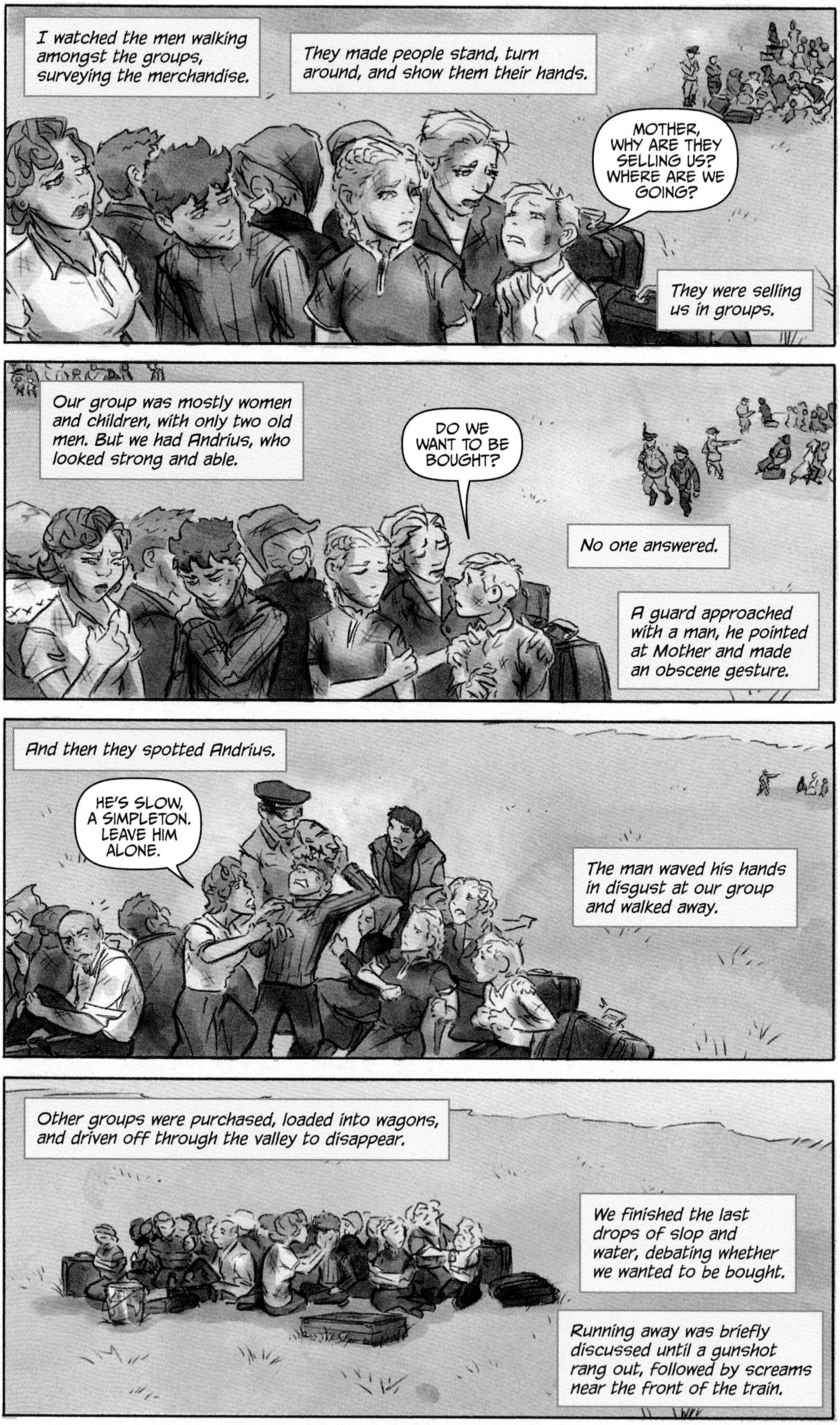

I watched the men walking amongst the groups, surveying the merchandise.
They made people stand, turn around, and show them their hands.
MOTHER, WHY ARE THEY SELLING US? WHERE ARE WE GOING?
They were selling us in groups.
Our group was mostly women and children, with only two old men. But we had Andrius, who looked strong and able.
DO WE WANT TO BE BOUGHT?
No one answered.
A guard approached with a man, he pointed at Mother and made an obscene gesture.
And then they spotted Andrius.
HE'S SLOW, A SIMPLETON. LEAVE HIM ALONE.
The man waved his hands in disgust at our group and walked away.
Other groups were purchased, loaded into wagons, and driven off through the valley to disappear.
We finished the last drops of slop and water, debating whether we wanted to be bought.
Running away was briefly discussed until a gunshot rang out, followed by screams near the front of the train.

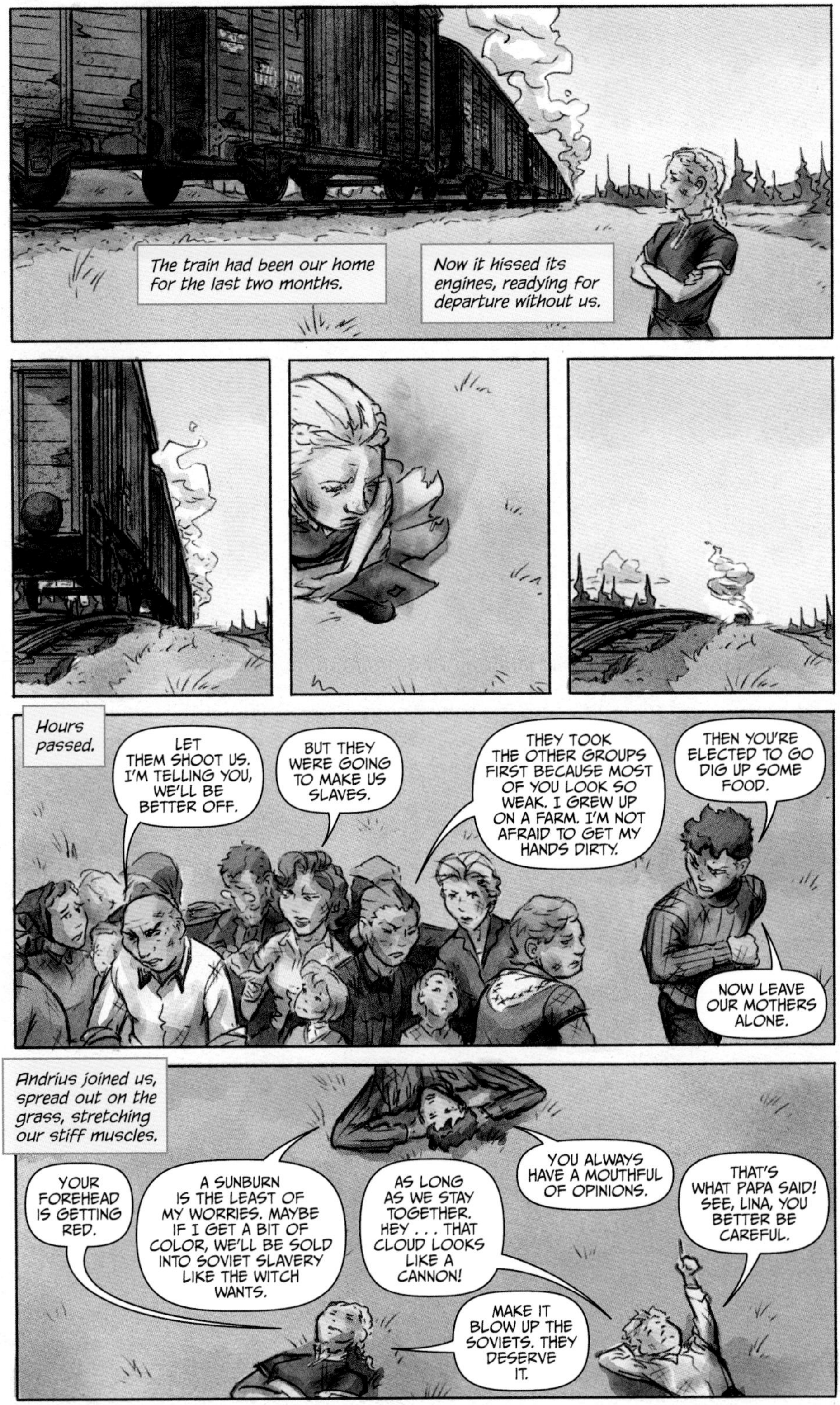
The train had been our home for the last two months.
Now it hissed its engines, readying for departure without us.
Hours passed.
LET THEM SHOOT US. I'M TELLING YOU, WE'LL BE BETTER OFF.
BUT THEY WERE GOING TO MAKE US SLAVES.
THEY TOOK THE OTHER GROUPS FIRST BECAUSE MOST OF YOU LOOK SO WEAK. I GREW UP ON A FARM. I'M NOT AFRAID TO GET MY HANDS DIRTY.
THEN YOU'RE ELECTED TO GO DIG UP SOME FOOD.
NOW LEAVE OUR MOTHERS ALONE.
Andrius joined us, spread out on the grass, stretching our stiff muscles.
YOUR FOREHEAD IS GETTING RED.
A SUNBURN IS THE LEAST OF MY WORRIES. MAYBE IF I GET A BIT OF COLOR, WE'LL BE SOLD INTO SOVIET SLAVERY LIKE THE WITCH WANTS.
AS LONG AS WE STAY TOGETHER. HEY . . . THAT CLOUD LOOKS LIKE A CANNON!
YOU ALWAYS HAVE A MOUTHFUL OF OPINIONS.
THAT'S WHAT PAPA SAID! SEE, LINA, YOU BETTER BE CAREFUL.
MAKE IT BLOW UP THE SOVIETS. THEY DESERVE IT.

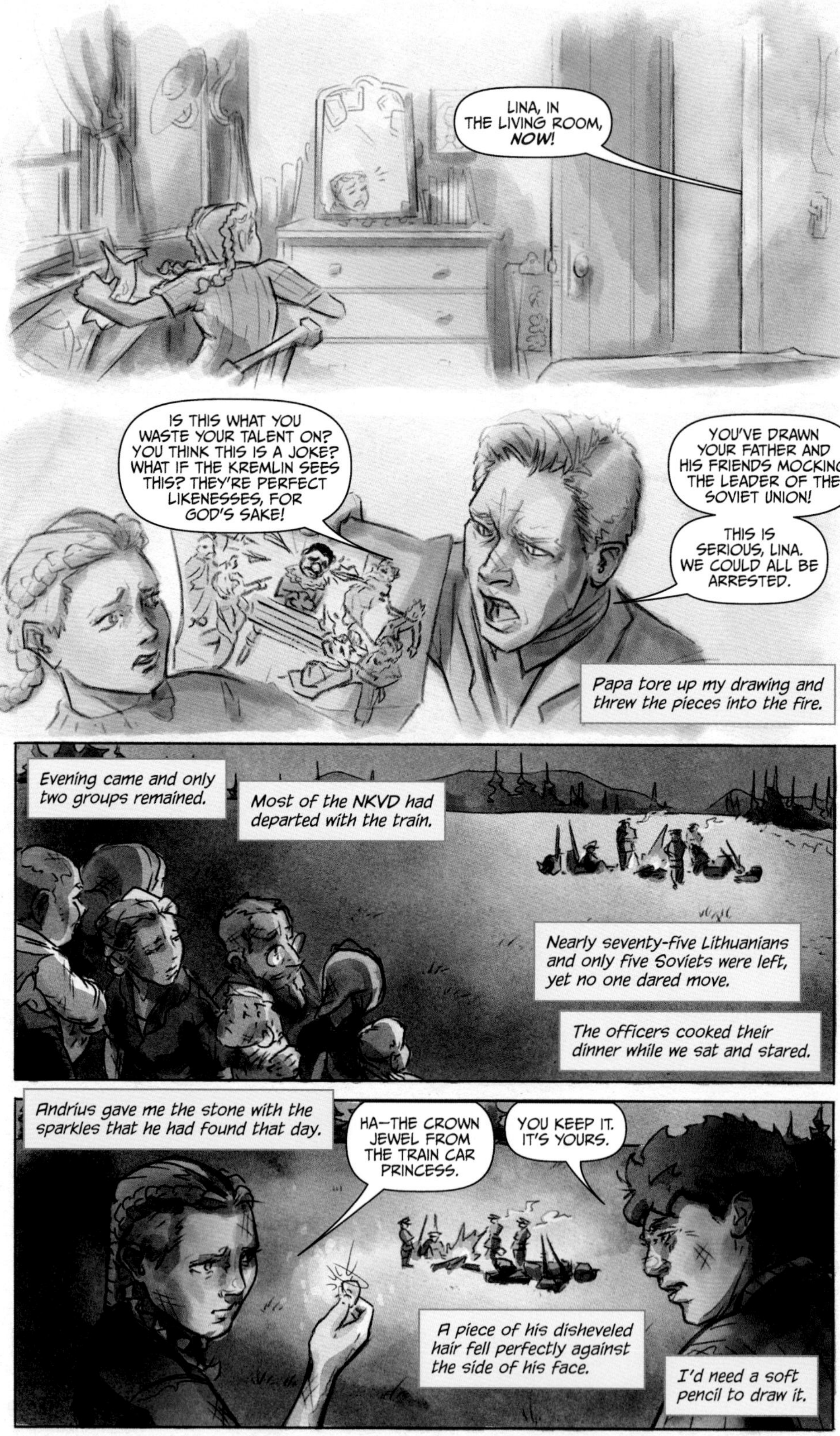
LINA, IN THE LIVING ROOM, NOW!
IS THIS WHAT YOU WASTE YOUR TALENT ON? YOU THINK THIS IS A JOKE? WHAT IF THE KREMLIN SEES THIS? THEY'RE PERFECT LIKENESSES, FOR GOD'S SAKE!
YOU'VE DRAWN YOUR FATHER AND HIS FRIENDS MOCKING THE LEADER OF THE SOVIET UNION!
THIS IS SERIOUS, LINA. WE COULD ALL BE ARRESTED.
Papa tore up my drawing and threw the pieces into the fire.
Evening came and only two groups remained.
Most of the NKVD had departed with the train.
Nearly seventy-five Lithuanians and only five Soviets were left, yet no one dared move.
The officers cooked their dinner while we sat and stared.
Andrius gave me the stone with the sparkles that he had found that day.
HA—THE CROWN JEWEL FROM THE TRAIN CAR PRINCESS.
YOU KEEP IT. IT'S YOURS.
A piece of his disheveled hair fell perfectly against the side of his face.
I'd need a soft pencil to draw it.

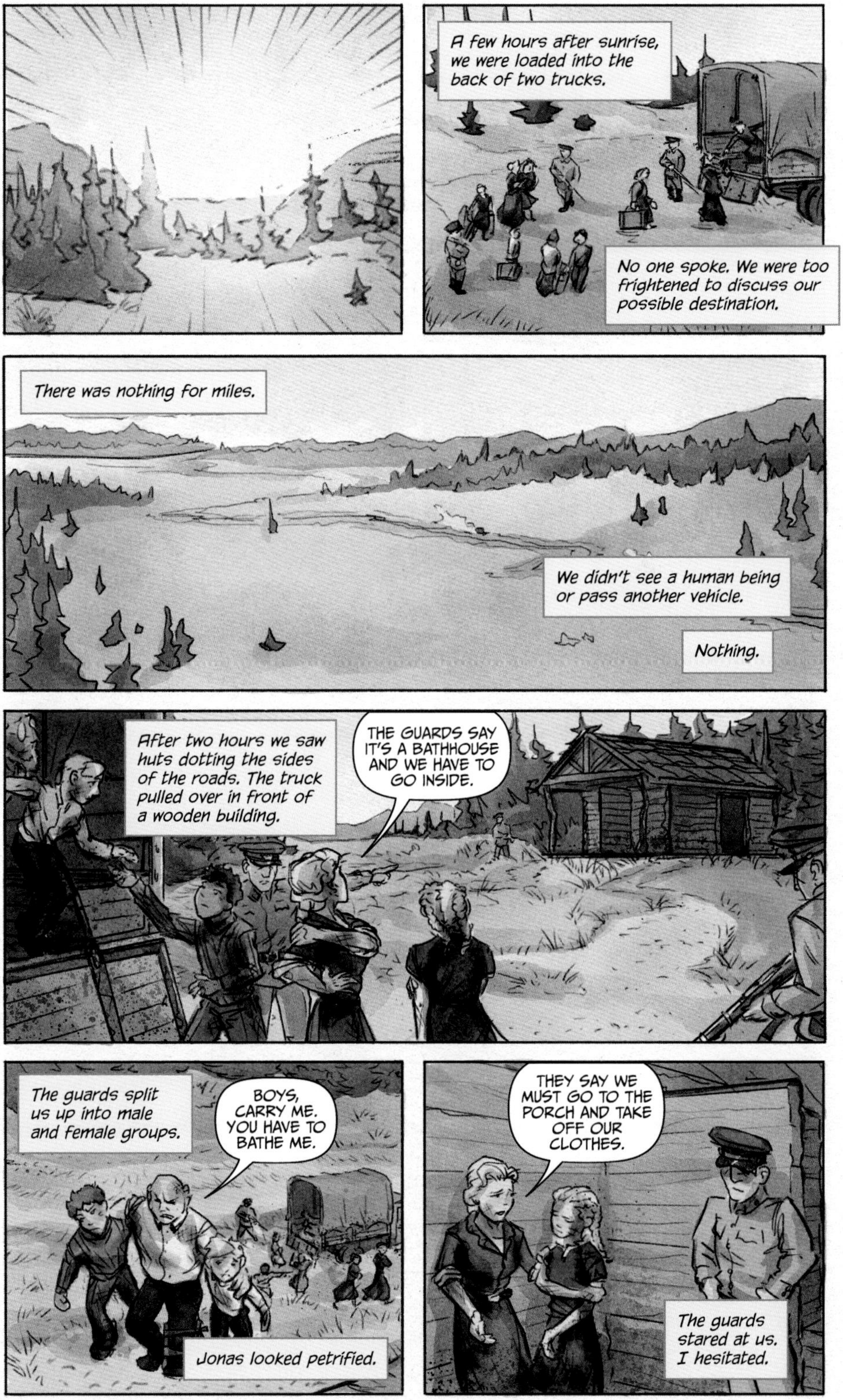
A few hours after sunrise, we were loaded into the back of two trucks.
No one spoke. We were too frightened to discuss our possible destination.
There was nothing for miles.
We didn't see a human being or pass another vehicle.
Nothing.
After two hours we saw huts dotting the sides of the roads. The truck pulled over in front of a wooden building.
THE GUARDS SAY IT'S A BATHHOUSE AND WE HAVE TO GO INSIDE.
The guards split us up into male and female groups.
BOYS, CARRY ME. YOU HAVE TO BATHE ME.
Jonas looked petrified.
THEY SAY WE MUST GO TO THE PORCH AND TAKE OFF OUR CLOTHES.
The guards stared at us. I hesitated.

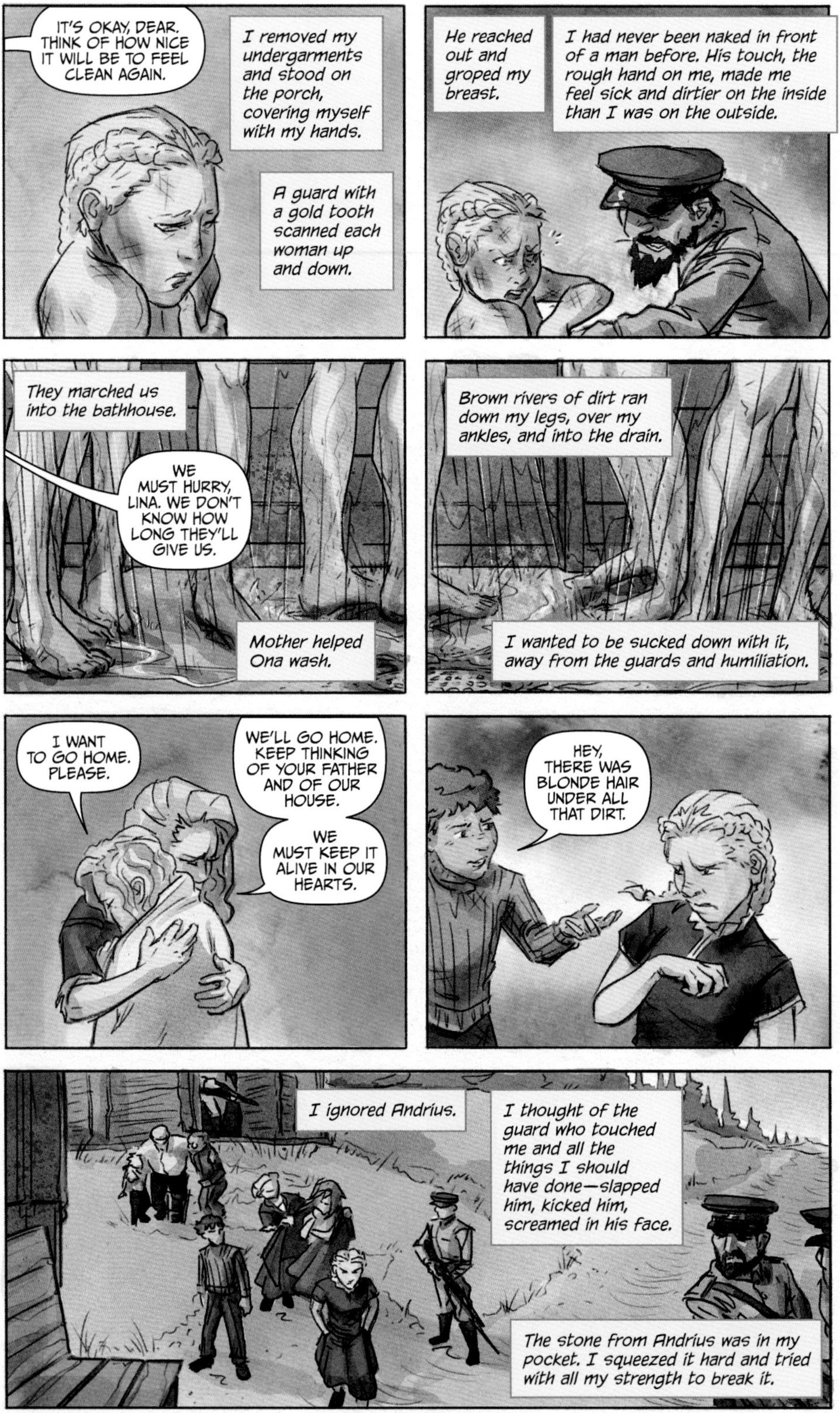
IT'S OKAY, DEAR. THINK OF HOW NICE IT WILL BE TO FEEL CLEAN AGAIN.
I removed my undergarments and stood on the porch, covering myself with my hands.
A guard with a gold tooth scanned each woman up and down.
He reached out and groped my breast.
I had never been naked in front of a man before. His touch, the rough hand on me, made me feel sick and dirtier on the inside than I was on the outside.
They marched us into the bathhouse.
WE MUST HURRY, LINA. WE DON'T KNOW HOW LONG THEY'LL GIVE US.
Mother helped Ona wash.
Brown rivers of dirt ran down my legs, over my ankles, and into the drain.
I wanted to be sucked down with it, away from the guards and humiliation.
I WANT TO GO HOME. PLEASE.
WE'LL GO HOME. KEEP THINKING OF YOUR FATHER AND OF OUR HOUSE.
WE MUST KEEP IT ALIVE IN OUR HEARTS.
HEY, THERE WAS BLONDE HAIR UNDER ALL THAT DIRT.
I ignored Andrius.
I thought of the guard who touched me and all the things I should have done—slapped him, kicked him, screamed in his face.
The stone from Andrius was in my pocket. I squeezed it hard and tried with all my strength to break it.

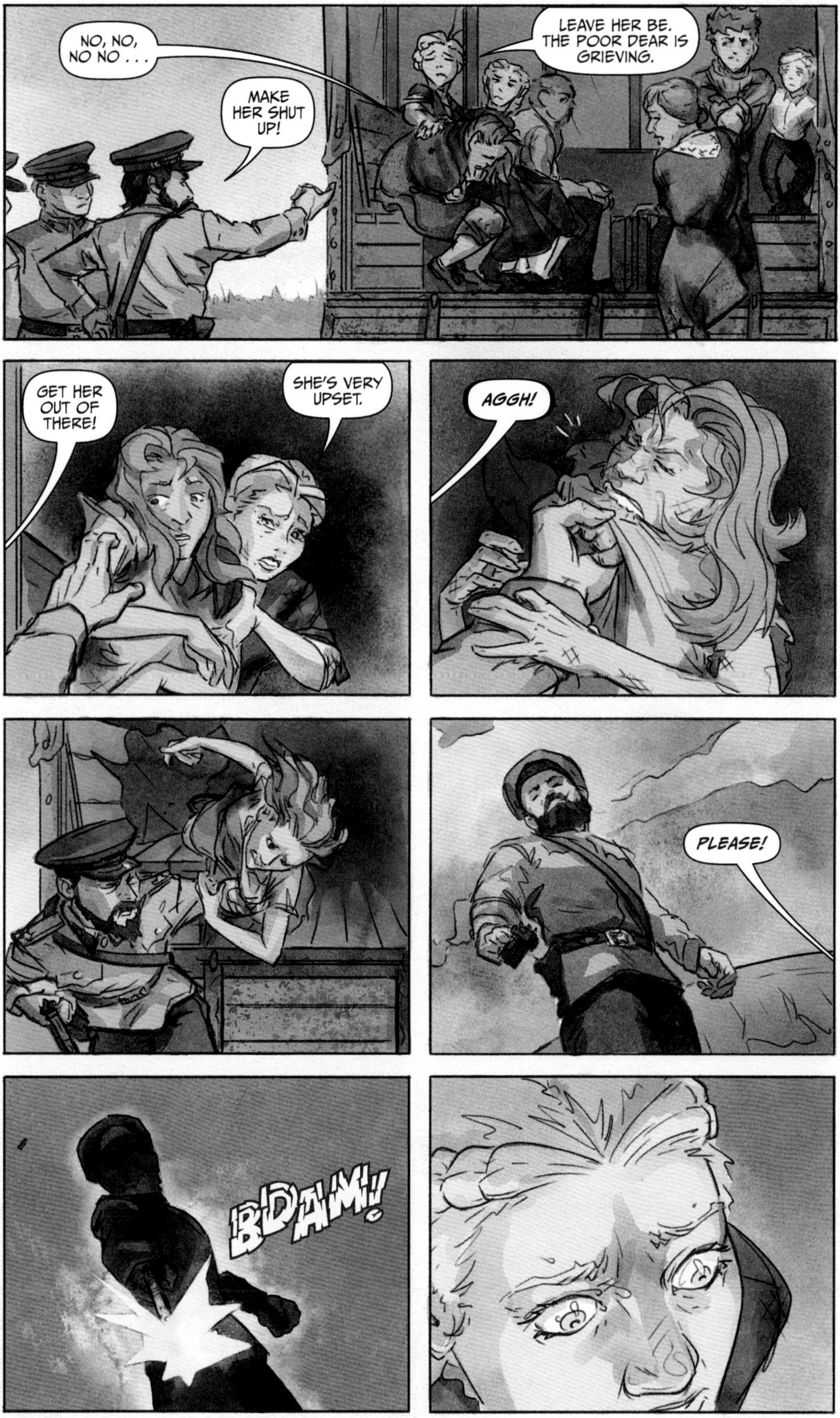
NO, NO,
NO NO . . .
LEAVE HER BE. THE POOR DEAR IS GRIEVING.
MAKE HER SHUT UP!
GET HER OUT OF THERE!
SHE'S VERY UPSET.
AGGH!
PLEASE!
BDAM!!

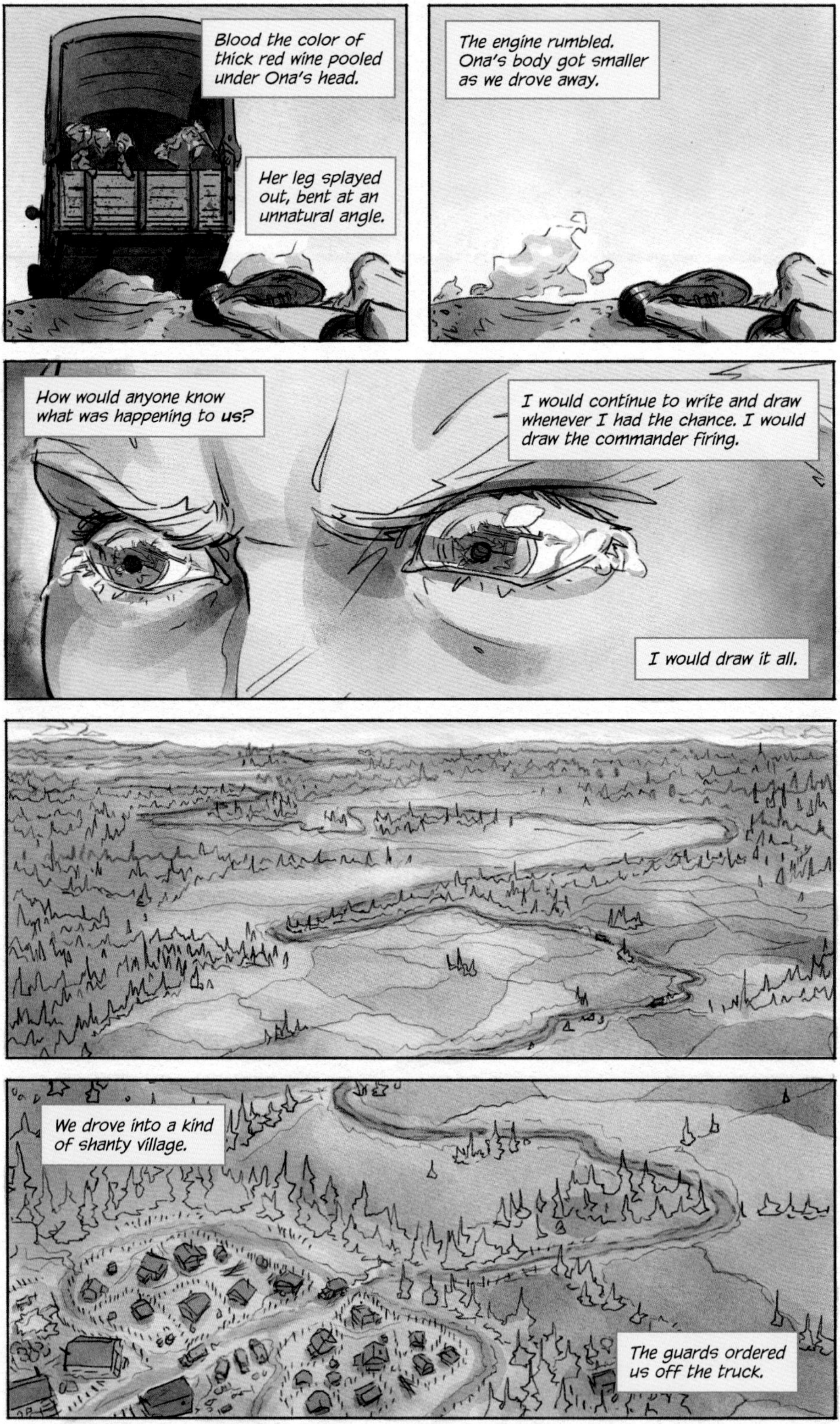
Blood the color of thick red wine pooled under Ona's head.
Her leg splayed out, bent at an unnatural angle.
The engine rumbled. Ona's body got smaller as we drove away.
How would anyone know what was happening to **us**?
I would continue to write and draw whenever I had the chance. I would draw the commander firing.
I would draw it all.
We drove into a kind of shanty village.
The guards ordered us off the truck.

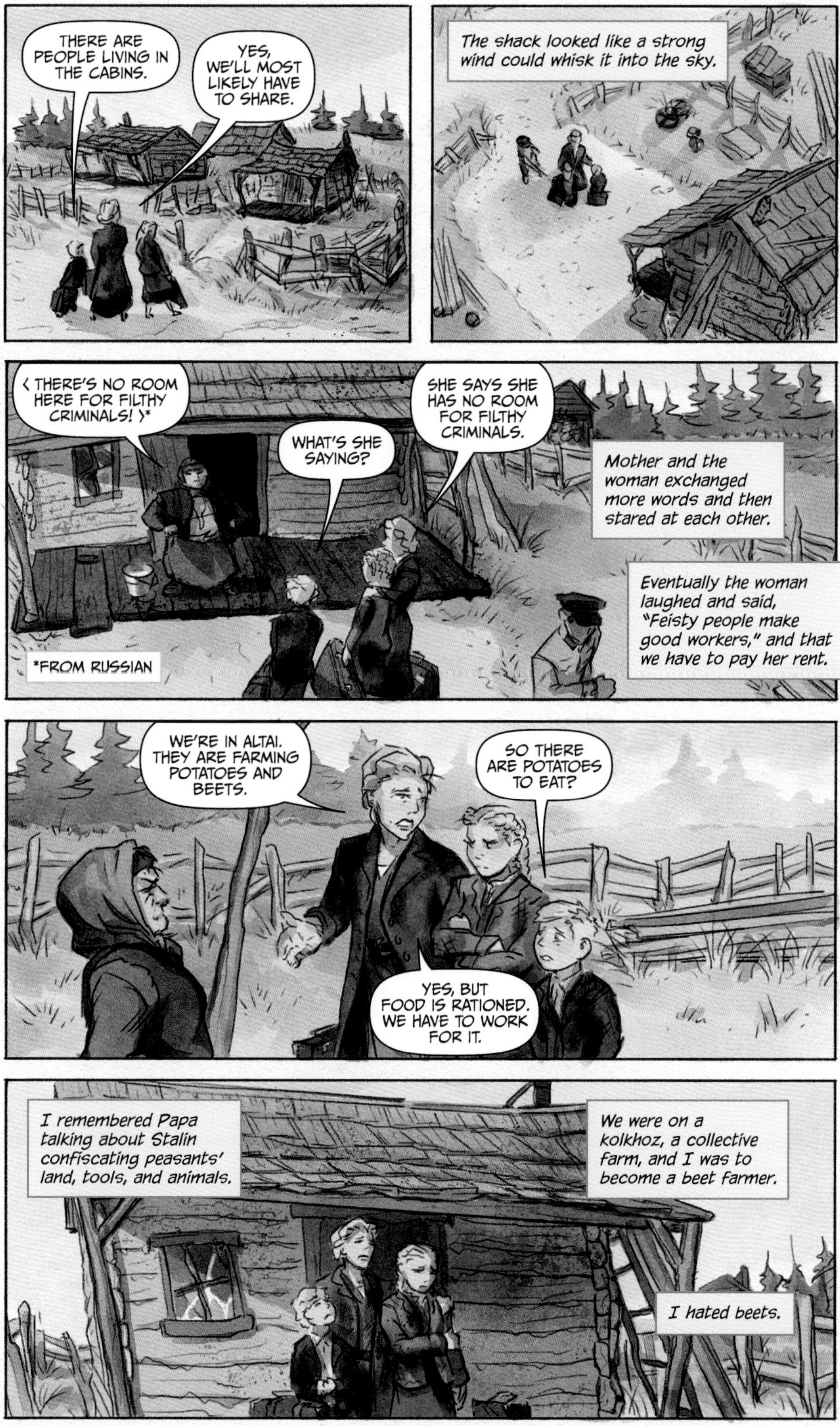
THERE ARE PEOPLE LIVING IN THE CABINS.
YES, WE'LL MOST LIKELY HAVE TO SHARE.
The shack looked like a strong wind could whisk it into the sky.
‹ THERE'S NO ROOM HERE FOR FILTHY CRIMINALS! ›*
WHAT'S SHE SAYING?
SHE SAYS SHE HAS NO ROOM FOR FILTHY CRIMINALS.
Mother and the woman exchanged more words and then stared at each other.
Eventually the woman laughed and said, "Feisty people make good workers," and that we have to pay her rent.
*FROM RUSSIAN
WE'RE IN ALTAI. THEY ARE FARMING POTATOES AND BEETS.
SO THERE ARE POTATOES TO EAT?
YES, BUT FOOD IS RATIONED. WE HAVE TO WORK FOR IT.
I remembered Papa talking about Stalin confiscating peasants' land, tools, and animals.
We were on a kolkhoz, a collective farm, and I was to become a beet farmer.
I hated beets.

MAPS
& SNAKES

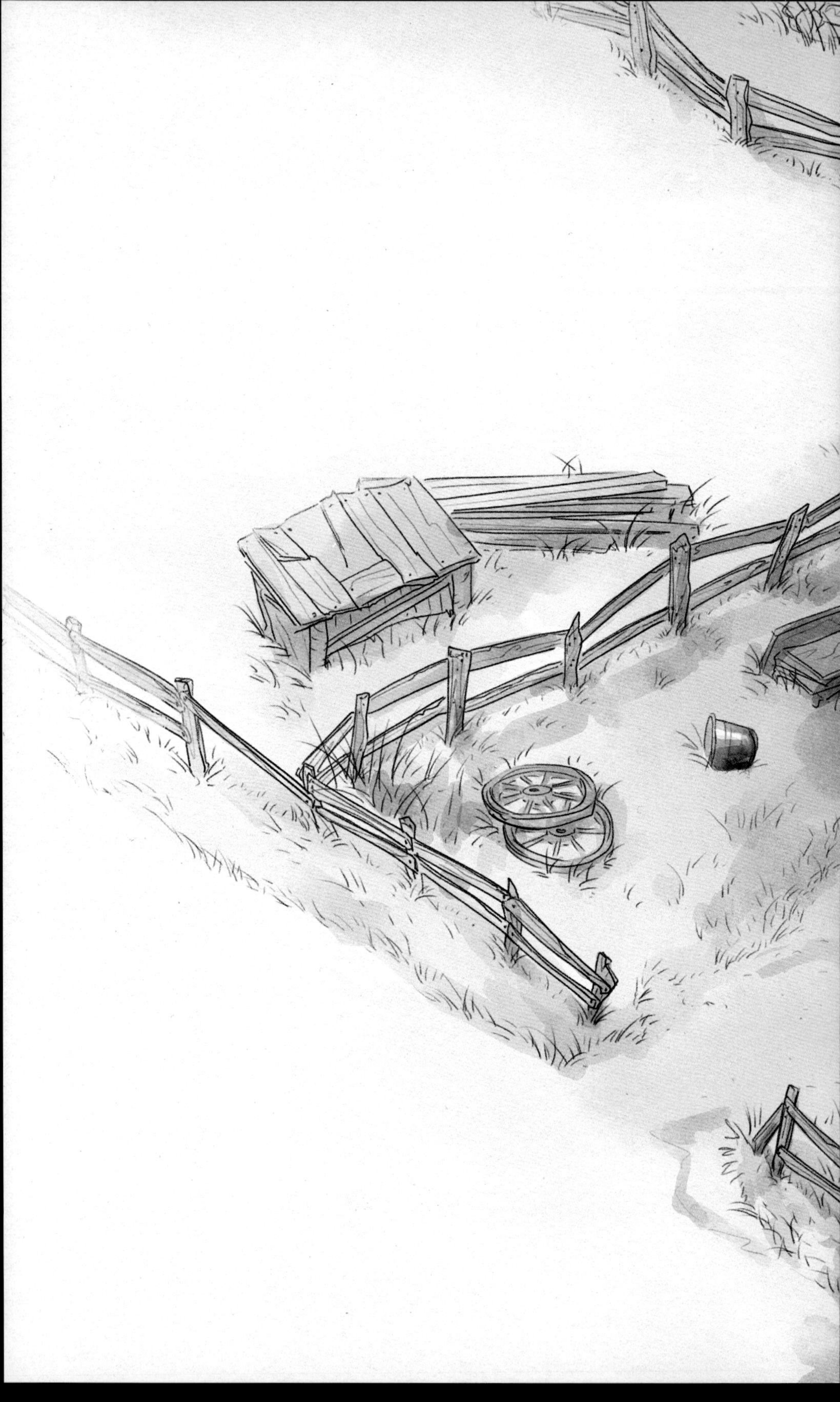

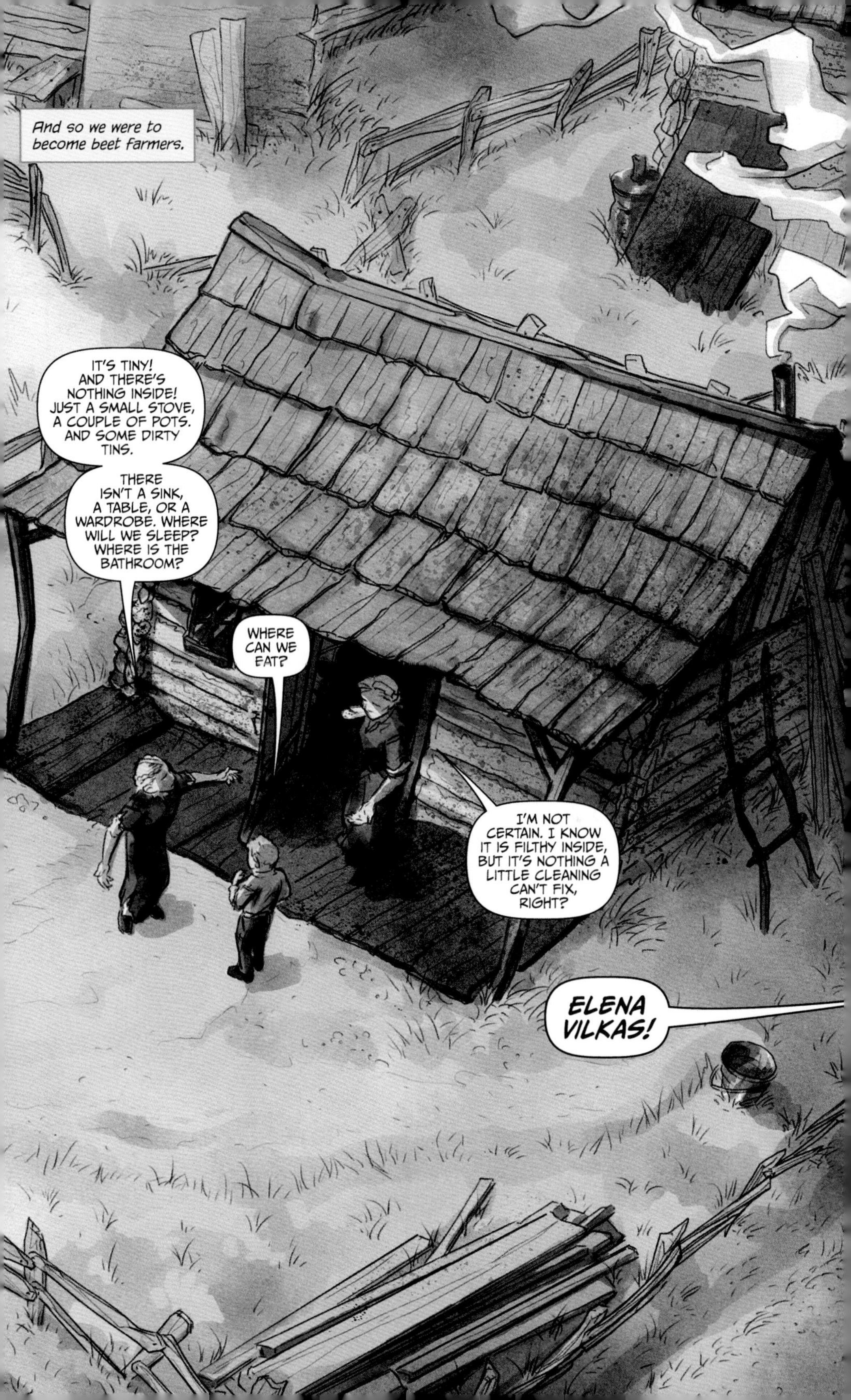
And so we were to become beet farmers.
IT'S TINY! AND THERE'S NOTHING INSIDE! JUST A SMALL STOVE, A COUPLE OF POTS. AND SOME DIRTY TINS.
THERE ISN'T A SINK, A TABLE, OR A WARDROBE. WHERE WILL WE SLEEP? WHERE IS THE BATHROOM?
WHERE CAN WE EAT?
I'M NOT CERTAIN. I KNOW IT IS FILTHY INSIDE, BUT IT'S NOTHING A LITTLE CLEANING CAN'T FIX, RIGHT?
ELENA VILKAS!

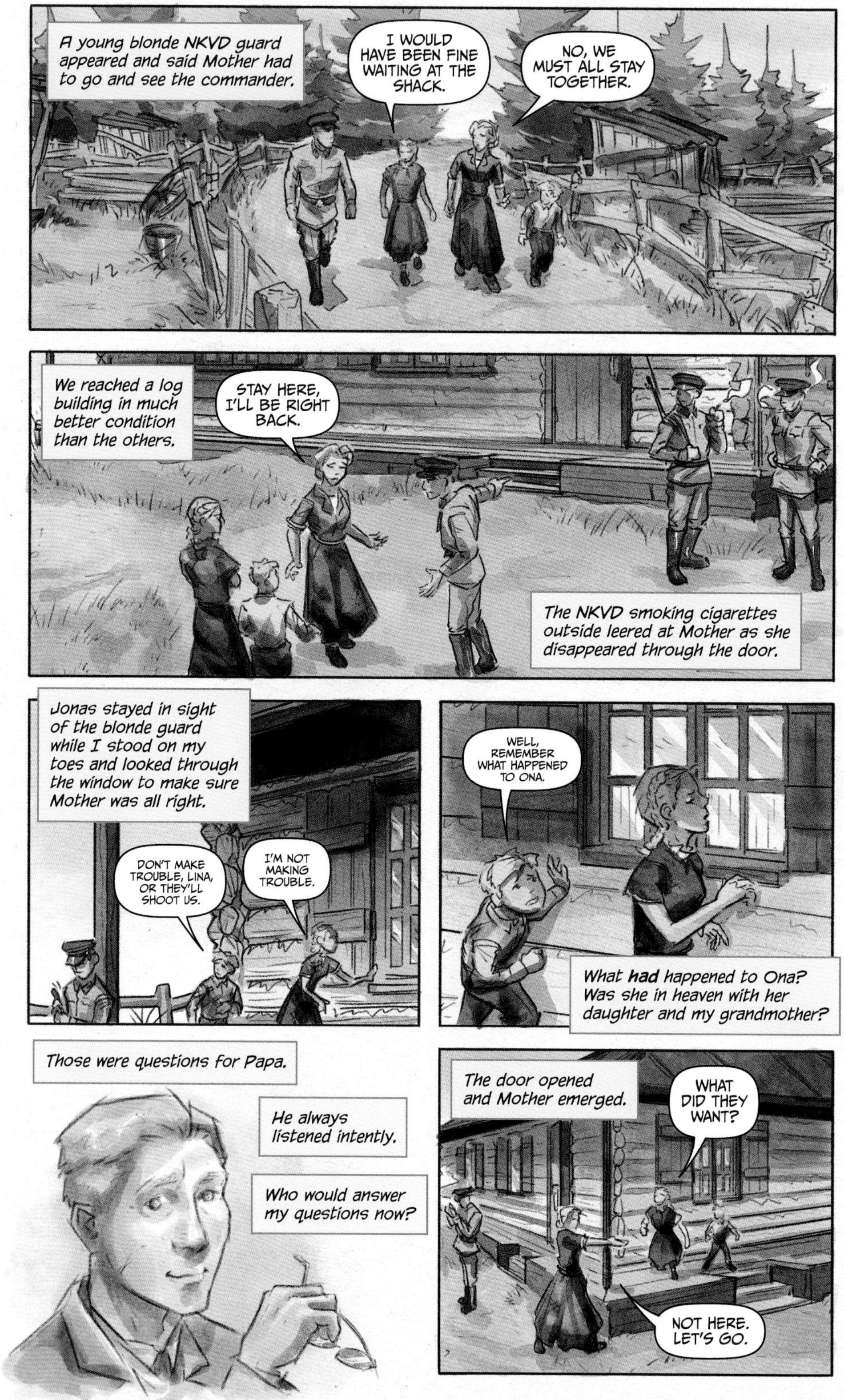
A young blonde NKVD guard appeared and said Mother had to go and see the commander.
I WOULD HAVE BEEN FINE WAITING AT THE SHACK.
NO, WE MUST ALL STAY TOGETHER.
We reached a log building in much better condition than the others.
STAY HERE, I'LL BE RIGHT BACK.
The NKVD smoking cigarettes outside leered at Mother as she disappeared through the door.
Jonas stayed in sight of the blonde guard while I stood on my toes and looked through the window to make sure Mother was all right.
DON'T MAKE TROUBLE, LINA, OR THEY'LL SHOOT US.
I'M NOT MAKING TROUBLE.
WELL, REMEMBER WHAT HAPPENED TO ONA.
What **had** happened to Ona? Was she in heaven with her daughter and my grandmother?
Those were questions for Papa.
He always listened intently.
Who would answer my questions now?
The door opened and Mother emerged.
WHAT DID THEY WANT?
NOT HERE. LET'S GO.

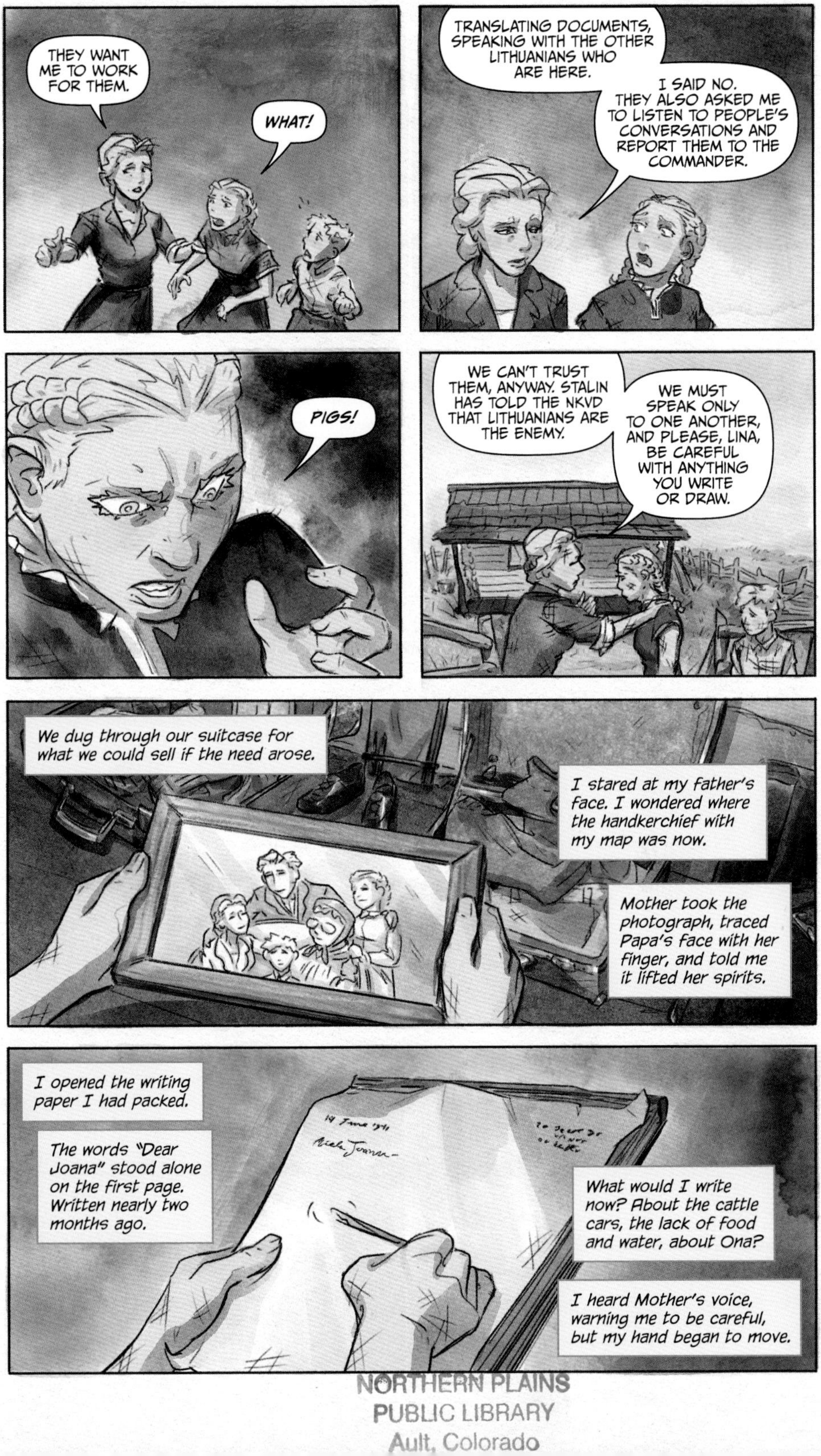
THEY WANT ME TO WORK FOR THEM.
WHAT!
TRANSLATING DOCUMENTS, SPEAKING WITH THE OTHER LITHUANIANS WHO ARE HERE.
I SAID NO. THEY ALSO ASKED ME TO LISTEN TO PEOPLE'S CONVERSATIONS AND REPORT THEM TO THE COMMANDER.
PIGS!
WE CAN'T TRUST THEM, ANYWAY. STALIN HAS TOLD THE NKVD THAT LITHUANIANS ARE THE ENEMY.
WE MUST SPEAK ONLY TO ONE ANOTHER, AND PLEASE, LINA, BE CAREFUL WITH ANYTHING YOU WRITE OR DRAW.
We dug through our suitcase for what we could sell if the need arose.
I stared at my father's face. I wondered where the handkerchief with my map was now.
Mother took the photograph, traced Papa's face with her finger, and told me it lifted her spirits.
I opened the writing paper I had packed.
The words "Dear Joana" stood alone on the first page. Written nearly two months ago.
What would I write now? About the cattle cars, the lack of food and water, about Ona?
I heard Mother's voice, warning me to be careful, but my hand began to move.

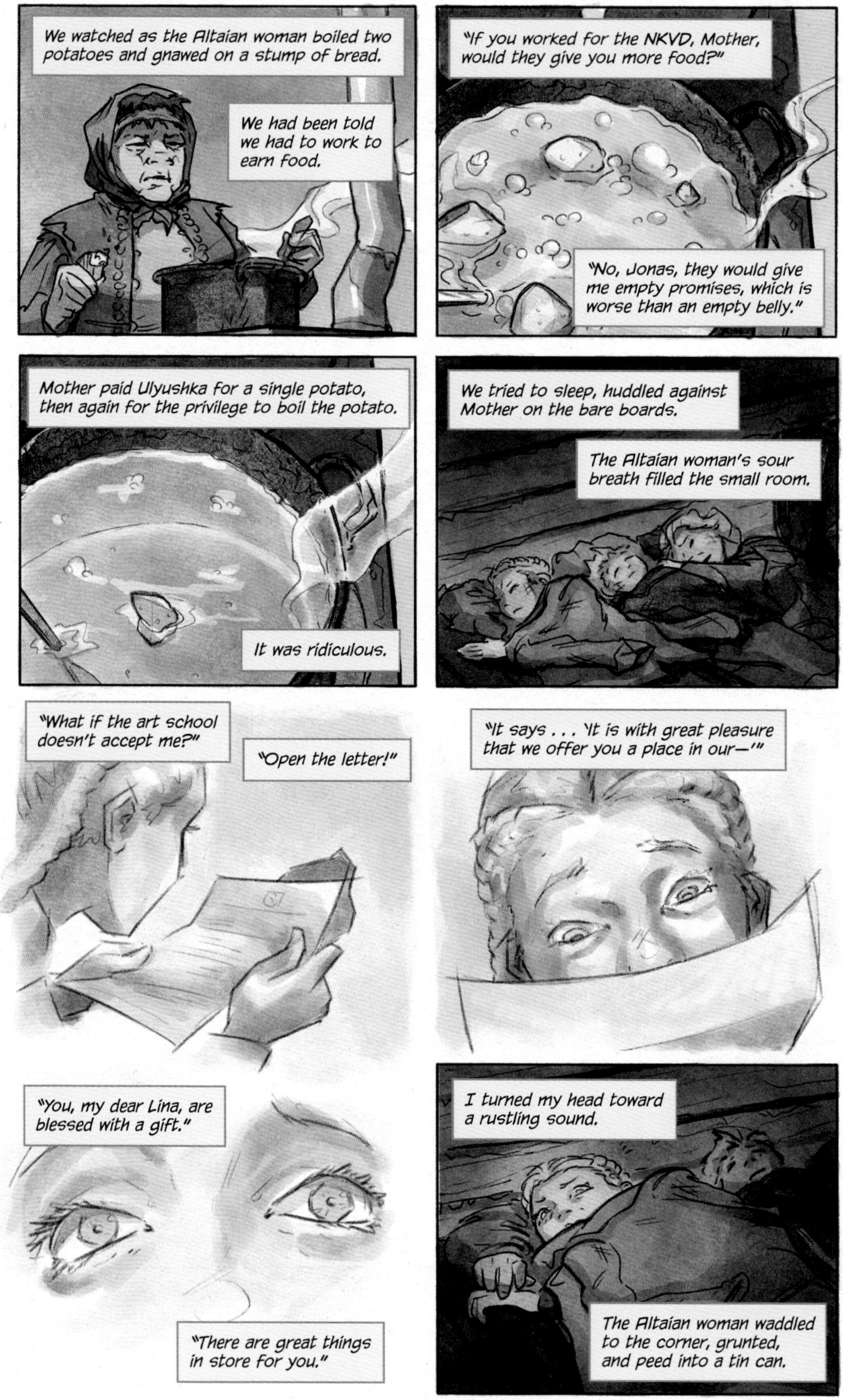
We watched as the Altaian woman boiled two potatoes and gnawed on a stump of bread.
We had been told we had to work to earn food.
"If you worked for the NKVD, Mother, would they give you more food?"
"No, Jonas, they would give me empty promises, which is worse than an empty belly."
Mother paid Ulyushka for a single potato, then again for the privilege to boil the potato.
It was ridiculous.
We tried to sleep, huddled against Mother on the bare boards.
The Altaian woman's sour breath filled the small room.
"What if the art school doesn't accept me?"
"Open the letter!"
"It says . . . 'It is with great pleasure that we offer you a place in our—'"
"You, my dear Lina, are blessed with a gift."
"There are great things in store for you."
I turned my head toward a rustling sound.
The Altaian woman waddled to the corner, grunted, and peed into a tin can.

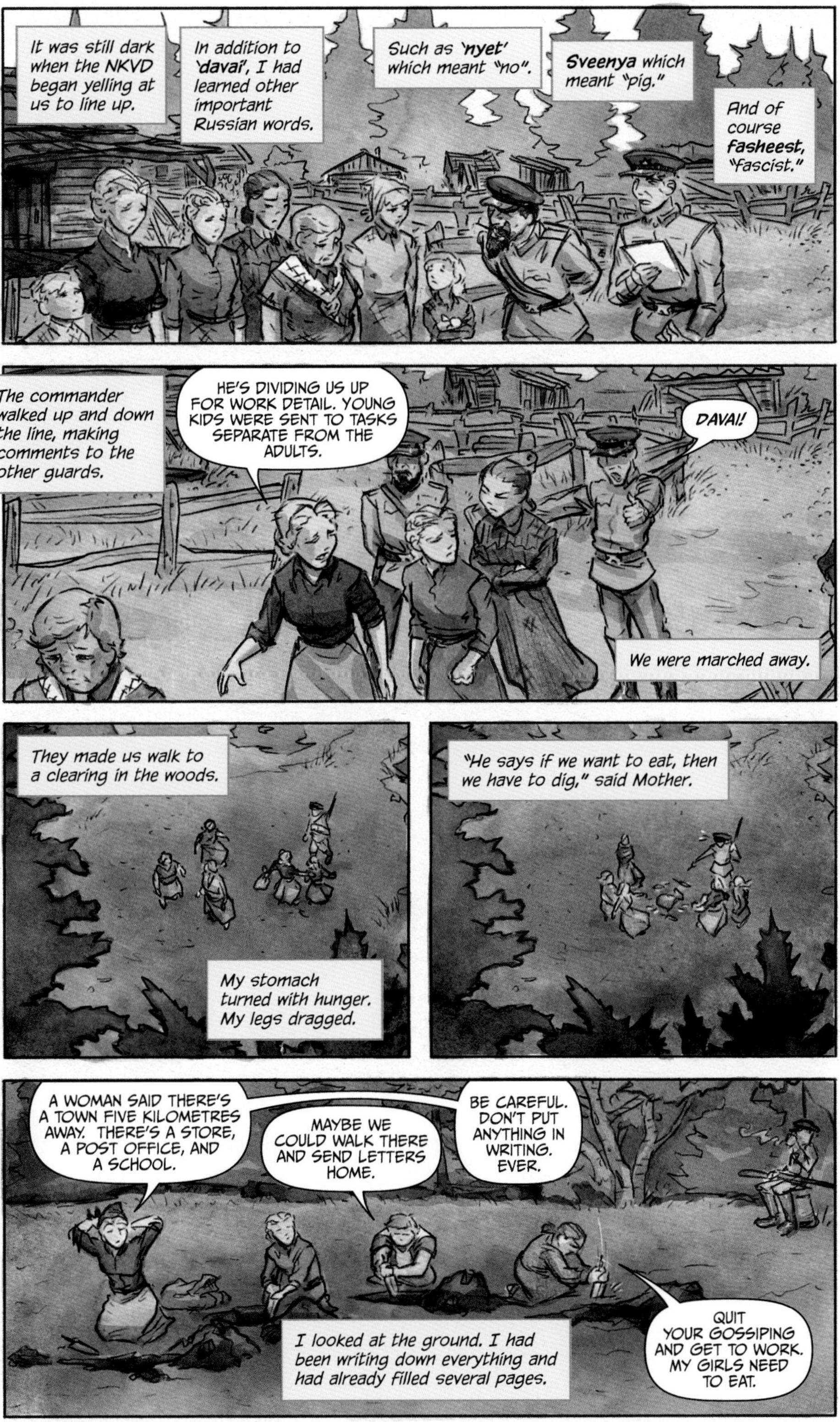
It was still dark when the NKVD began yelling at us to line up.
In addition to 'davai', I had learned other important Russian words.
Such as 'nyet' which meant "no".
Sveenya which meant "pig."
And of course fasheest, "fascist."
The commander walked up and down the line, making comments to the other guards.
HE'S DIVIDING US UP FOR WORK DETAIL. YOUNG KIDS WERE SENT TO TASKS SEPARATE FROM THE ADULTS.
DAVAI!
We were marched away.
They made us walk to a clearing in the woods.
My stomach turned with hunger. My legs dragged.
"He says if we want to eat, then we have to dig," said Mother.
A WOMAN SAID THERE'S A TOWN FIVE KILOMETRES AWAY. THERE'S A STORE, A POST OFFICE, AND A SCHOOL.
MAYBE WE COULD WALK THERE AND SEND LETTERS HOME.
BE CAREFUL. DON'T PUT ANYTHING IN WRITING. EVER.
I looked at the ground. I had been writing down everything and had already filled several pages.
QUIT YOUR GOSSIPING AND GET TO WORK. MY GIRLS NEED TO EAT.

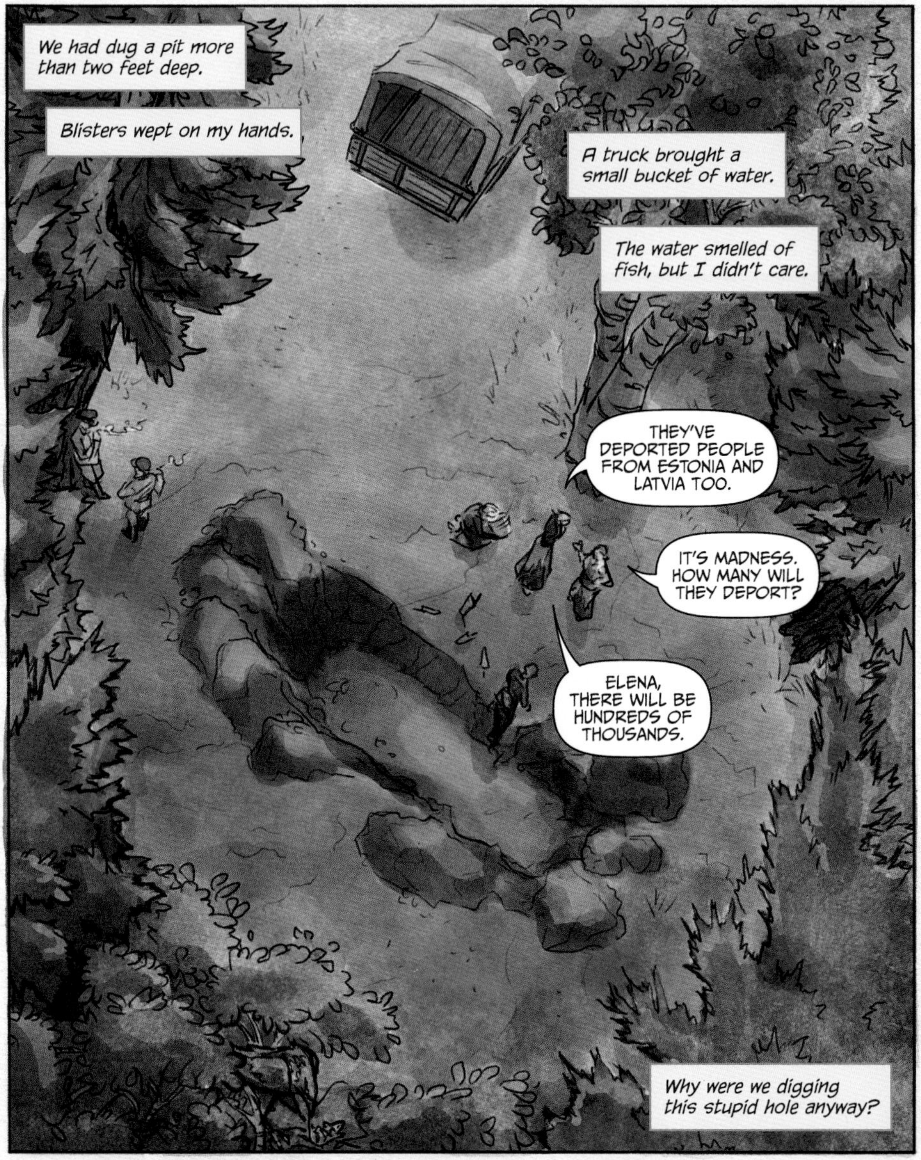
We had dug a pit more than two feet deep.
Blisters wept on my hands.
A truck brought a small bucket of water.
The water smelled of fish, but I didn't care.
THEY'VE DEPORTED PEOPLE FROM ESTONIA AND LATVIA TOO.
IT'S MADNESS. HOW MANY WILL THEY DEPORT?
ELENA, THERE WILL BE HUNDREDS OF THOUSANDS.
Why were we digging this stupid hole anyway?

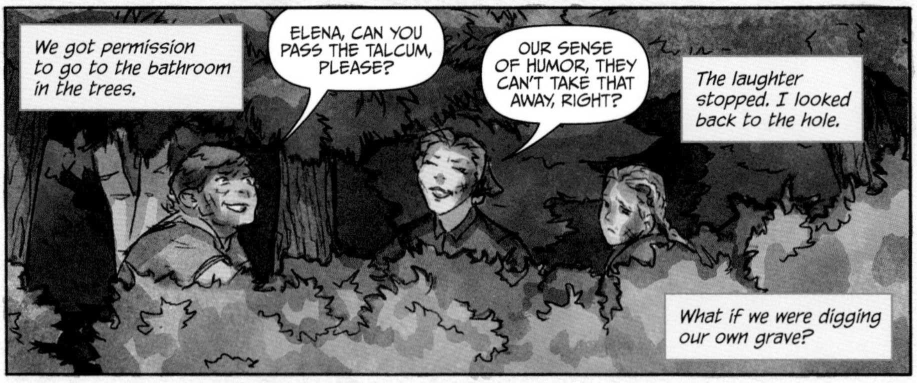
We got permission to go to the bathroom in the trees.
ELENA, CAN YOU PASS THE TALCUM, PLEASE?
OUR SENSE OF HUMOR, THEY CAN'T TAKE THAT AWAY, RIGHT?
The laughter stopped. I looked back to the hole.
What if we were digging our own grave?

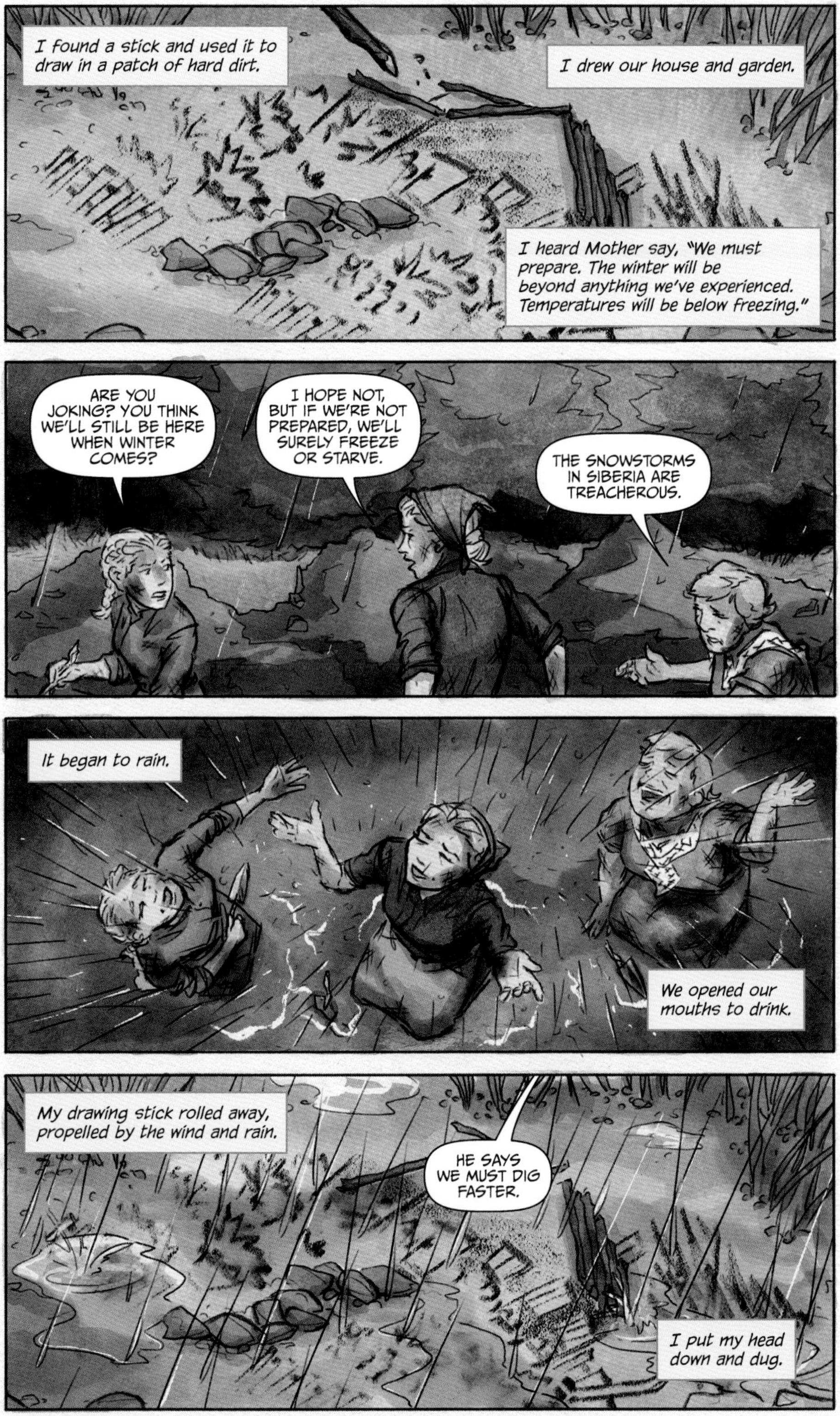
I found a stick and used it to draw in a patch of hard dirt.
I drew our house and garden.
I heard Mother say, "We must prepare. The winter will be beyond anything we've experienced. Temperatures will be below freezing."
ARE YOU JOKING? YOU THINK WE'LL STILL BE HERE WHEN WINTER COMES?
I HOPE NOT, BUT IF WE'RE NOT PREPARED, WE'LL SURELY FREEZE OR STARVE.
THE SNOWSTORMS IN SIBERIA ARE TREACHEROUS.
It began to rain.
We opened our mouths to drink.
My drawing stick rolled away, propelled by the wind and rain.
HE SAYS WE MUST DIG FASTER.
I put my head down and dug.

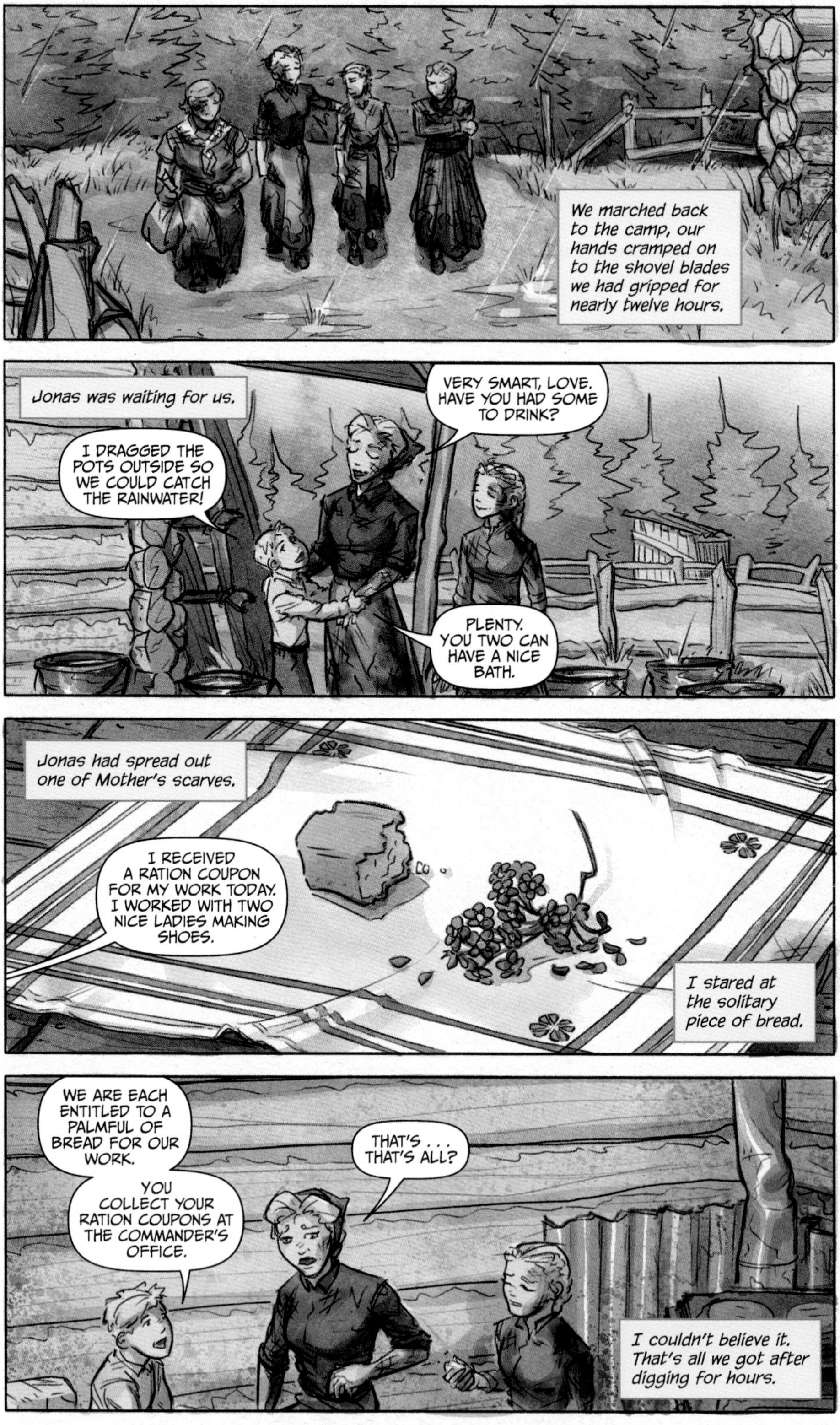
We marched back to the camp, our hands cramped on to the shovel blades we had gripped for nearly twelve hours.
Jonas was waiting for us.
I DRAGGED THE POTS OUTSIDE SO WE COULD CATCH THE RAINWATER!
VERY SMART, LOVE. HAVE YOU HAD SOME TO DRINK?
PLENTY. YOU TWO CAN HAVE A NICE BATH.
Jonas had spread out one of Mother's scarves.
I RECEIVED A RATION COUPON FOR MY WORK TODAY. I WORKED WITH TWO NICE LADIES MAKING SHOES.
I stared at the solitary piece of bread.
WE ARE EACH ENTITLED TO A PALMFUL OF BREAD FOR OUR WORK.
YOU COLLECT YOUR RATION COUPONS AT THE COMMANDER'S OFFICE.
THAT'S . . . THAT'S ALL?
I couldn't believe it. That's all we got after digging for hours.

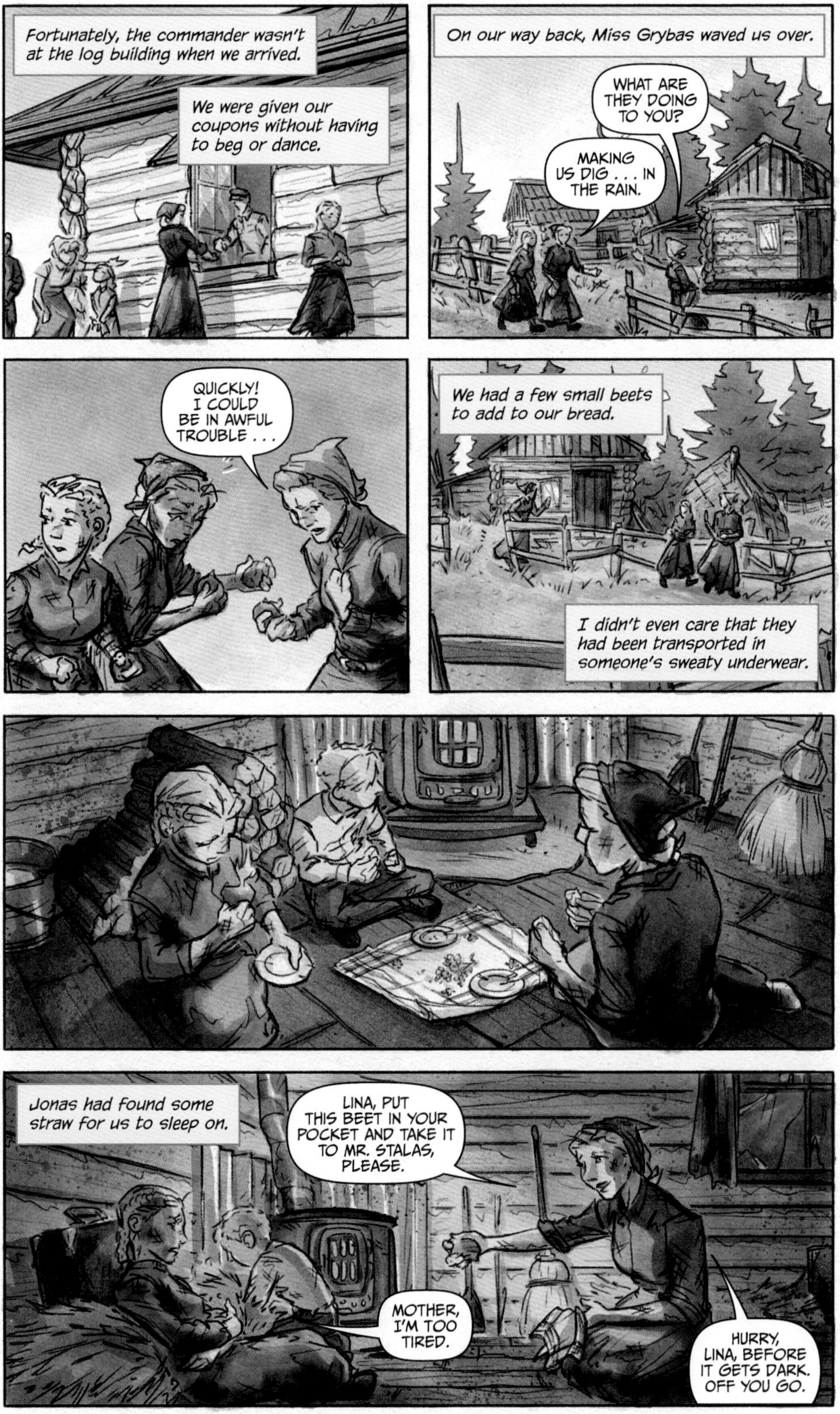
Fortunately, the commander wasn't at the log building when we arrived.
We were given our coupons without having to beg or dance.
On our way back, Miss Grybas waved us over.
WHAT ARE THEY DOING TO YOU?
MAKING US DIG . . . IN THE RAIN.
QUICKLY! I COULD BE IN AWFUL TROUBLE . . .
We had a few small beets to add to our bread.
I didn't even care that they had been transported in someone's sweaty underwear.
Jonas had found some straw for us to sleep on.
LINA, PUT THIS BEET IN YOUR POCKET AND TAKE IT TO MR. STALAS, PLEASE.
MOTHER, I'M TOO TIRED.
HURRY, LINA, BEFORE IT GETS DARK. OFF YOU GO.

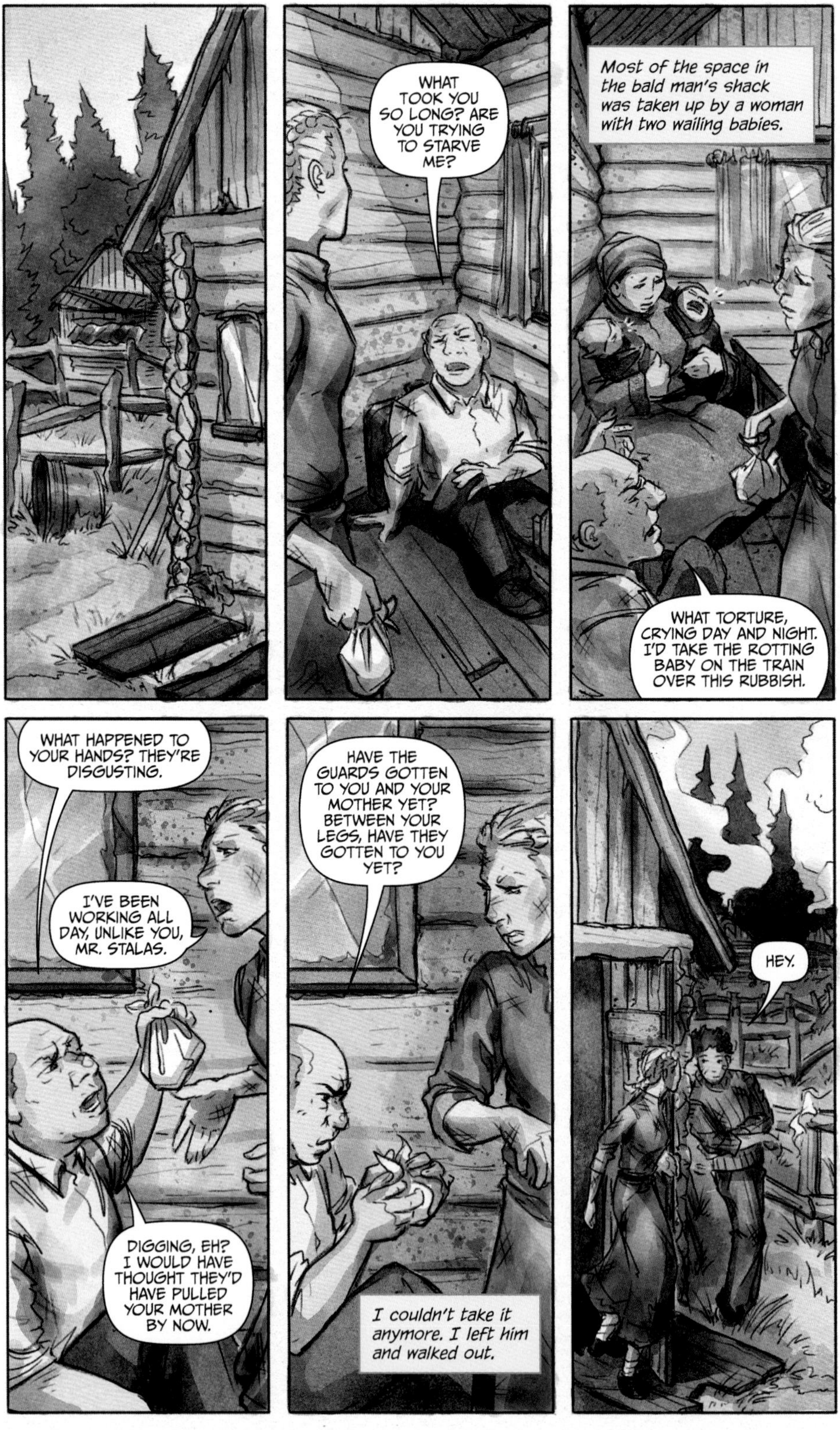
WHAT TOOK YOU SO LONG? ARE YOU TRYING TO STARVE ME?
Most of the space in the bald man's shack was taken up by a woman with two wailing babies.
WHAT TORTURE, CRYING DAY AND NIGHT. I'D TAKE THE ROTTING BABY ON THE TRAIN OVER THIS RUBBISH.
WHAT HAPPENED TO YOUR HANDS? THEY'RE DISGUSTING.
I'VE BEEN WORKING ALL DAY, UNLIKE YOU, MR. STALAS.
DIGGING, EH? I WOULD HAVE THOUGHT THEY'D HAVE PULLED YOUR MOTHER BY NOW.
HAVE THE GUARDS GOTTEN TO YOU AND YOUR MOTHER YET? BETWEEN YOUR LEGS, HAVE THEY GOTTEN TO YOU YET?
I couldn't take it anymore. I left him and walked out.
HEY.

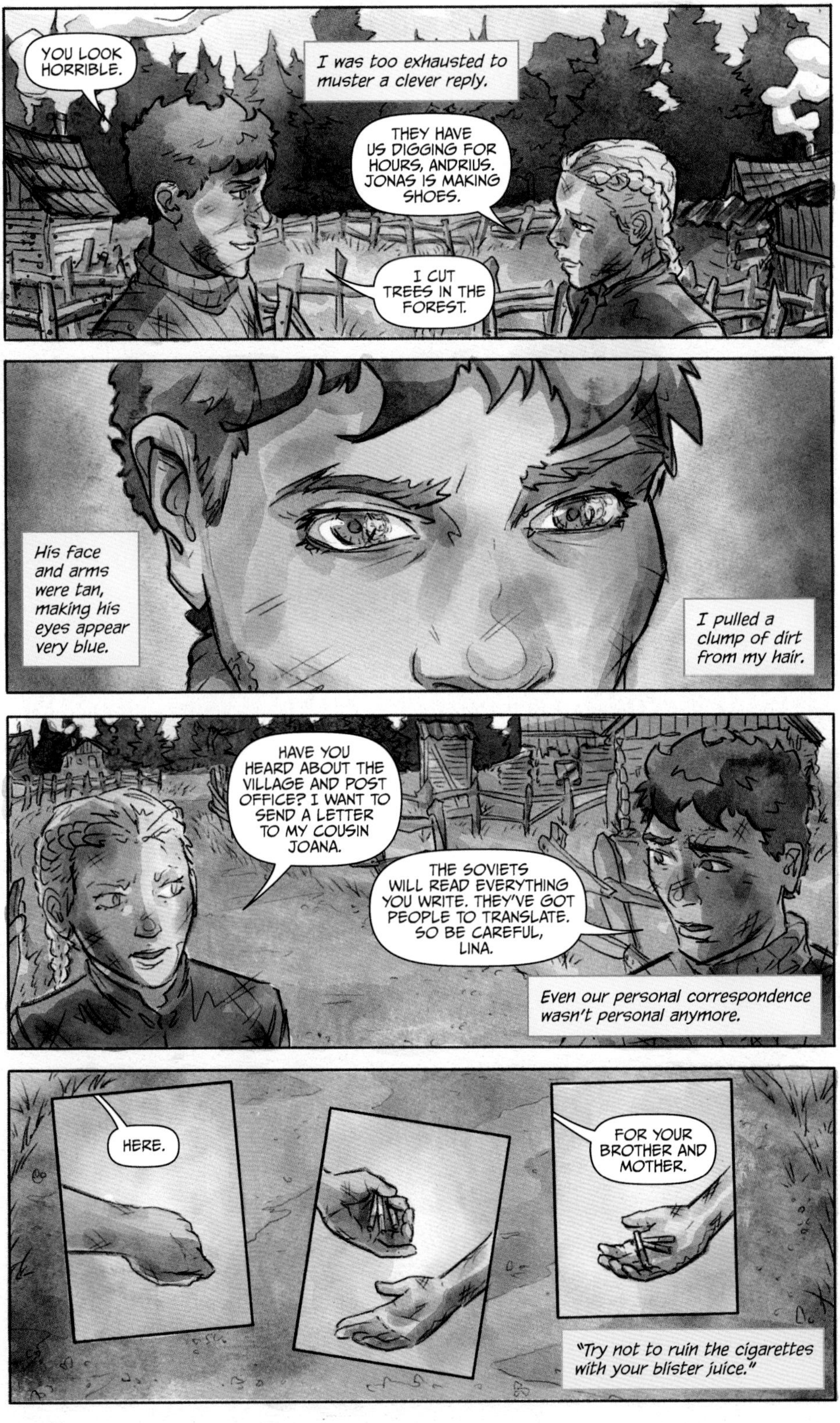
YOU LOOK HORRIBLE.
I was too exhausted to muster a clever reply.
THEY HAVE US DIGGING FOR HOURS, ANDRIUS. JONAS IS MAKING SHOES.
I CUT TREES IN THE FOREST.
His face and arms were tan, making his eyes appear very blue.
I pulled a clump of dirt from my hair.
HAVE YOU HEARD ABOUT THE VILLAGE AND POST OFFICE? I WANT TO SEND A LETTER TO MY COUSIN JOANA.
THE SOVIETS WILL READ EVERYTHING YOU WRITE. THEY'VE GOT PEOPLE TO TRANSLATE. SO BE CAREFUL, LINA.
Even our personal correspondence wasn't personal anymore.
HERE.
FOR YOUR BROTHER AND MOTHER.
"Try not to ruin the cigarettes with your blister juice."

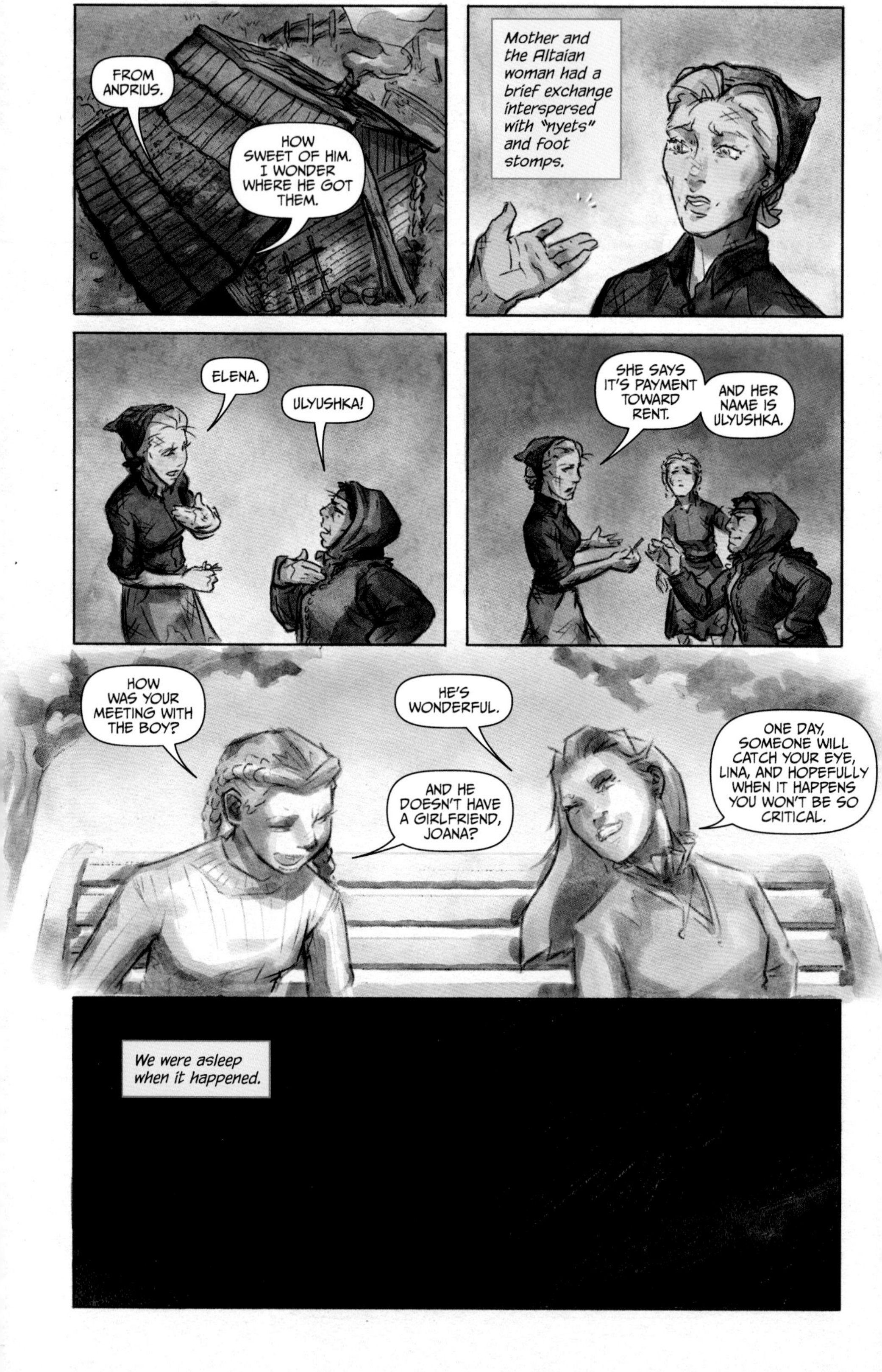
FROM ANDRIUS.
HOW SWEET OF HIM. I WONDER WHERE HE GOT THEM.
Mother and the Altaian woman had a brief exchange interspersed with "nyets" and foot stomps.
ELENA.
ULYUSHKA!
SHE SAYS IT'S PAYMENT TOWARD RENT.
AND HER NAME IS ULYUSHKA.
HOW WAS YOUR MEETING WITH THE BOY?
HE'S WONDERFUL.
AND HE DOESN'T HAVE A GIRLFRIEND, JOANA?
ONE DAY, SOMEONE WILL CATCH YOUR EYE, LINA, AND HOPEFULLY WHEN IT HAPPENS YOU WON'T BE SO CRITICAL.
We were asleep when it happened.

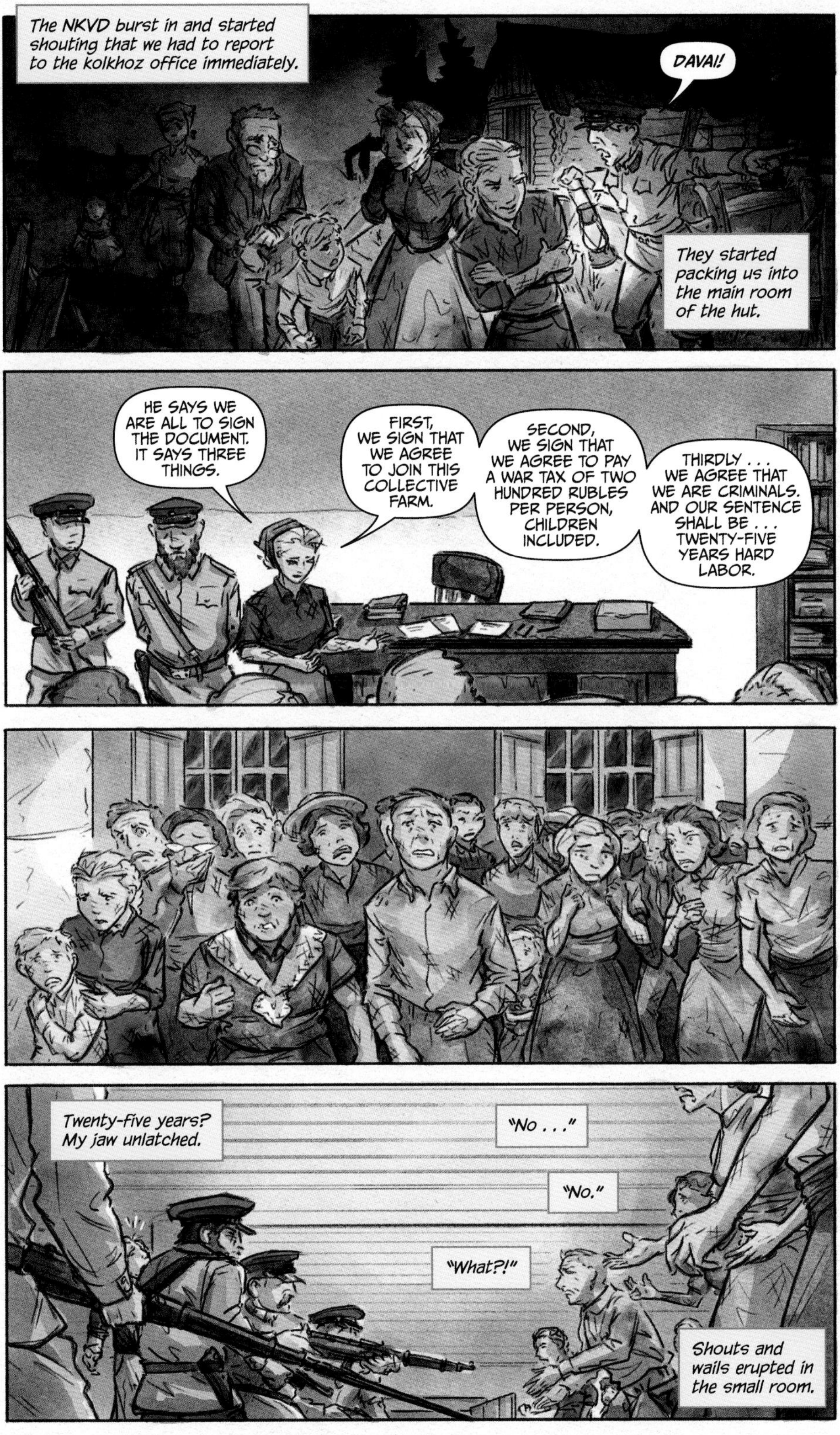

The NKVD burst in and started shouting that we had to report to the kolkhoz office immediately.
DAVAI!
They started packing us into the main room of the hut.
HE SAYS WE ARE ALL TO SIGN THE DOCUMENT. IT SAYS THREE THINGS.
FIRST, WE SIGN THAT WE AGREE TO JOIN THIS COLLECTIVE FARM.
SECOND, WE SIGN THAT WE AGREE TO PAY A WAR TAX OF TWO HUNDRED RUBLES PER PERSON, CHILDREN INCLUDED.
THIRDLY . . . WE AGREE THAT WE ARE CRIMINALS. AND OUR SENTENCE SHALL BE . . . TWENTY-FIVE YEARS HARD LABOR.
Twenty-five years? My jaw unlatched.
"No . . ."
"No."
"What?!"
Shouts and wails erupted in the small room.

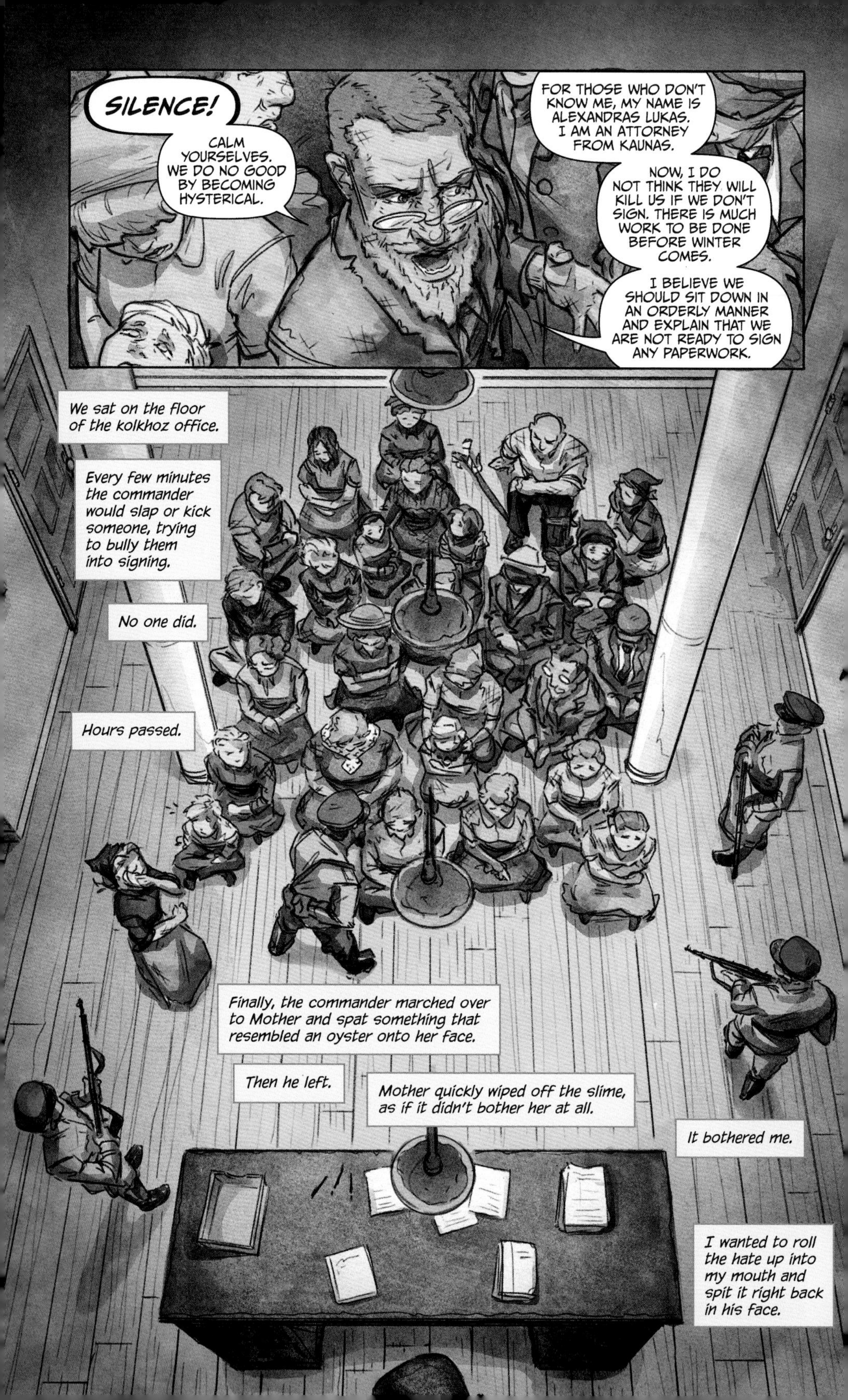
SILENCE!
CALM YOURSELVES. WE DO NO GOOD BY BECOMING HYSTERICAL.
FOR THOSE WHO DON'T KNOW ME, MY NAME IS ALEXANDRAS LUKAS. I AM AN ATTORNEY FROM KAUNAS.
NOW, I DO NOT THINK THEY WILL KILL US IF WE DON'T SIGN. THERE IS MUCH WORK TO BE DONE BEFORE WINTER COMES.
I BELIEVE WE SHOULD SIT DOWN IN AN ORDERLY MANNER AND EXPLAIN THAT WE ARE NOT READY TO SIGN ANY PAPERWORK.
We sat on the floor of the kolkhoz office.
Every few minutes the commander would slap or kick someone, trying to bully them into signing.
No one did.
Hours passed.
Finally, the commander marched over to Mother and spat something that resembled an oyster onto her face.
Then he left.
Mother quickly wiped off the slime, as if it didn't bother her at all.
It bothered me.
I wanted to roll the hate up into my mouth and spit it right back in his face.

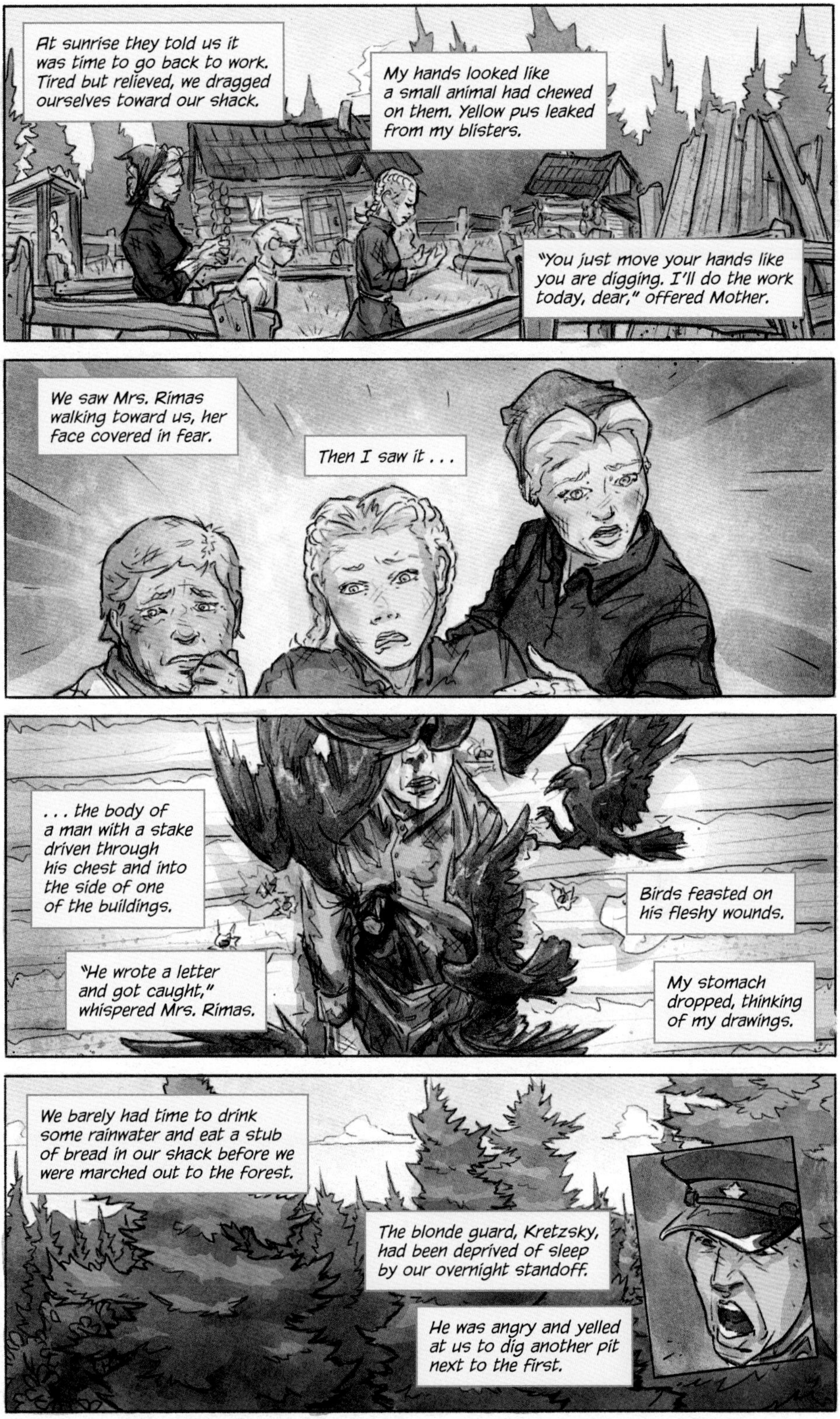
At sunrise they told us it was time to go back to work. Tired but relieved, we dragged ourselves toward our shack.
My hands looked like a small animal had chewed on them. Yellow pus leaked from my blisters.
"You just move your hands like you are digging. I'll do the work today, dear," offered Mother.
We saw Mrs. Rimas walking toward us, her face covered in fear.
Then I saw it . . .
. . . the body of a man with a stake driven through his chest and into the side of one of the buildings.
Birds feasted on his fleshy wounds.
"He wrote a letter and got caught," whispered Mrs. Rimas.
My stomach dropped, thinking of my drawings.
We barely had time to drink some rainwater and eat a stub of bread in our shack before we were marched out to the forest.
The blonde guard, Kretzsky, had been deprived of sleep by our overnight standoff.
He was angry and yelled at us to dig another pit next to the first.

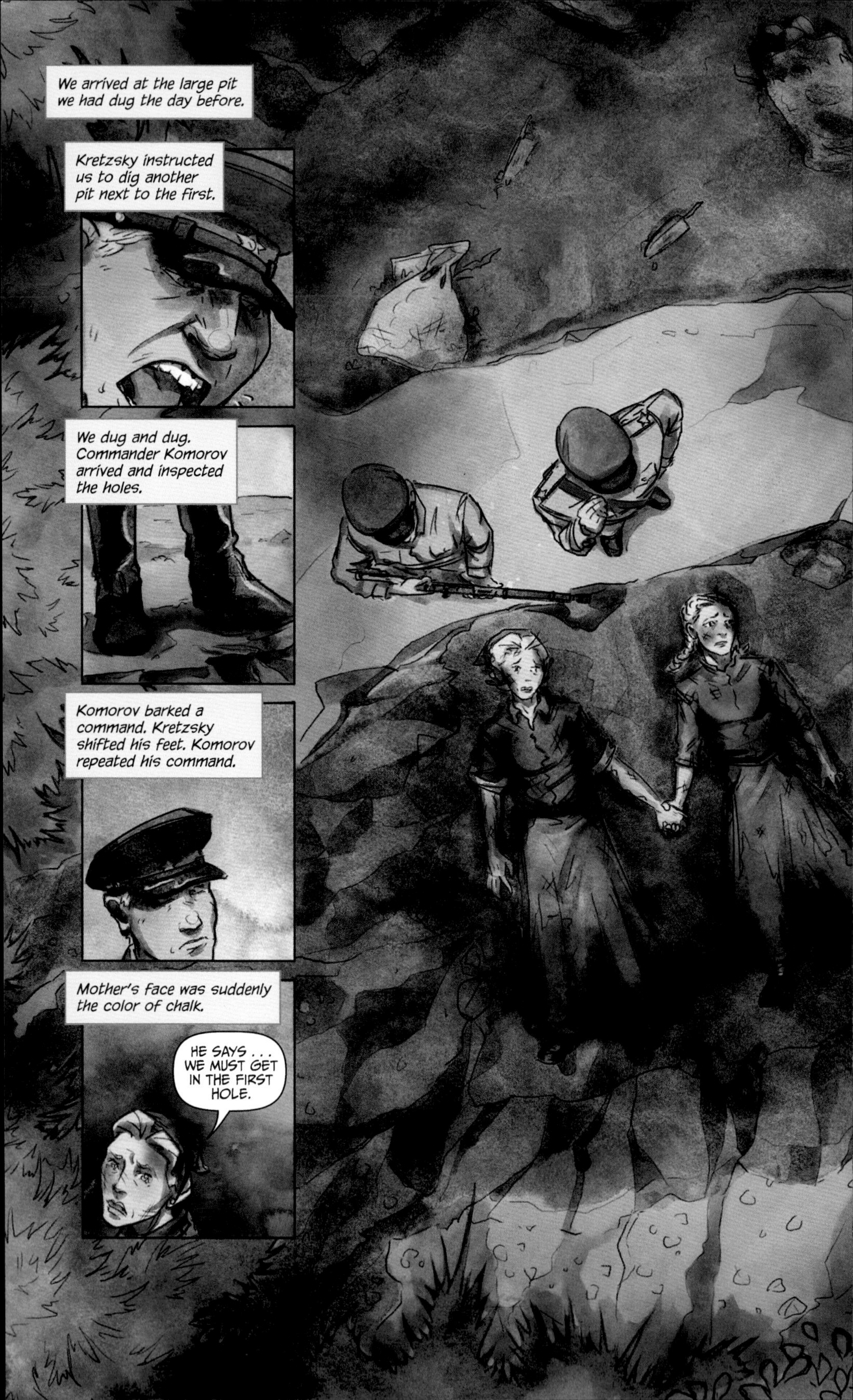
We arrived at the large pit we had dug the day before.
Kretzsky instructed us to dig another pit next to the first.
We dug and dug. Commander Komorov arrived and inspected the holes.
Komorov barked a command. Kretzsky shifted his feet. Komorov repeated his command.
Mother's face was suddenly the color of chalk.
HE SAYS . . . WE MUST GET IN THE FIRST HOLE.

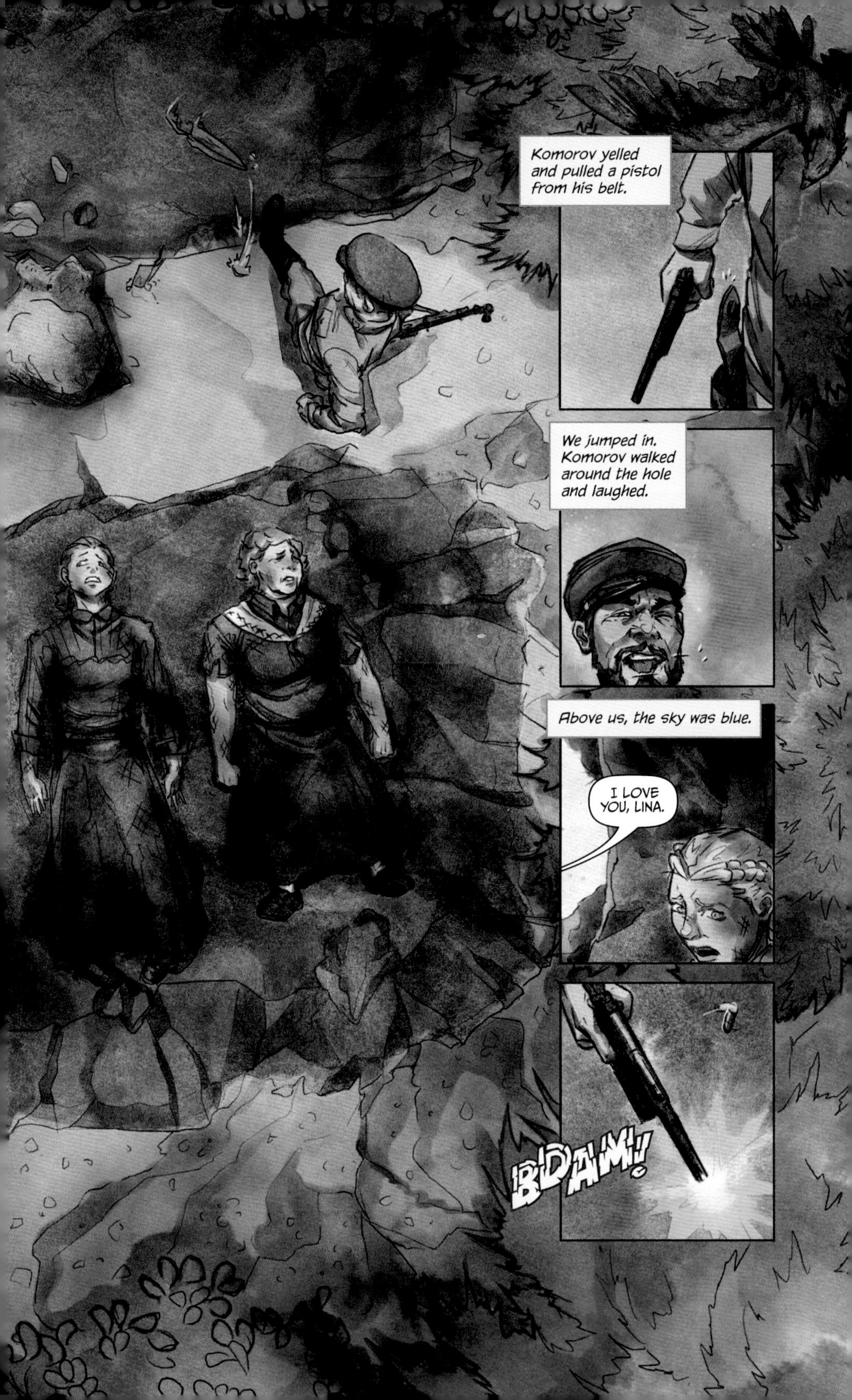
Komorov yelled and pulled a pistol from his belt.
We jumped in. Komorov walked around the hole and laughed.
Above us, the sky was blue.
I LOVE YOU, LINA.
BDAM!

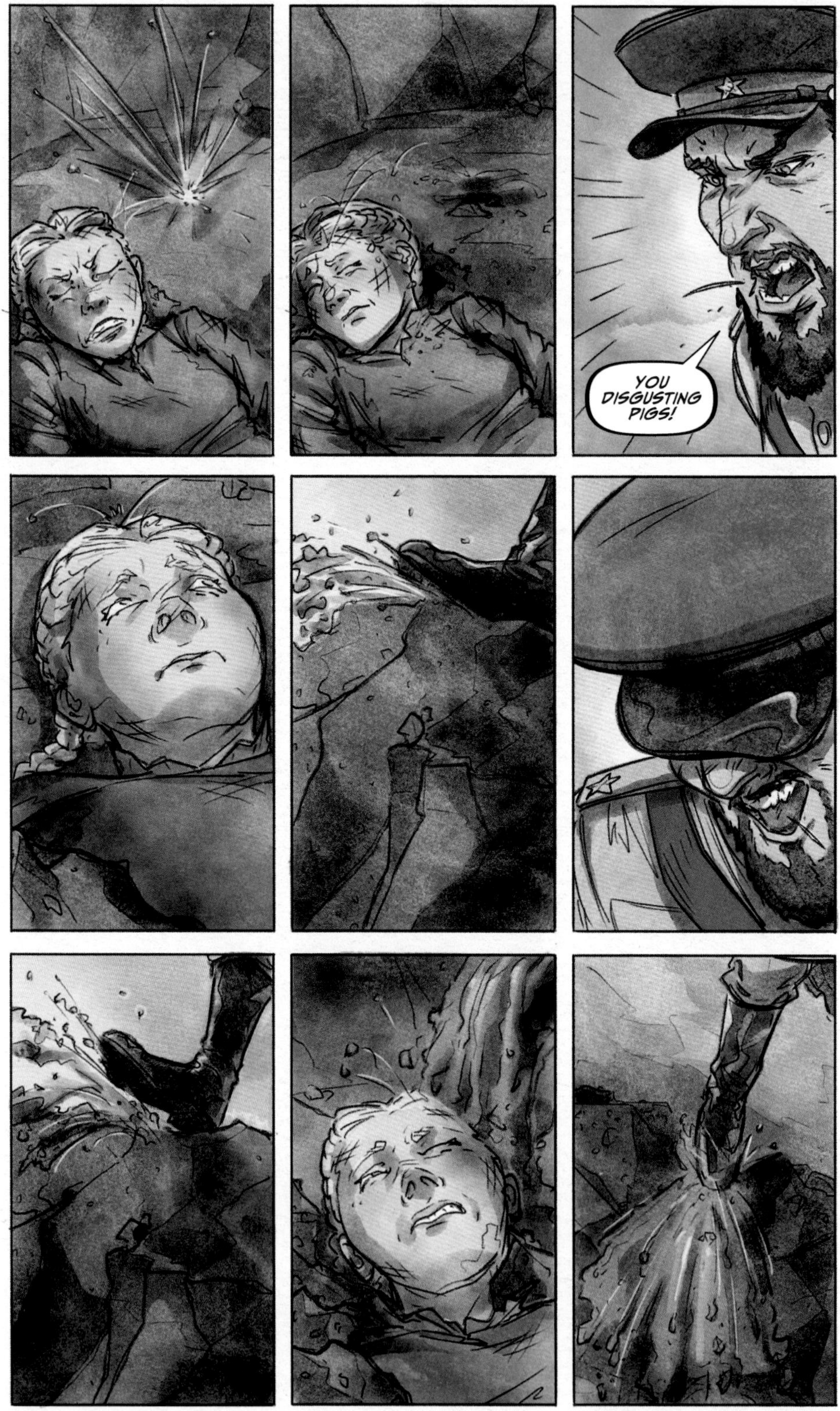
YOU DISGUSTING PIGS!

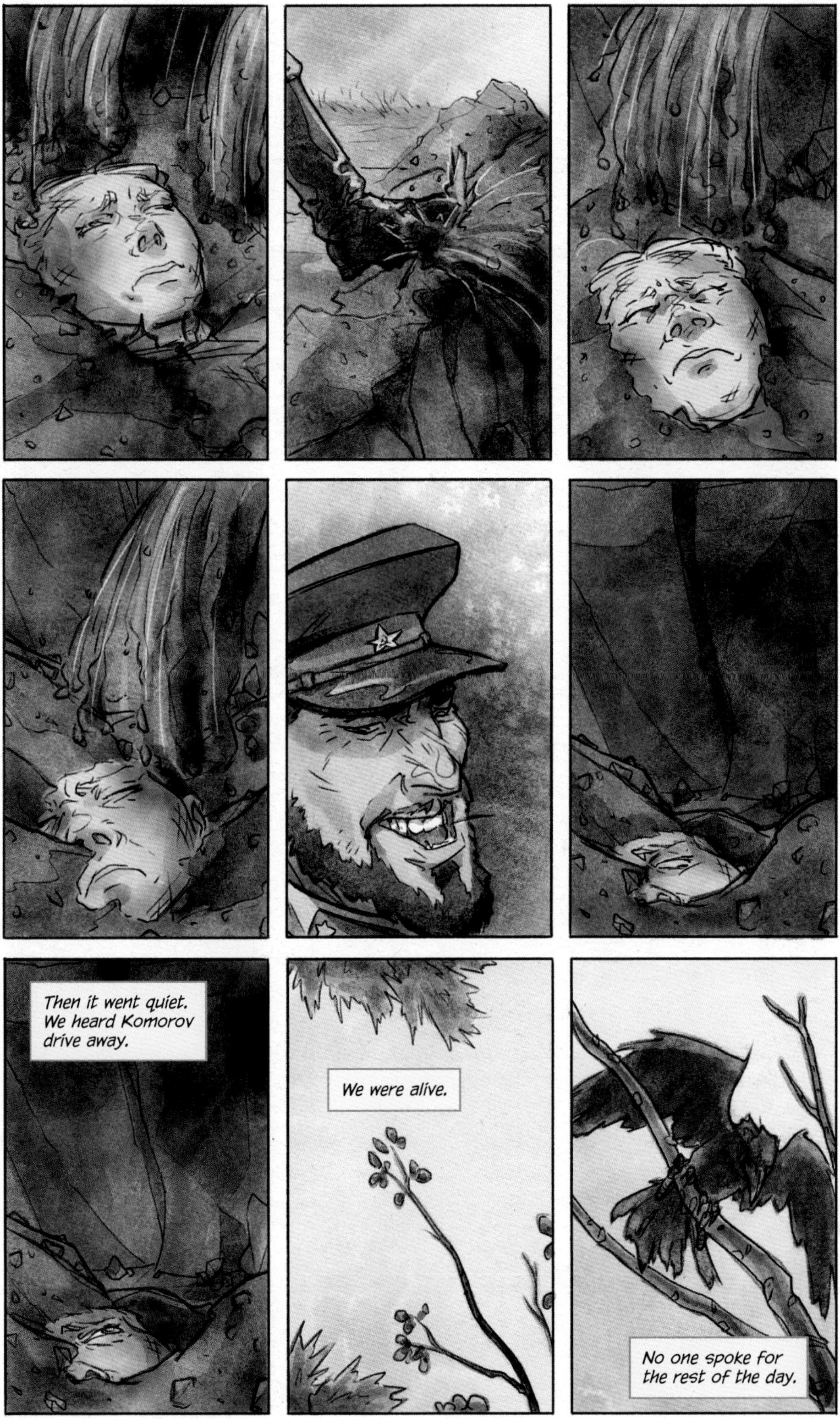
Then it went quiet. We heard Komorov drive away.
We were alive.
No one spoke for the rest of the day.

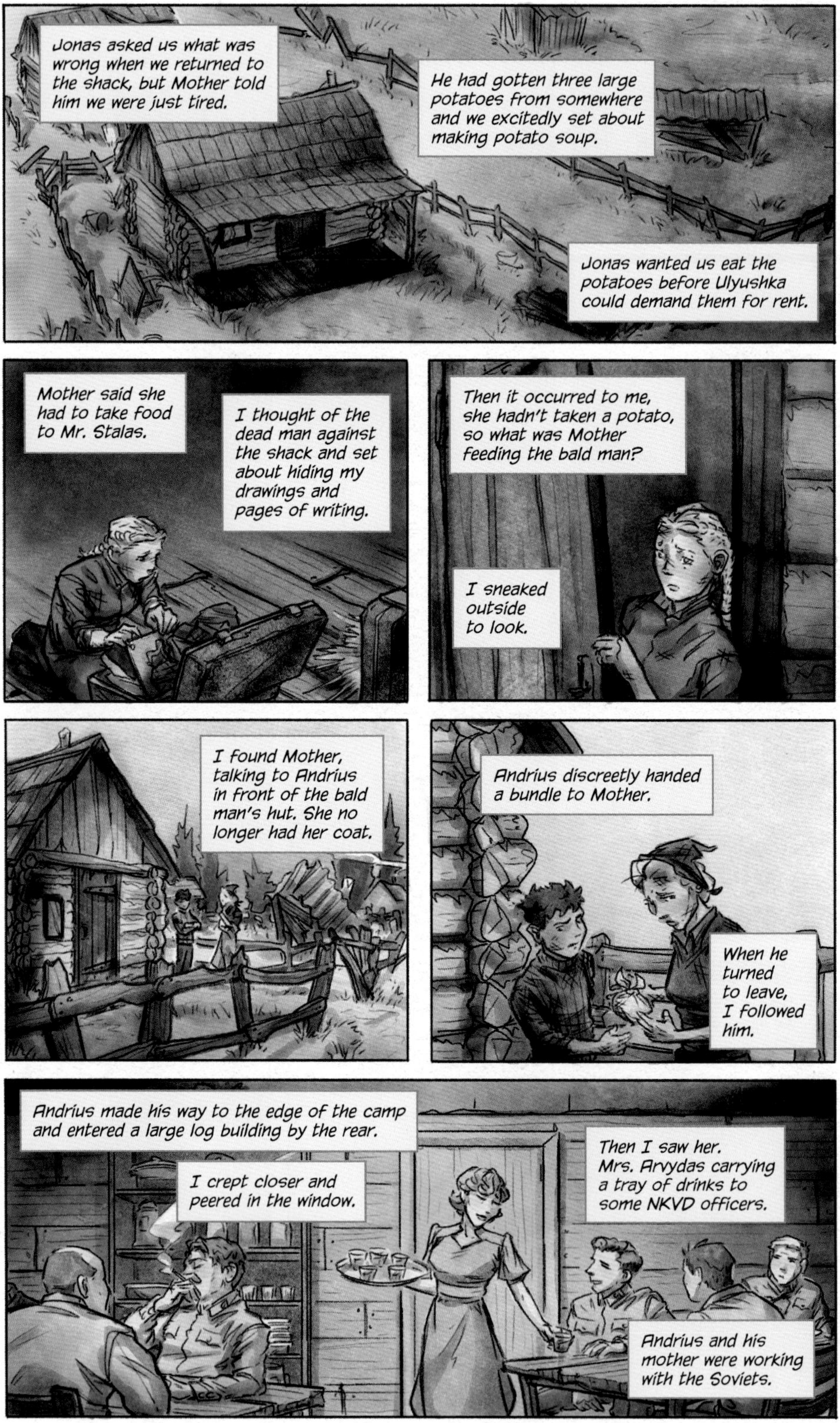
Jonas asked us what was wrong when we returned to the shack, but Mother told him we were just tired.
He had gotten three large potatoes from somewhere and we excitedly set about making potato soup.
Jonas wanted us eat the potatoes before Ulyushka could demand them for rent.
Mother said she had to take food to Mr. Stalas.
I thought of the dead man against the shack and set about hiding my drawings and pages of writing.
Then it occurred to me, she hadn't taken a potato, so what was Mother feeding the bald man?
I sneaked outside to look.
I found Mother, talking to Andrius in front of the bald man's hut. She no longer had her coat.
Andrius discreetly handed a bundle to Mother.
When he turned to leave, I followed him.
Andrius made his way to the edge of the camp and entered a large log building by the rear.
I crept closer and peered in the window.
Then I saw her. Mrs. Arvydas carrying a tray of drinks to some NKVD officers.
Andrius and his mother were working with the Soviets.

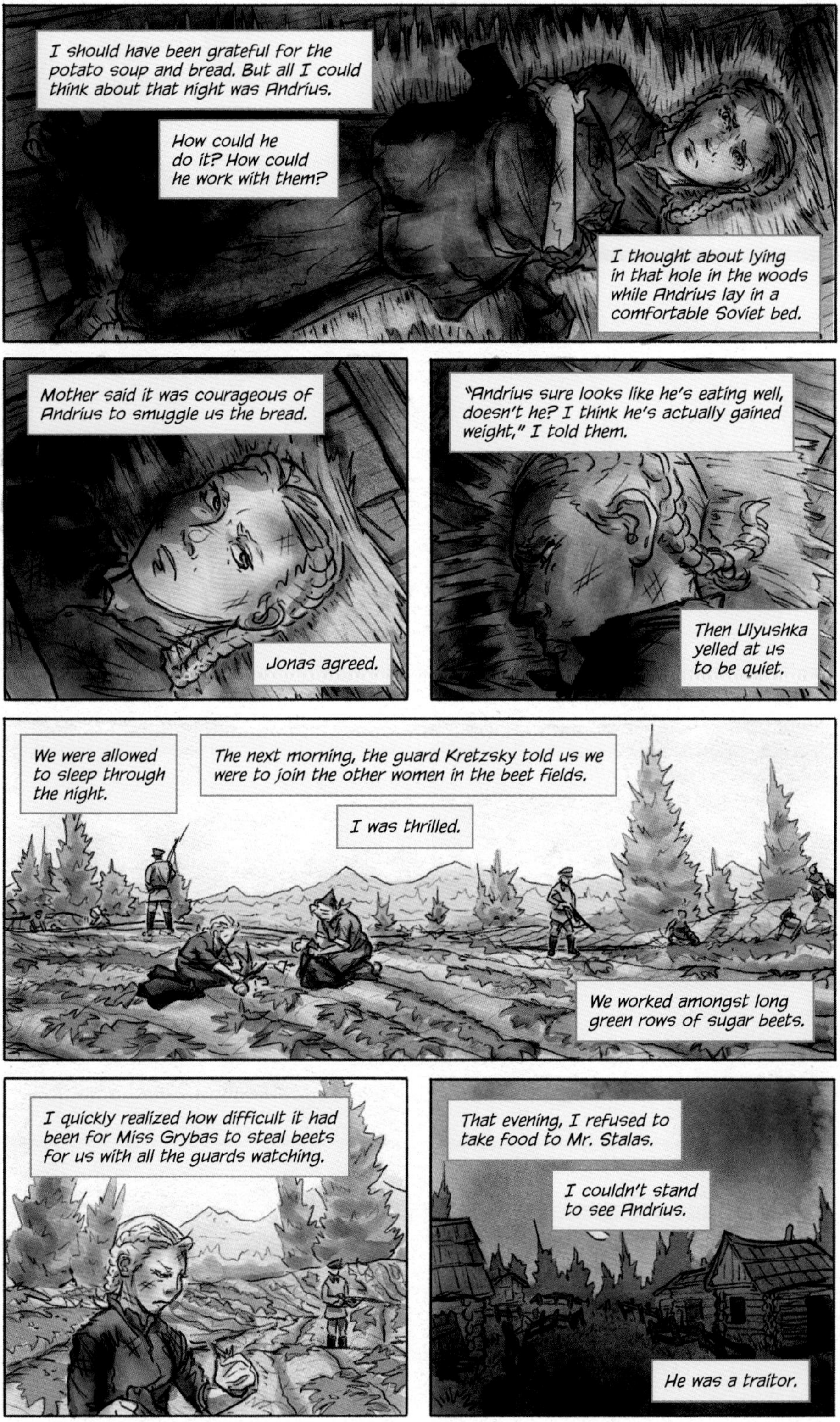

I should have been grateful for the potato soup and bread. But all I could think about that night was Andrius.
How could he do it? How could he work with them?
I thought about lying in that hole in the woods while Andrius lay in a comfortable Soviet bed.
Mother said it was courageous of Andrius to smuggle us the bread.
Jonas agreed.
"Andrius sure looks like he's eating well, doesn't he? I think he's actually gained weight," I told them.
Then Ulyushka yelled at us to be quiet.
We were allowed to sleep through the night.
The next morning, the guard Kretzsky told us we were to join the other women in the beet fields.
I was thrilled.
We worked amongst long green rows of sugar beets.
I quickly realized how difficult it had been for Miss Grybas to steal beets for us with all the guards watching.
That evening, I refused to take food to Mr. Stalas.
I couldn't stand to see Andrius.
He was a traitor.

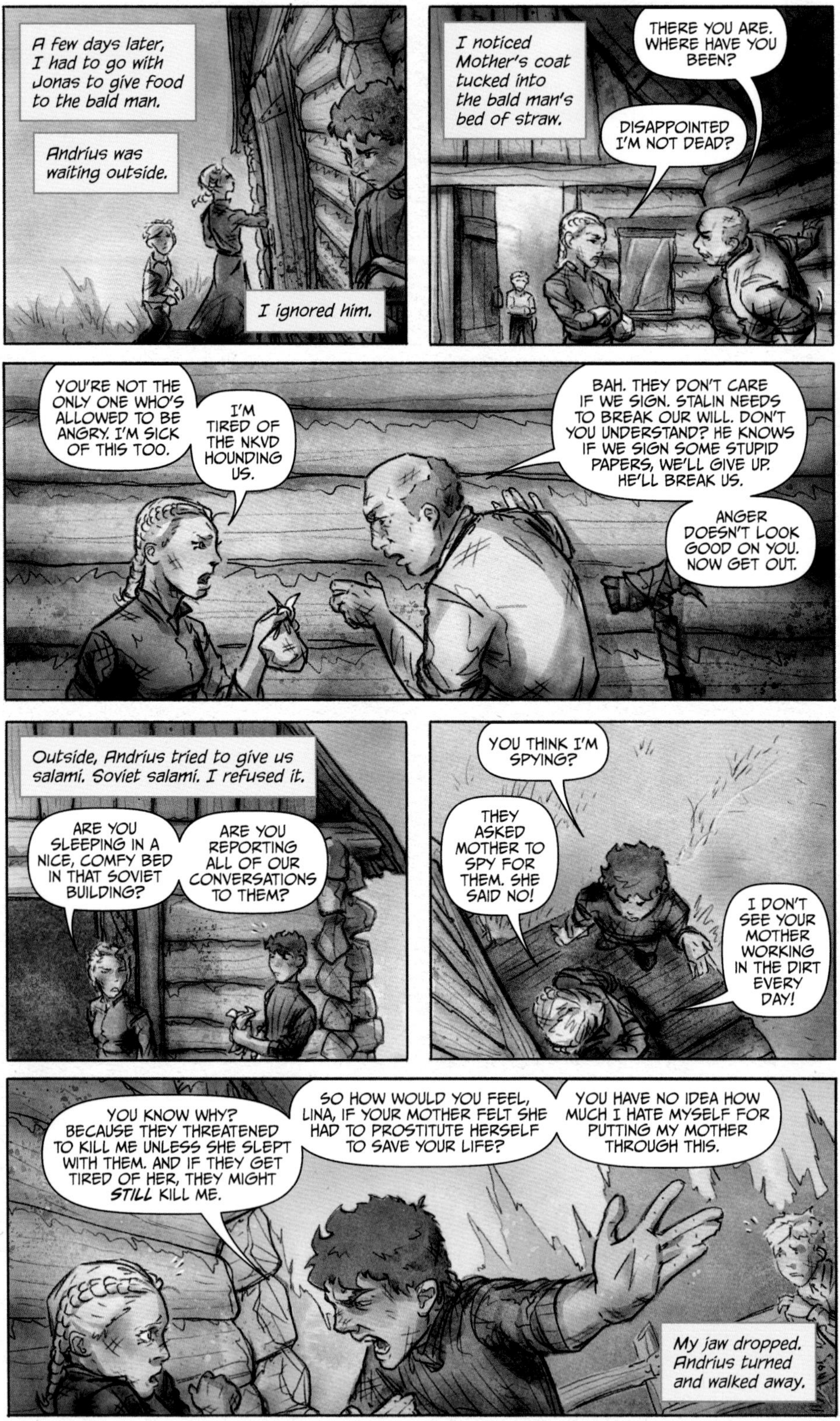
A few days later, I had to go with Jonas to give food to the bald man.
Andrius was waiting outside.
I ignored him.
I noticed Mother's coat tucked into the bald man's bed of straw.
THERE YOU ARE. WHERE HAVE YOU BEEN?
DISAPPOINTED I'M NOT DEAD?
YOU'RE NOT THE ONLY ONE WHO'S ALLOWED TO BE ANGRY. I'M SICK OF THIS TOO.
I'M TIRED OF THE NKVD HOUNDING US.
BAH. THEY DON'T CARE IF WE SIGN. STALIN NEEDS TO BREAK OUR WILL. DON'T YOU UNDERSTAND? HE KNOWS IF WE SIGN SOME STUPID PAPERS, WE'LL GIVE UP. HE'LL BREAK US.
ANGER DOESN'T LOOK GOOD ON YOU. NOW GET OUT.
Outside, Andrius tried to give us salami. Soviet salami. I refused it.
ARE YOU SLEEPING IN A NICE, COMFY BED IN THAT SOVIET BUILDING?
ARE YOU REPORTING ALL OF OUR CONVERSATIONS TO THEM?
YOU THINK I'M SPYING?
THEY ASKED MOTHER TO SPY FOR THEM. SHE SAID NO!
I DON'T SEE YOUR MOTHER WORKING IN THE DIRT EVERY DAY!
YOU KNOW WHY? BECAUSE THEY THREATENED TO KILL ME UNLESS SHE SLEPT WITH THEM. AND IF THEY GET TIRED OF HER, THEY MIGHT *STILL* KILL ME.
SO HOW WOULD YOU FEEL, LINA, IF YOUR MOTHER FELT SHE HAD TO PROSTITUTE HERSELF TO SAVE YOUR LIFE?
YOU HAVE NO IDEA HOW MUCH I HATE MYSELF FOR PUTTING MY MOTHER THROUGH THIS.
My jaw dropped. Andrius turned and walked away.

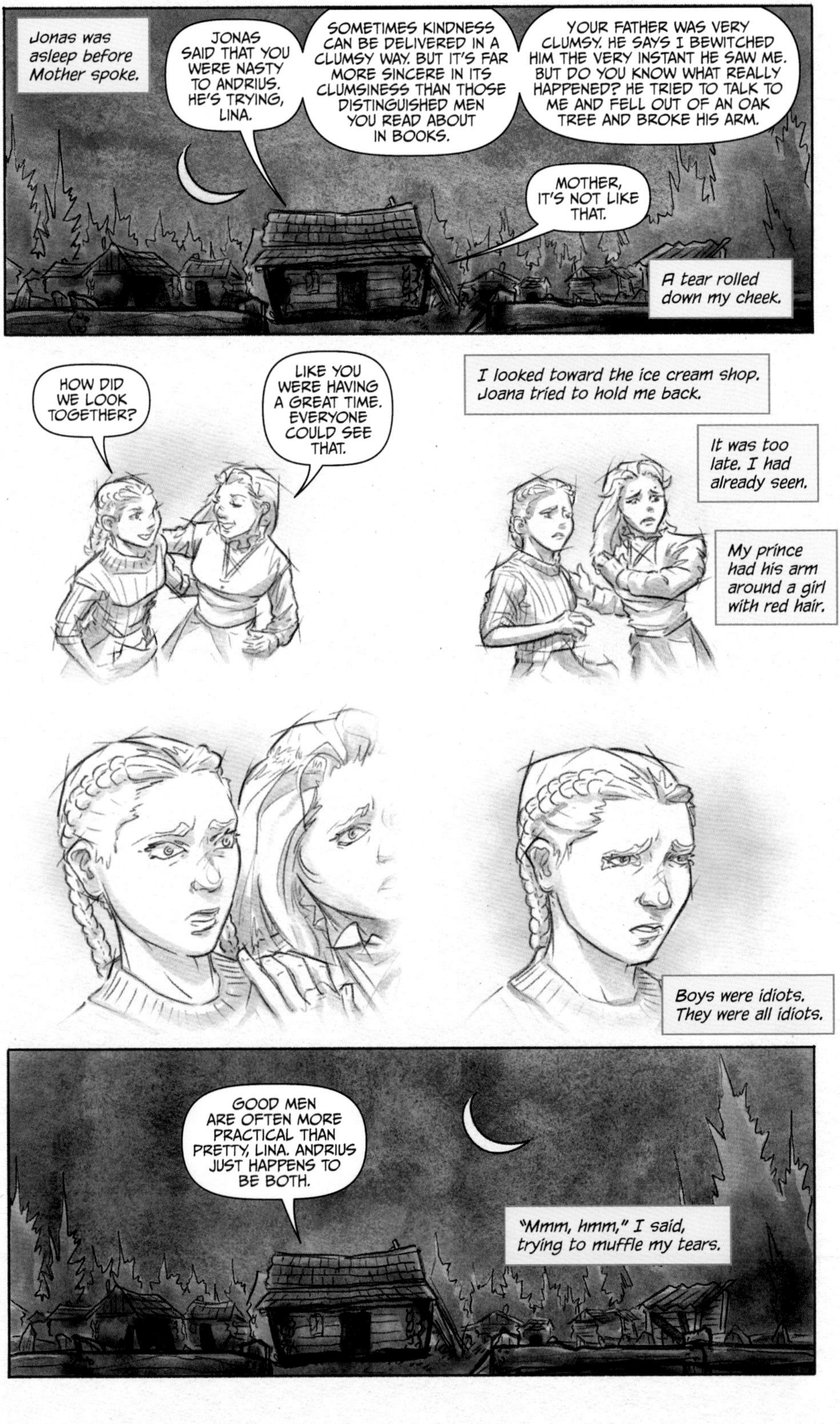
Jonas was asleep before Mother spoke.
JONAS SAID THAT YOU WERE NASTY TO ANDRIUS. HE'S TRYING, LINA.
SOMETIMES KINDNESS CAN BE DELIVERED IN A CLUMSY WAY. BUT IT'S FAR MORE SINCERE IN ITS CLUMSINESS THAN THOSE DISTINGUISHED MEN YOU READ ABOUT IN BOOKS.
YOUR FATHER WAS VERY CLUMSY. HE SAYS I BEWITCHED HIM THE VERY INSTANT HE SAW ME. BUT DO YOU KNOW WHAT REALLY HAPPENED? HE TRIED TO TALK TO ME AND FELL OUT OF AN OAK TREE AND BROKE HIS ARM.
MOTHER, IT'S NOT LIKE THAT.
A tear rolled down my cheek.
HOW DID WE LOOK TOGETHER?
LIKE YOU WERE HAVING A GREAT TIME. EVERYONE COULD SEE THAT.
I looked toward the ice cream shop. Joana tried to hold me back.
It was too late. I had already seen.
My prince had his arm around a girl with red hair.
Boys were idiots. They were all idiots.
GOOD MEN ARE OFTEN MORE PRACTICAL THAN PRETTY, LINA. ANDRIUS JUST HAPPENS TO BE BOTH.
"Mmm, hmm," I said, trying to muffle my tears.

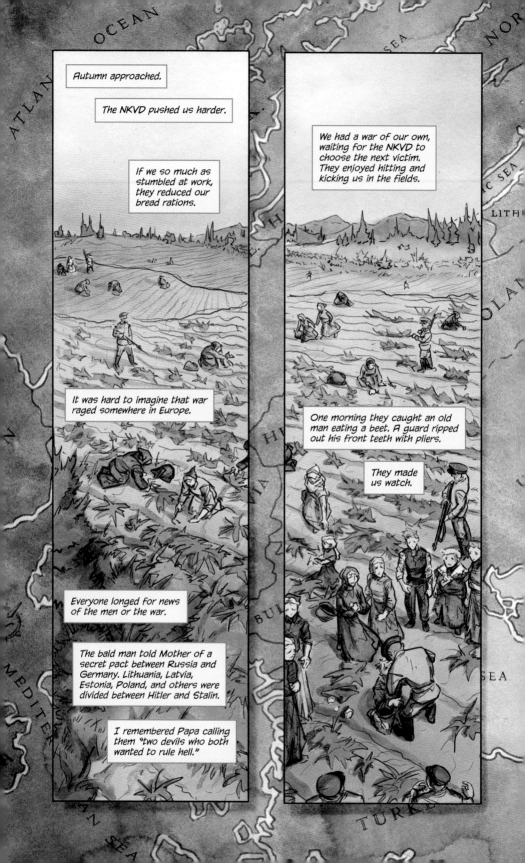

Autumn approached.

The NKVD pushed us harder.

If we so much as stumbled at work, they reduced our bread rations.

We had a war of our own, waiting for the NKVD to choose the next victim. They enjoyed hitting and kicking us in the fields.

It was hard to imagine that war raged somewhere in Europe.

One morning they caught an old man eating a beet. A guard ripped out his front teeth with pliers.

They made us watch.

Everyone longed for news of the men or the war.

The bald man told Mother of a secret pact between Russia and Germany. Lithuania, Latvia, Estonia, Poland, and others were divided between Hitler and Stalin.

I remembered Papa calling them "two devils who both wanted to rule hell."

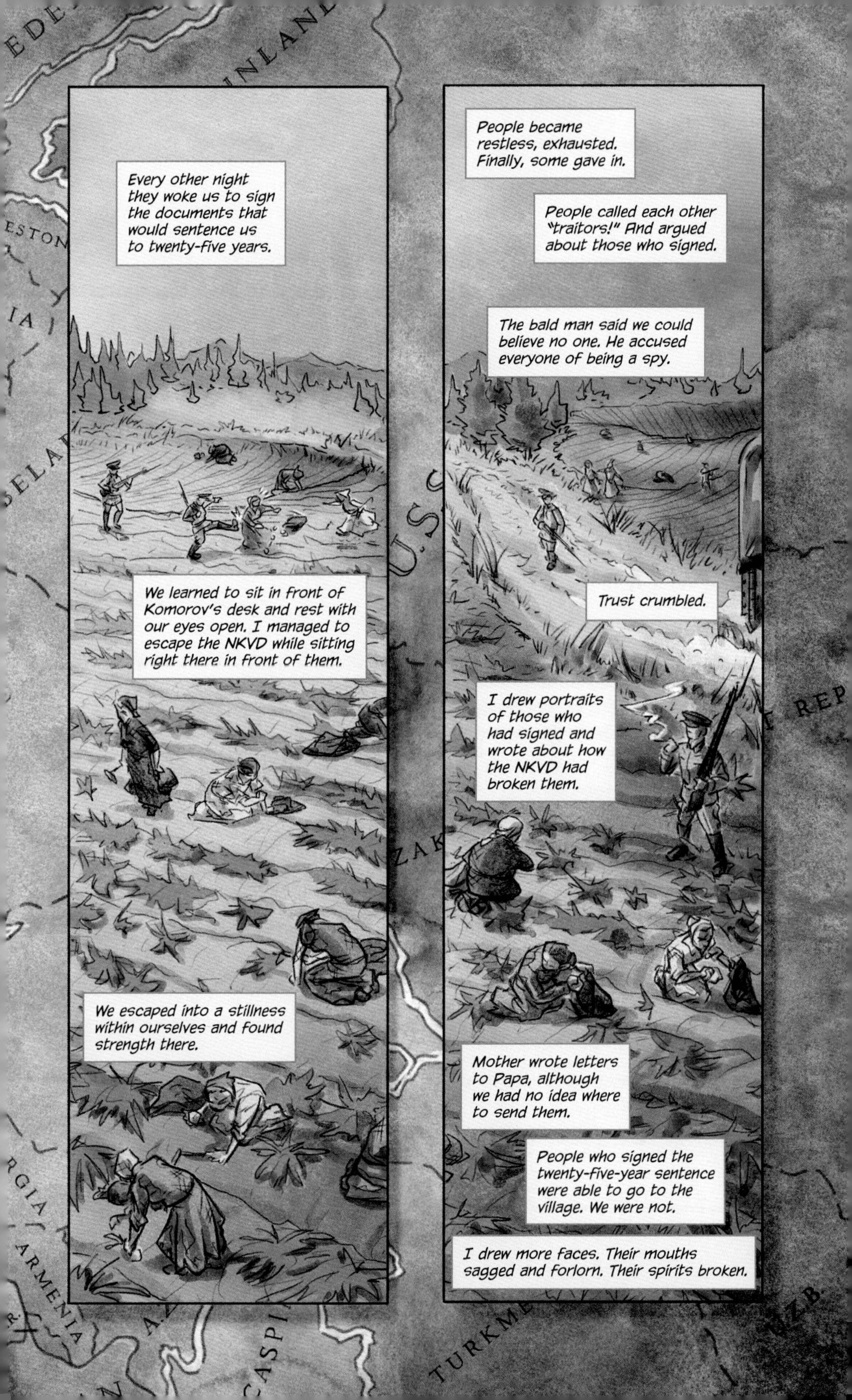
Every other night they woke us to sign the documents that would sentence us to twenty-five years.
We learned to sit in front of Komorov's desk and rest with our eyes open. I managed to escape the NKVD while sitting right there in front of them.
We escaped into a stillness within ourselves and found strength there.
People became restless, exhausted. Finally, some gave in.
People called each other "traitors!" And argued about those who signed.
The bald man said we could believe no one. He accused everyone of being a spy.
Trust crumbled.
I drew portraits of those who had signed and wrote about how the NKVD had broken them.
Mother wrote letters to Papa, although we had no idea where to send them.
People who signed the twenty-five-year sentence were able to go to the village. We were not.
I drew more faces. Their mouths sagged and forlorn. Their spirits broken.

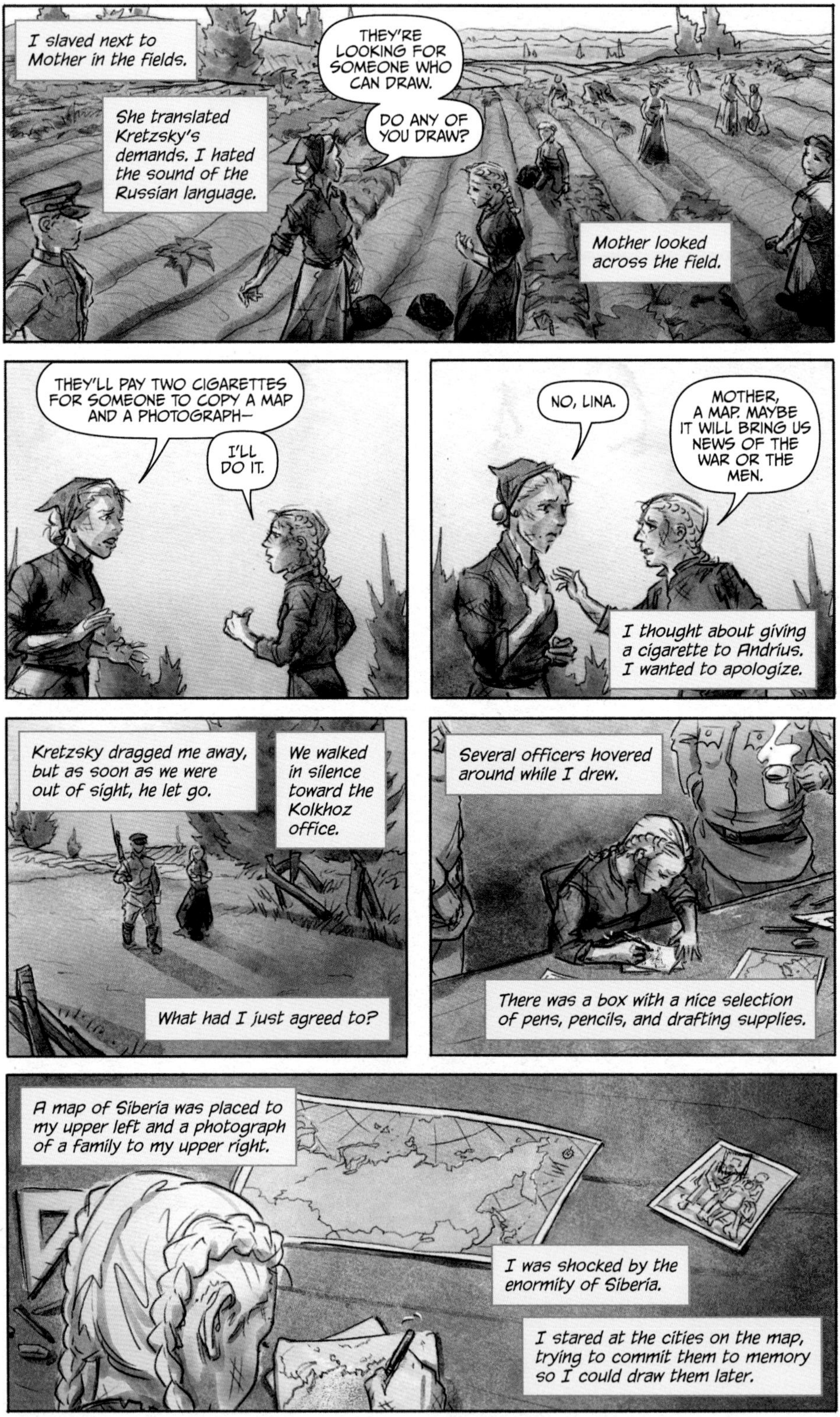
I slaved next to Mother in the fields.
She translated Kretzsky's demands. I hated the sound of the Russian language.
THEY'RE LOOKING FOR SOMEONE WHO CAN DRAW.
DO ANY OF YOU DRAW?
Mother looked across the field.
THEY'LL PAY TWO CIGARETTES FOR SOMEONE TO COPY A MAP AND A PHOTOGRAPH—
I'LL DO IT.
NO, LINA.
MOTHER, A MAP. MAYBE IT WILL BRING US NEWS OF THE WAR OR THE MEN.
I thought about giving a cigarette to Andrius. I wanted to apologize.
Kretzsky dragged me away, but as soon as we were out of sight, he let go.
We walked in silence toward the Kolkhoz office.
What had I just agreed to?
Several officers hovered around while I drew.
There was a box with a nice selection of pens, pencils, and drafting supplies.
A map of Siberia was placed to my upper left and a photograph of a family to my upper right.
I was shocked by the enormity of Siberia.
I stared at the cities on the map, trying to commit them to memory so I could draw them later.

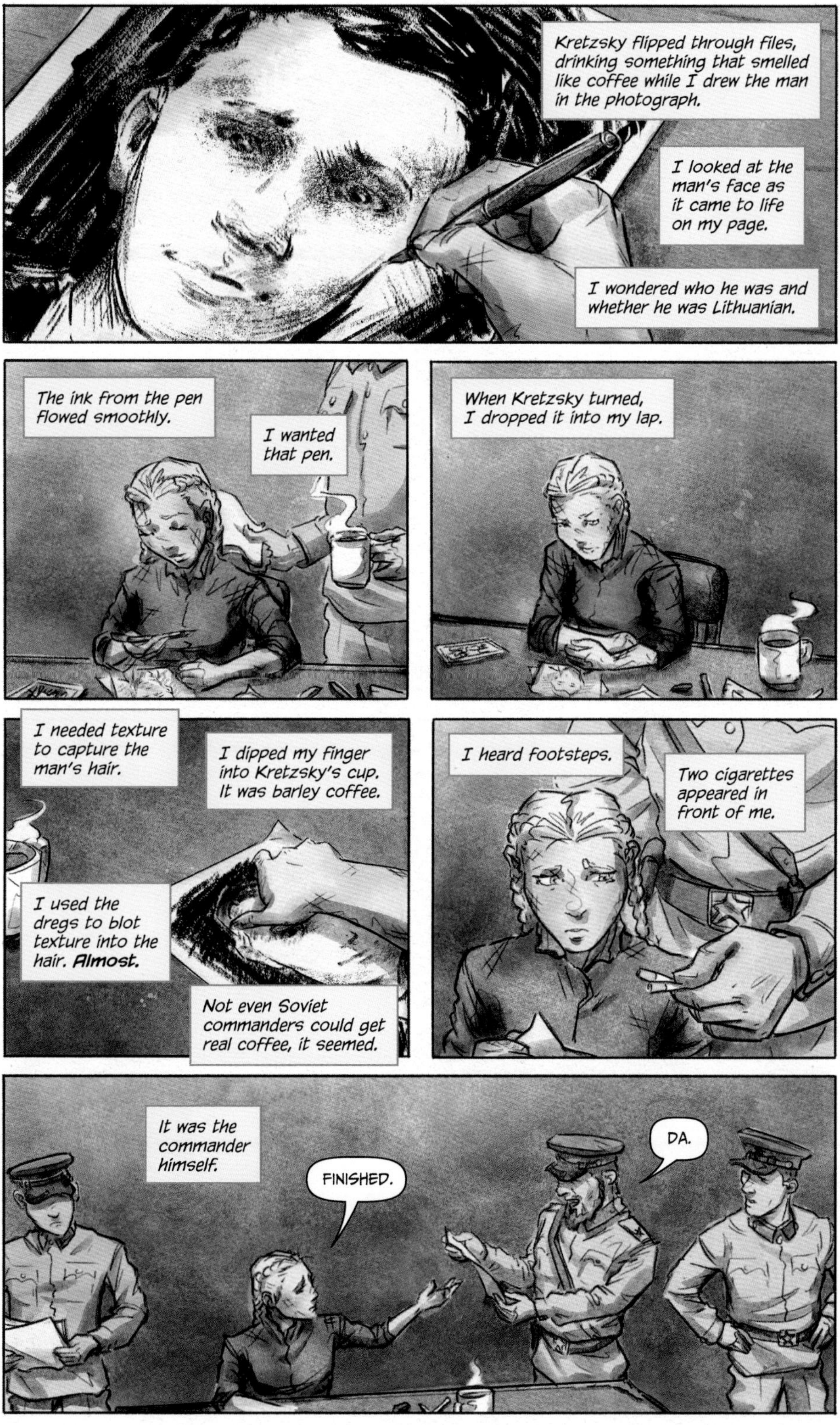

Kretzsky flipped through files, drinking something that smelled like coffee while I drew the man in the photograph.
I looked at the man's face as it came to life on my page.
I wondered who he was and whether he was Lithuanian.
The ink from the pen flowed smoothly.
I wanted that pen.
When Kretzsky turned, I dropped it into my lap.
I needed texture to capture the man's hair.
I dipped my finger into Kretzsky's cup. It was barley coffee.
I used the dregs to blot texture into the hair. **Almost.**
Not even Soviet commanders could get real coffee, it seemed.
I heard footsteps.
Two cigarettes appeared in front of me.
It was the commander himself.
FINISHED.
DA.

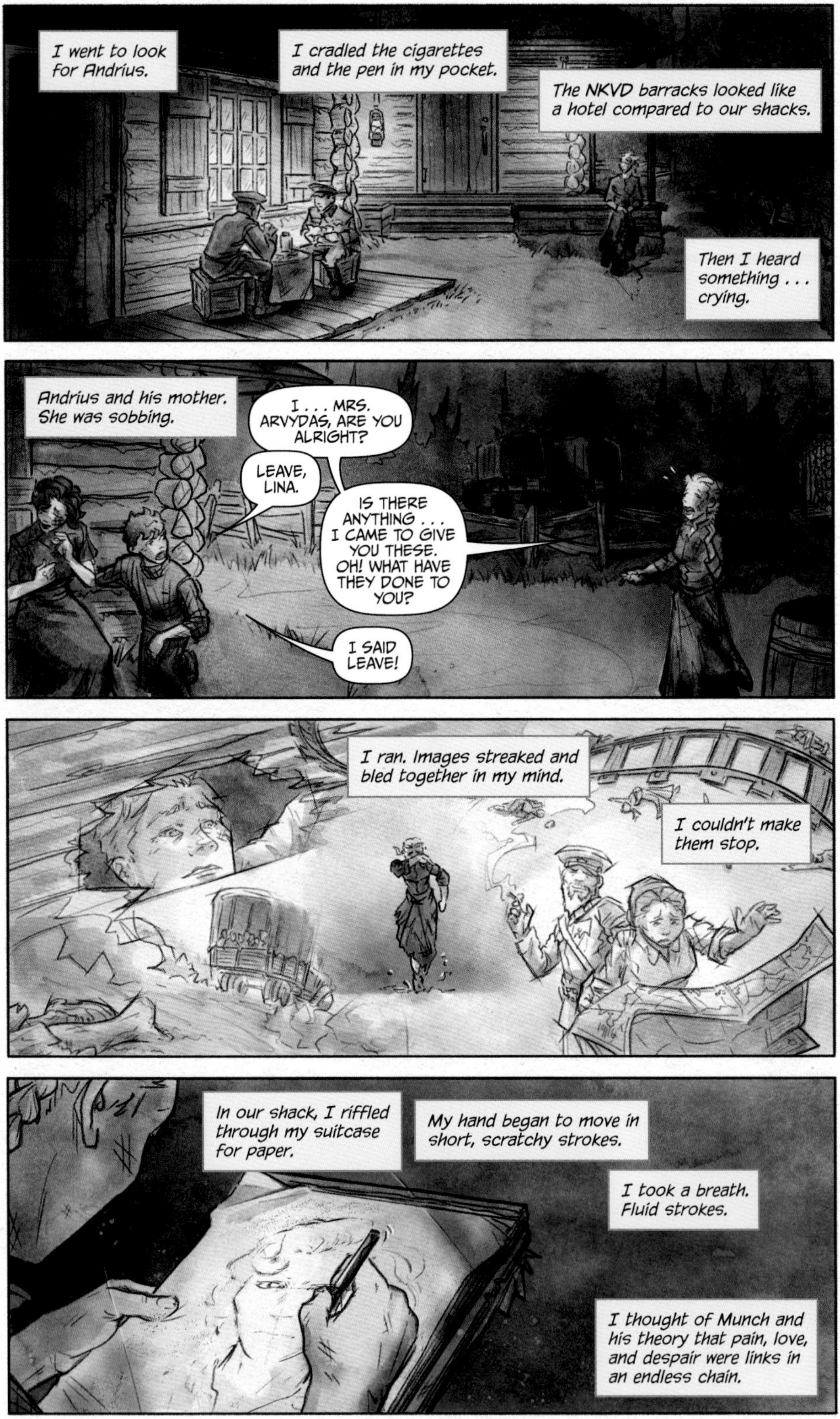
I went to look for Andrius.
I cradled the cigarettes and the pen in my pocket.
The NKVD barracks looked like a hotel compared to our shacks.
Then I heard something . . . crying.
Andrius and his mother. She was sobbing.
I . . . MRS. ARVYDAS, ARE YOU ALRIGHT?
LEAVE, LINA.
IS THERE ANYTHING . . . I CAME TO GIVE YOU THESE. OH! WHAT HAVE THEY DONE TO YOU?
I SAID LEAVE!
I ran. Images streaked and bled together in my mind.
I couldn't make them stop.
In our shack, I riffled through my suitcase for paper.
My hand began to move in short, scratchy strokes.
I took a breath. Fluid strokes.
I thought of Munch and his theory that pain, love, and despair were links in an endless chain.

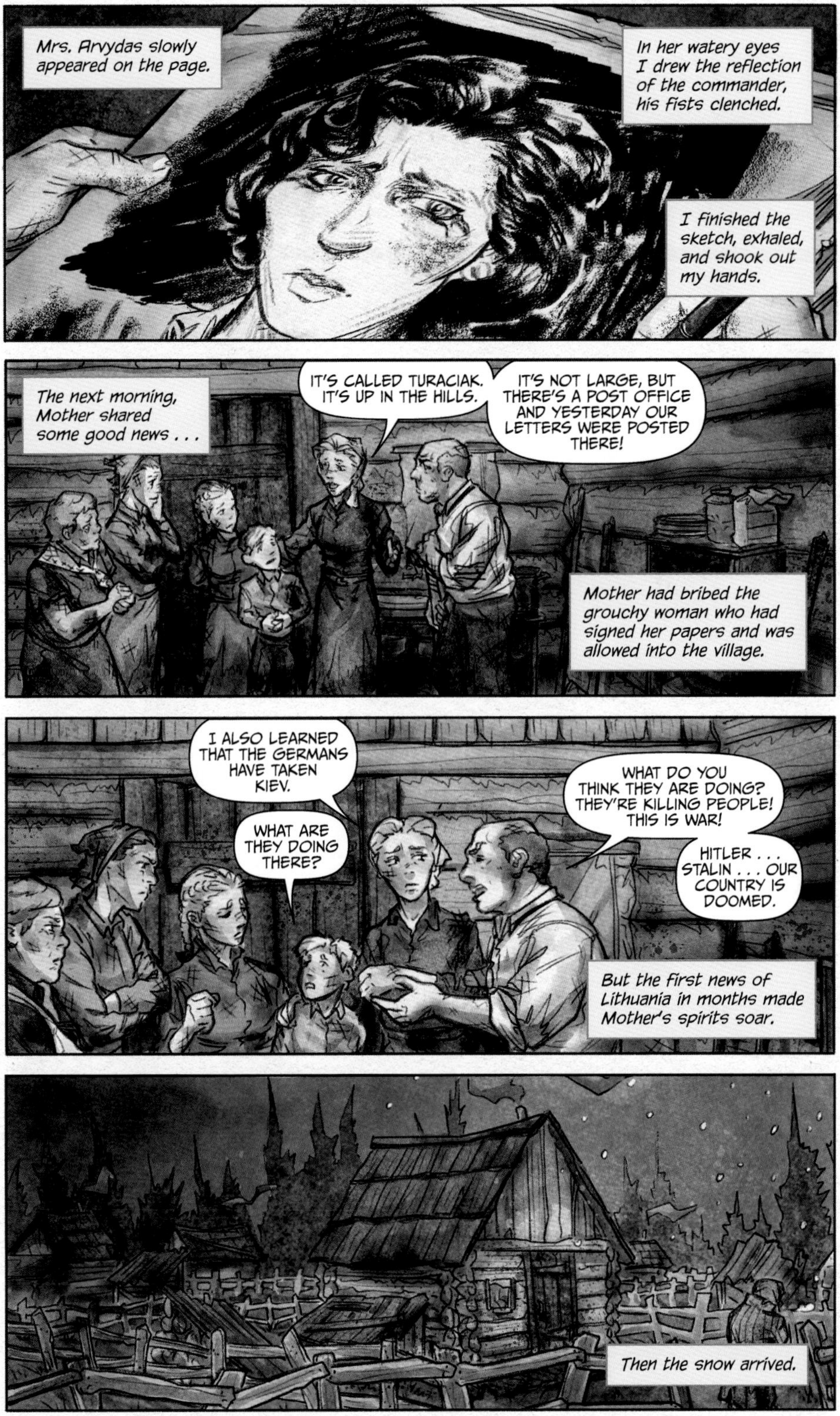
Mrs. Arvydas slowly appeared on the page.
In her watery eyes I drew the reflection of the commander, his fists clenched.
I finished the sketch, exhaled, and shook out my hands.
The next morning, Mother shared some good news . . .
IT'S CALLED TURACIAK. IT'S UP IN THE HILLS.
IT'S NOT LARGE, BUT THERE'S A POST OFFICE AND YESTERDAY OUR LETTERS WERE POSTED THERE!
Mother had bribed the grouchy woman who had signed her papers and was allowed into the village.
I ALSO LEARNED THAT THE GERMANS HAVE TAKEN KIEV.
WHAT ARE THEY DOING THERE?
WHAT DO YOU THINK THEY ARE DOING? THEY'RE KILLING PEOPLE! THIS IS WAR!
HITLER . . . STALIN . . . OUR COUNTRY IS DOOMED.
But the first news of Lithuania in months made Mother's spirits soar.
Then the snow arrived.

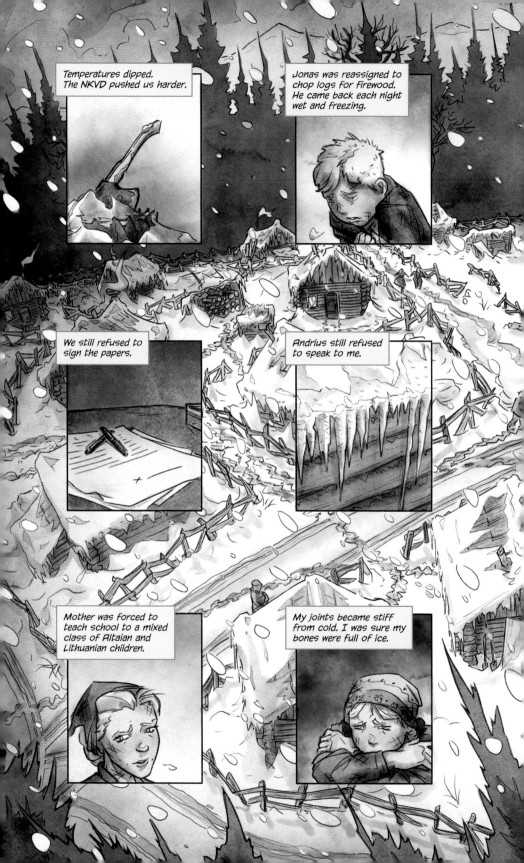

Temperatures dipped. The NKVD pushed us harder.

Jonas was reassigned to chop logs for firewood. He came back each night wet and freezing.

We still refused to sign the papers.

Andrius still refused to speak to me.

Mother was forced to teach school to a mixed class of Altaian and Lithuanian children.

My joints became stiff from cold. I was sure my bones were full of ice.

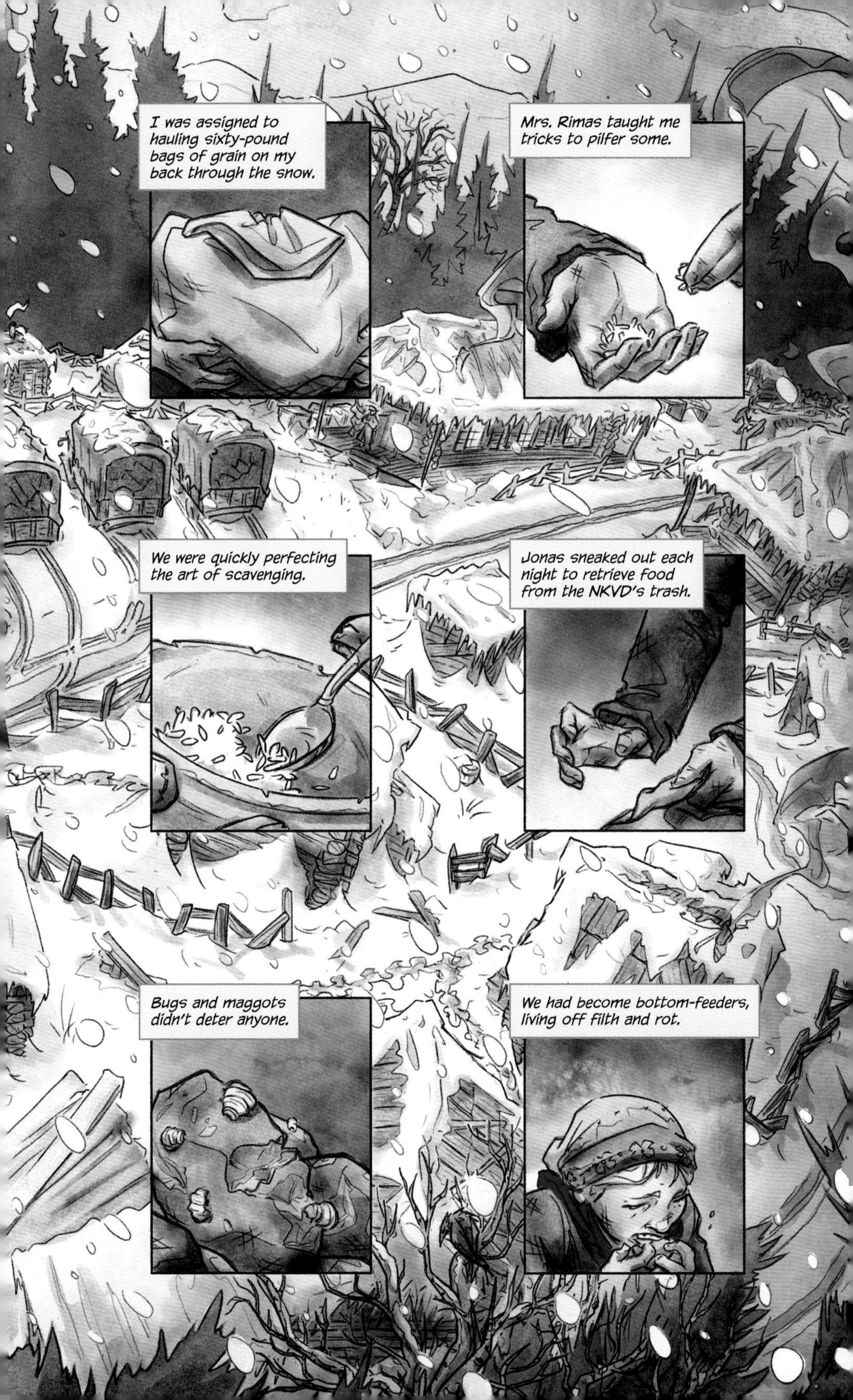
I was assigned to hauling sixty-pound bags of grain on my back through the snow.
Mrs. Rimas taught me tricks to pilfer some.
We were quickly perfecting the art of scavenging.
Jonas sneaked out each night to retrieve food from the NKVD's trash.
Bugs and maggots didn't deter anyone.
We had become bottom-feeders, living off filth and rot.

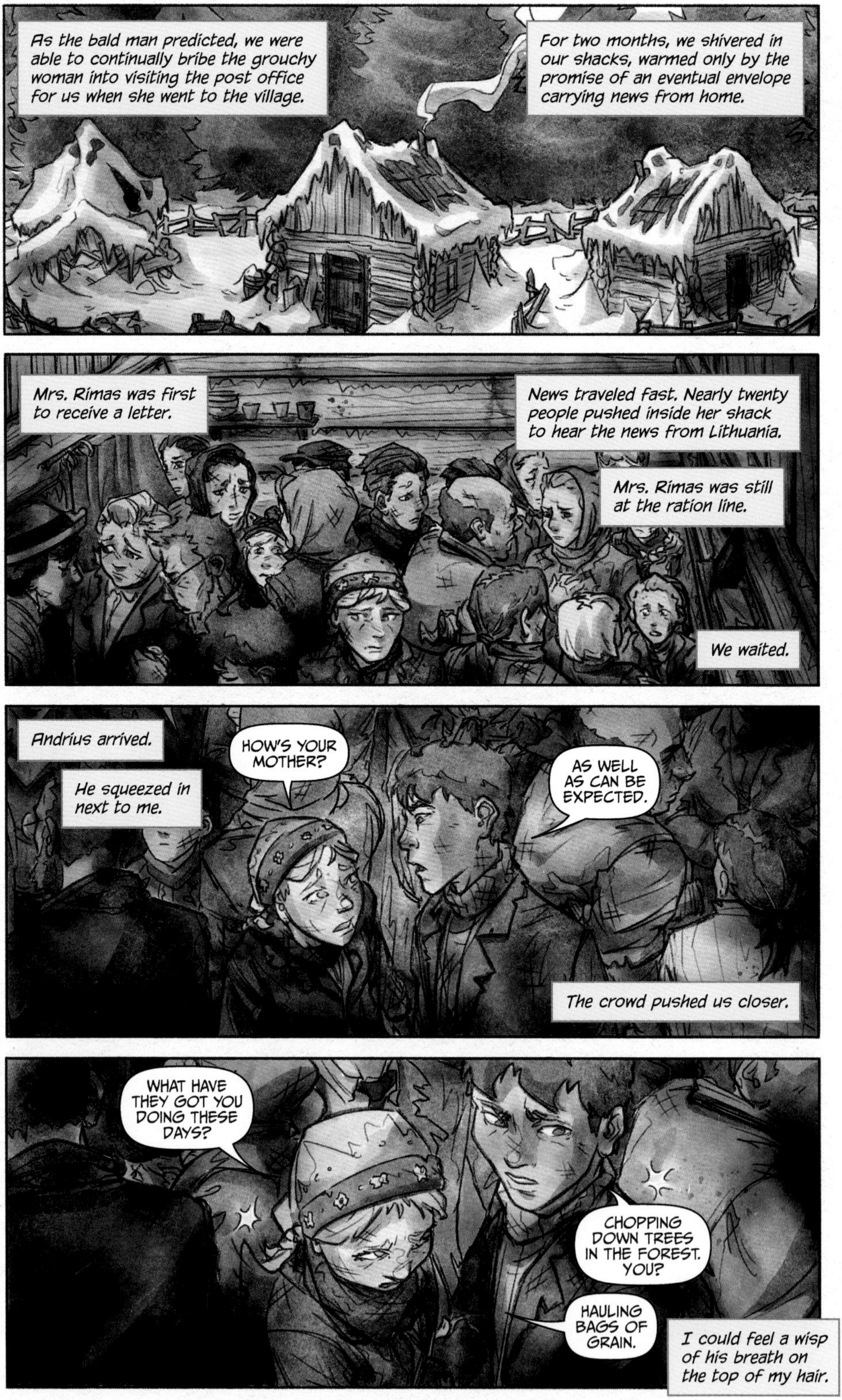
As the bald man predicted, we were able to continually bribe the grouchy woman into visiting the post office for us when she went to the village.
For two months, we shivered in our shacks, warmed only by the promise of an eventual envelope carrying news from home.
Mrs. Rimas was first to receive a letter.
News traveled fast. Nearly twenty people pushed inside her shack to hear the news from Lithuania.
Mrs. Rimas was still at the ration line.
We waited.
Andrius arrived.
He squeezed in next to me.
HOW'S YOUR MOTHER?
AS WELL AS CAN BE EXPECTED.
The crowd pushed us closer.
WHAT HAVE THEY GOT YOU DOING THESE DAYS?
CHOPPING DOWN TREES IN THE FOREST. YOU?
HAULING BAGS OF GRAIN.
I could feel a wisp of his breath on the top of my hair.

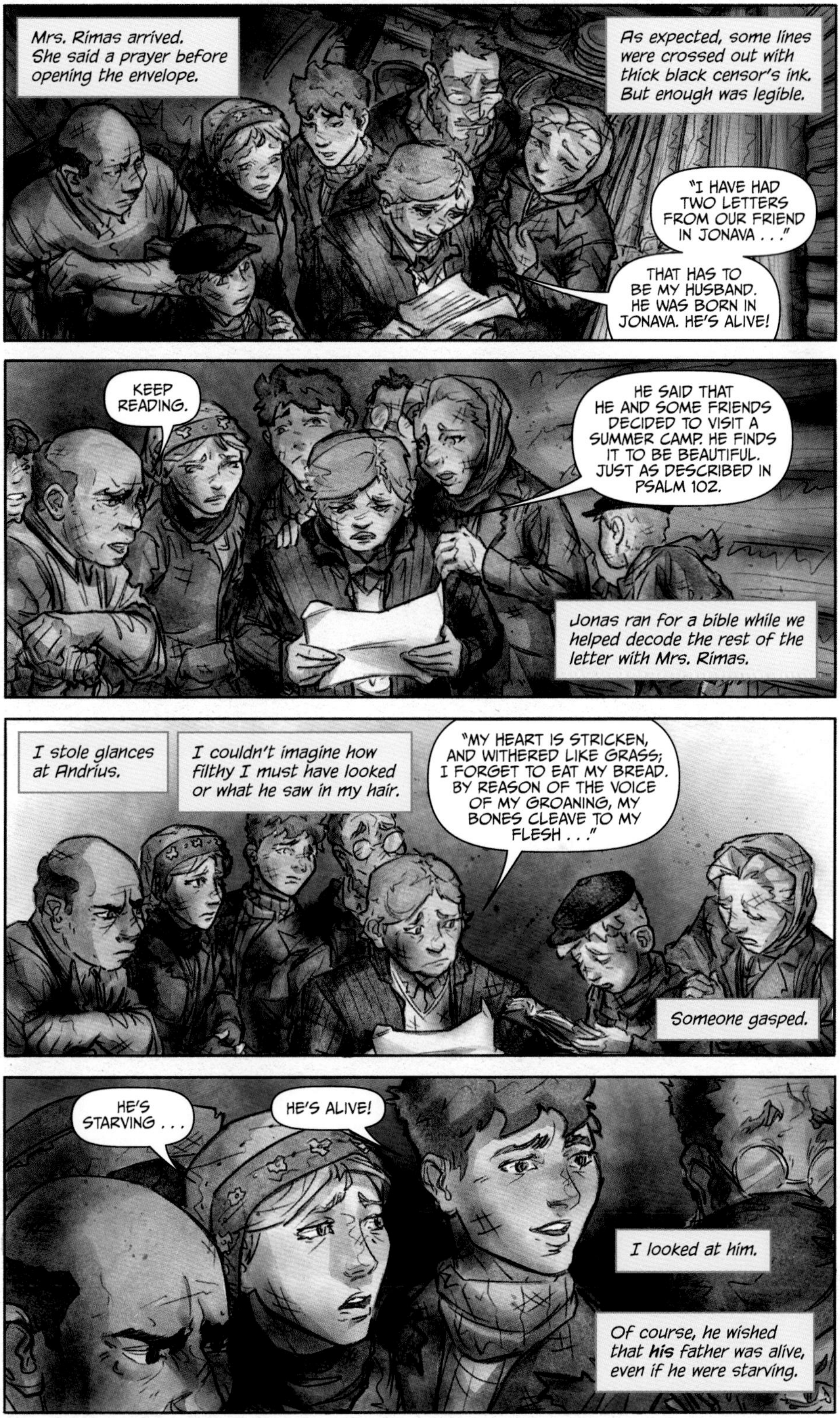

Mrs. Rimas arrived. She said a prayer before opening the envelope.
As expected, some lines were crossed out with thick black censor's ink. But enough was legible.
"I HAVE HAD TWO LETTERS FROM OUR FRIEND IN JONAVA . . ."
THAT HAS TO BE MY HUSBAND. HE WAS BORN IN JONAVA. HE'S ALIVE!
KEEP READING.
HE SAID THAT HE AND SOME FRIENDS DECIDED TO VISIT A SUMMER CAMP. HE FINDS IT TO BE BEAUTIFUL. JUST AS DESCRIBED IN PSALM 102.
Jonas ran for a bible while we helped decode the rest of the letter with Mrs. Rimas.
I stole glances at Andrius.
I couldn't imagine how filthy I must have looked or what he saw in my hair.
"MY HEART IS STRICKEN, AND WITHERED LIKE GRASS; I FORGET TO EAT MY BREAD. BY REASON OF THE VOICE OF MY GROANING, MY BONES CLEAVE TO MY FLESH . . ."
Someone gasped.
HE'S STARVING . . .
HE'S ALIVE!
I looked at him.
Of course, he wished that **his** father was alive, even if he were starving.

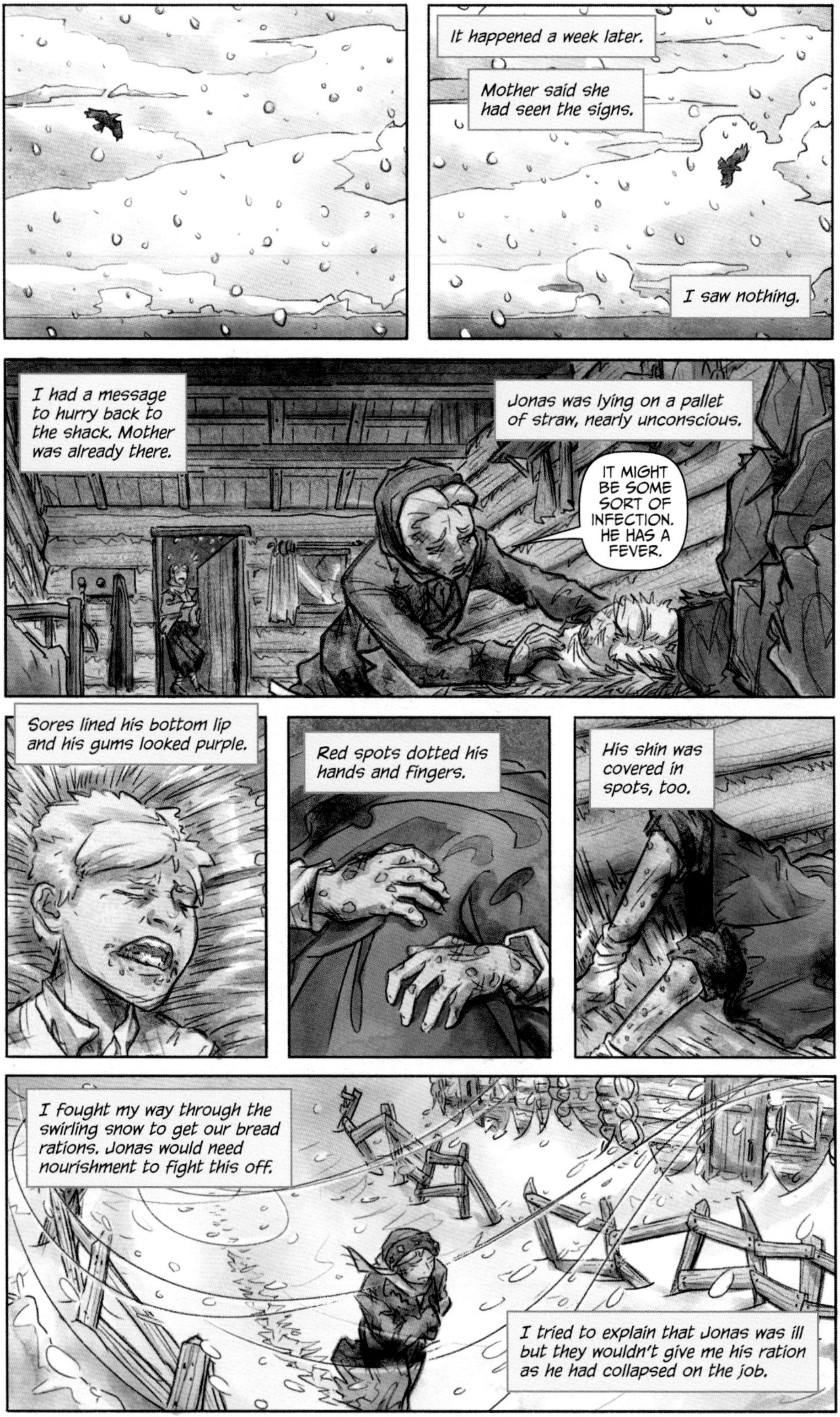
It happened a week later.
Mother said she had seen the signs.
I saw nothing.
I had a message to hurry back to the shack. Mother was already there.
Jonas was lying on a pallet of straw, nearly unconscious.
IT MIGHT BE SOME SORT OF INFECTION. HE HAS A FEVER.
Sores lined his bottom lip and his gums looked purple.
Red spots dotted his hands and fingers.
His shin was covered in spots, too.
I fought my way through the swirling snow to get our bread rations. Jonas would need nourishment to fight this off.
I tried to explain that Jonas was ill but they wouldn't give me his ration as he had collapsed on the job.

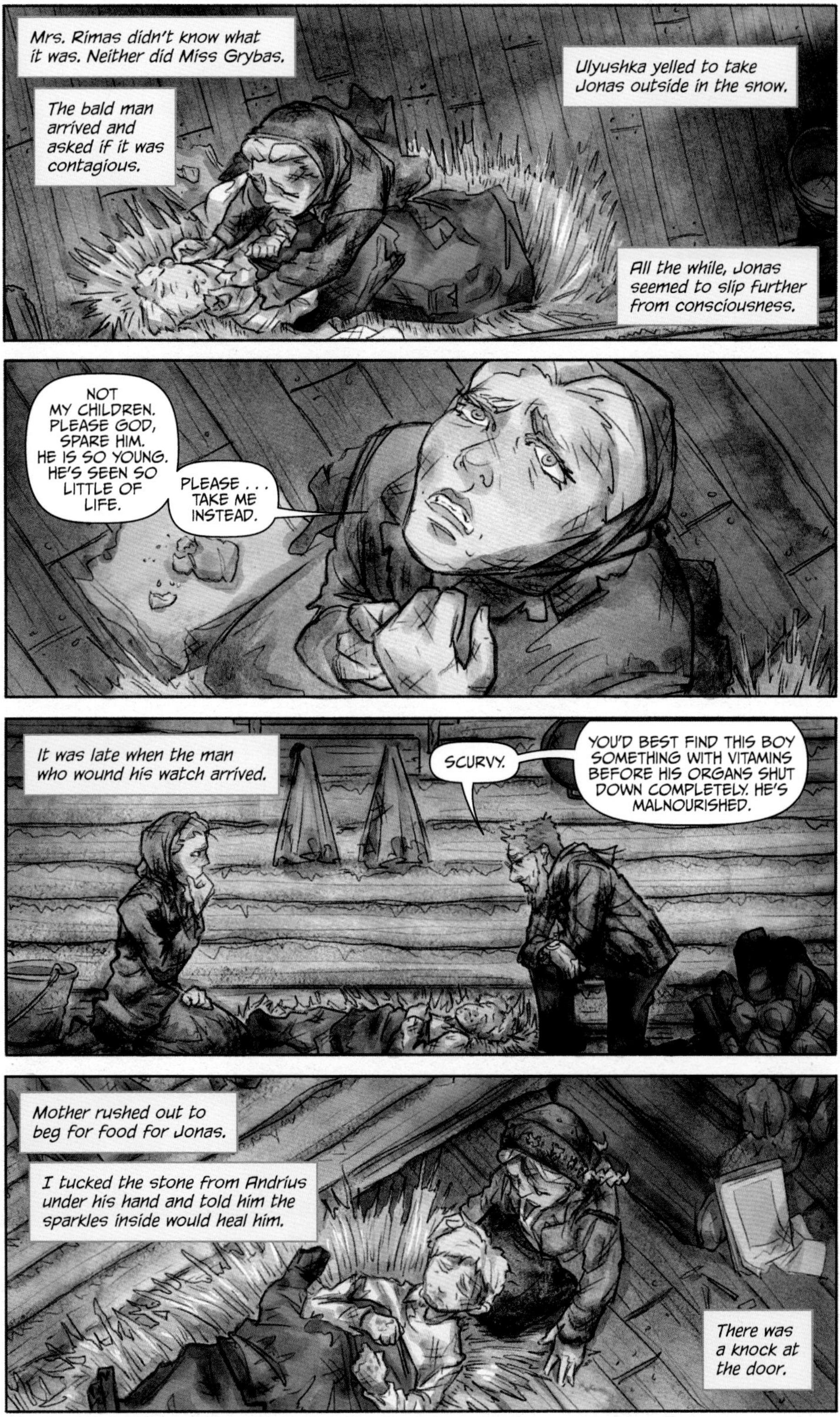
Mrs. Rimas didn't know what it was. Neither did Miss Grybas.
The bald man arrived and asked if it was contagious.
Ulyushka yelled to take Jonas outside in the snow.
All the while, Jonas seemed to slip further from consciousness.
NOT MY CHILDREN. PLEASE GOD, SPARE HIM. HE IS SO YOUNG. HE'S SEEN SO LITTLE OF LIFE.
PLEASE . . . TAKE ME INSTEAD.
It was late when the man who wound his watch arrived.
SCURVY.
YOU'D BEST FIND THIS BOY SOMETHING WITH VITAMINS BEFORE HIS ORGANS SHUT DOWN COMPLETELY. HE'S MALNOURISHED.
Mother rushed out to beg for food for Jonas.
I tucked the stone from Andrius under his hand and told him the sparkles inside would heal him.
There was a knock at the door.

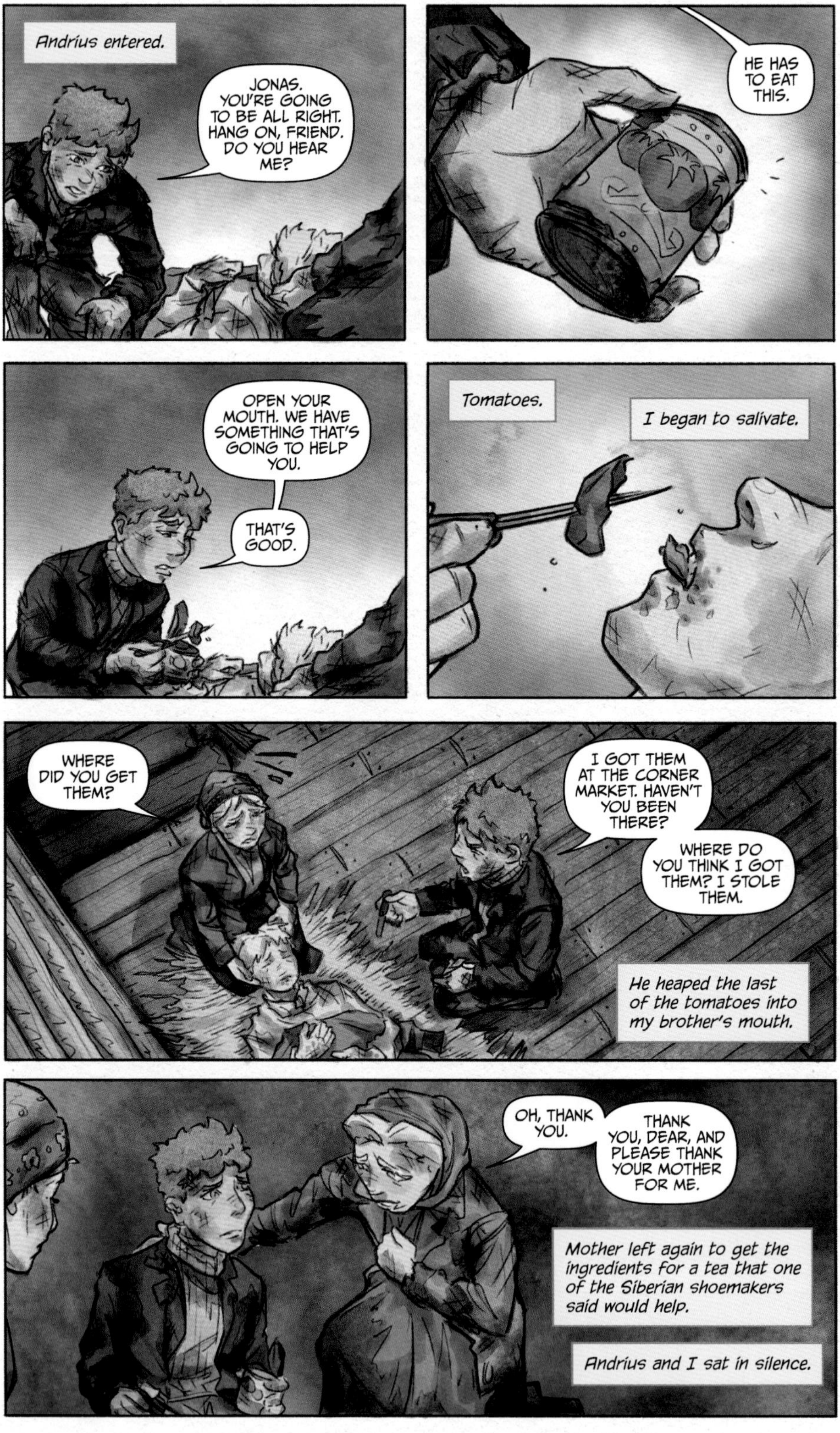
Andrius entered.
JONAS. YOU'RE GOING TO BE ALL RIGHT. HANG ON, FRIEND. DO YOU HEAR ME?
HE HAS TO EAT THIS.
OPEN YOUR MOUTH. WE HAVE SOMETHING THAT'S GOING TO HELP YOU.
THAT'S GOOD.
Tomatoes.
I began to salivate.
WHERE DID YOU GET THEM?
I GOT THEM AT THE CORNER MARKET. HAVEN'T YOU BEEN THERE?
WHERE DO YOU THINK I GOT THEM? I STOLE THEM.
He heaped the last of the tomatoes into my brother's mouth.
OH, THANK YOU.
THANK YOU, DEAR, AND PLEASE THANK YOUR MOTHER FOR ME.
Mother left again to get the ingredients for a tea that one of the Siberian shoemakers said would help.
Andrius and I sat in silence.

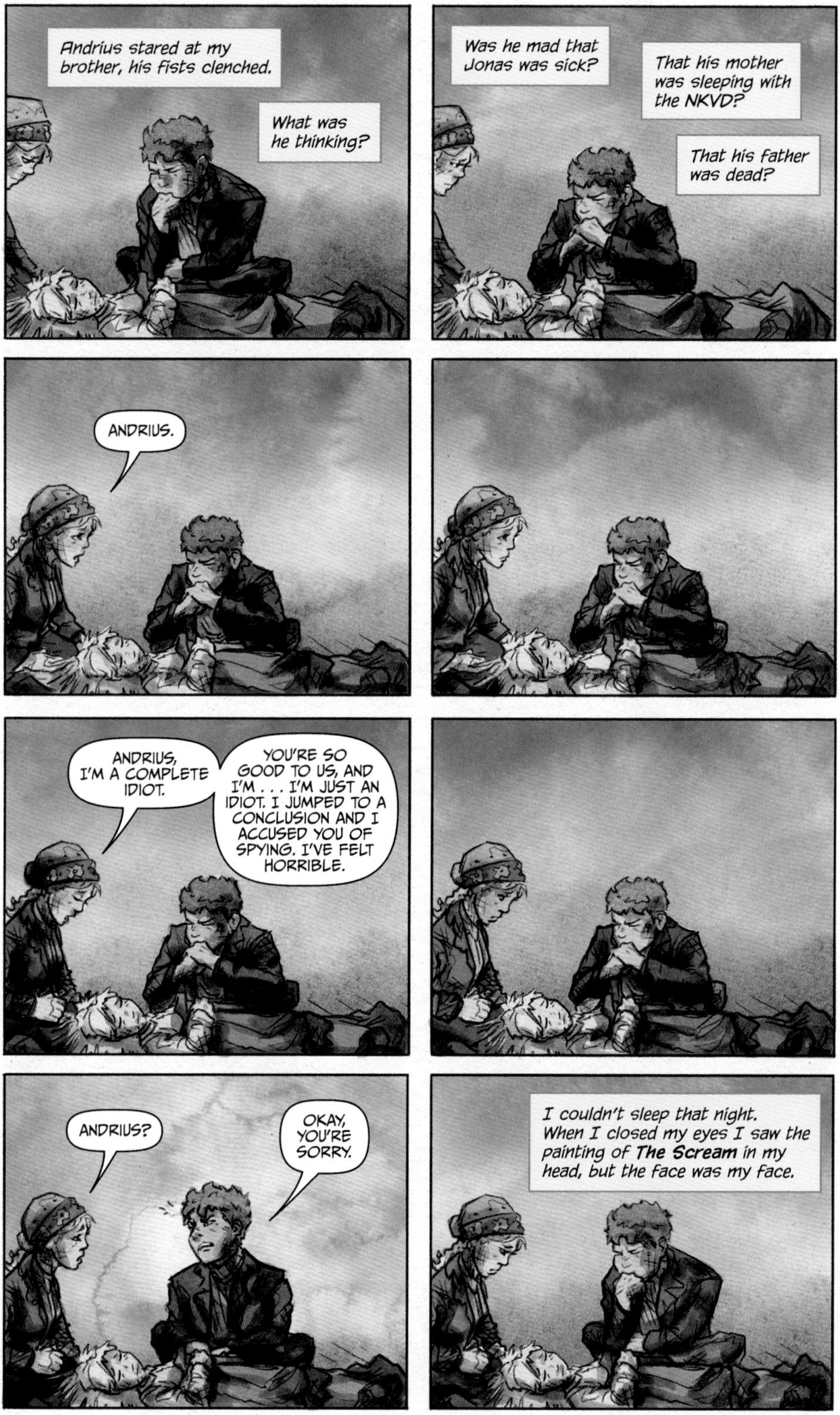
Andrius stared at my brother, his fists clenched.
What was he thinking?
Was he mad that Jonas was sick?
That his mother was sleeping with the NKVD?
That his father was dead?
ANDRIUS.
ANDRIUS, I'M A COMPLETE IDIOT.
YOU'RE SO GOOD TO US, AND I'M . . . I'M JUST AN IDIOT. I JUMPED TO A CONCLUSION AND I ACCUSED YOU OF SPYING. I'VE FELT HORRIBLE.
ANDRIUS?
OKAY, YOU'RE SORRY.
I couldn't sleep that night. When I closed my eyes I saw the painting of **The Scream** in my head, but the face was my face.

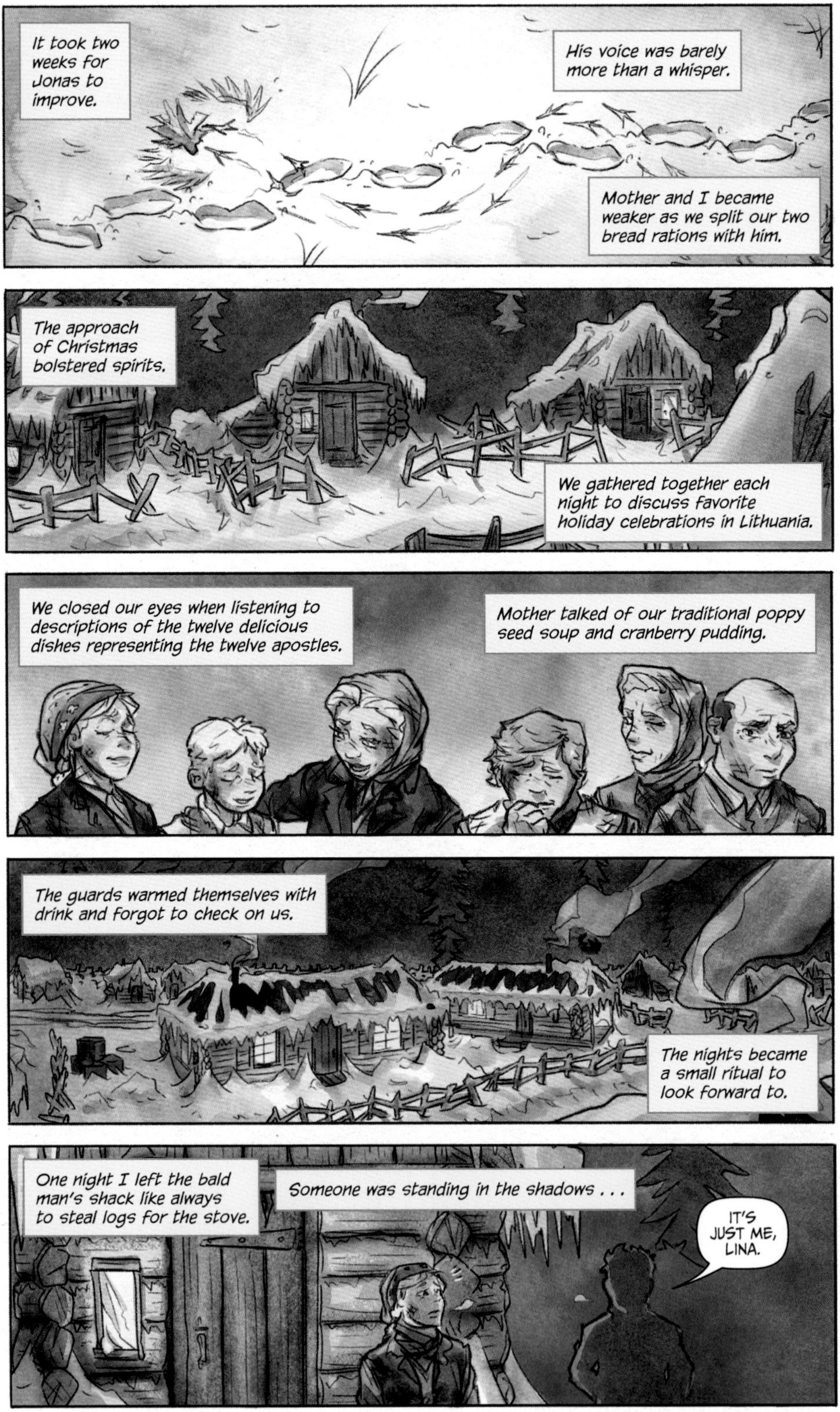
It took two weeks for Jonas to improve.
His voice was barely more than a whisper.
Mother and I became weaker as we split our two bread rations with him.
The approach of Christmas bolstered spirits.
We gathered together each night to discuss favorite holiday celebrations in Lithuania.
We closed our eyes when listening to descriptions of the twelve delicious dishes representing the twelve apostles.
Mother talked of our traditional poppy seed soup and cranberry pudding.
The guards warmed themselves with drink and forgot to check on us.
The nights became a small ritual to look forward to.
One night I left the bald man's shack like always to steal logs for the stove.
Someone was standing in the shadows . . .
IT'S JUST ME, LINA.

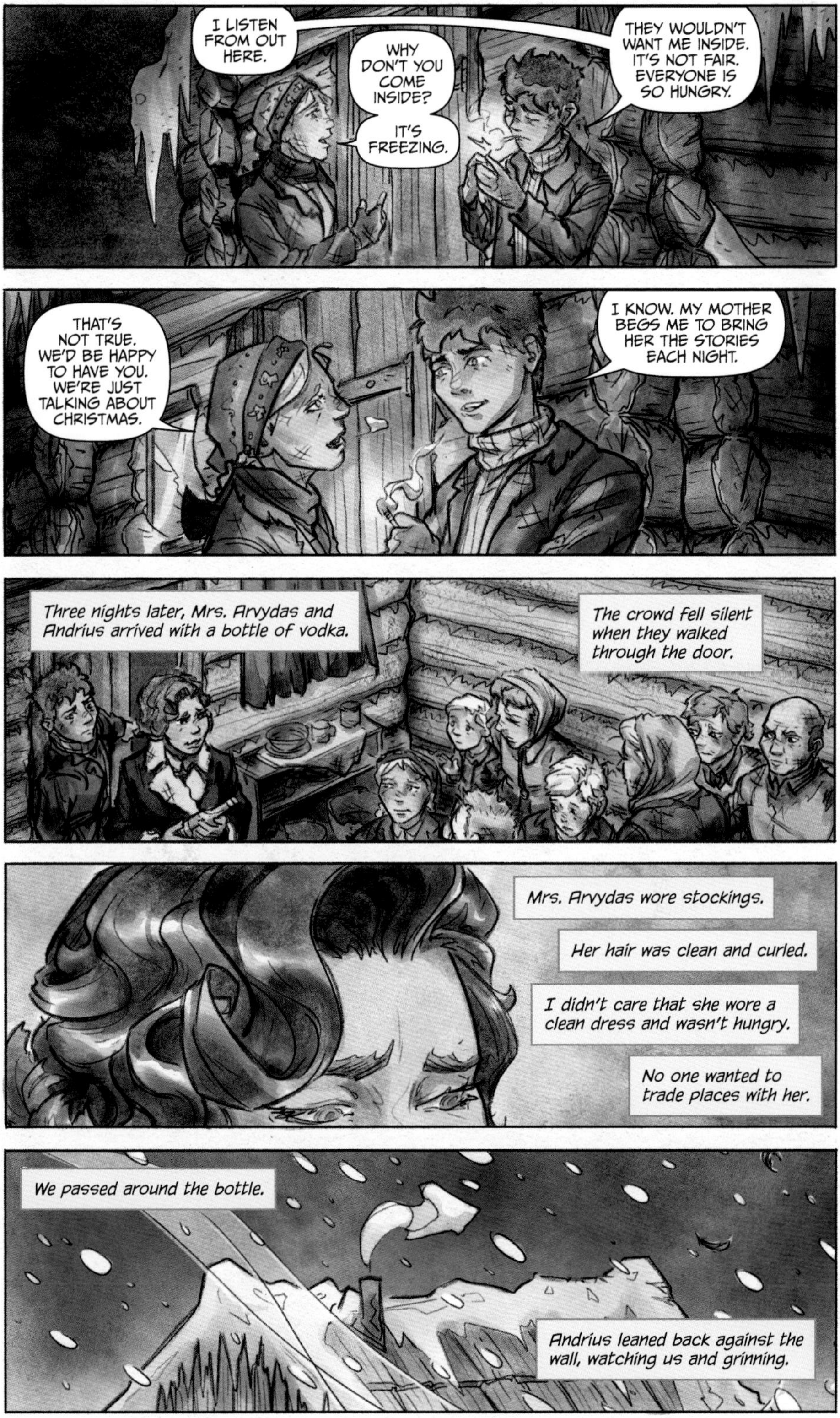
I LISTEN FROM OUT HERE.
WHY DON'T YOU COME INSIDE?
IT'S FREEZING.
THEY WOULDN'T WANT ME INSIDE. IT'S NOT FAIR. EVERYONE IS SO HUNGRY.
THAT'S NOT TRUE. WE'D BE HAPPY TO HAVE YOU. WE'RE JUST TALKING ABOUT CHRISTMAS.
I KNOW. MY MOTHER BEGS ME TO BRING HER THE STORIES EACH NIGHT.
Three nights later, Mrs. Arvydas and Andrius arrived with a bottle of vodka.
The crowd fell silent when they walked through the door.
Mrs. Arvydas wore stockings.
Her hair was clean and curled.
I didn't care that she wore a clean dress and wasn't hungry.
No one wanted to trade places with her.
We passed around the bottle.
Andrius leaned back against the wall, watching us and grinning.

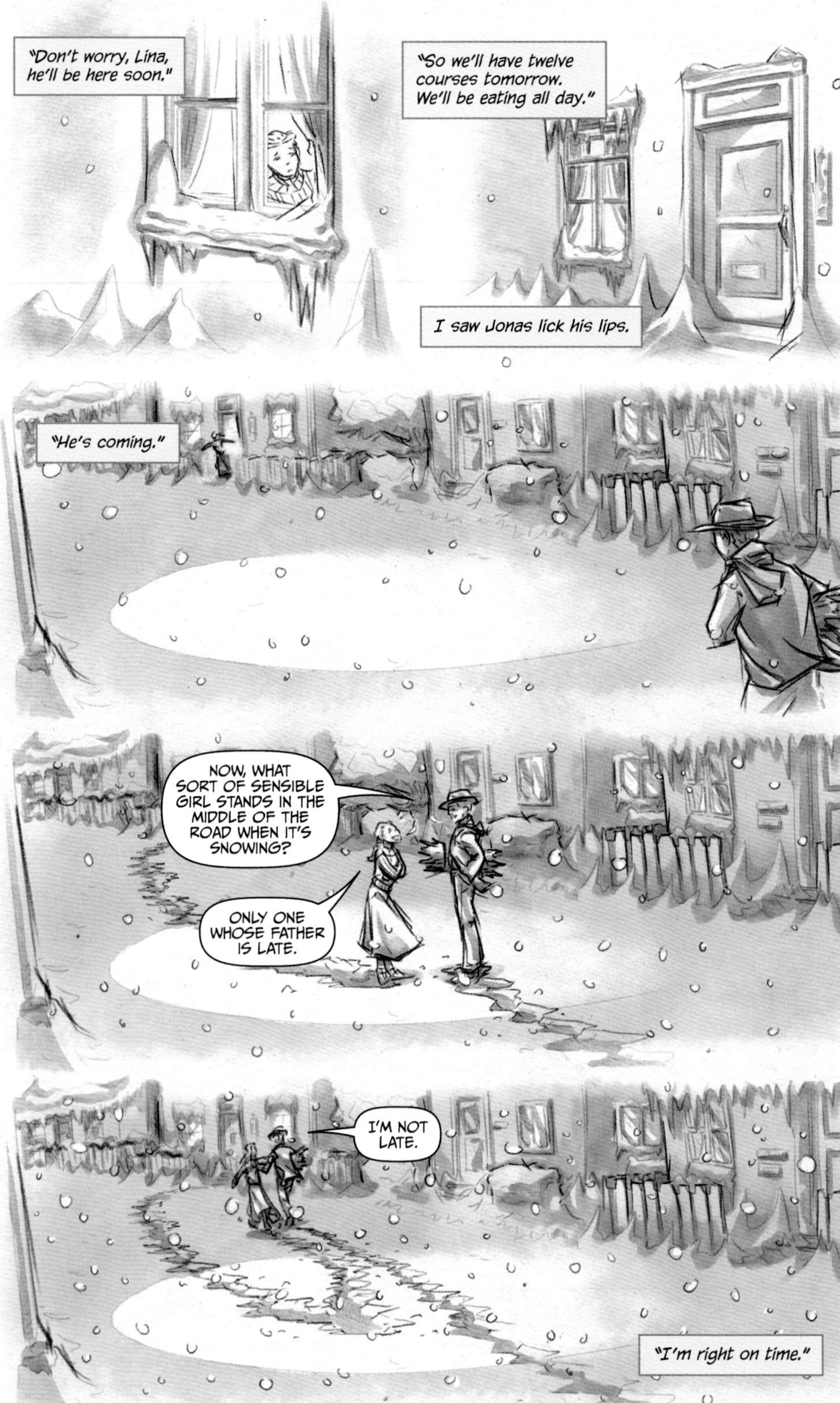
"Don't worry, Lina, he'll be here soon."
"So we'll have twelve courses tomorrow. We'll be eating all day."
I saw Jonas lick his lips.
"He's coming."
NOW, WHAT SORT OF SENSIBLE GIRL STANDS IN THE MIDDLE OF THE ROAD WHEN IT'S SNOWING?
ONLY ONE WHOSE FATHER IS LATE.
I'M NOT LATE.
"I'm right on time."

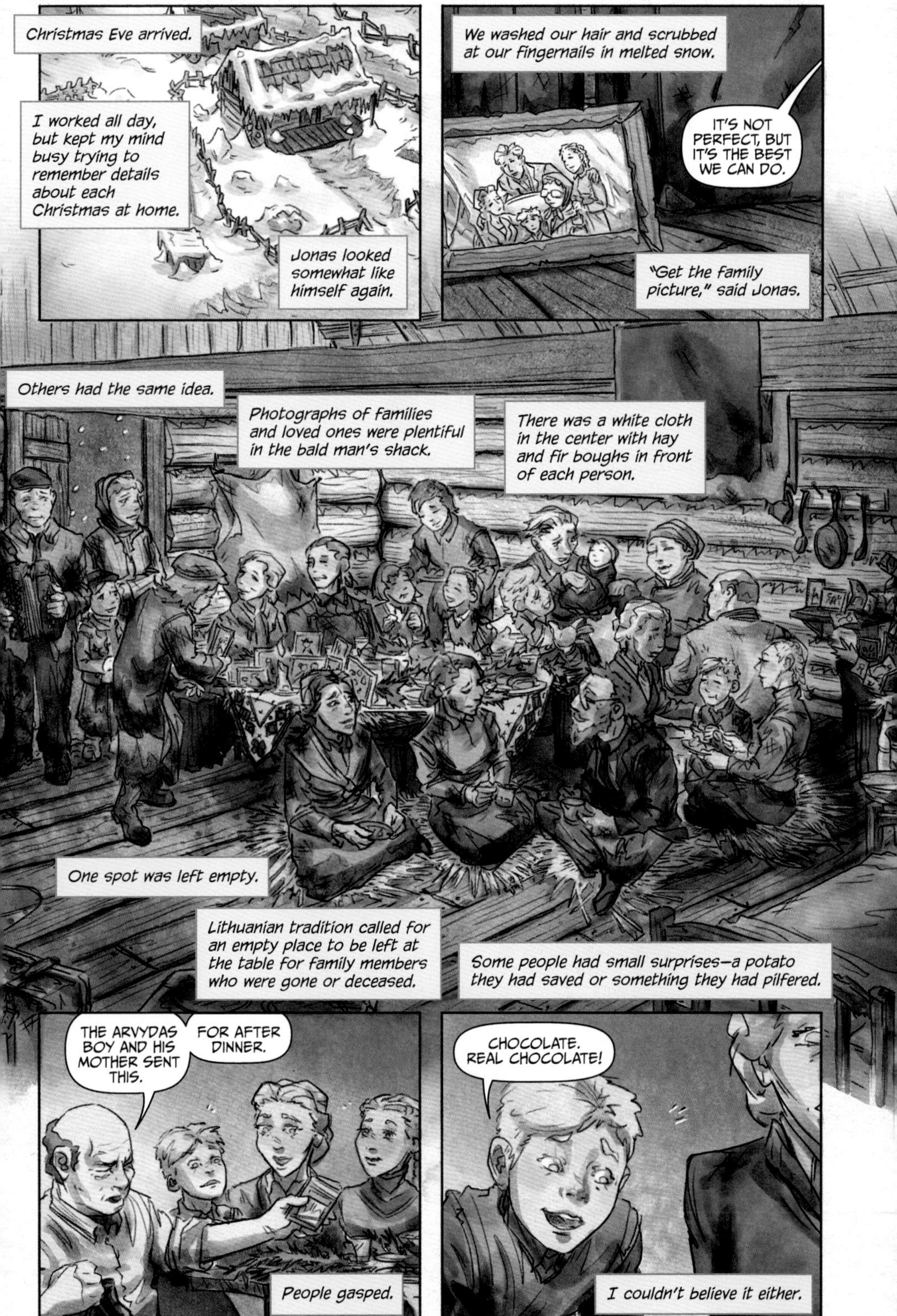
Christmas Eve arrived.
I worked all day, but kept my mind busy trying to remember details about each Christmas at home.
Jonas looked somewhat like himself again.
We washed our hair and scrubbed at our fingernails in melted snow.
"Get the family picture," said Jonas.
IT'S NOT PERFECT, BUT IT'S THE BEST WE CAN DO.
Others had the same idea.
Photographs of families and loved ones were plentiful in the bald man's shack.
There was a white cloth in the center with hay and fir boughs in front of each person.
One spot was left empty.
Lithuanian tradition called for an empty place to be left at the table for family members who were gone or deceased.
Some people had small surprises—a potato they had saved or something they had pilfered.
THE ARVYDAS BOY AND HIS MOTHER SENT THIS.
FOR AFTER DINNER.
People gasped.
CHOCOLATE. REAL CHOCOLATE!
I couldn't believe it either.

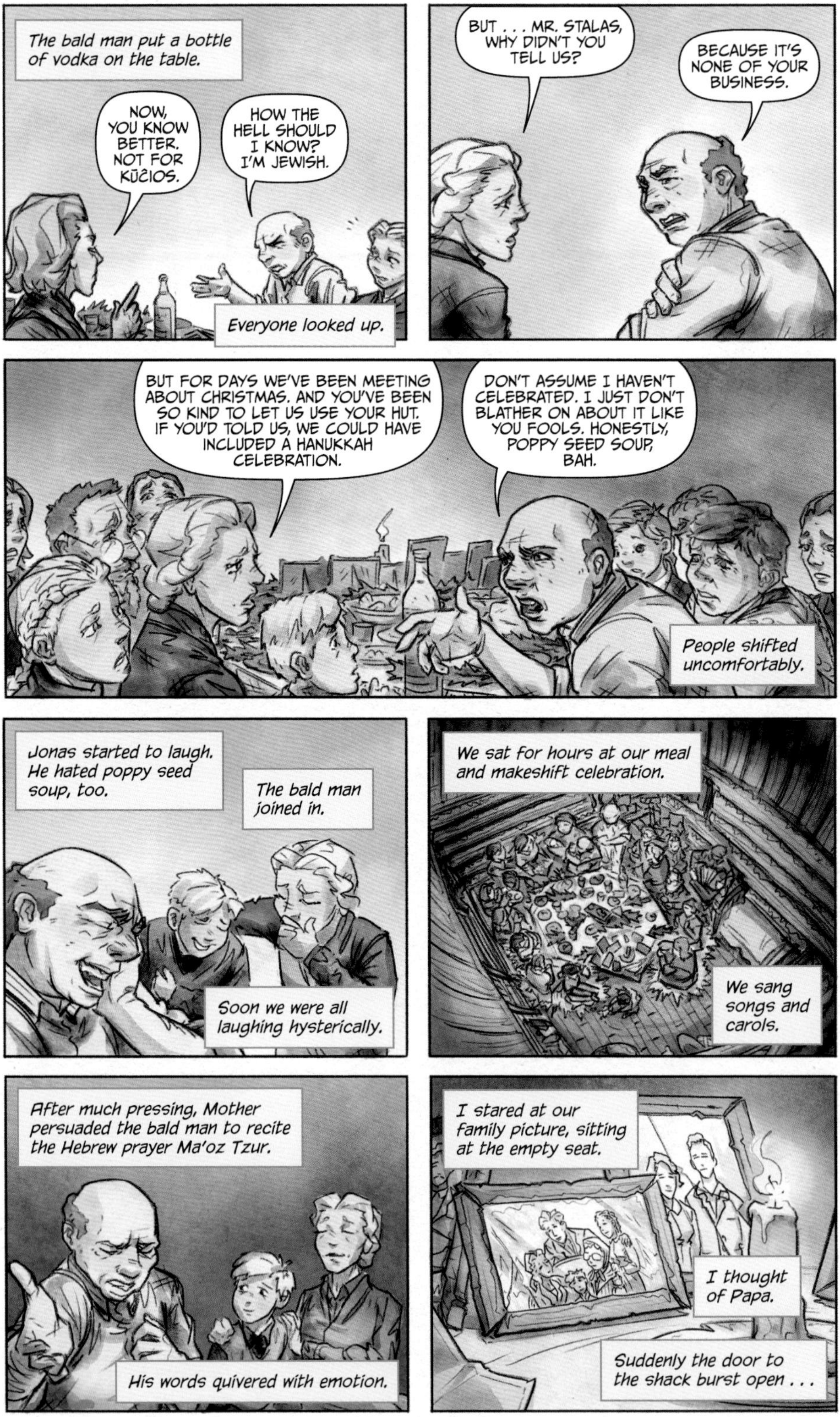

The bald man put a bottle of vodka on the table.
NOW, YOU KNOW BETTER. NOT FOR KŪČIOS.
HOW THE HELL SHOULD I KNOW? I'M JEWISH.
Everyone looked up.
BUT . . . MR. STALAS, WHY DIDN'T YOU TELL US?
BECAUSE IT'S NONE OF YOUR BUSINESS.
BUT FOR DAYS WE'VE BEEN MEETING ABOUT CHRISTMAS. AND YOU'VE BEEN SO KIND TO LET US USE YOUR HUT. IF YOU'D TOLD US, WE COULD HAVE INCLUDED A HANUKKAH CELEBRATION.
DON'T ASSUME I HAVEN'T CELEBRATED. I JUST DON'T BLATHER ON ABOUT IT LIKE YOU FOOLS. HONESTLY, POPPY SEED SOUP, BAH.
People shifted uncomfortably.
Jonas started to laugh. He hated poppy seed soup, too.
The bald man joined in.
Soon we were all laughing hysterically.
We sat for hours at our meal and makeshift celebration.
We sang songs and carols.
After much pressing, Mother persuaded the bald man to recite the Hebrew prayer Ma'oz Tzur.
His words quivered with emotion.
I stared at our family picture, sitting at the empty seat.
I thought of Papa.
Suddenly the door to the shack burst open . . .

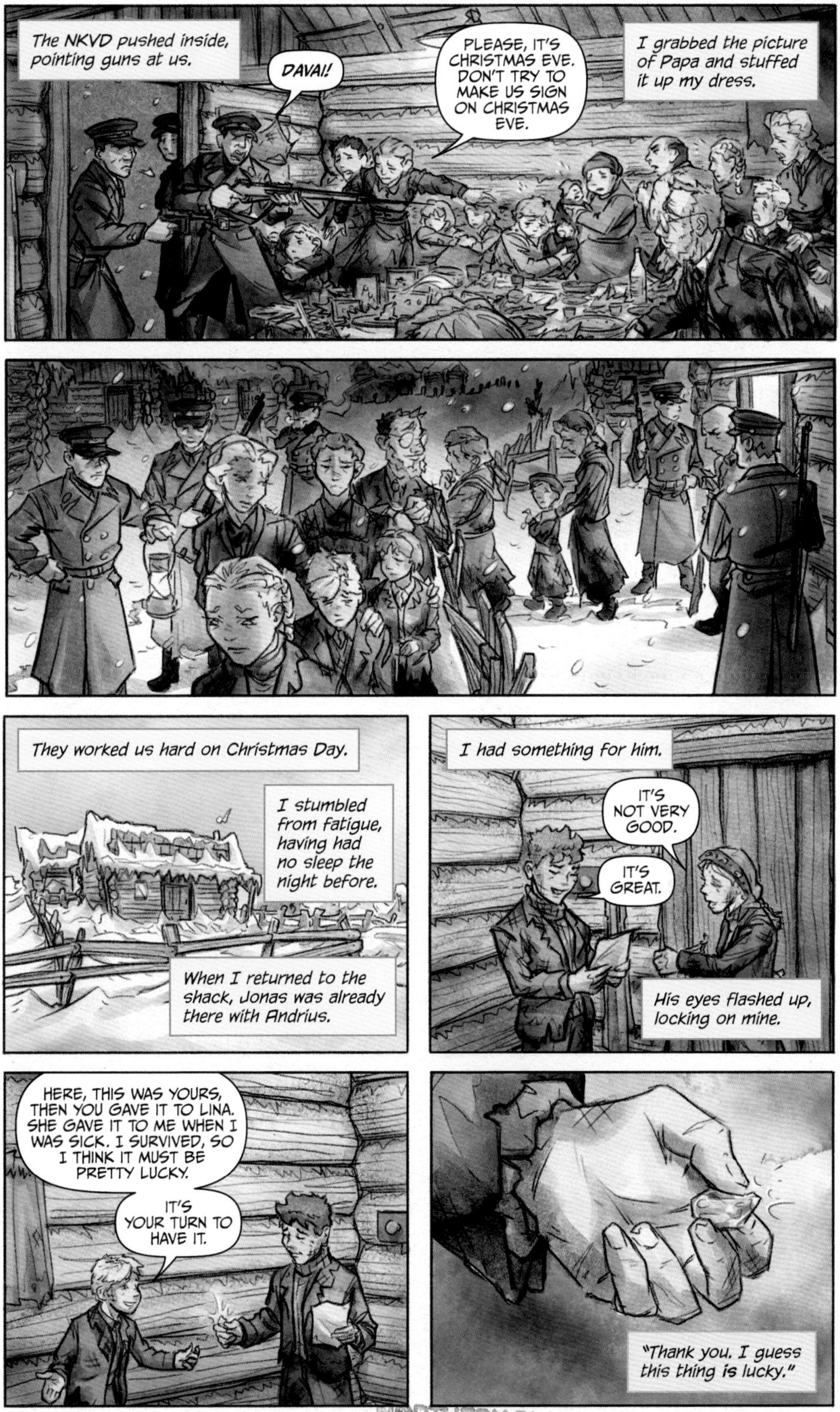
The NKVD pushed inside, pointing guns at us.
DAVAI!
PLEASE, IT'S CHRISTMAS EVE. DON'T TRY TO MAKE US SIGN ON CHRISTMAS EVE.
I grabbed the picture of Papa and stuffed it up my dress.
They worked us hard on Christmas Day.
I stumbled from fatigue, having had no sleep the night before.
When I returned to the shack, Jonas was already there with Andrius.
I had something for him.
IT'S NOT VERY GOOD.
IT'S GREAT.
His eyes flashed up, locking on mine.
HERE, THIS WAS YOURS, THEN YOU GAVE IT TO LINA. SHE GAVE IT TO ME WHEN I WAS SICK. I SURVIVED, SO I THINK IT MUST BE PRETTY LUCKY.
IT'S YOUR TURN TO HAVE IT.
"Thank you. I guess this thing is lucky."

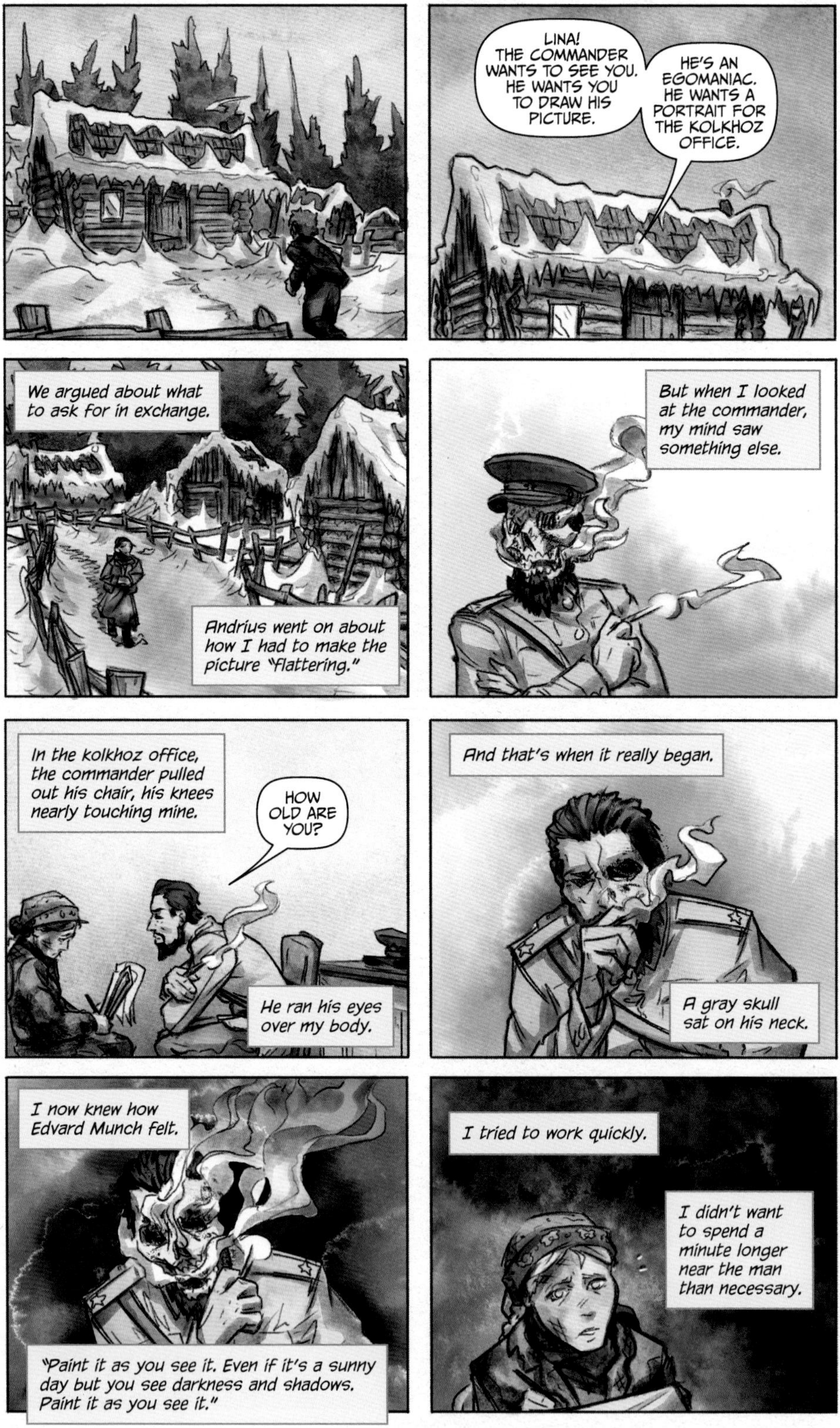
LINA! THE COMMANDER WANTS TO SEE YOU. HE WANTS YOU TO DRAW HIS PICTURE.
HE'S AN EGOMANIAC. HE WANTS A PORTRAIT FOR THE KOLKHOZ OFFICE.
We argued about what to ask for in exchange.
Andrius went on about how I had to make the picture "flattering."
But when I looked at the commander, my mind saw something else.
In the kolkhoz office, the commander pulled out his chair, his knees nearly touching mine.
HOW OLD ARE YOU?
He ran his eyes over my body.
And that's when it really began.
A gray skull sat on his neck.
I now knew how Edvard Munch felt.
"Paint it as you see it. Even if it's a sunny day but you see darkness and shadows. Paint it as you see it."
I tried to work quickly.
I didn't want to spend a minute longer near the man than necessary.

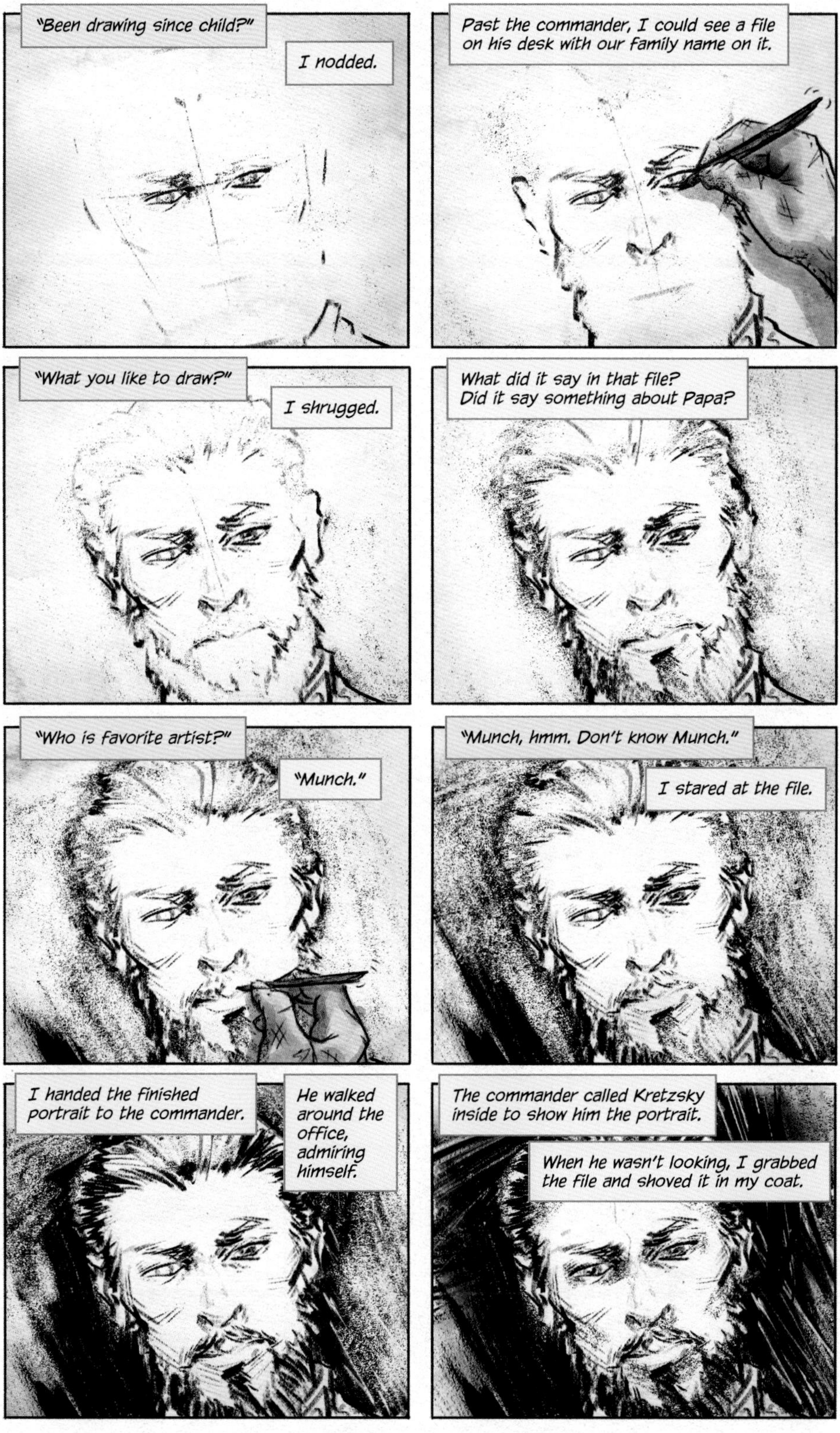
"Been drawing since child?"
I nodded.
Past the commander, I could see a file on his desk with our family name on it.
"What you like to draw?"
I shrugged.
What did it say in that file? Did it say something about Papa?
"Who is favorite artist?"
"Munch."
"Munch, hmm. Don't know Munch."
I stared at the file.
I handed the finished portrait to the commander.
He walked around the office, admiring himself.
The commander called Kretzsky inside to show him the portrait.
When he wasn't looking, I grabbed the file and shoved it in my coat.

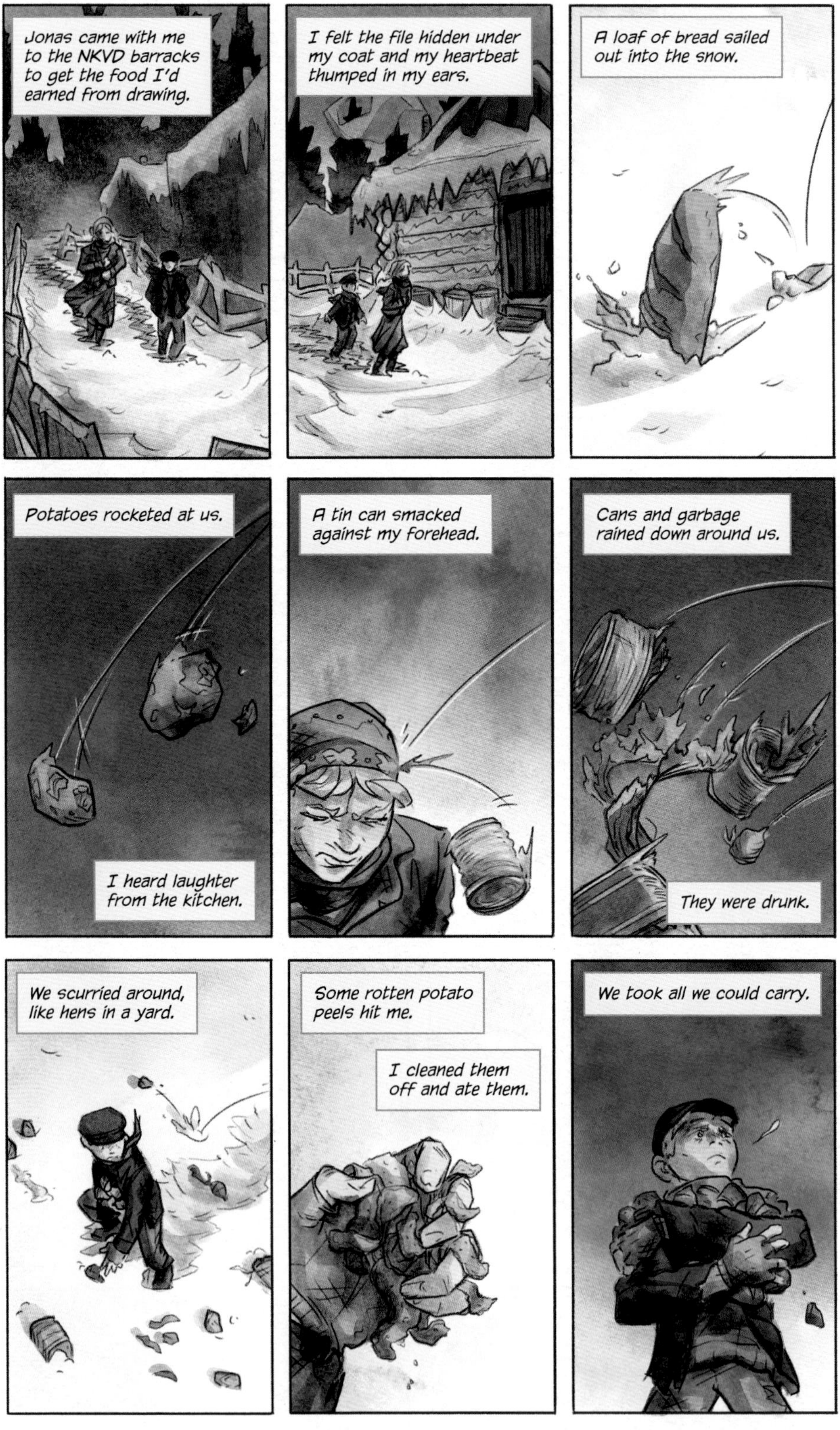
Jonas came with me to the NKVD barracks to get the food I'd earned from drawing.
I felt the file hidden under my coat and my heartbeat thumped in my ears.
A loaf of bread sailed out into the snow.
Potatoes rocketed at us.
I heard laughter from the kitchen.
A tin can smacked against my forehead.
Cans and garbage rained down around us.
They were drunk.
We scurried around, like hens in a yard.
Some rotten potato peels hit me.
I cleaned them off and ate them.
We took all we could carry.

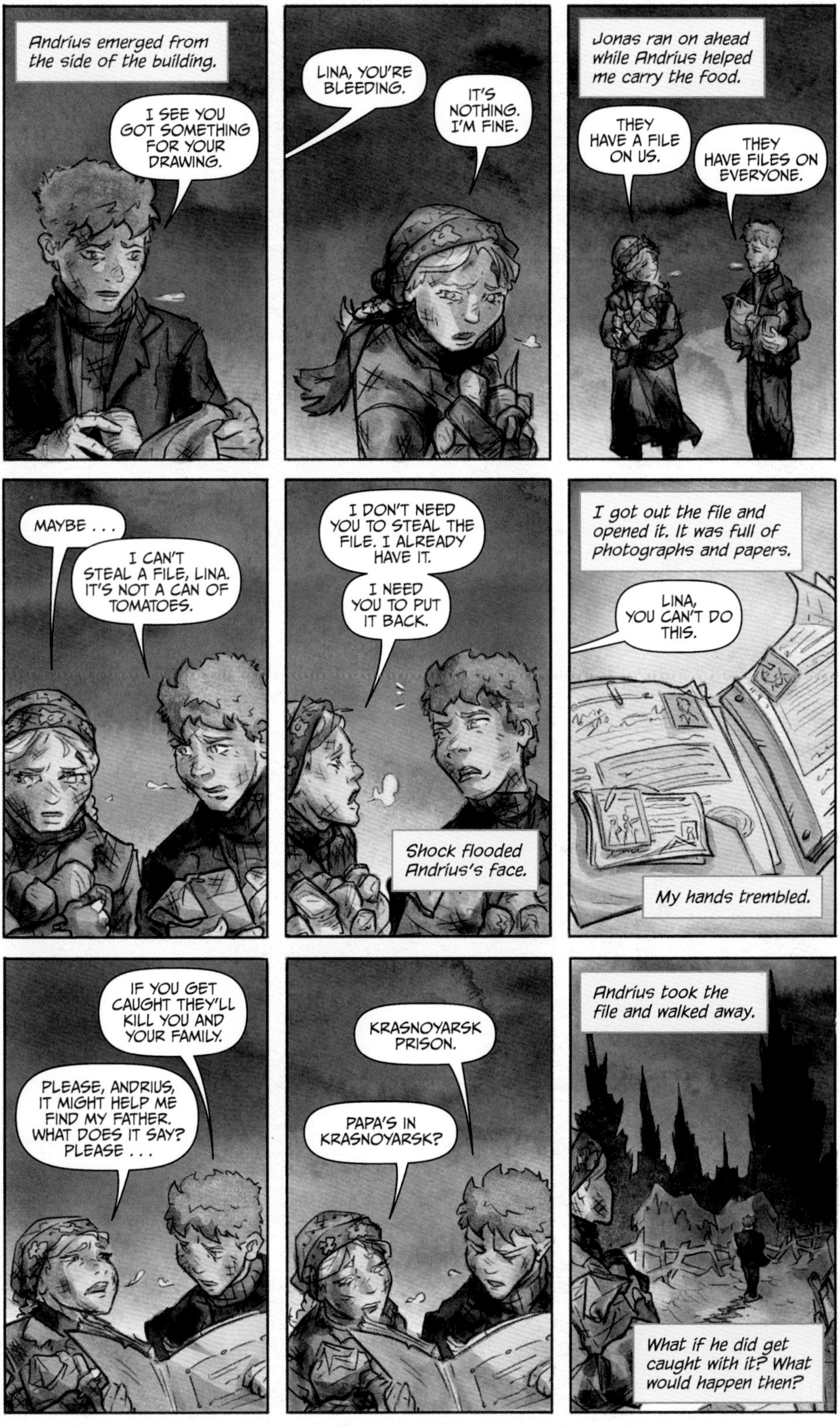
Andrius emerged from the side of the building.
I SEE YOU GOT SOMETHING FOR YOUR DRAWING.
LINA, YOU'RE BLEEDING.
IT'S NOTHING. I'M FINE.
Jonas ran on ahead while Andrius helped me carry the food.
THEY HAVE A FILE ON US.
THEY HAVE FILES ON EVERYONE.
MAYBE . . .
I CAN'T STEAL A FILE, LINA. IT'S NOT A CAN OF TOMATOES.
I DON'T NEED YOU TO STEAL THE FILE. I ALREADY HAVE IT.
I NEED YOU TO PUT IT BACK.
Shock flooded Andrius's face.
I got out the file and opened it. It was full of photographs and papers.
LINA, YOU CAN'T DO THIS.
My hands trembled.
IF YOU GET CAUGHT THEY'LL KILL YOU AND YOUR FAMILY.
PLEASE, ANDRIUS, IT MIGHT HELP ME FIND MY FATHER. WHAT DOES IT SAY? PLEASE . . .
KRASNOYARSK PRISON.
PAPA'S IN KRASNOYARSK?
Andrius took the file and walked away.
What if he did get caught with it? What would happen then?

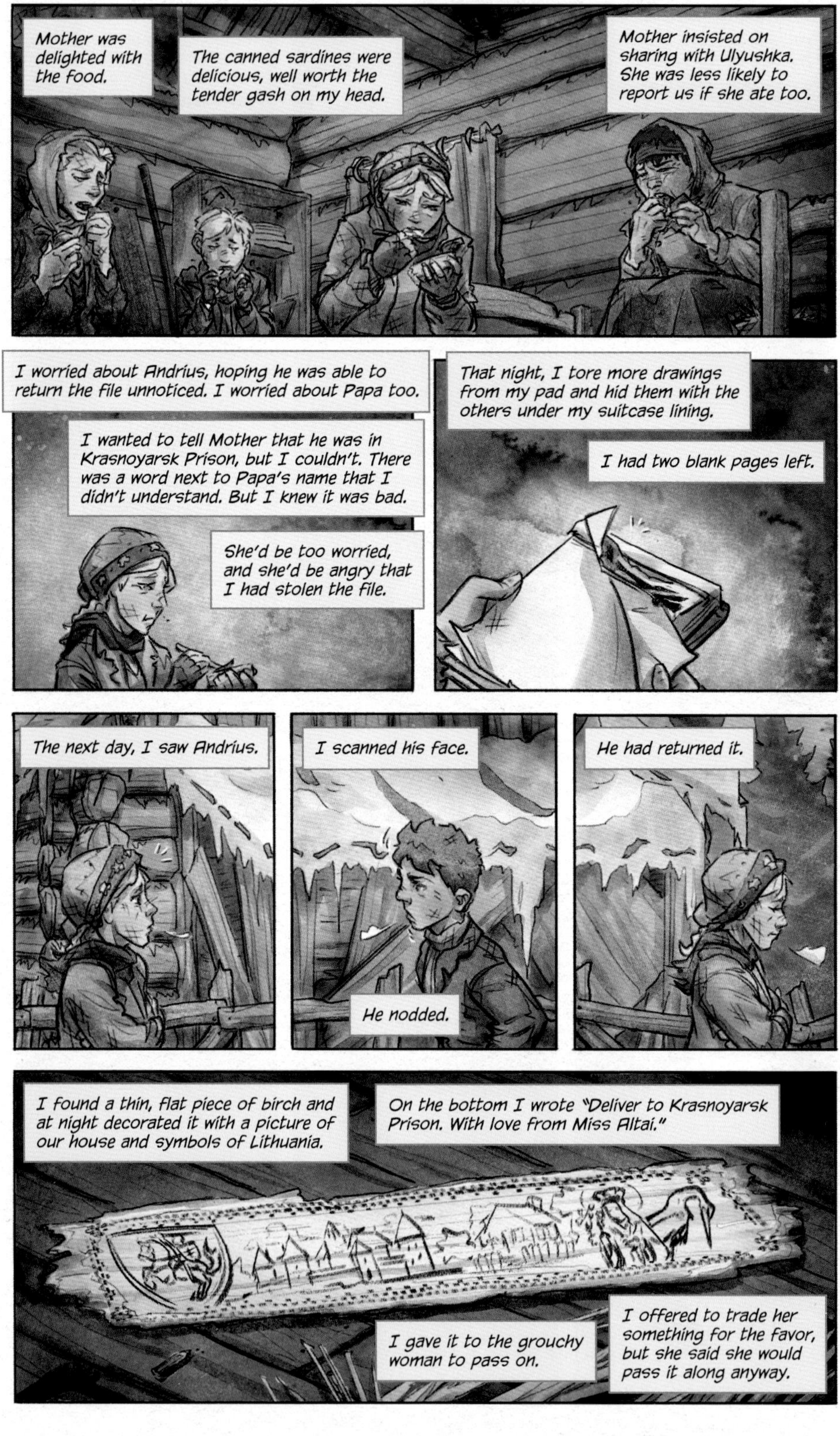
Mother was delighted with the food.
The canned sardines were delicious, well worth the tender gash on my head.
Mother insisted on sharing with Ulyushka. She was less likely to report us if she ate too.
I worried about Andrius, hoping he was able to return the file unnoticed. I worried about Papa too.
I wanted to tell Mother that he was in Krasnoyarsk Prison, but I couldn't. There was a word next to Papa's name that I didn't understand. But I knew it was bad.
She'd be too worried, and she'd be angry that I had stolen the file.
That night, I tore more drawings from my pad and hid them with the others under my suitcase lining.
I had two blank pages left.
The next day, I saw Andrius.
I scanned his face.
He nodded.
He had returned it.
I found a thin, flat piece of birch and at night decorated it with a picture of our house and symbols of Lithuania.
On the bottom I wrote "Deliver to Krasnoyarsk Prison. With love from Miss Altai."
I gave it to the grouchy woman to pass on.
I offered to trade her something for the favor, but she said she would pass it along anyway.

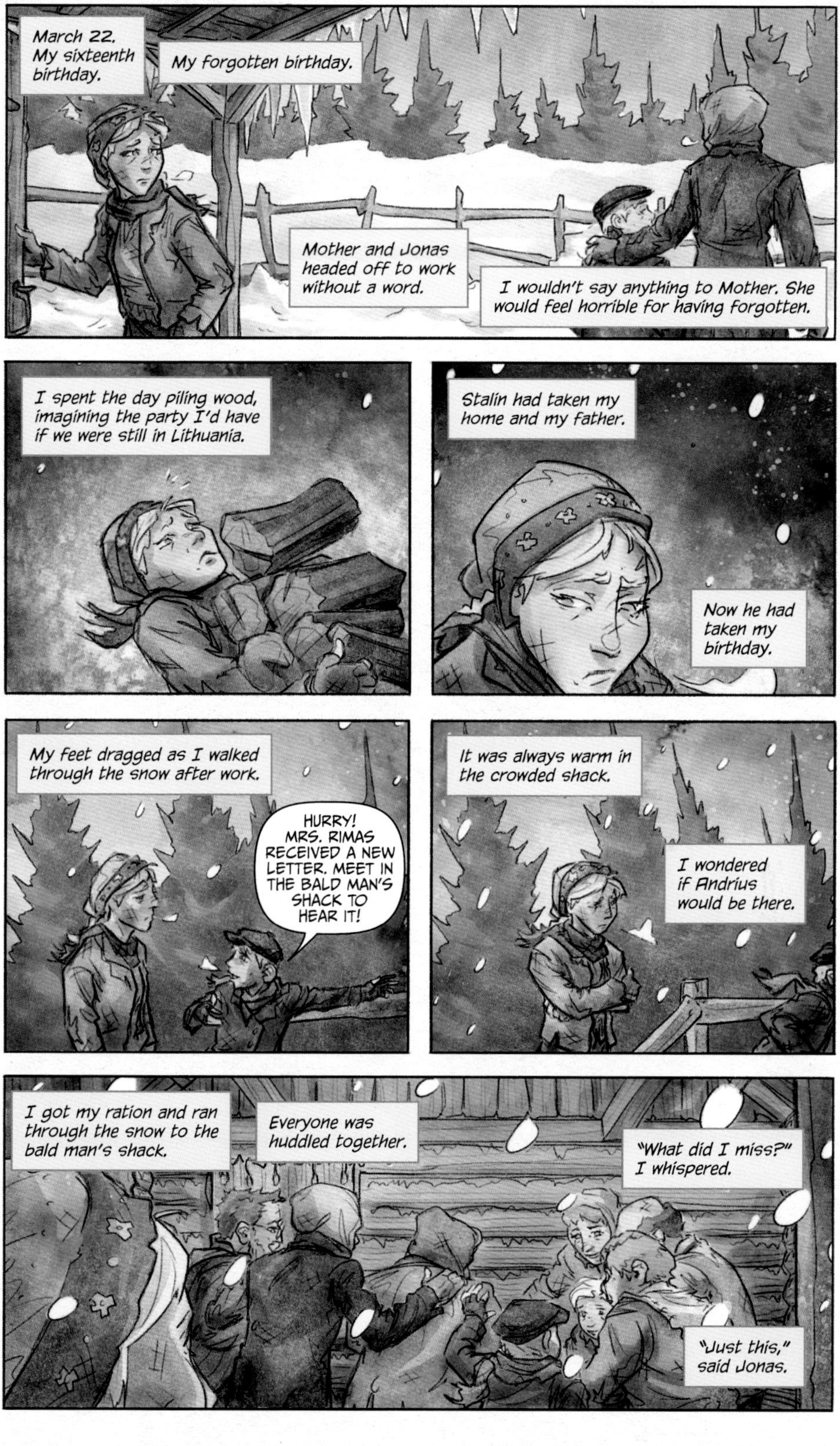
March 22. My sixteenth birthday.
My forgotten birthday.
Mother and Jonas headed off to work without a word.
I wouldn't say anything to Mother. She would feel horrible for having forgotten.
I spent the day piling wood, imagining the party I'd have if we were still in Lithuania.
Stalin had taken my home and my father.
Now he had taken my birthday.
My feet dragged as I walked through the snow after work.
HURRY! MRS. RIMAS RECEIVED A NEW LETTER. MEET IN THE BALD MAN'S SHACK TO HEAR IT!
It was always warm in the crowded shack.
I wondered if Andrius would be there.
I got my ration and ran through the snow to the bald man's shack.
Everyone was huddled together.
"What did I miss?" I whispered.
"Just this," said Jonas.

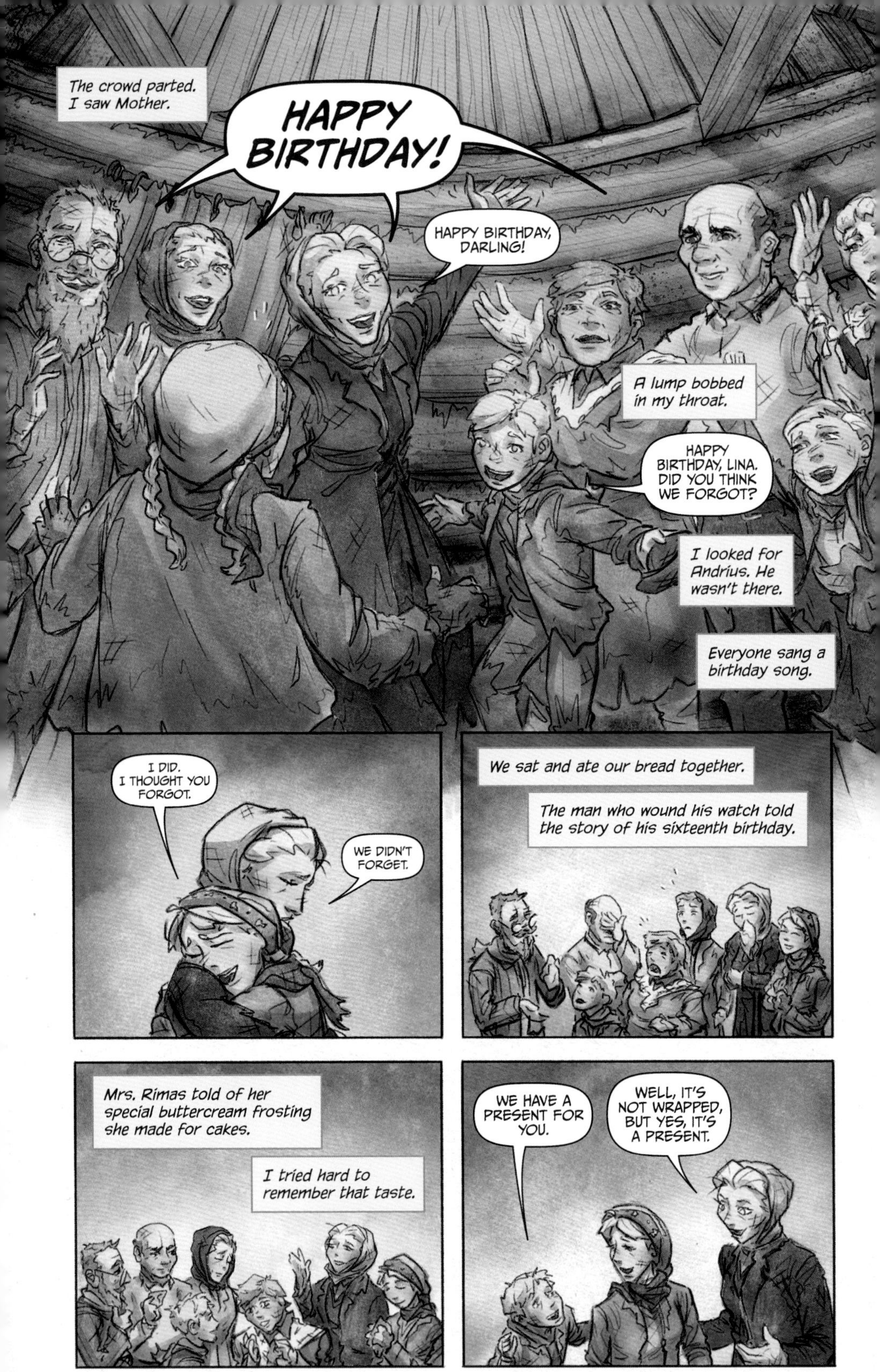

The crowd parted. I saw Mother.
HAPPY BIRTHDAY!
HAPPY BIRTHDAY, DARLING!
A lump bobbed in my throat.
HAPPY BIRTHDAY, LINA. DID YOU THINK WE FORGOT?
I looked for Andrius. He wasn't there.
Everyone sang a birthday song.
I DID. I THOUGHT YOU FORGOT.
WE DIDN'T FORGET.
We sat and ate our bread together.
The man who wound his watch told the story of his sixteenth birthday.
Mrs. Rimas told of her special buttercream frosting she made for cakes.
I tried hard to remember that taste.
WE HAVE A PRESENT FOR YOU.
WELL, IT'S NOT WRAPPED, BUT YES, IT'S A PRESENT.

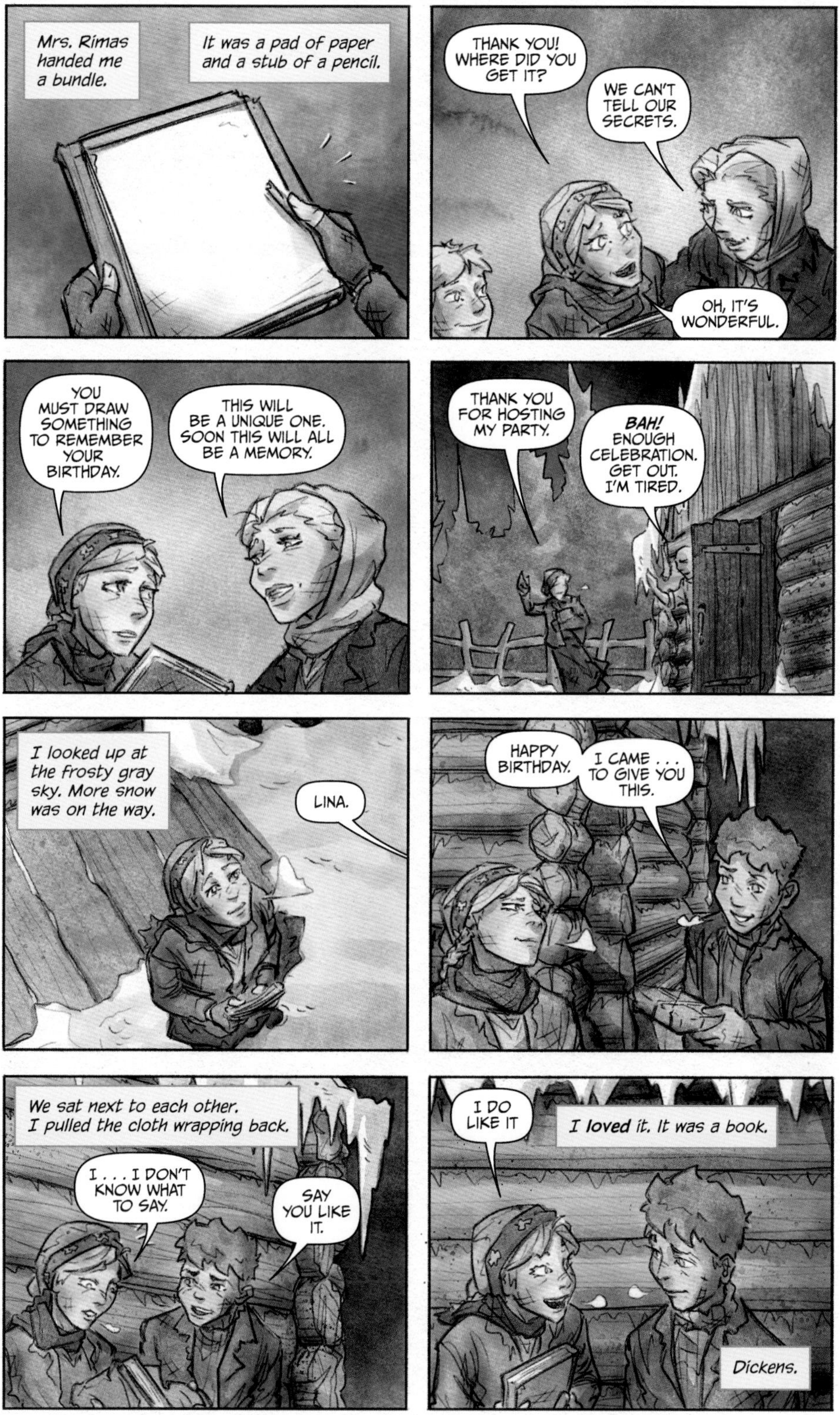
Mrs. Rimas handed me a bundle.
It was a pad of paper and a stub of a pencil.
THANK YOU! WHERE DID YOU GET IT?
WE CAN'T TELL OUR SECRETS.
OH, IT'S WONDERFUL.
YOU MUST DRAW SOMETHING TO REMEMBER YOUR BIRTHDAY.
THIS WILL BE A UNIQUE ONE. SOON THIS WILL ALL BE A MEMORY.
THANK YOU FOR HOSTING MY PARTY.
BAH! ENOUGH CELEBRATION. GET OUT. I'M TIRED.
I looked up at the frosty gray sky. More snow was on the way.
LINA.
HAPPY BIRTHDAY.
I CAME . . . TO GIVE YOU THIS.
We sat next to each other. I pulled the cloth wrapping back.
I . . . I DON'T KNOW WHAT TO SAY.
SAY YOU LIKE IT.
I DO LIKE IT
I loved it. It was a book.
Dickens.

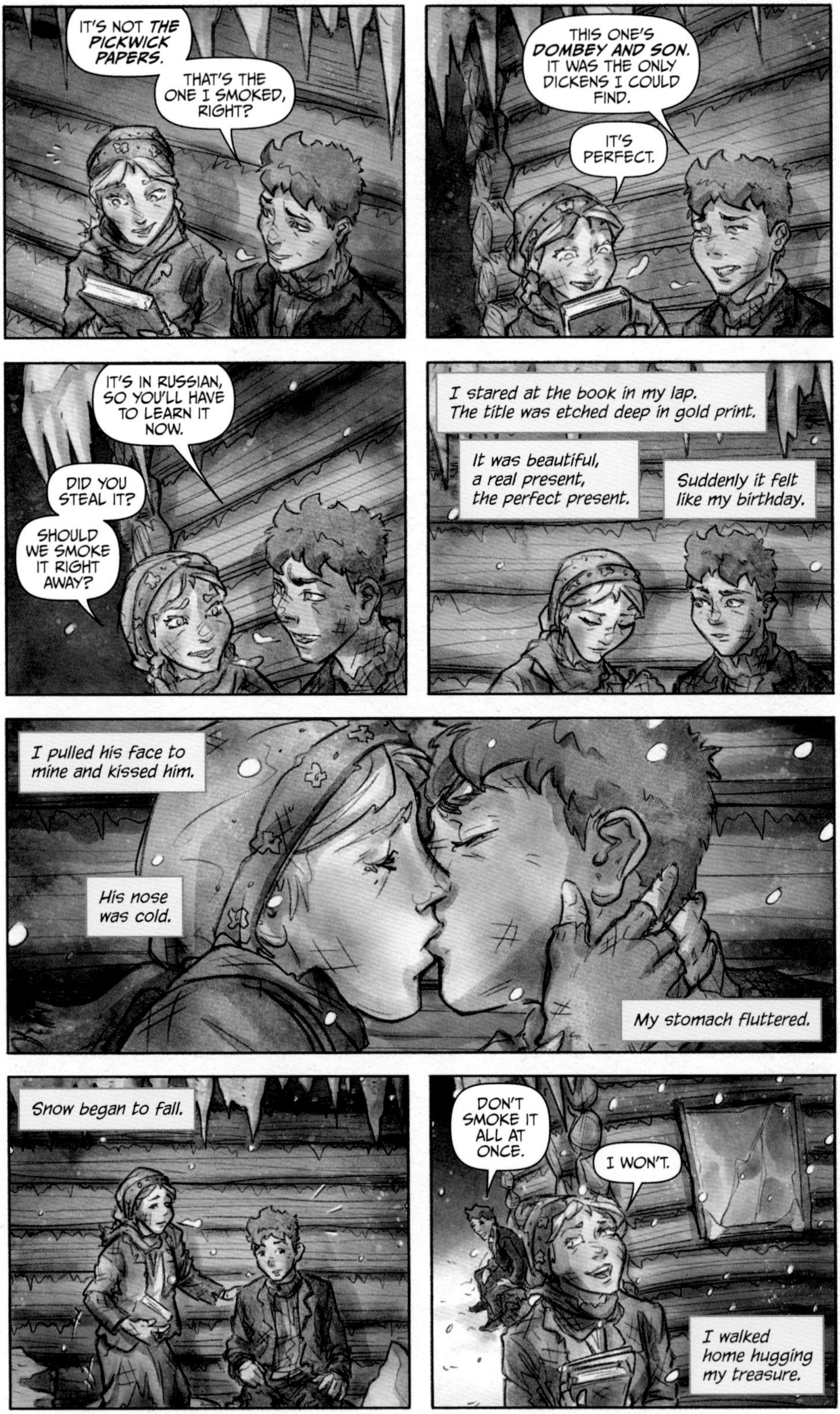
IT'S NOT *THE PICKWICK PAPERS.*
THAT'S THE ONE I SMOKED, RIGHT?
THIS ONE'S *DOMBEY AND SON.* IT WAS THE ONLY DICKENS I COULD FIND.
IT'S PERFECT.
IT'S IN RUSSIAN, SO YOU'LL HAVE TO LEARN IT NOW.
DID YOU STEAL IT?
SHOULD WE SMOKE IT RIGHT AWAY?
I stared at the book in my lap. The title was etched deep in gold print.
It was beautiful, a real present, the perfect present.
Suddenly it felt like my birthday.
I pulled his face to mine and kissed him.
His nose was cold.
My stomach fluttered.
Snow began to fall.
DON'T SMOKE IT ALL AT ONCE.
I WON'T.
I walked home hugging my treasure.

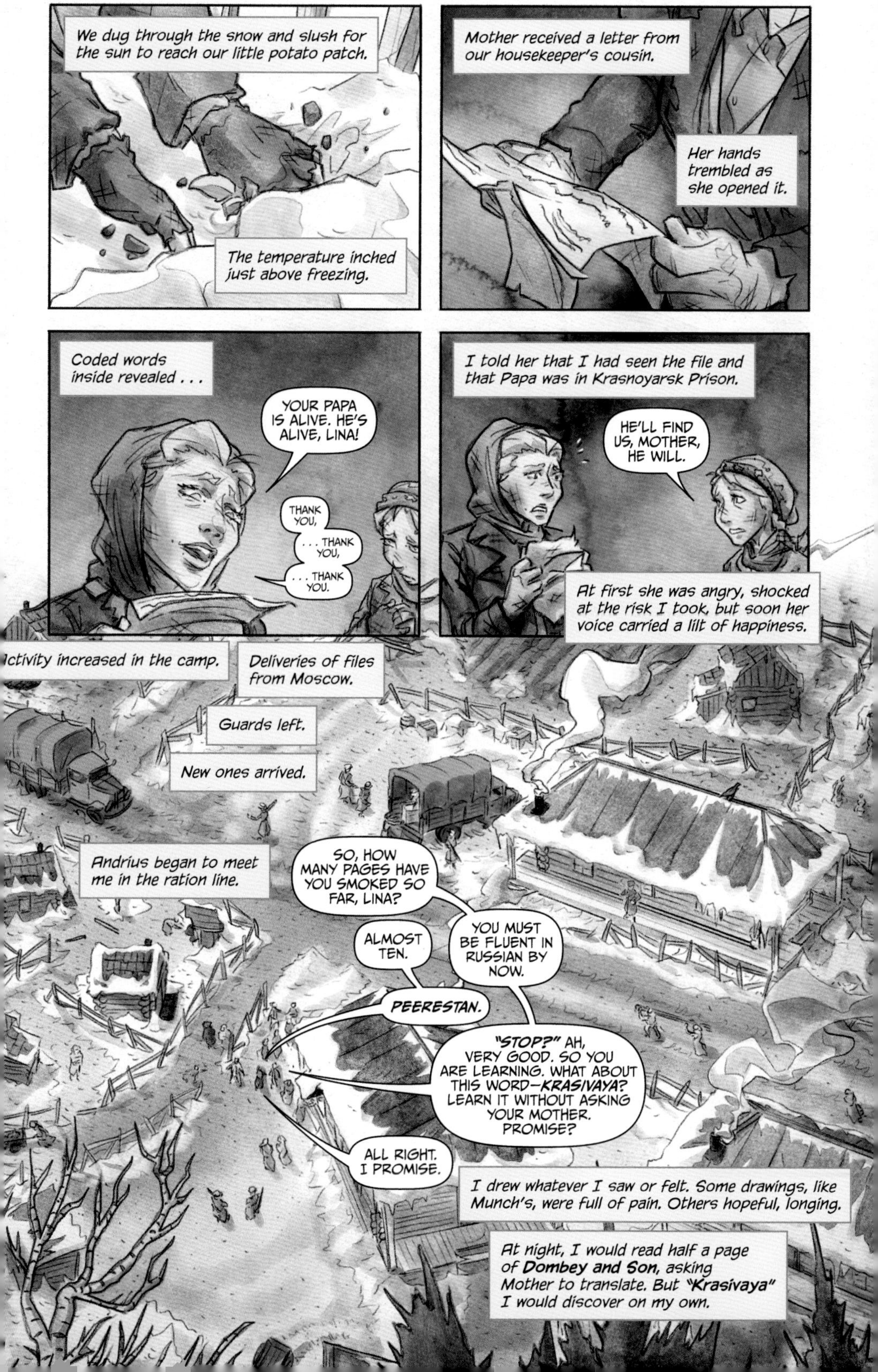
We dug through the snow and slush for the sun to reach our little potato patch.
The temperature inched just above freezing.
Mother received a letter from our housekeeper's cousin.
Her hands trembled as she opened it.
Coded words inside revealed . . .
YOUR PAPA IS ALIVE. HE'S ALIVE, LINA!
THANK YOU,
. . . THANK YOU,
. . . THANK YOU.
I told her that I had seen the file and that Papa was in Krasnoyarsk Prison.
HE'LL FIND US, MOTHER, HE WILL.
At first she was angry, shocked at the risk I took, but soon her voice carried a lilt of happiness.
ctivity increased in the camp.
Deliveries of files from Moscow.
Guards left.
New ones arrived.
Andrius began to meet me in the ration line.
SO, HOW MANY PAGES HAVE YOU SMOKED SO FAR, LINA?
ALMOST TEN.
YOU MUST BE FLUENT IN RUSSIAN BY NOW.
PEERESTAN.
"STOP?" AH, VERY GOOD. SO YOU ARE LEARNING. WHAT ABOUT THIS WORD—KRASIVAYA? LEARN IT WITHOUT ASKING YOUR MOTHER. PROMISE?
ALL RIGHT. I PROMISE.
I drew whatever I saw or felt. Some drawings, like Munch's, were full of pain. Others hopeful, longing.
At night, I would read half a page of Dombey and Son, asking Mother to translate. But "Krasivaya" I would discover on my own.

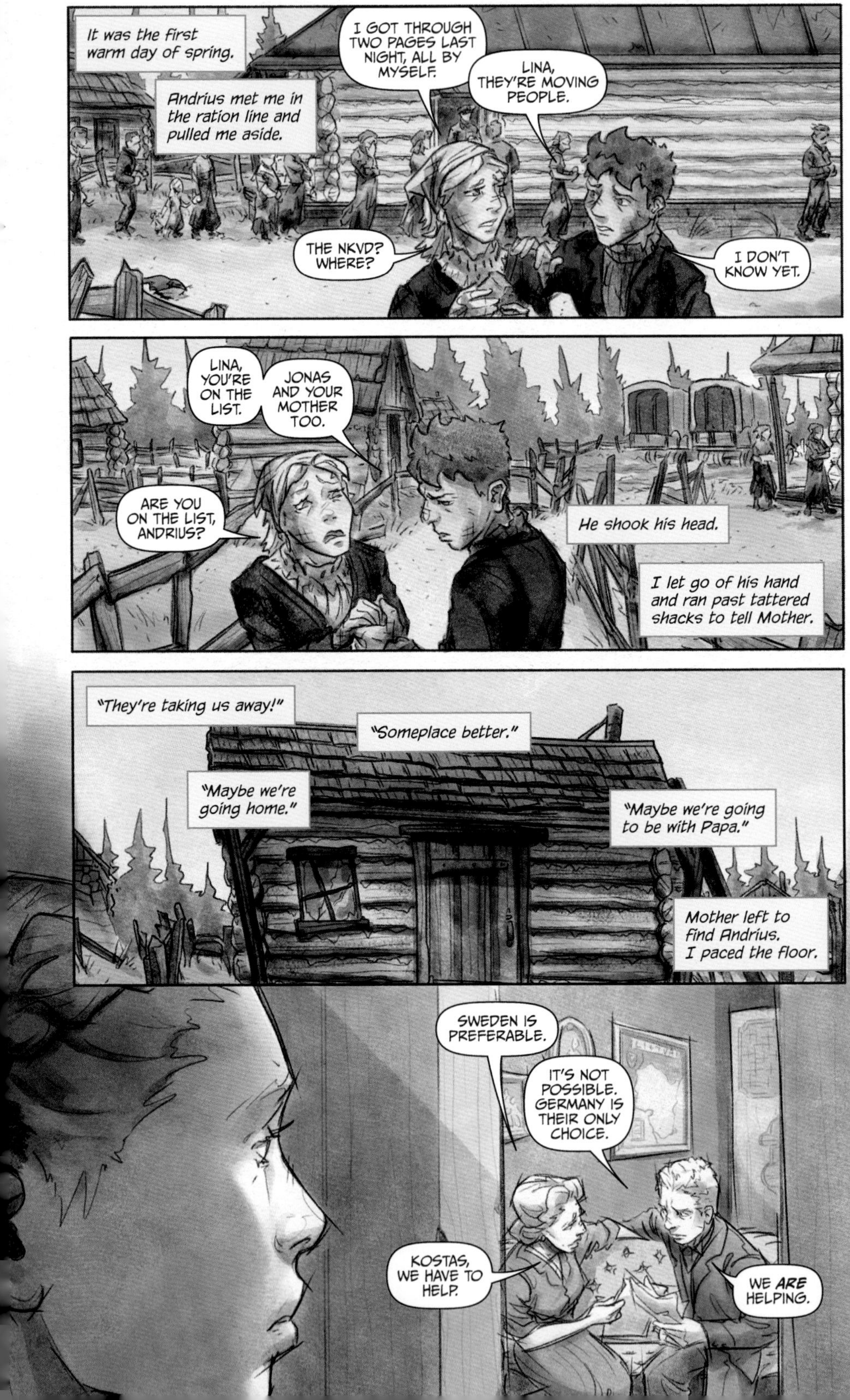

It was the first warm day of spring.
Andrius met me in the ration line and pulled me aside.
I GOT THROUGH TWO PAGES LAST NIGHT, ALL BY MYSELF.
LINA, THEY'RE MOVING PEOPLE.
THE NKVD? WHERE?
I DON'T KNOW YET.
LINA, YOU'RE ON THE LIST.
JONAS AND YOUR MOTHER TOO.
ARE YOU ON THE LIST, ANDRIUS?
He shook his head.
I let go of his hand and ran past tattered shacks to tell Mother.
"They're taking us away!"
"Someplace better."
"Maybe we're going home."
"Maybe we're going to be with Papa."
Mother left to find Andrius. I paced the floor.
SWEDEN IS PREFERABLE.
IT'S NOT POSSIBLE. GERMANY IS THEIR ONLY CHOICE.
KOSTAS, WE HAVE TO HELP.
WE ARE HELPING.

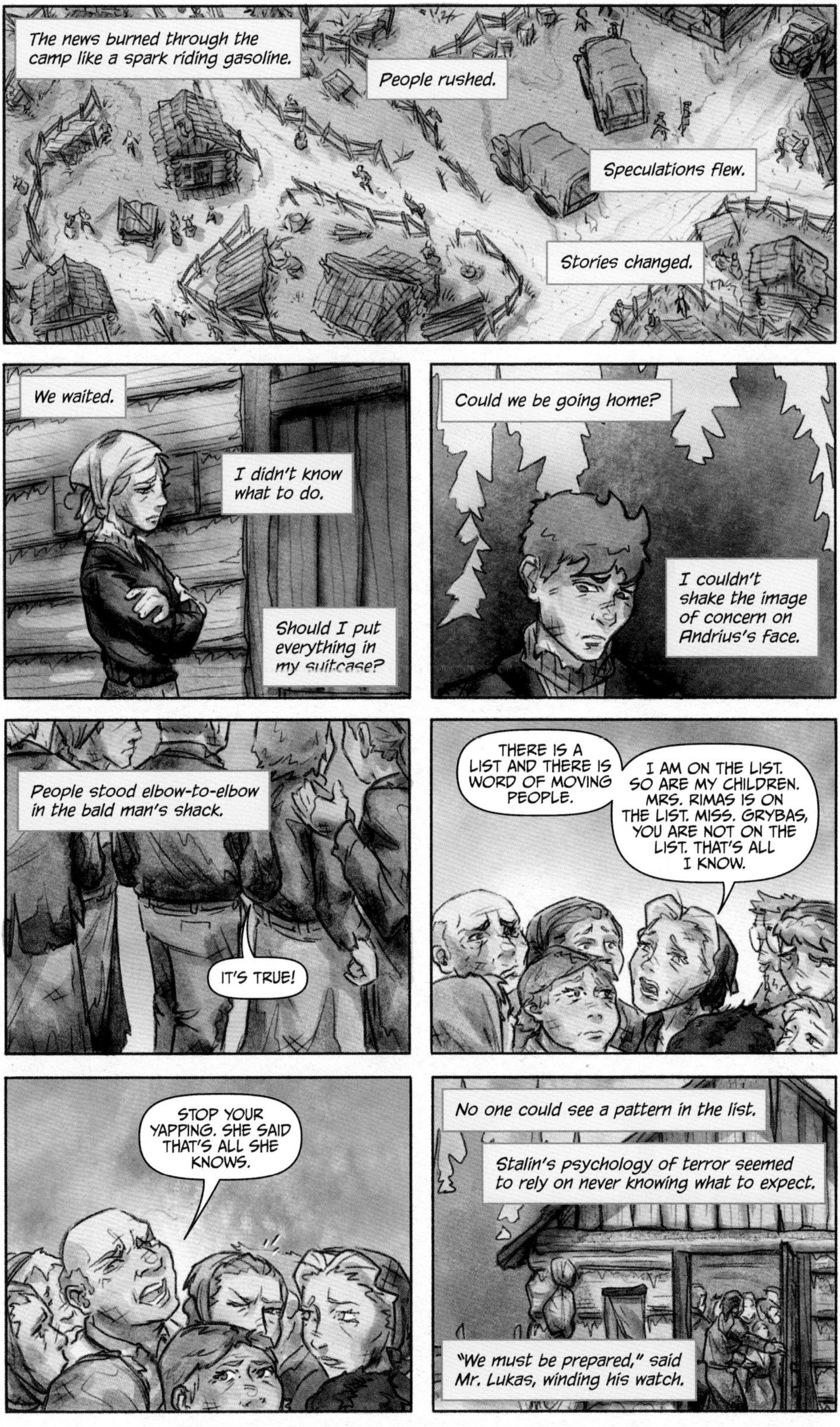
The news burned through the camp like a spark riding gasoline.
People rushed.
Speculations flew.
Stories changed.
We waited.
I didn't know what to do.
Should I put everything in my suitcase?
Could we be going home?
I couldn't shake the image of concern on Andrius's face.
People stood elbow-to-elbow in the bald man's shack.
IT'S TRUE!
THERE IS A LIST AND THERE IS WORD OF MOVING PEOPLE.
I AM ON THE LIST. SO ARE MY CHILDREN. MRS. RIMAS IS ON THE LIST. MISS. GRYBAS, YOU ARE NOT ON THE LIST. THAT'S ALL I KNOW.
STOP YOUR YAPPING. SHE SAID THAT'S ALL SHE KNOWS.
No one could see a pattern in the list.
Stalin's psychology of terror seemed to rely on never knowing what to expect.
"We must be prepared," said Mr. Lukas, winding his watch.

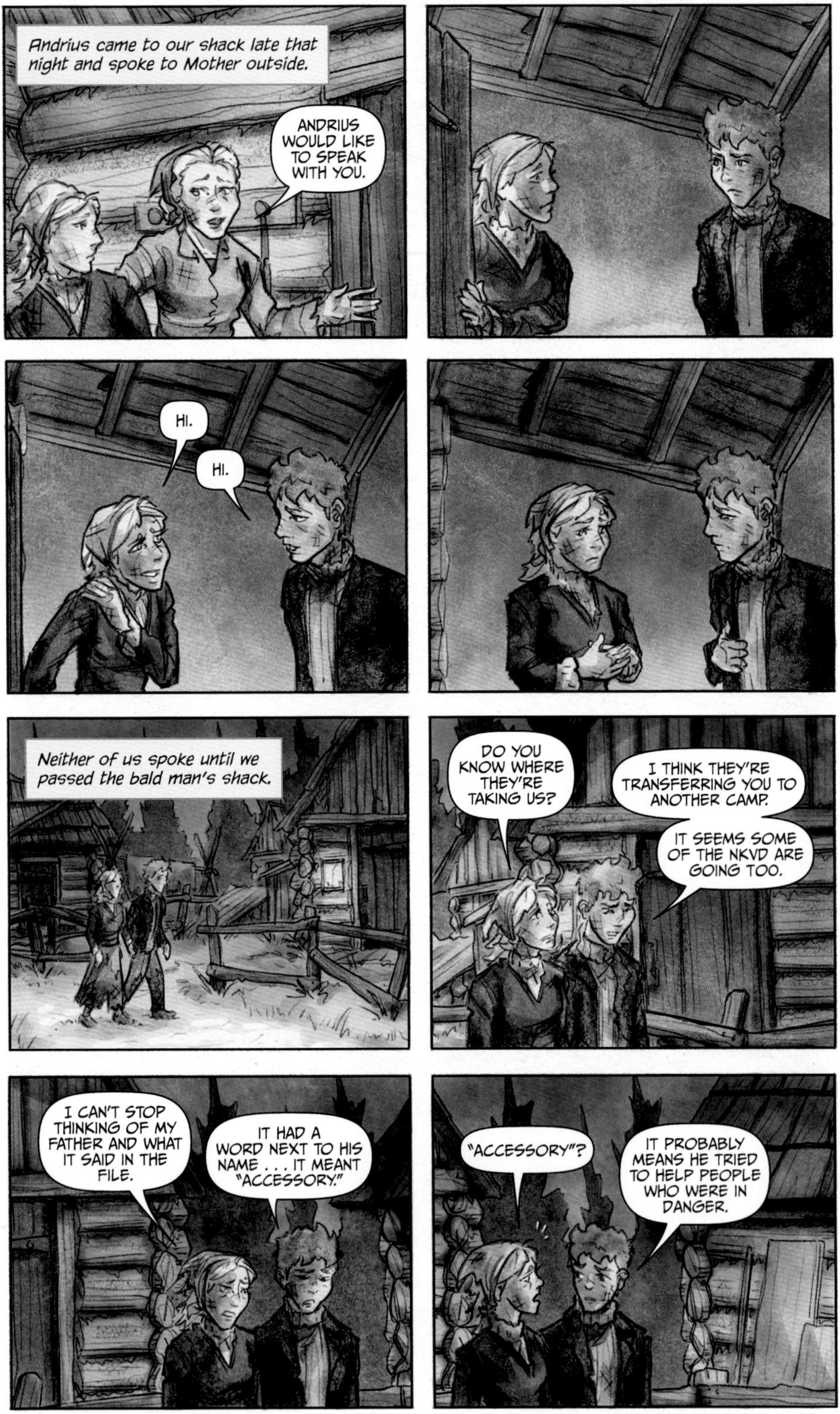
Andrius came to our shack late that night and spoke to Mother outside.
ANDRIUS WOULD LIKE TO SPEAK WITH YOU.
HI.
HI.
Neither of us spoke until we passed the bald man's shack.
DO YOU KNOW WHERE THEY'RE TAKING US?
I THINK THEY'RE TRANSFERRING YOU TO ANOTHER CAMP.
IT SEEMS SOME OF THE NKVD ARE GOING TOO.
I CAN'T STOP THINKING OF MY FATHER AND WHAT IT SAID IN THE FILE.
IT HAD A WORD NEXT TO HIS NAME . . . IT MEANT "ACCESSORY."
"ACCESSORY"?
IT PROBABLY MEANS HE TRIED TO HELP PEOPLE WHO WERE IN DANGER.

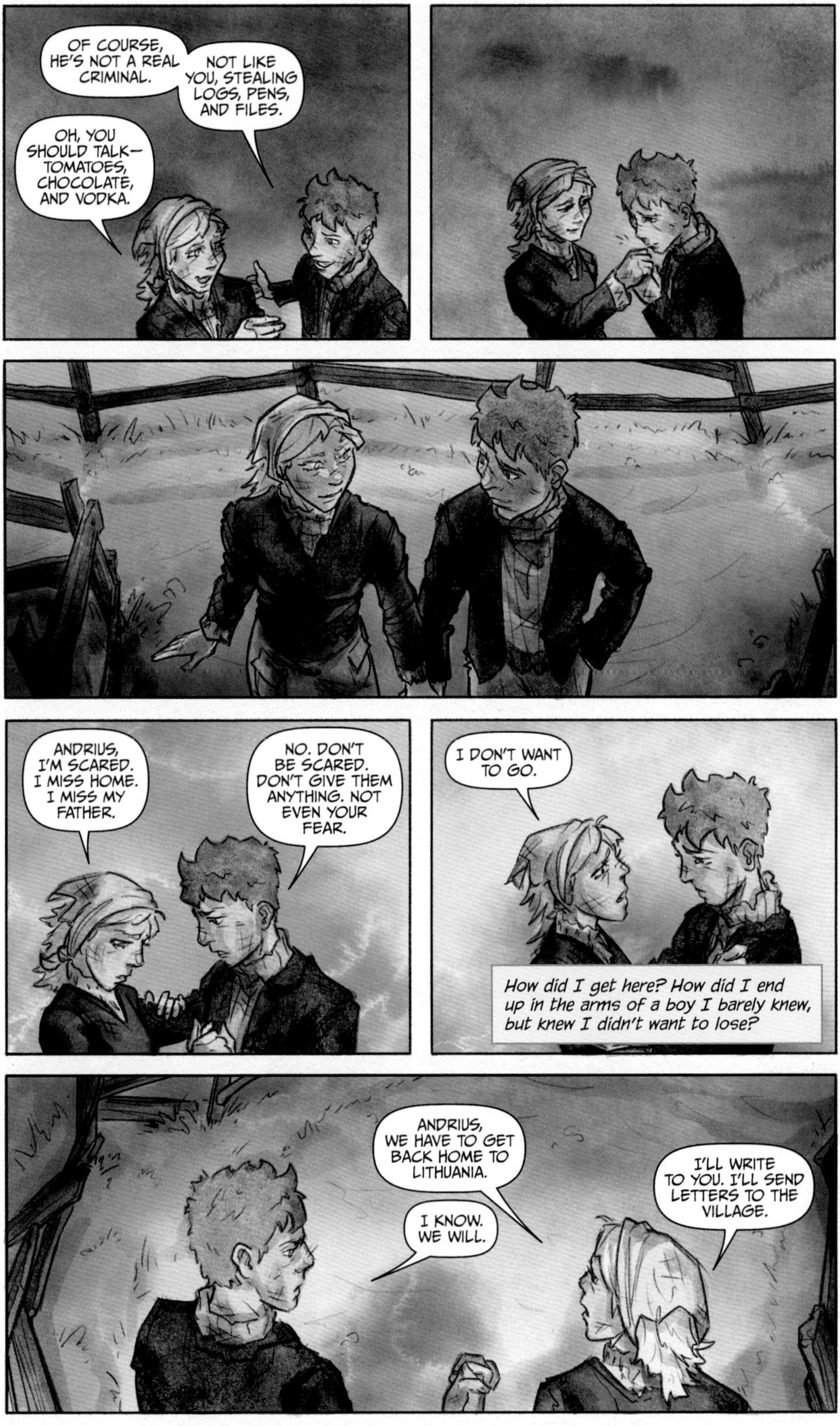
OF COURSE, HE'S NOT A REAL CRIMINAL.
NOT LIKE YOU, STEALING LOGS, PENS, AND FILES.
OH, YOU SHOULD TALK—TOMATOES, CHOCOLATE, AND VODKA.
ANDRIUS, I'M SCARED. I MISS HOME. I MISS MY FATHER.
NO. DON'T BE SCARED. DON'T GIVE THEM ANYTHING. NOT EVEN YOUR FEAR.
I DON'T WANT TO GO.
How did I get here? How did I end up in the arms of a boy I barely knew, but knew I didn't want to lose?
ANDRIUS, WE HAVE TO GET BACK HOME TO LITHUANIA.
I KNOW. WE WILL.
I'LL WRITE TO YOU. I'LL SEND LETTERS TO THE VILLAGE.

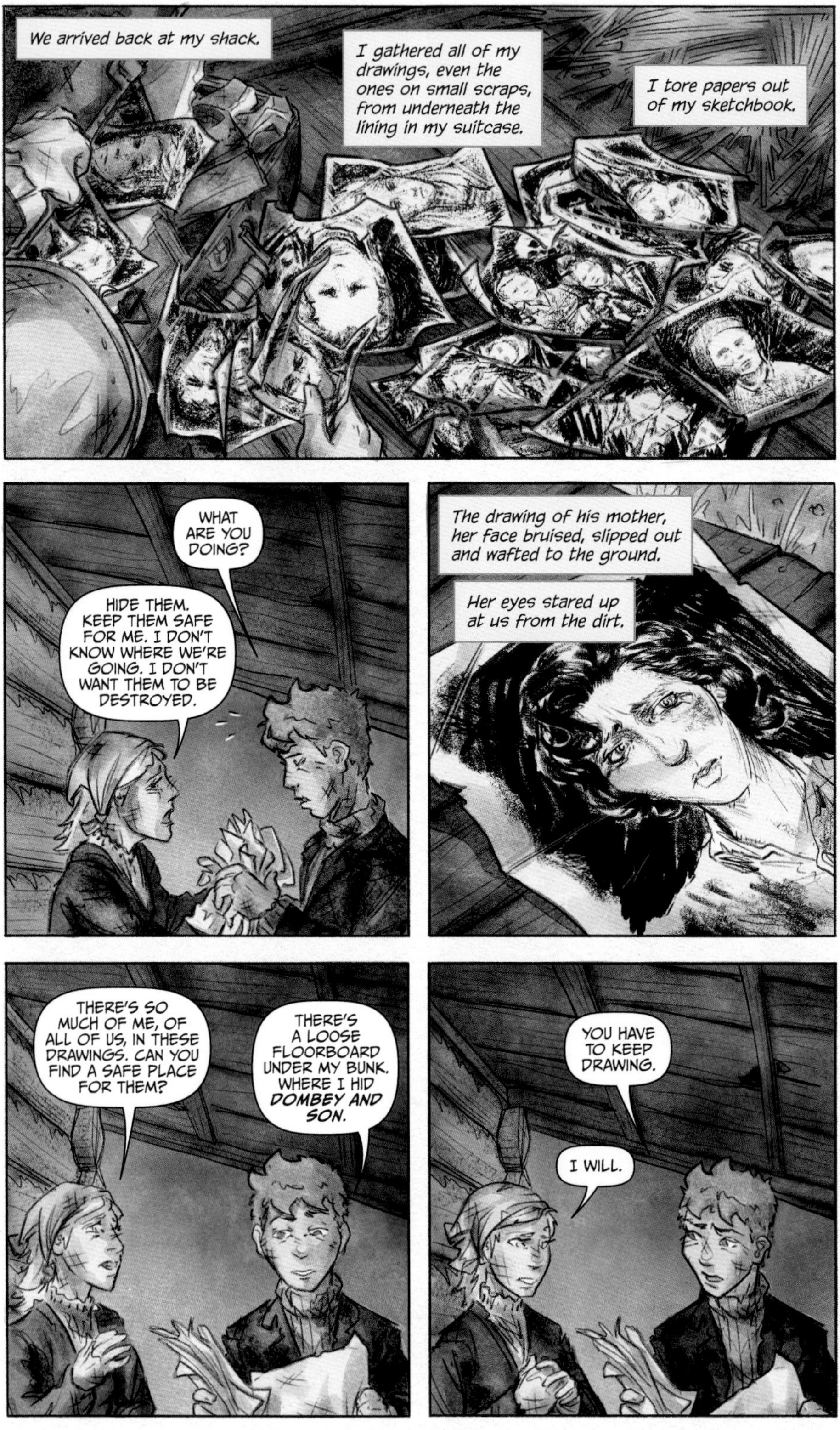
We arrived back at my shack.
I gathered all of my drawings, even the ones on small scraps, from underneath the lining in my suitcase.
I tore papers out of my sketchbook.
WHAT ARE YOU DOING?
HIDE THEM. KEEP THEM SAFE FOR ME. I DON'T KNOW WHERE WE'RE GOING. I DON'T WANT THEM TO BE DESTROYED.
The drawing of his mother, her face bruised, slipped out and wafted to the ground.
Her eyes stared up at us from the dirt.
THERE'S SO MUCH OF ME, OF ALL OF US, IN THESE DRAWINGS. CAN YOU FIND A SAFE PLACE FOR THEM?
THERE'S A LOOSE FLOORBOARD UNDER MY BUNK. WHERE I HID *DOMBEY AND SON.*
YOU HAVE TO KEEP DRAWING.
I WILL.

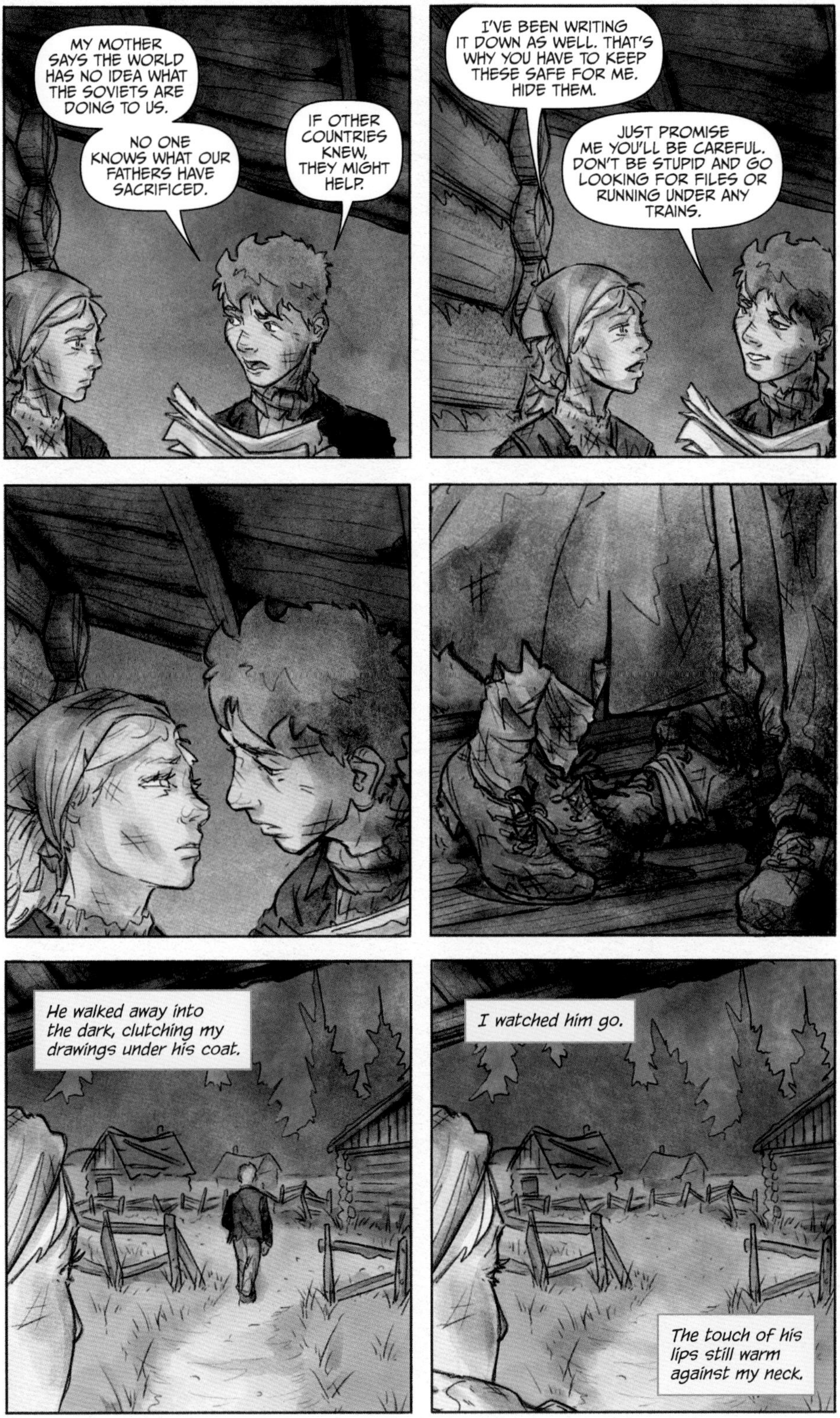
MY MOTHER SAYS THE WORLD HAS NO IDEA WHAT THE SOVIETS ARE DOING TO US.
NO ONE KNOWS WHAT OUR FATHERS HAVE SACRIFICED.
IF OTHER COUNTRIES KNEW, THEY MIGHT HELP.
I'VE BEEN WRITING IT DOWN AS WELL. THAT'S WHY YOU HAVE TO KEEP THESE SAFE FOR ME. HIDE THEM.
JUST PROMISE ME YOU'LL BE CAREFUL. DON'T BE STUPID AND GO LOOKING FOR FILES OR RUNNING UNDER ANY TRAINS.
He walked away into the dark, clutching my drawings under his coat.
I watched him go.
The touch of his lips still warm against my neck.

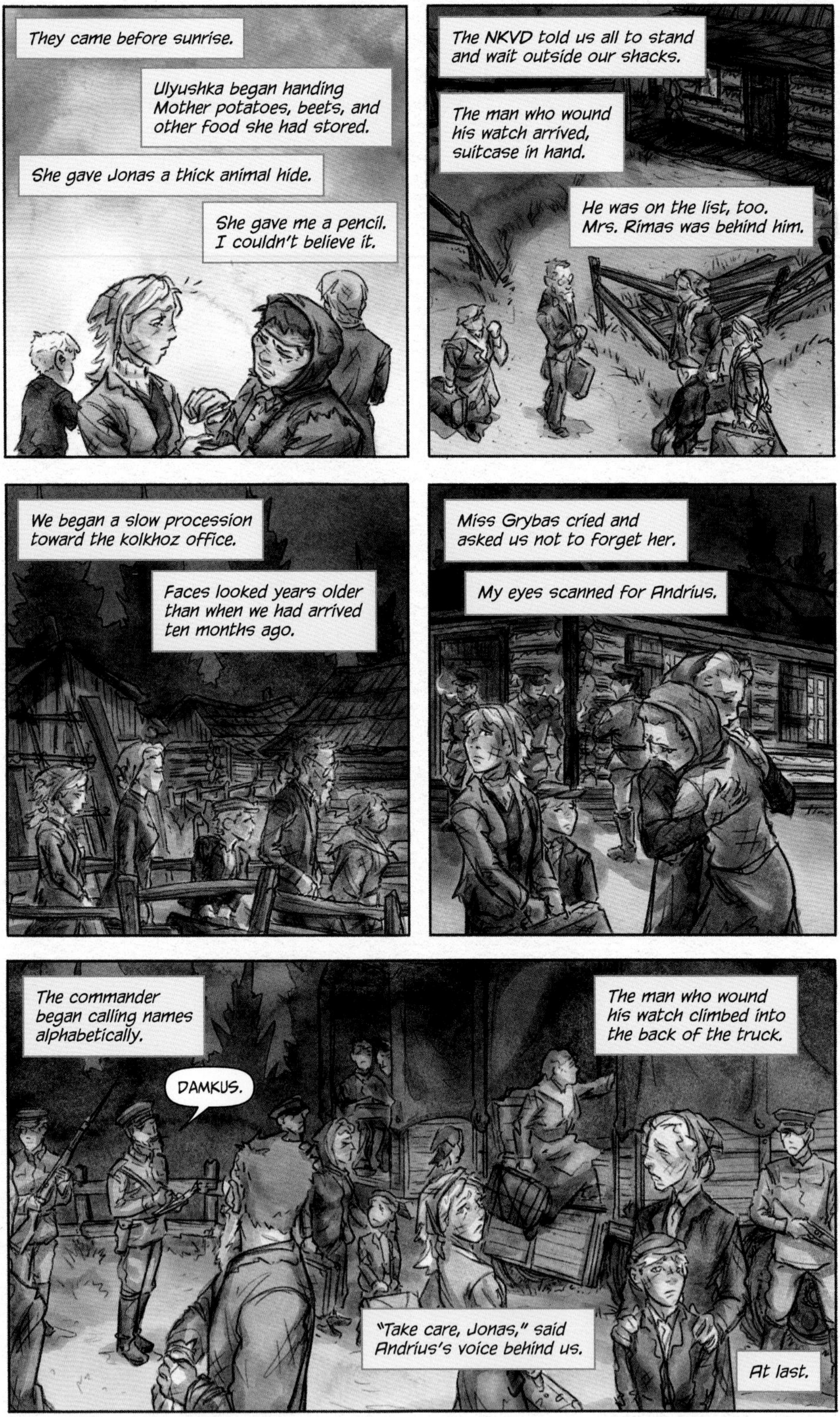
They came before sunrise.
Ulyushka began handing Mother potatoes, beets, and other food she had stored.
She gave Jonas a thick animal hide.
She gave me a pencil. I couldn't believe it.
The NKVD told us all to stand and wait outside our shacks.
The man who wound his watch arrived, suitcase in hand.
He was on the list, too. Mrs. Rimas was behind him.
We began a slow procession toward the kolkhoz office.
Faces looked years older than when we had arrived ten months ago.
Miss Grybas cried and asked us not to forget her.
My eyes scanned for Andrius.
The commander began calling names alphabetically.
DAMKUS.
The man who wound his watch climbed into the back of the truck.
"Take care, Jonas," said Andrius's voice behind us.
At last.

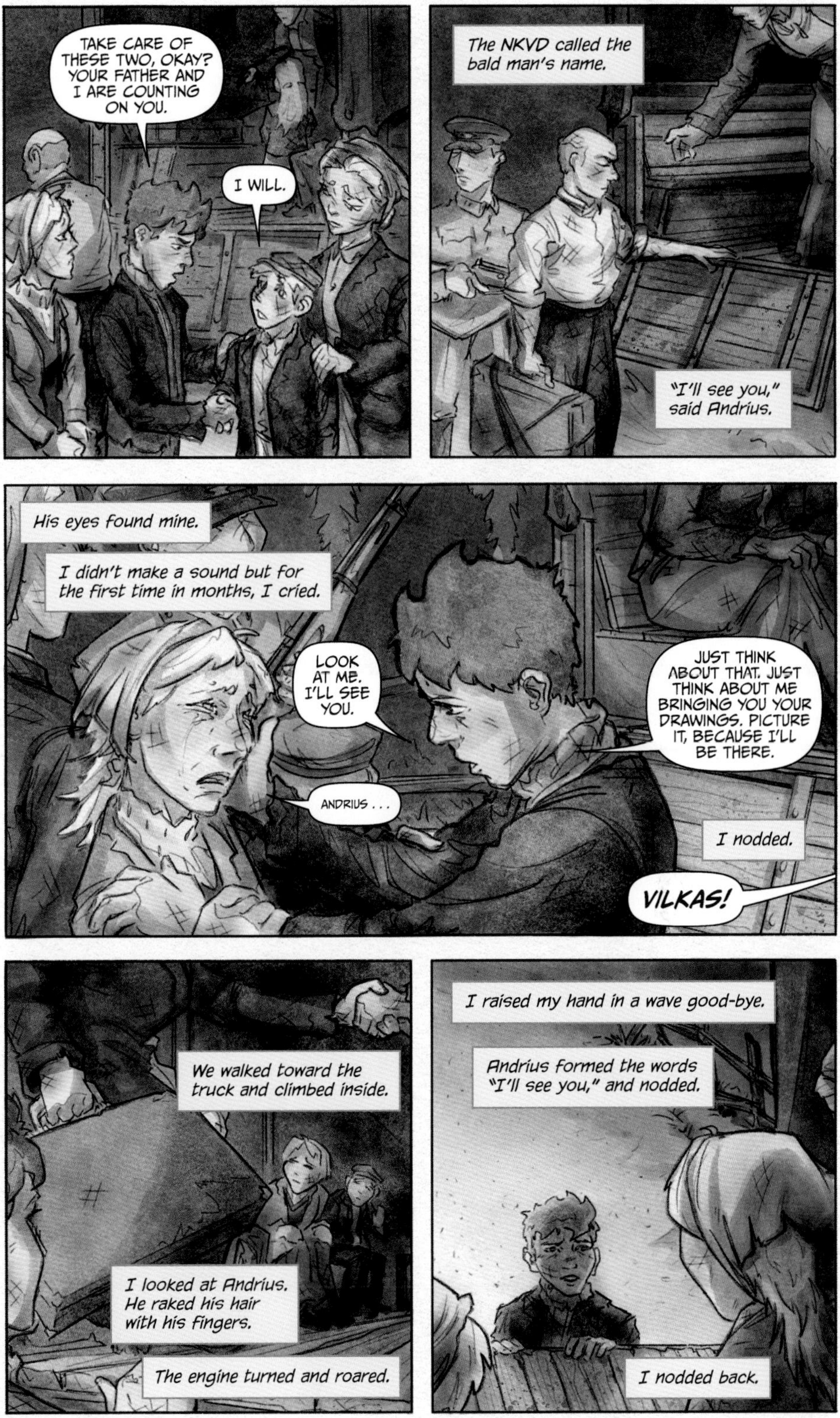
TAKE CARE OF THESE TWO, OKAY? YOUR FATHER AND I ARE COUNTING ON YOU.
I WILL.
The NKVD called the bald man's name.
"I'll see you," said Andrius.
His eyes found mine.
I didn't make a sound but for the first time in months, I cried.
LOOK AT ME. I'LL SEE YOU.
JUST THINK ABOUT THAT. JUST THINK ABOUT ME BRINGING YOU YOUR DRAWINGS. PICTURE IT, BECAUSE I'LL BE THERE.
ANDRIUS . . .
I nodded.
VILKAS!
We walked toward the truck and climbed inside.
I looked at Andrius. He raked his hair with his fingers.
The engine turned and roared.
I raised my hand in a wave good-bye.
Andrius formed the words "I'll see you," and nodded.
I nodded back.

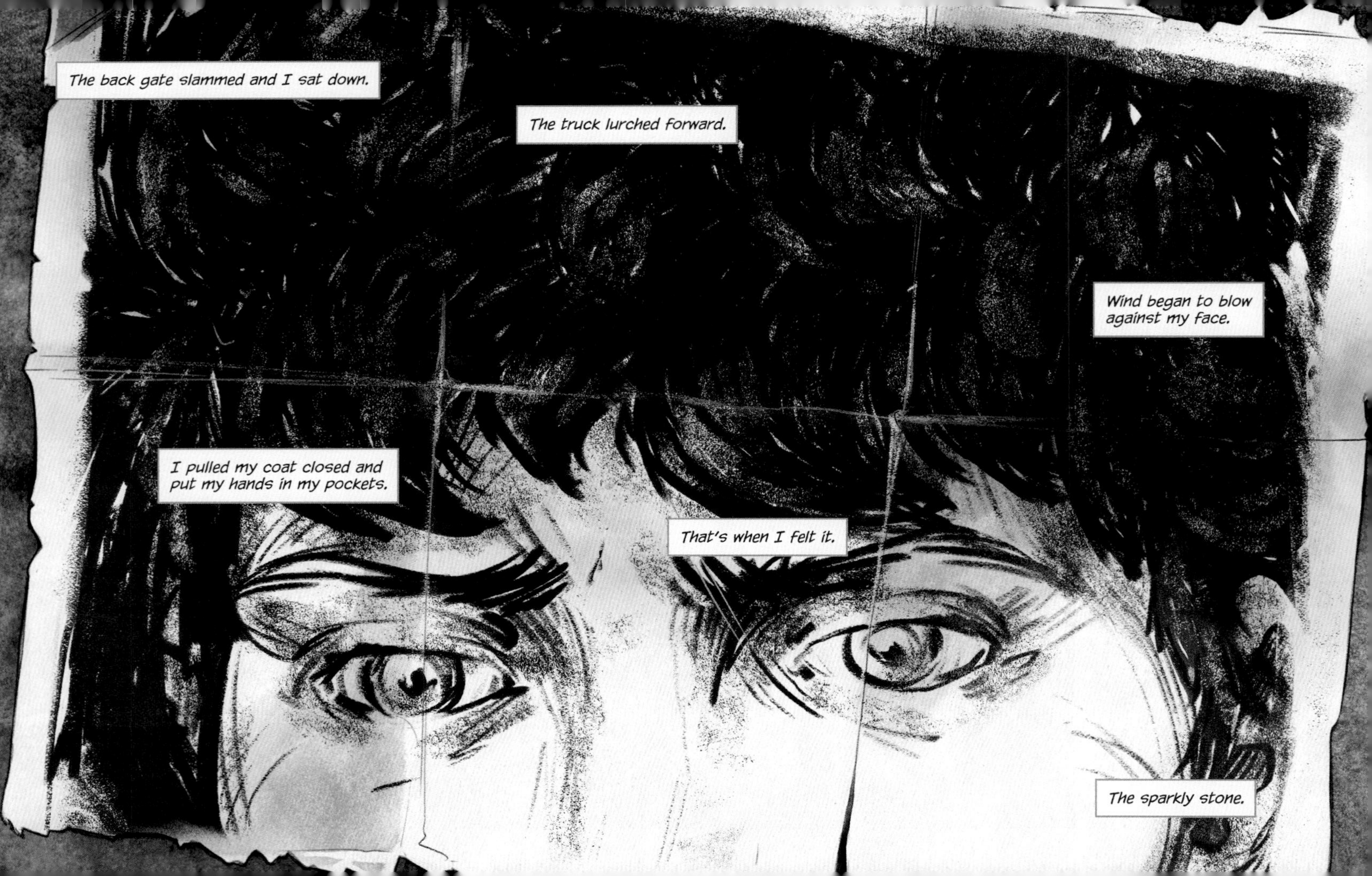
The back gate slammed and I sat down.
The truck lurched forward.
Wind began to blow against my face.
I pulled my coat closed and put my hands in my pockets.
That's when I felt it.
The sparkly stone.

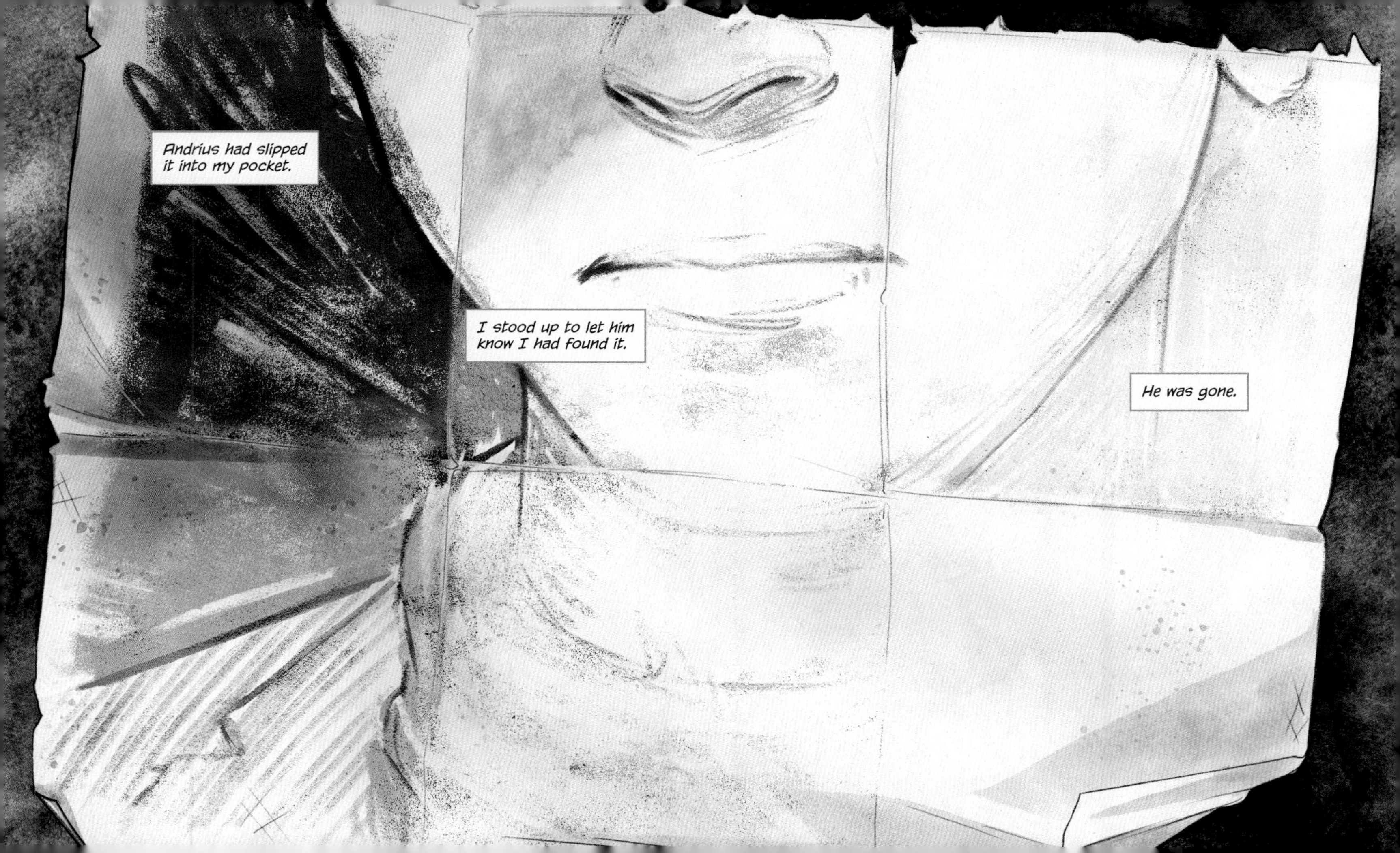
Andrius had slipped it into my pocket.
I stood up to let him know I had found it.
He was gone.

ICE
& ASHES

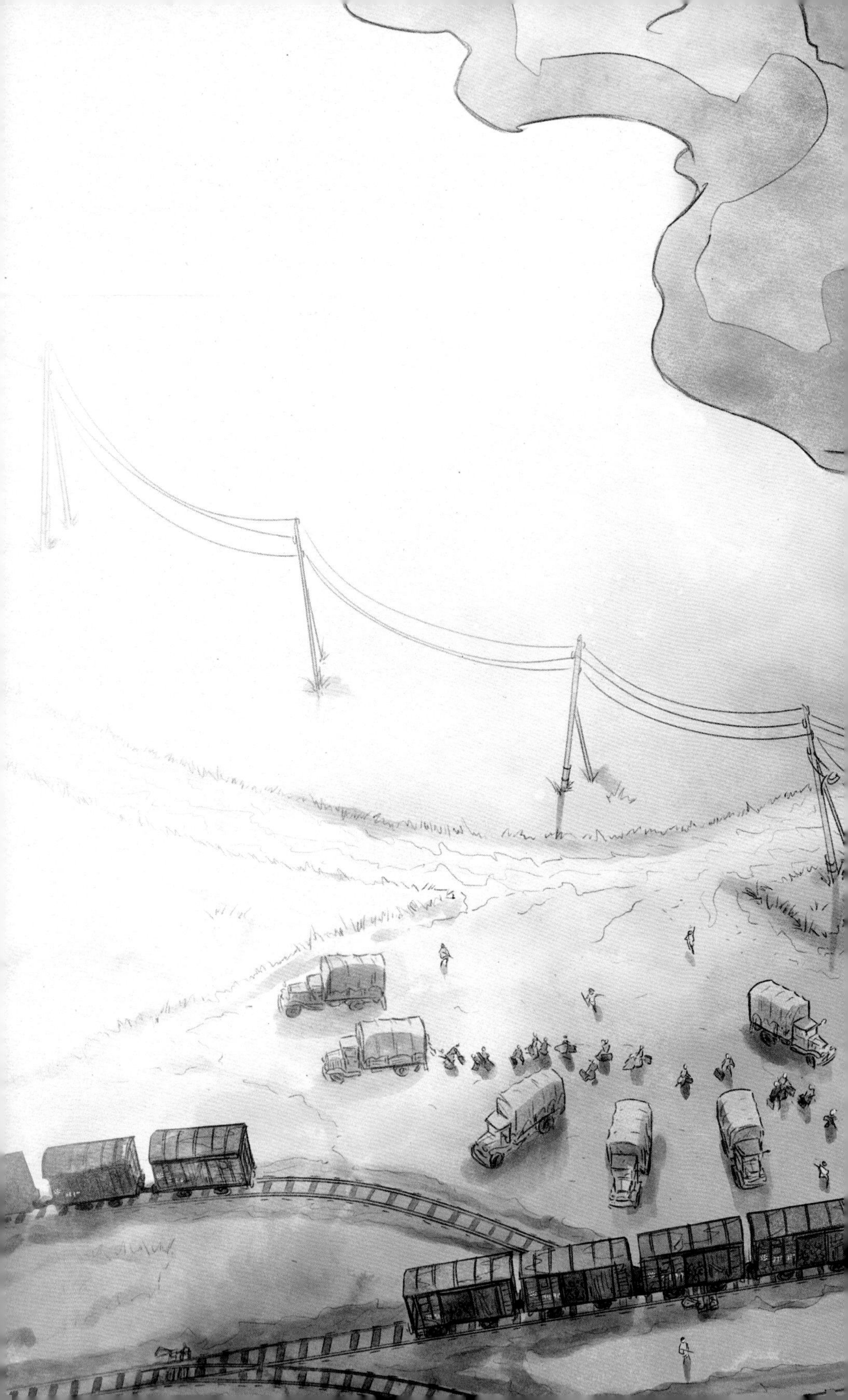

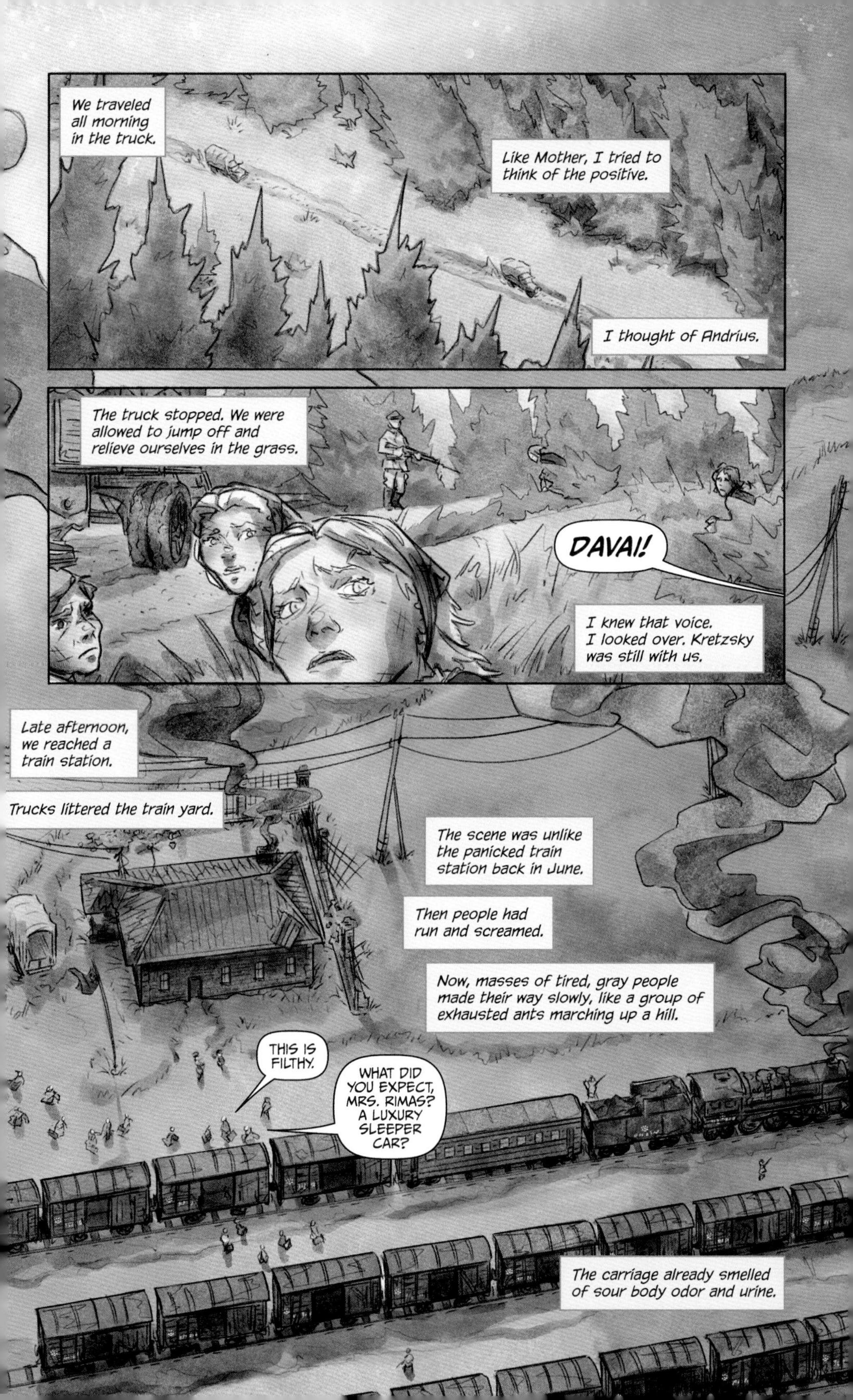
We traveled all morning in the truck.
Like Mother, I tried to think of the positive.
I thought of Andrius.
The truck stopped. We were allowed to jump off and relieve ourselves in the grass.
DAVAI!
I knew that voice. I looked over. Kretzsky was still with us.
Late afternoon, we reached a train station.
Trucks littered the train yard.
The scene was unlike the panicked train station back in June.
Then people had run and screamed.
Now, masses of tired, gray people made their way slowly, like a group of exhausted ants marching up a hill.
THIS IS FILTHY.
WHAT DID YOU EXPECT, MRS. RIMAS? A LUXURY SLEEPER CAR?
The carriage already smelled of sour body odor and urine.

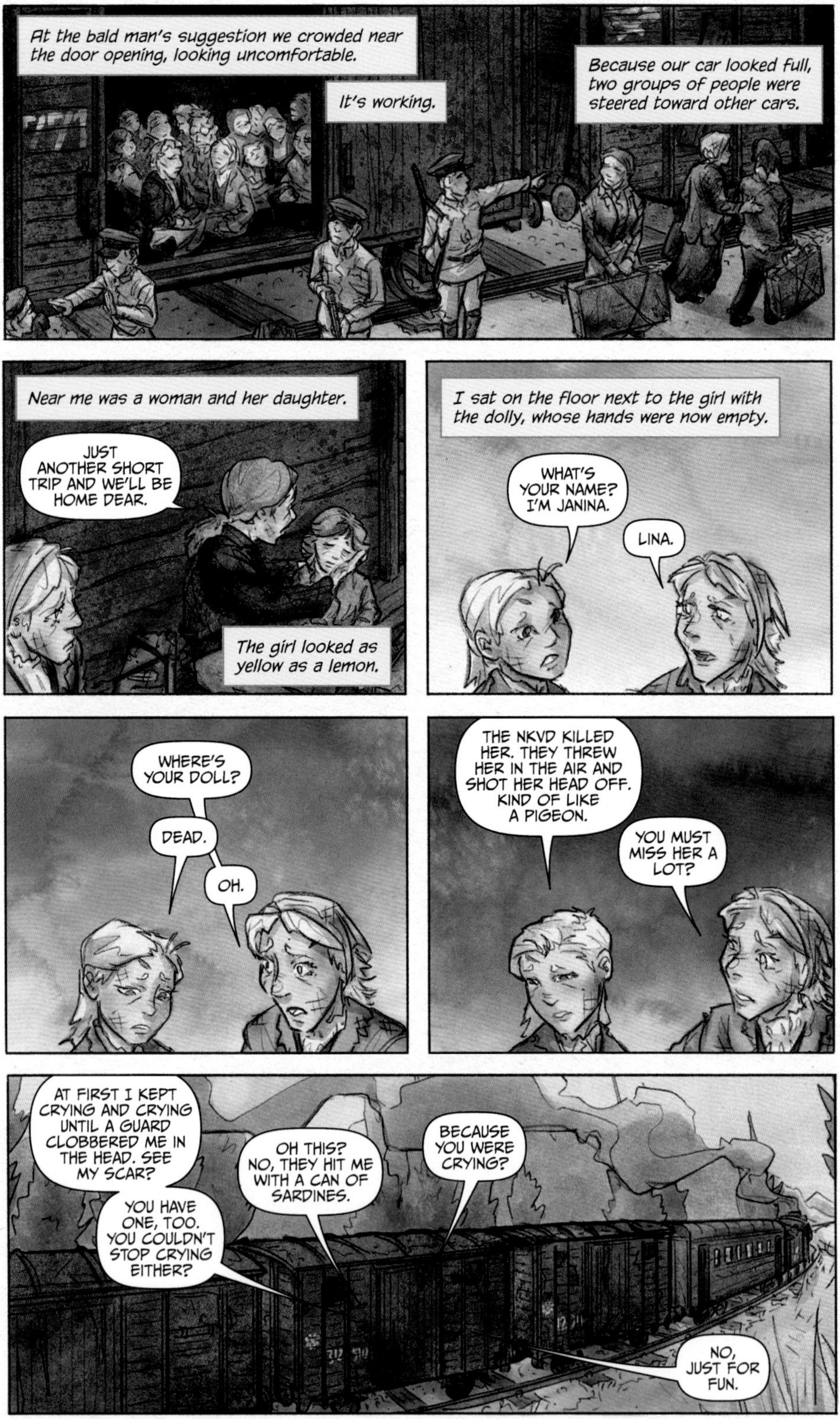
At the bald man's suggestion we crowded near the door opening, looking uncomfortable.
It's working.
Because our car looked full, two groups of people were steered toward other cars.
Near me was a woman and her daughter.
JUST ANOTHER SHORT TRIP AND WE'LL BE HOME DEAR.
The girl looked as yellow as a lemon.
I sat on the floor next to the girl with the dolly, whose hands were now empty.
WHAT'S YOUR NAME? I'M JANINA.
LINA.
WHERE'S YOUR DOLL?
DEAD.
OH.
THE NKVD KILLED HER. THEY THREW HER IN THE AIR AND SHOT HER HEAD OFF. KIND OF LIKE A PIGEON.
YOU MUST MISS HER A LOT?
AT FIRST I KEPT CRYING AND CRYING UNTIL A GUARD CLOBBERED ME IN THE HEAD. SEE MY SCAR?
YOU HAVE ONE, TOO. YOU COULDN'T STOP CRYING EITHER?
OH THIS? NO, THEY HIT ME WITH A CAN OF SARDINES.
BECAUSE YOU WERE CRYING?
NO, JUST FOR FUN.

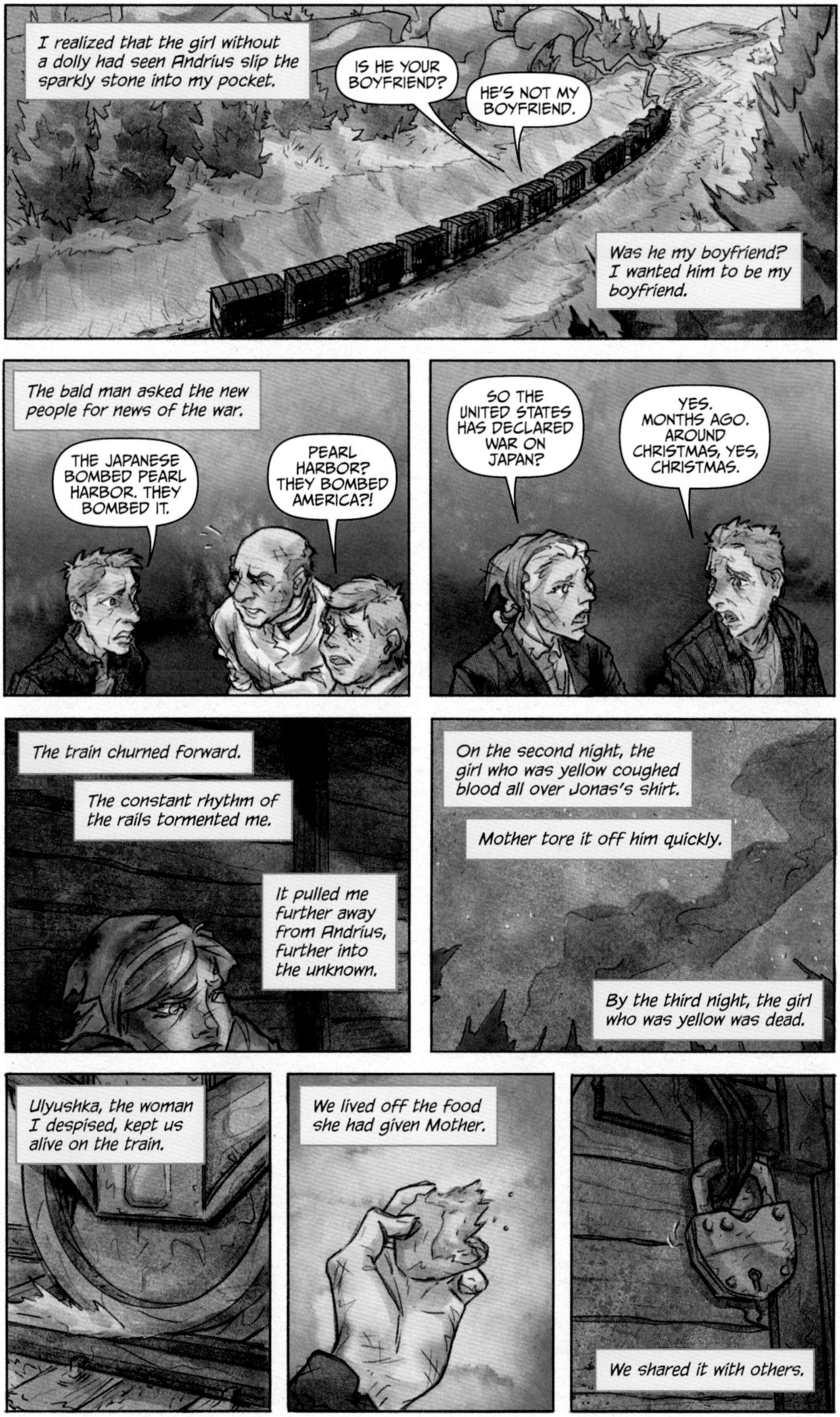
I realized that the girl without a dolly had seen Andrius slip the sparkly stone into my pocket.
IS HE YOUR BOYFRIEND?
HE'S NOT MY BOYFRIEND.
Was he my boyfriend? I wanted him to be my boyfriend.
The bald man asked the new people for news of the war.
THE JAPANESE BOMBED PEARL HARBOR. THEY BOMBED IT.
PEARL HARBOR? THEY BOMBED AMERICA?!
SO THE UNITED STATES HAS DECLARED WAR ON JAPAN?
YES. MONTHS AGO. AROUND CHRISTMAS, YES, CHRISTMAS.
The train churned forward.
The constant rhythm of the rails tormented me.
It pulled me further away from Andrius, further into the unknown.
On the second night, the girl who was yellow coughed blood all over Jonas's shirt.
Mother tore it off him quickly.
By the third night, the girl who was yellow was dead.
Ulyushka, the woman I despised, kept us alive on the train.
We lived off the food she had given Mother.
We shared it with others.

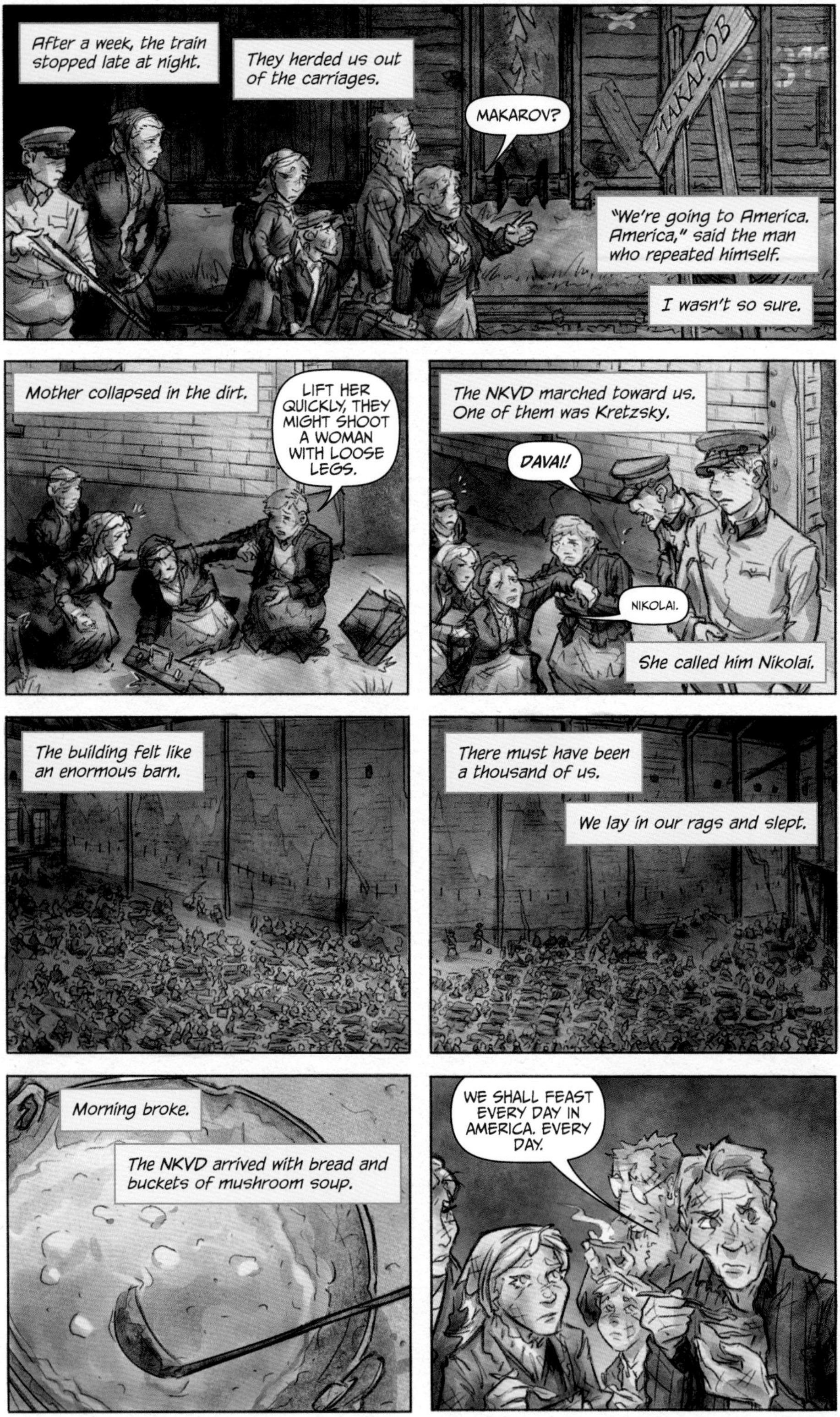
After a week, the train stopped late at night.
They herded us out of the carriages.
MAKAROV?
МАКАРОВ
"We're going to America. America," said the man who repeated himself.
I wasn't so sure.
Mother collapsed in the dirt.
LIFT HER QUICKLY, THEY MIGHT SHOOT A WOMAN WITH LOOSE LEGS.
The NKVD marched toward us. One of them was Kretzsky.
DAVAI!
NIKOLAI.
She called him Nikolai.
The building felt like an enormous barn.
There must have been a thousand of us.
We lay in our rags and slept.
Morning broke.
The NKVD arrived with bread and buckets of mushroom soup.
WE SHALL FEAST EVERY DAY IN AMERICA. EVERY DAY.

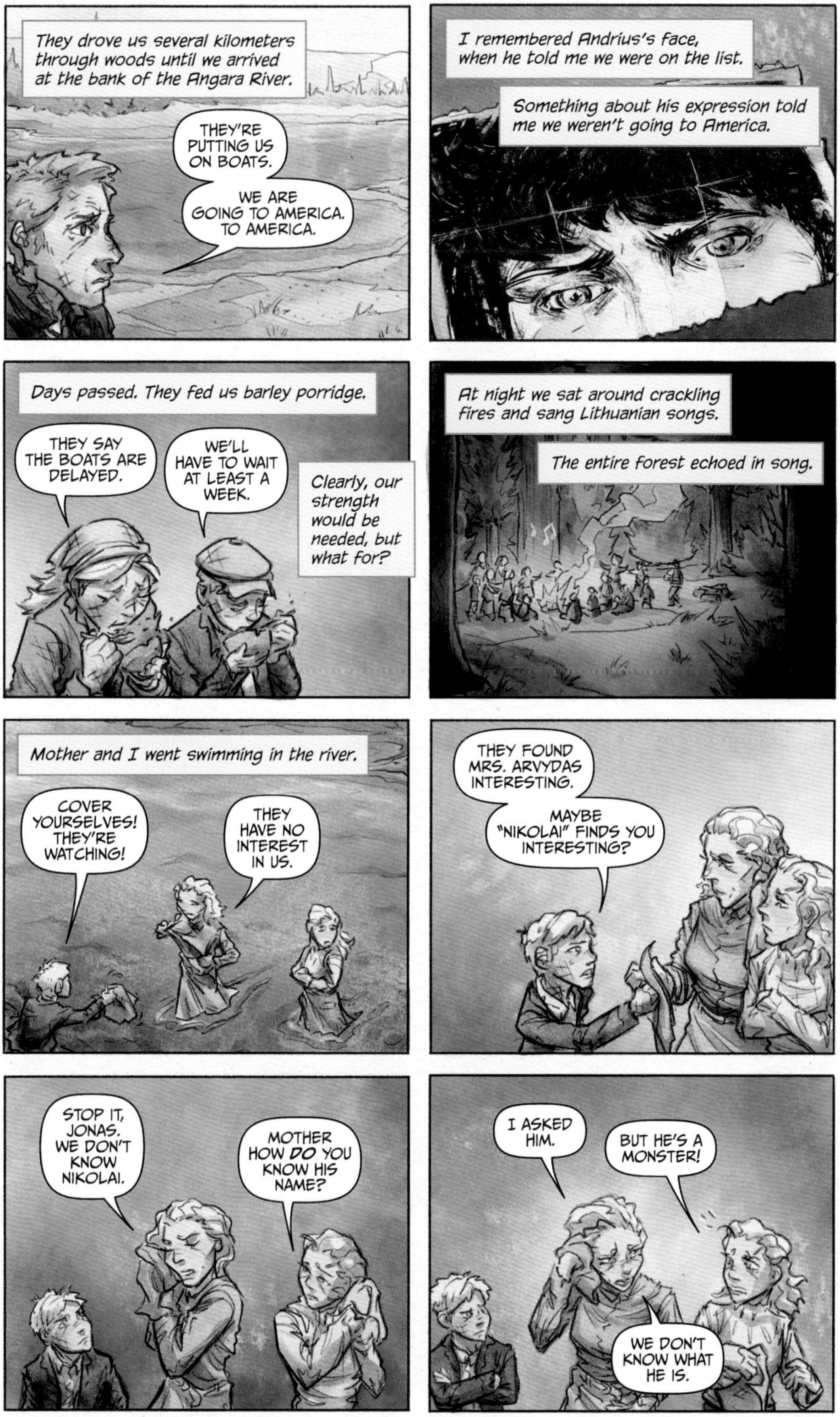

They drove us several kilometers through woods until we arrived at the bank of the Angara River.
THEY'RE PUTTING US ON BOATS.
WE ARE GOING TO AMERICA. TO AMERICA.
I remembered Andrius's face, when he told me we were on the list.
Something about his expression told me we weren't going to America.
Days passed. They fed us barley porridge.
THEY SAY THE BOATS ARE DELAYED.
WE'LL HAVE TO WAIT AT LEAST A WEEK.
Clearly, our strength would be needed, but what for?
At night we sat around crackling fires and sang Lithuanian songs.
The entire forest echoed in song.
Mother and I went swimming in the river.
COVER YOURSELVES! THEY'RE WATCHING!
THEY HAVE NO INTEREST IN US.
THEY FOUND MRS. ARVYDAS INTERESTING.
MAYBE "NIKOLAI" FINDS YOU INTERESTING?
STOP IT, JONAS. WE DON'T KNOW NIKOLAI.
MOTHER HOW DO YOU KNOW HIS NAME?
I ASKED HIM.
BUT HE'S A MONSTER!
WE DON'T KNOW WHAT HE IS.

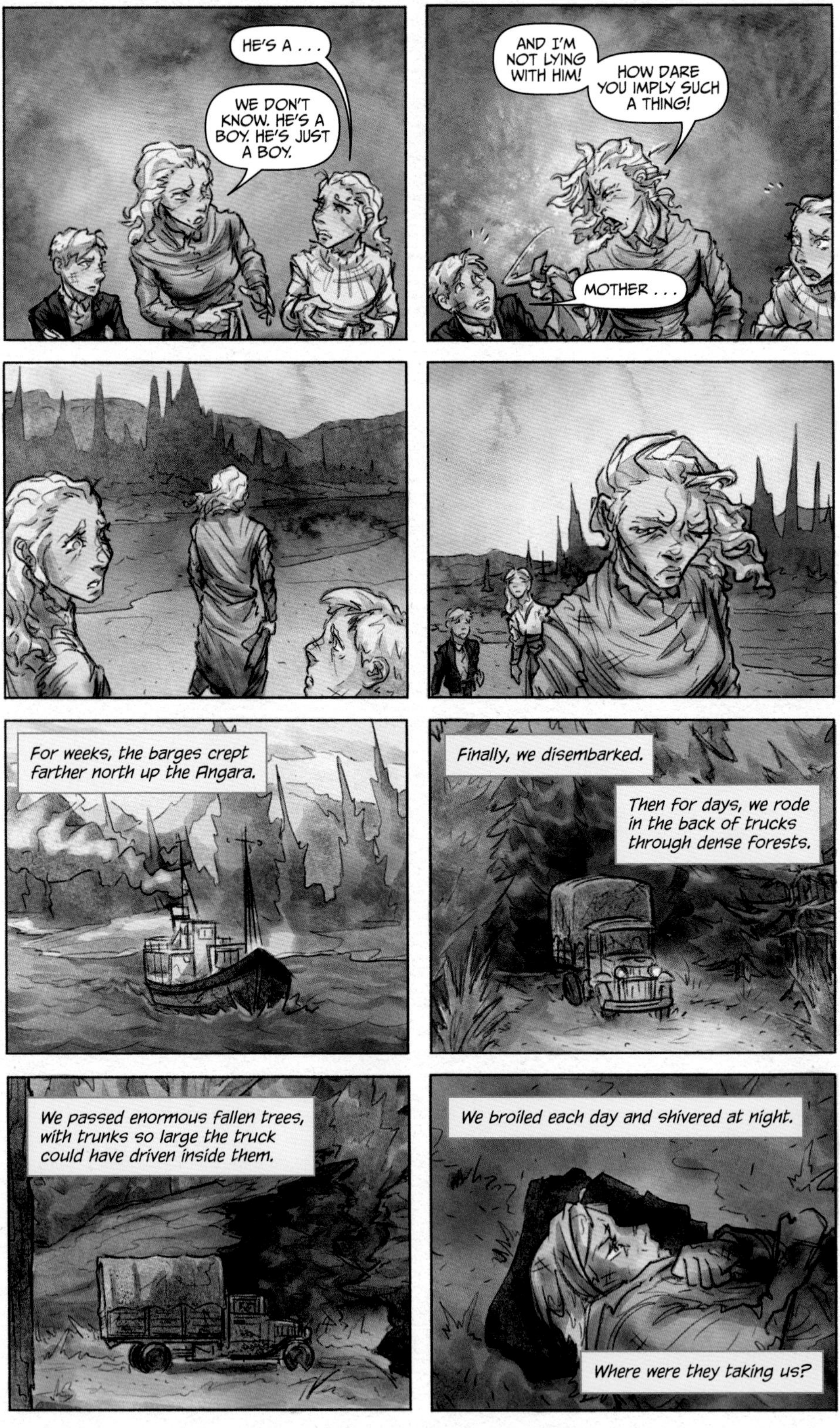
HE'S A . . .
WE DON'T KNOW. HE'S A BOY. HE'S JUST A BOY.
AND I'M NOT LYING WITH HIM!
HOW DARE YOU IMPLY SUCH A THING!
MOTHER . . .
For weeks, the barges crept farther north up the Angara.
Finally, we disembarked.
Then for days, we rode in the back of trucks through dense forests.
We passed enormous fallen trees, with trunks so large the truck could have driven inside them.
We broiled each day and shivered at night.
Where were they taking us?

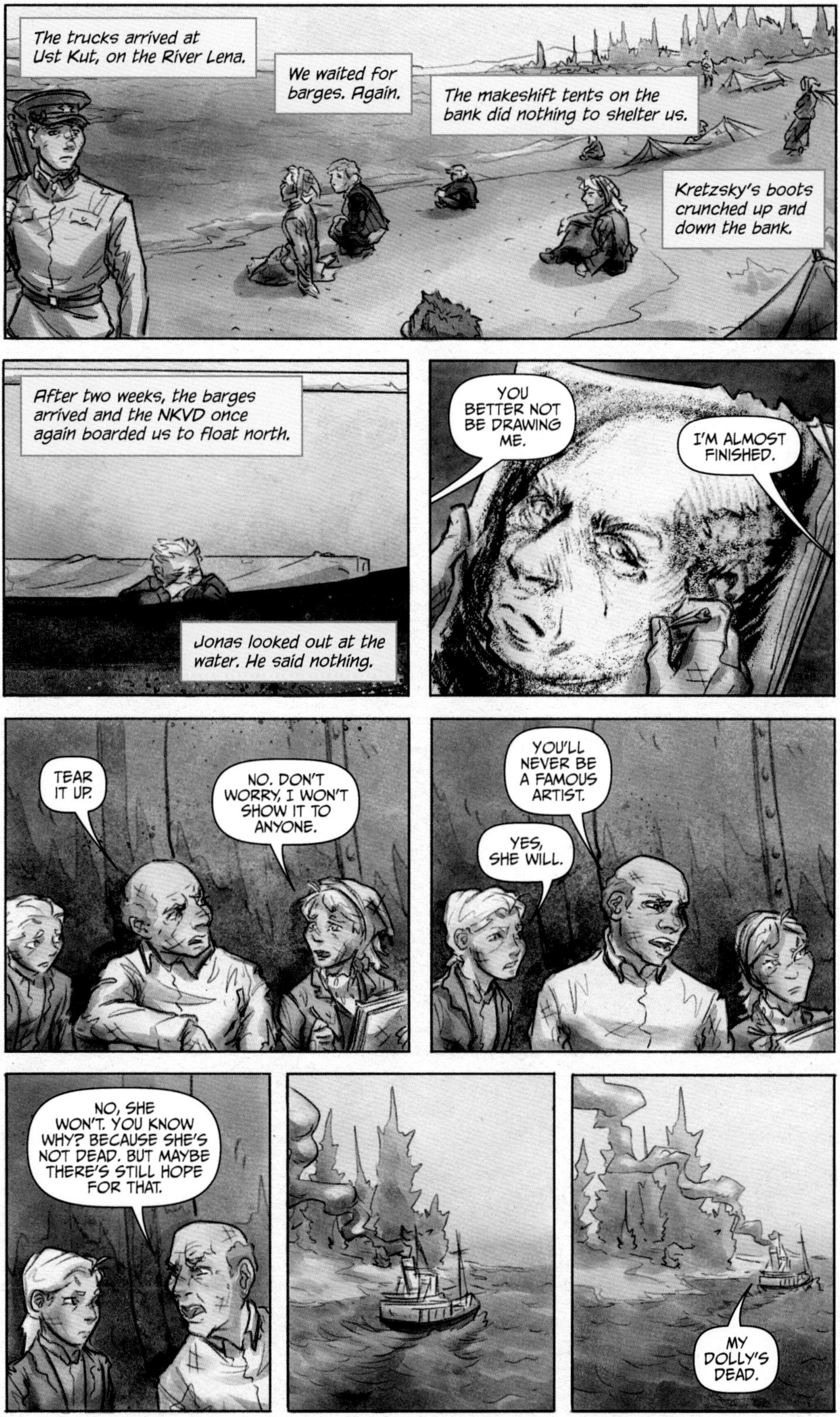
The trucks arrived at Ust Kut, on the River Lena.
We waited for barges. Again.
The makeshift tents on the bank did nothing to shelter us.
Kretzsky's boots crunched up and down the bank.
After two weeks, the barges arrived and the NKVD once again boarded us to float north.
Jonas looked out at the water. He said nothing.
YOU BETTER NOT BE DRAWING ME.
I'M ALMOST FINISHED.
TEAR IT UP.
NO. DON'T WORRY, I WON'T SHOW IT TO ANYONE.
YOU'LL NEVER BE A FAMOUS ARTIST.
YES, SHE WILL.
NO, SHE WON'T. YOU KNOW WHY? BECAUSE SHE'S NOT DEAD. BUT MAYBE THERE'S STILL HOPE FOR THAT.
MY DOLLY'S DEAD.

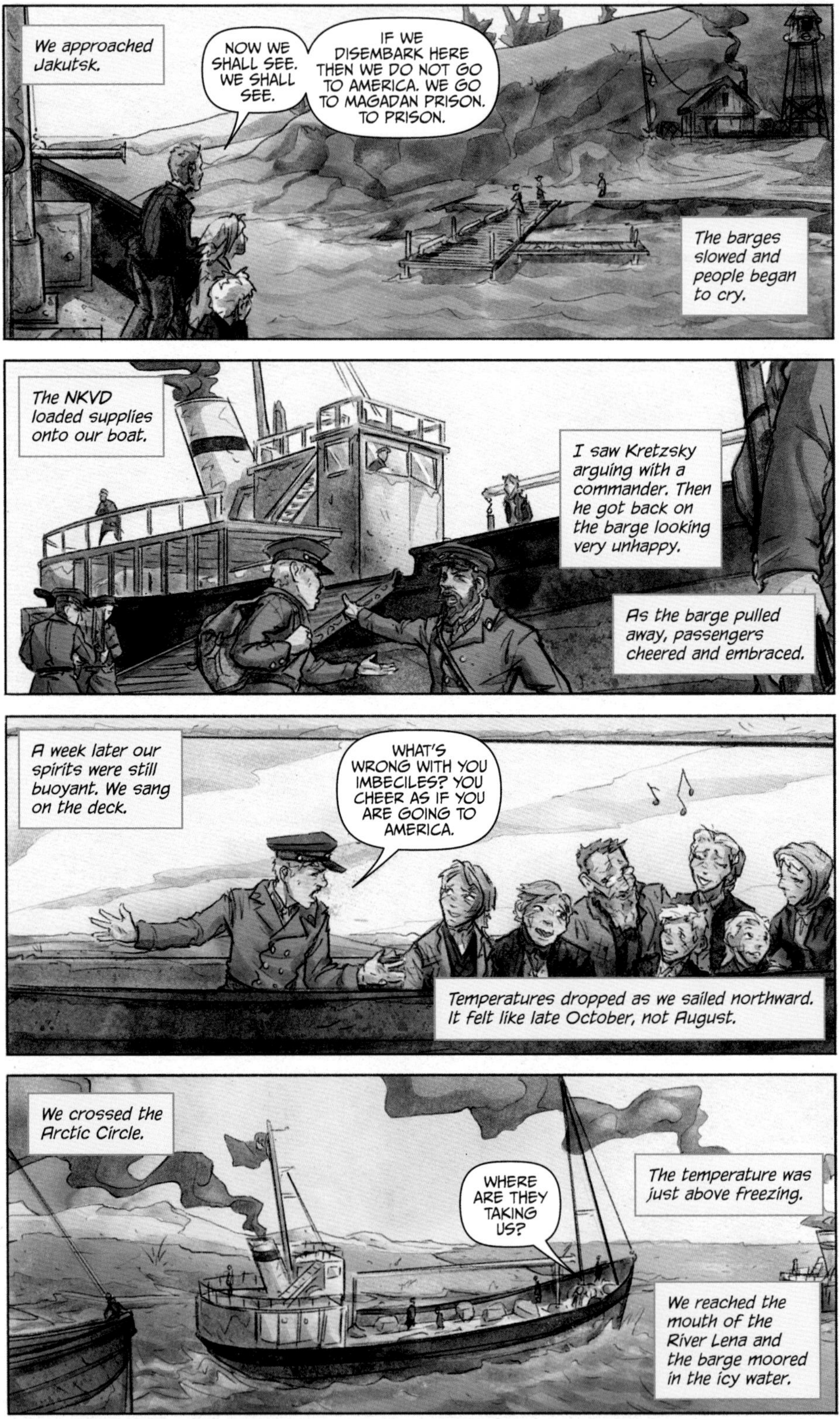
We approached Jakutsk.
NOW WE SHALL SEE. WE SHALL SEE.
IF WE DISEMBARK HERE THEN WE DO NOT GO TO AMERICA. WE GO TO MAGADAN PRISON. TO PRISON.
The barges slowed and people began to cry.
The NKVD loaded supplies onto our boat.
I saw Kretzsky arguing with a commander. Then he got back on the barge looking very unhappy.
As the barge pulled away, passengers cheered and embraced.
A week later our spirits were still buoyant. We sang on the deck.
WHAT'S WRONG WITH YOU IMBECILES? YOU CHEER AS IF YOU ARE GOING TO AMERICA.
Temperatures dropped as we sailed northward. It felt like late October, not August.
We crossed the Arctic Circle.
WHERE ARE THEY TAKING US?
The temperature was just above freezing.
We reached the mouth of the River Lena and the barge moored in the icy water.

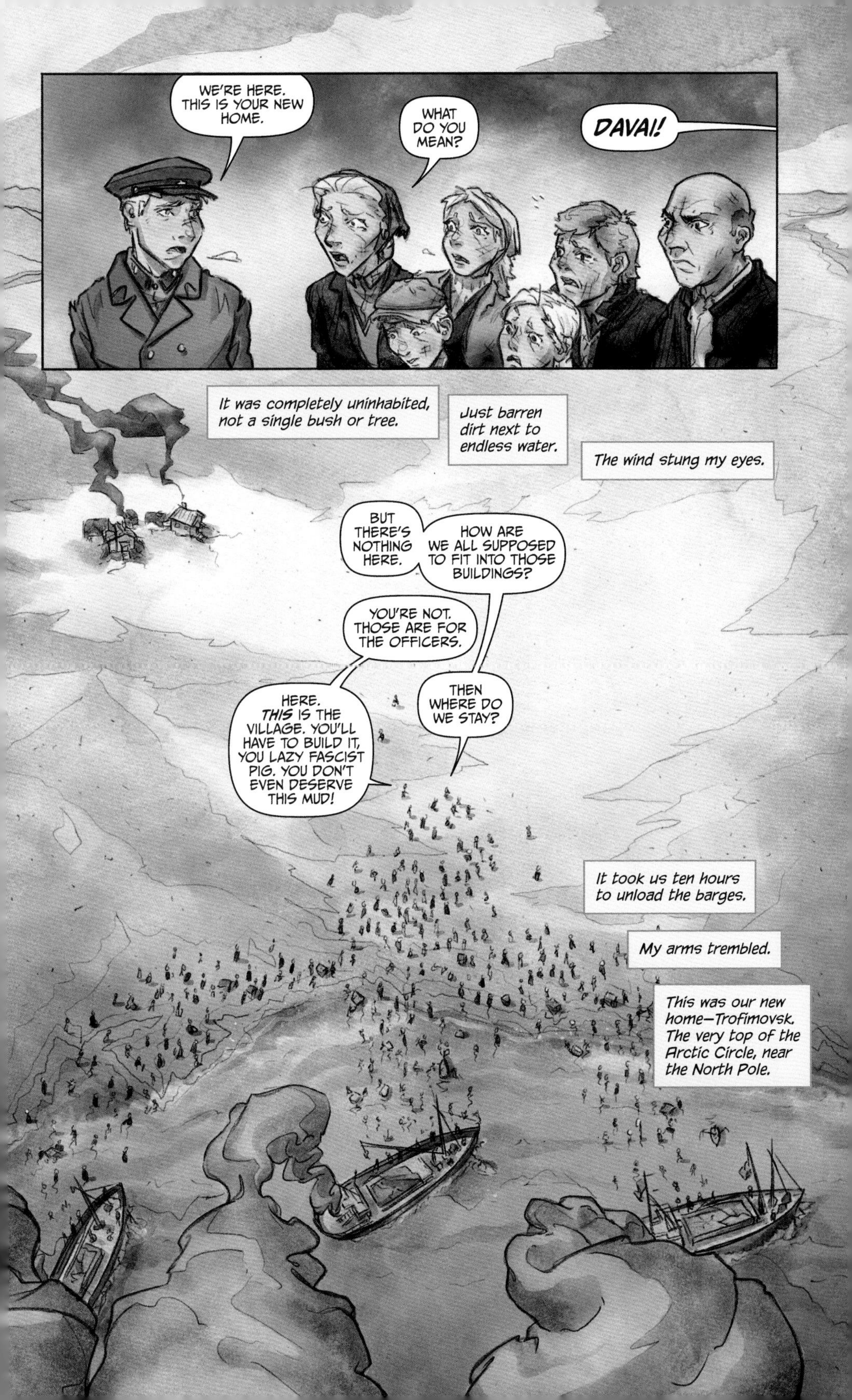
WE'RE HERE. THIS IS YOUR NEW HOME.
WHAT DO YOU MEAN?
DAVAI!
It was completely uninhabited, not a single bush or tree.
Just barren dirt next to endless water.
The wind stung my eyes.
BUT THERE'S NOTHING HERE.
HOW ARE WE ALL SUPPOSED TO FIT INTO THOSE BUILDINGS?
YOU'RE NOT. THOSE ARE FOR THE OFFICERS.
THEN WHERE DO WE STAY?
HERE. THIS IS THE VILLAGE. YOU'LL HAVE TO BUILD IT, YOU LAZY FASCIST PIG. YOU DON'T EVEN DESERVE THIS MUD!
It took us ten hours to unload the barges.
My arms trembled.
This was our new home—Trofimovsk. The very top of the Arctic Circle, near the North Pole.

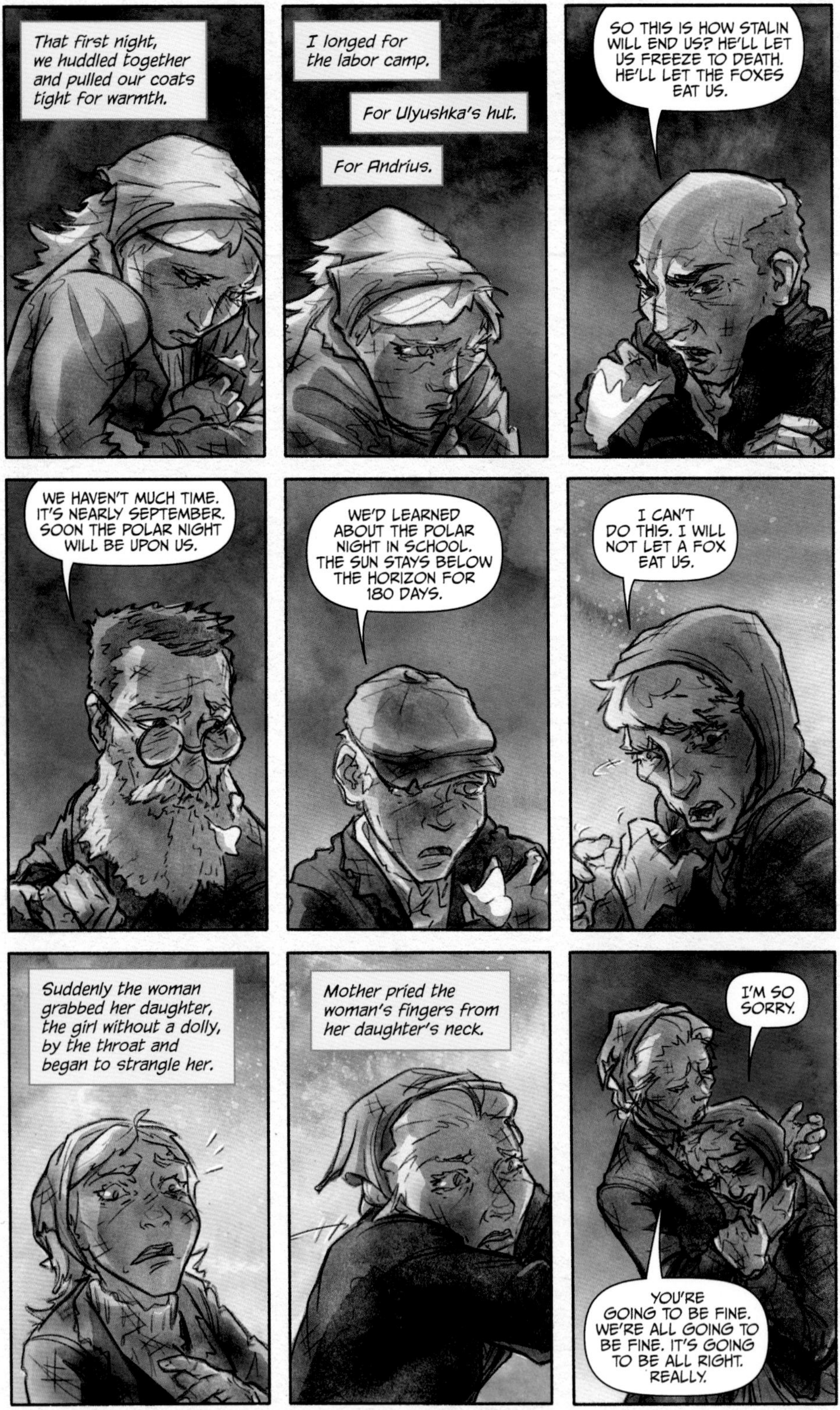

That first night, we huddled together and pulled our coats tight for warmth.
I longed for the labor camp.
For Ulyushka's hut.
For Andrius.
SO THIS IS HOW STALIN WILL END US? HE'LL LET US FREEZE TO DEATH. HE'LL LET THE FOXES EAT US.
WE HAVEN'T MUCH TIME. IT'S NEARLY SEPTEMBER. SOON THE POLAR NIGHT WILL BE UPON US.
WE'D LEARNED ABOUT THE POLAR NIGHT IN SCHOOL. THE SUN STAYS BELOW THE HORIZON FOR 180 DAYS.
I CAN'T DO THIS. I WILL NOT LET A FOX EAT US.
Suddenly the woman grabbed her daughter, the girl without a dolly, by the throat and began to strangle her.
Mother pried the woman's fingers from her daughter's neck.
I'M SO SORRY.
YOU'RE GOING TO BE FINE. WE'RE ALL GOING TO BE FINE. IT'S GOING TO BE ALL RIGHT. REALLY.

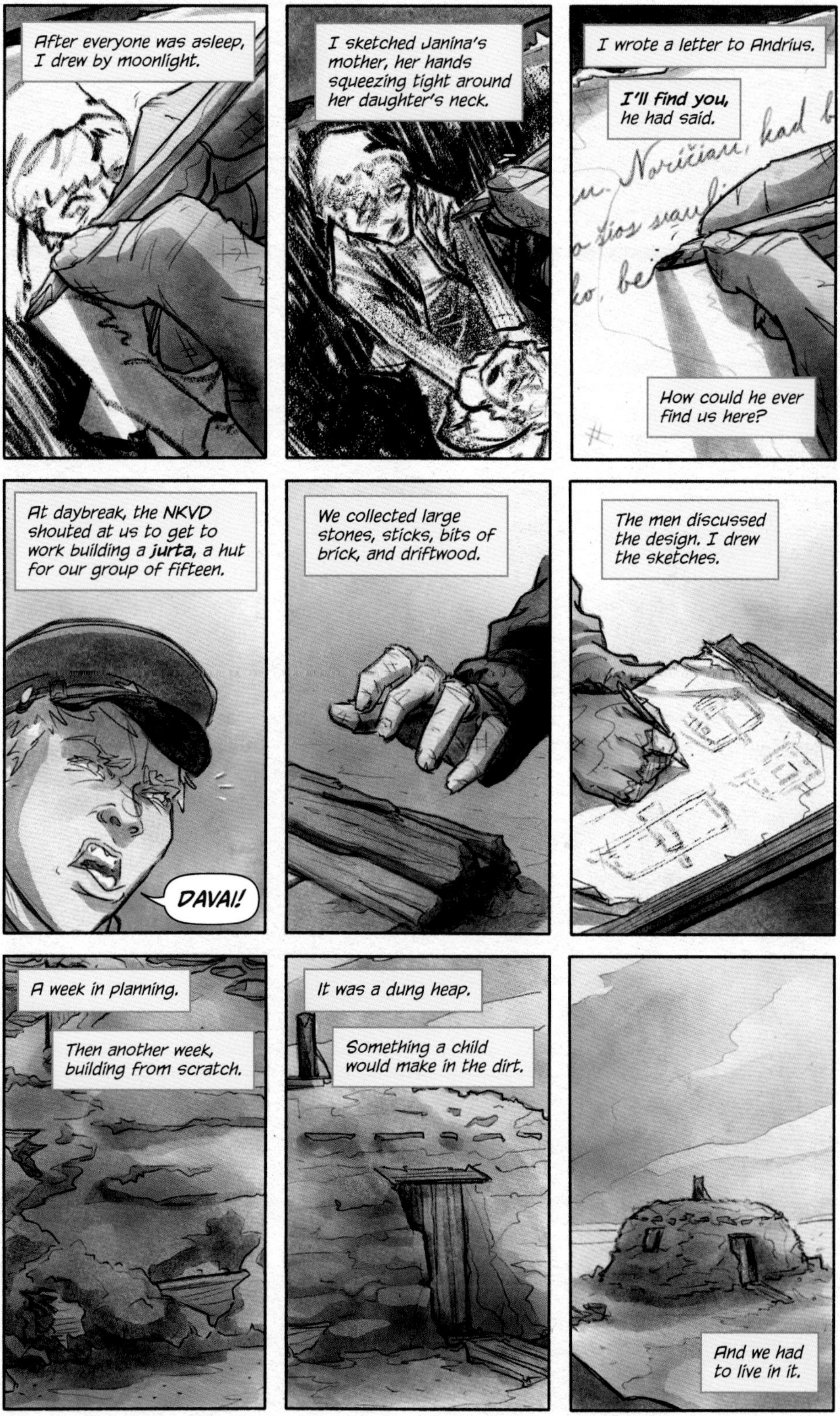
After everyone was asleep, I drew by moonlight.
I sketched Janina's mother, her hands squeezing tight around her daughter's neck.
I wrote a letter to Andrius.
I'll find you, he had said.
How could he ever find us here?
At daybreak, the NKVD shouted at us to get to work building a **jurta**, a hut for our group of fifteen.
DAVAI!
We collected large stones, sticks, bits of brick, and driftwood.
The men discussed the design. I drew the sketches.
A week in planning.
Then another week, building from scratch.
It was a dung heap.
Something a child would make in the dirt.
And we had to live in it.

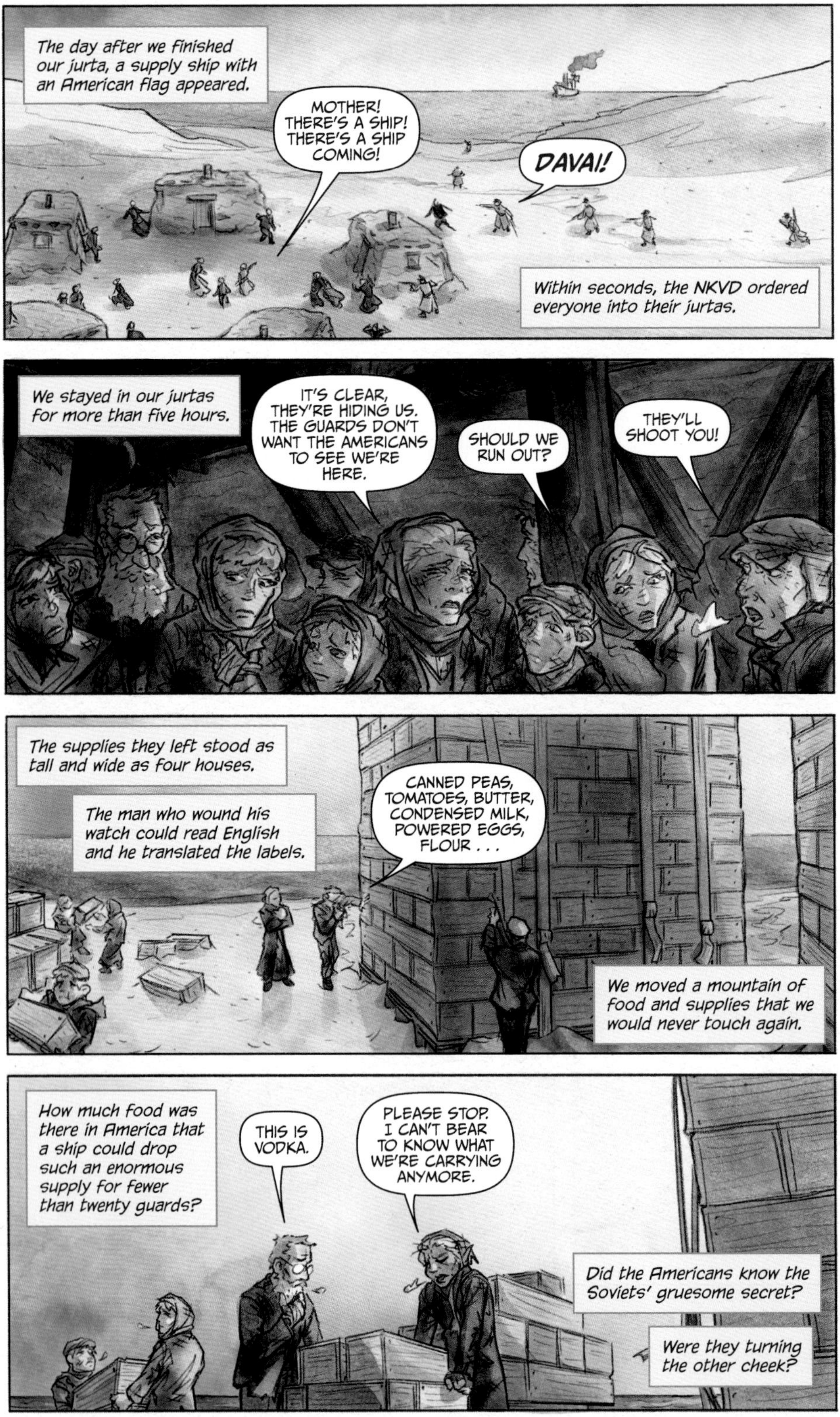
The day after we finished our jurta, a supply ship with an American flag appeared.
MOTHER! THERE'S A SHIP! THERE'S A SHIP COMING!
DAVAI!
Within seconds, the NKVD ordered everyone into their jurtas.
We stayed in our jurtas for more than five hours.
IT'S CLEAR, THEY'RE HIDING US. THE GUARDS DON'T WANT THE AMERICANS TO SEE WE'RE HERE.
SHOULD WE RUN OUT?
THEY'LL SHOOT YOU!
The supplies they left stood as tall and wide as four houses.
The man who wound his watch could read English and he translated the labels.
CANNED PEAS, TOMATOES, BUTTER, CONDENSED MILK, POWERED EGGS, FLOUR . . .
We moved a mountain of food and supplies that we would never touch again.
How much food was there in America that a ship could drop such an enormous supply for fewer than twenty guards?
THIS IS VODKA.
PLEASE STOP. I CAN'T BEAR TO KNOW WHAT WE'RE CARRYING ANYMORE.
Did the Americans know the Soviets' gruesome secret?
Were they turning the other cheek?

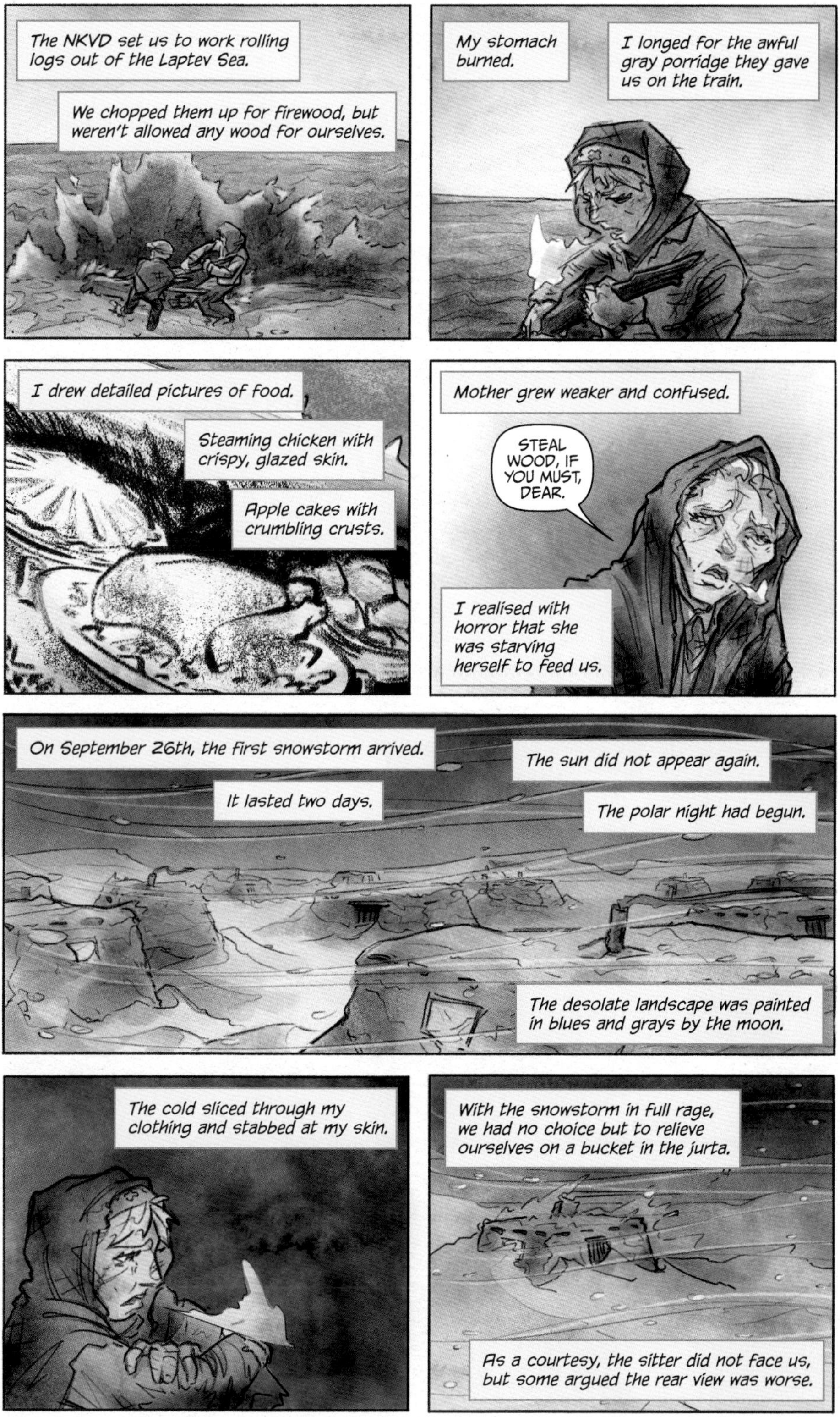
The NKVD set us to work rolling logs out of the Laptev Sea.
We chopped them up for firewood, but weren't allowed any wood for ourselves.
My stomach burned.
I longed for the awful gray porridge they gave us on the train.
I drew detailed pictures of food.
Steaming chicken with crispy, glazed skin.
Apple cakes with crumbling crusts.
Mother grew weaker and confused.
STEAL WOOD, IF YOU MUST, DEAR.
I realised with horror that she was starving herself to feed us.
On September 26th, the first snowstorm arrived.
It lasted two days.
The sun did not appear again.
The polar night had begun.
The desolate landscape was painted in blues and grays by the moon.
The cold sliced through my clothing and stabbed at my skin.
With the snowstorm in full rage, we had no choice but to relieve ourselves on a bucket in the jurta.
As a courtesy, the sitter did not face us, but some argued the rear view was worse.

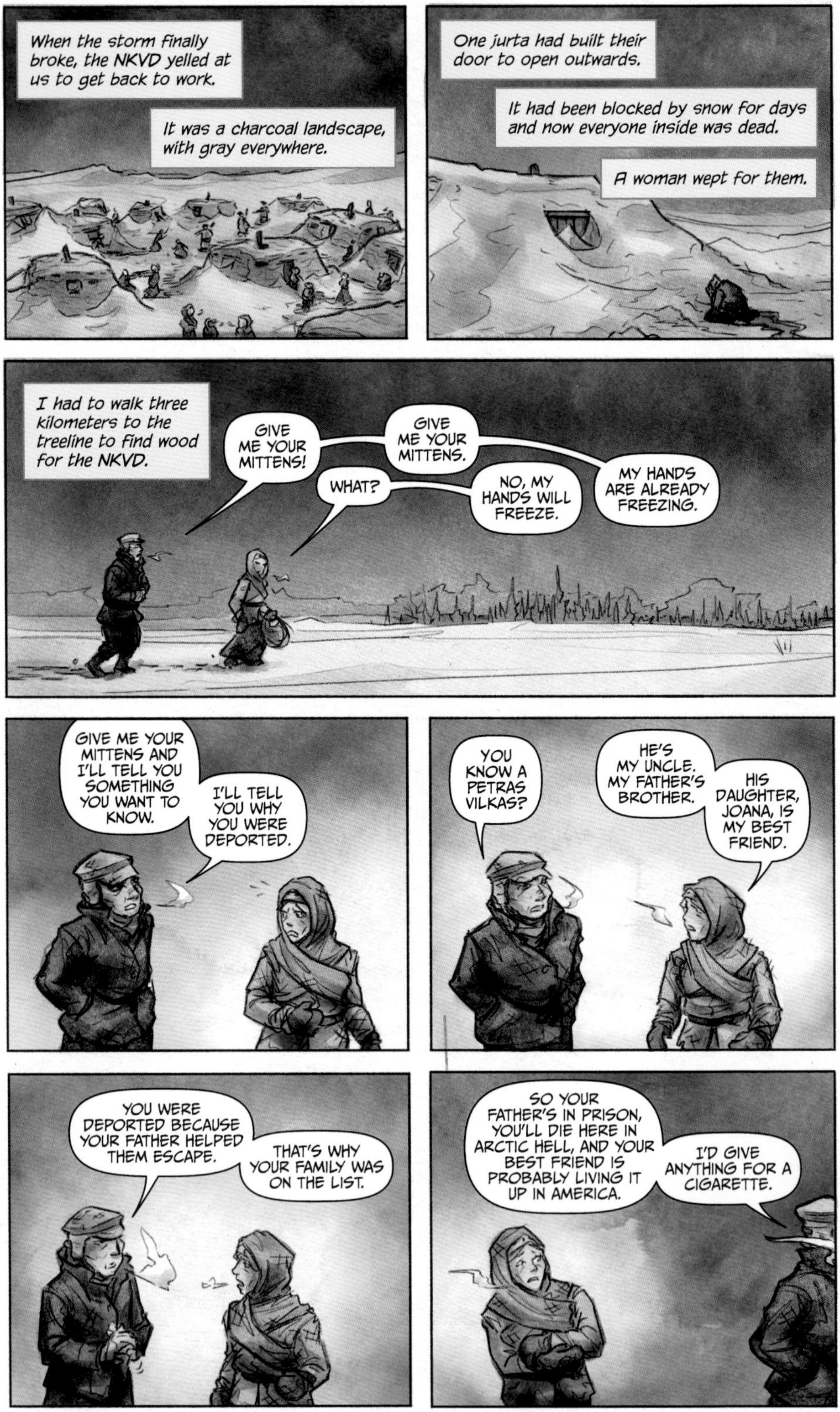
When the storm finally broke, the NKVD yelled at us to get back to work.
It was a charcoal landscape, with gray everywhere.
One jurta had built their door to open outwards.
It had been blocked by snow for days and now everyone inside was dead.
A woman wept for them.
I had to walk three kilometers to the treeline to find wood for the NKVD.
GIVE ME YOUR MITTENS!
WHAT?
GIVE ME YOUR MITTENS.
NO, MY HANDS WILL FREEZE.
MY HANDS ARE ALREADY FREEZING.
GIVE ME YOUR MITTENS AND I'LL TELL YOU SOMETHING YOU WANT TO KNOW.
I'LL TELL YOU WHY YOU WERE DEPORTED.
YOU KNOW A PETRAS VILKAS?
HE'S MY UNCLE. MY FATHER'S BROTHER.
HIS DAUGHTER, JOANA, IS MY BEST FRIEND.
YOU WERE DEPORTED BECAUSE YOUR FATHER HELPED THEM ESCAPE.
THAT'S WHY YOUR FAMILY WAS ON THE LIST.
SO YOUR FATHER'S IN PRISON, YOU'LL DIE HERE IN ARCTIC HELL, AND YOUR BEST FRIEND IS PROBABLY LIVING IT UP IN AMERICA.
I'D GIVE ANYTHING FOR A CIGARETTE.

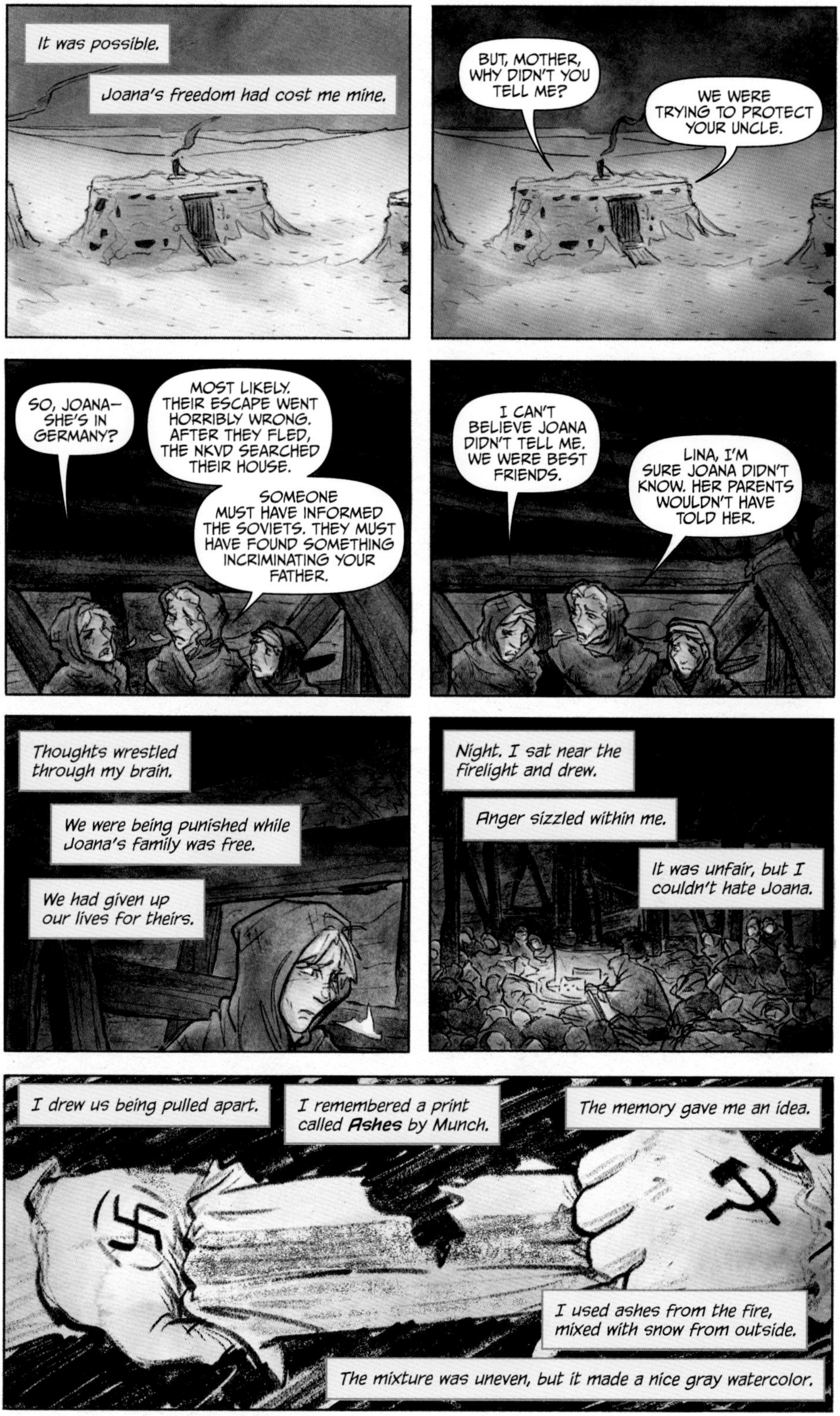
It was possible.
Joana's freedom had cost me mine.
BUT, MOTHER, WHY DIDN'T YOU TELL ME?
WE WERE TRYING TO PROTECT YOUR UNCLE.
SO, JOANA— SHE'S IN GERMANY?
MOST LIKELY. THEIR ESCAPE WENT HORRIBLY WRONG. AFTER THEY FLED, THE NKVD SEARCHED THEIR HOUSE.
SOMEONE MUST HAVE INFORMED THE SOVIETS. THEY MUST HAVE FOUND SOMETHING INCRIMINATING YOUR FATHER.
I CAN'T BELIEVE JOANA DIDN'T TELL ME. WE WERE BEST FRIENDS.
LINA, I'M SURE JOANA DIDN'T KNOW. HER PARENTS WOULDN'T HAVE TOLD HER.
Thoughts wrestled through my brain.
We were being punished while Joana's family was free.
We had given up our lives for theirs.
Night. I sat near the firelight and drew.
Anger sizzled within me.
It was unfair, but I couldn't hate Joana.
I drew us being pulled apart.
I remembered a print called **Ashes** by Munch.
The memory gave me an idea.
I used ashes from the fire, mixed with snow from outside.
The mixture was uneven, but it made a nice gray watercolor.

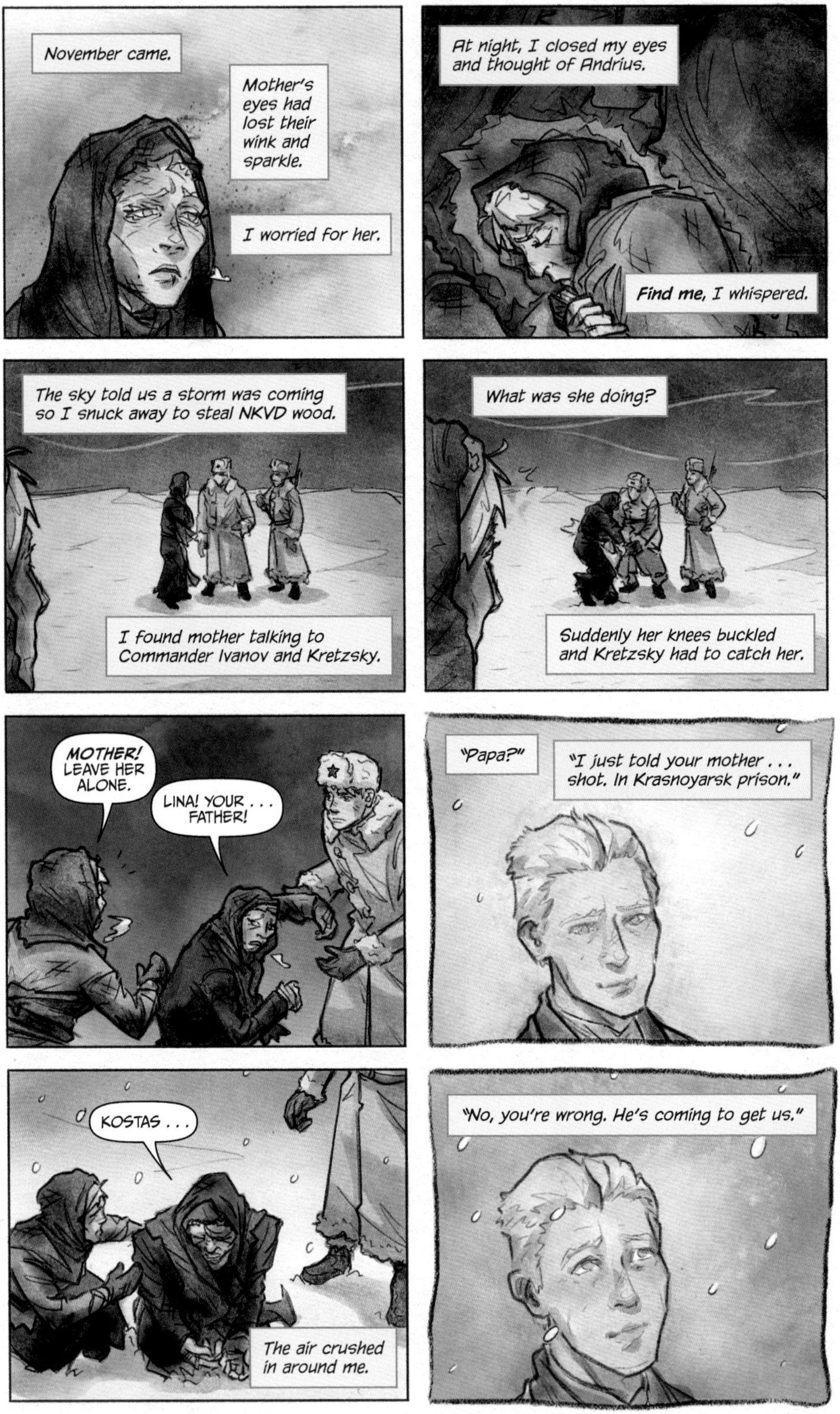
November came.
Mother's eyes had lost their wink and sparkle.
I worried for her.
At night, I closed my eyes and thought of Andrius.
Find me, I whispered.
The sky told us a storm was coming so I snuck away to steal NKVD wood.
I found mother talking to Commander Ivanov and Kretzsky.
What was she doing?
Suddenly her knees buckled and Kretzsky had to catch her.
MOTHER! LEAVE HER ALONE.
LINA! YOUR . . . FATHER!
"Papa?"
"I just told your mother . . . shot. In Krasnoyarsk prison."
KOSTAS . . .
The air crushed in around me.
"No, you're wrong. He's coming to get us."

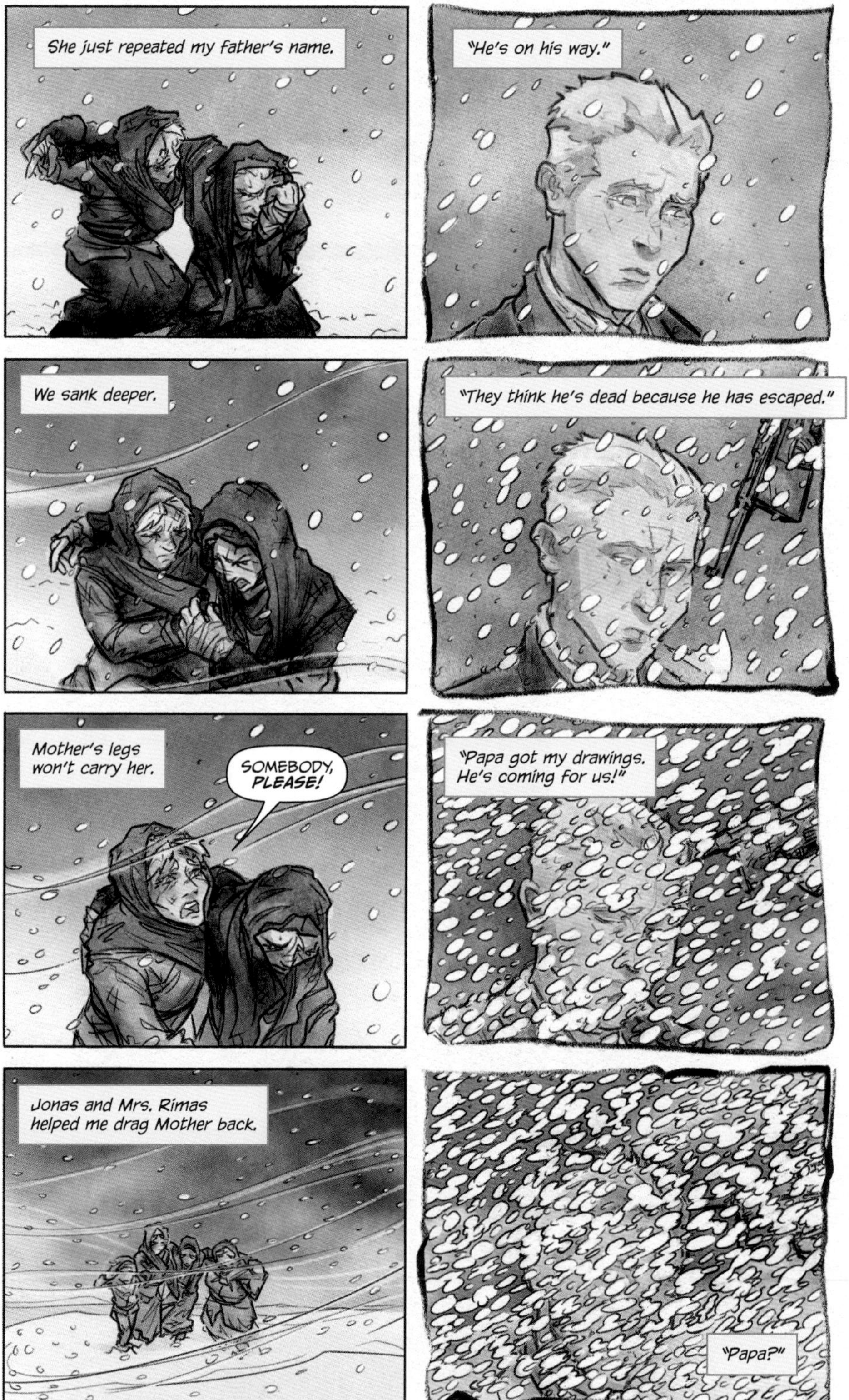
She just repeated my father's name.
"He's on his way."
We sank deeper.
"They think he's dead because he has escaped."
Mother's legs won't carry her.
SOMEBODY, PLEASE!
"Papa got my drawings. He's coming for us!"
Jonas and Mrs. Rimas helped me drag Mother back.
"Papa?"

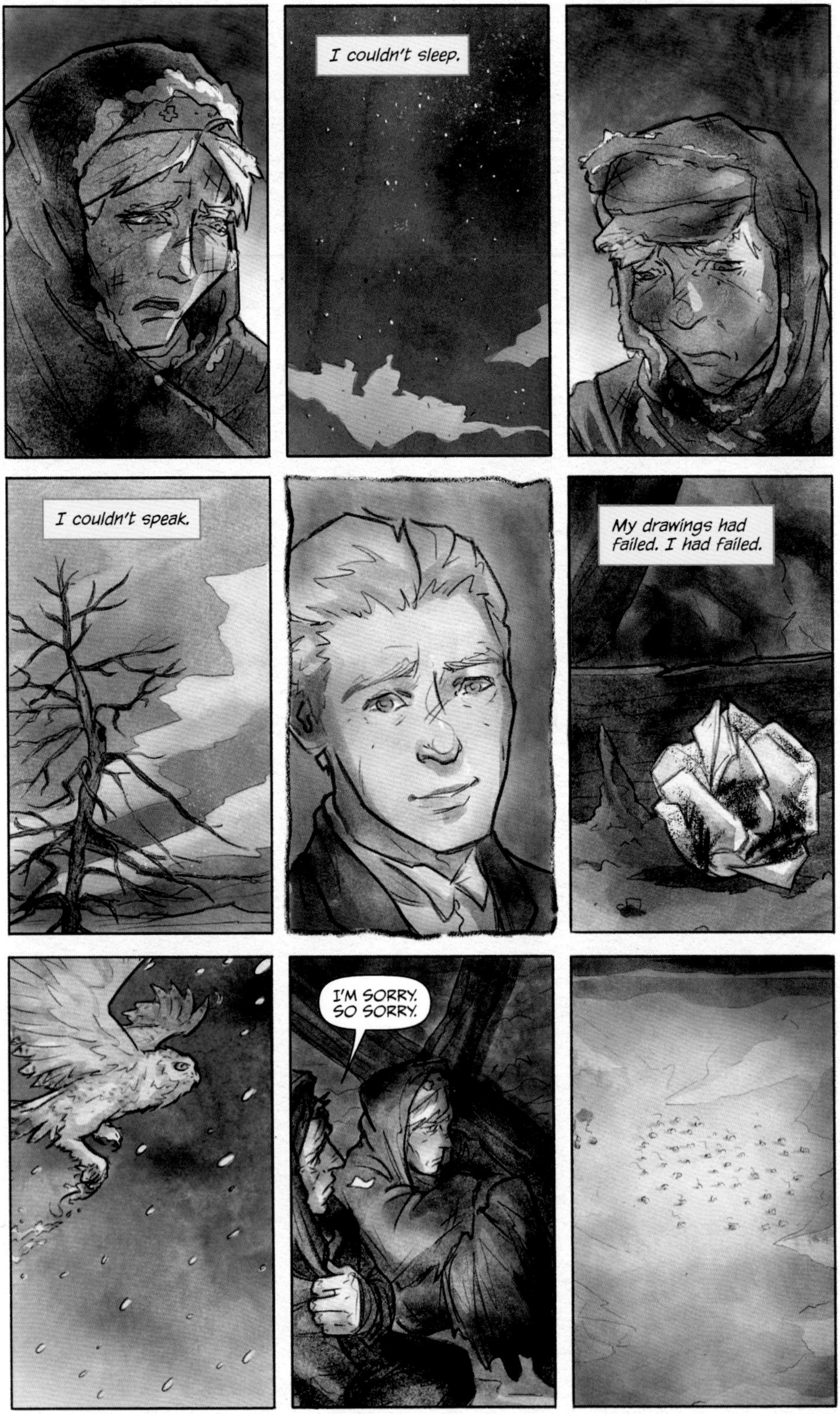
I couldn't sleep.
I couldn't speak.
My drawings had failed. I had failed.
I'M SORRY. SO SORRY.

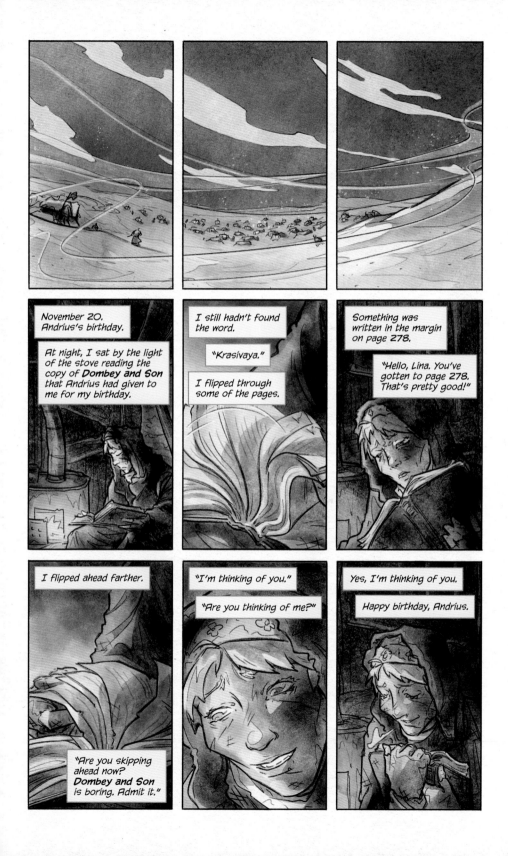

November 20.
Andrius's birthday.

At night, I sat by the light of the stove reading the copy of **Dombey and Son** that Andrius had given to me for my birthday.

I still hadn't found the word.

"Krasivaya."

I flipped through some of the pages.

Something was written in the margin on page 278.

"Hello, Lina. You've gotten to page 278. That's pretty good!"

I flipped ahead farther.

"Are you skipping ahead now? **Dombey and Son** is boring. Admit it."

"I'm thinking of you."

"Are you thinking of me?"

Yes, I'm thinking of you.

Happy birthday, Andrius.

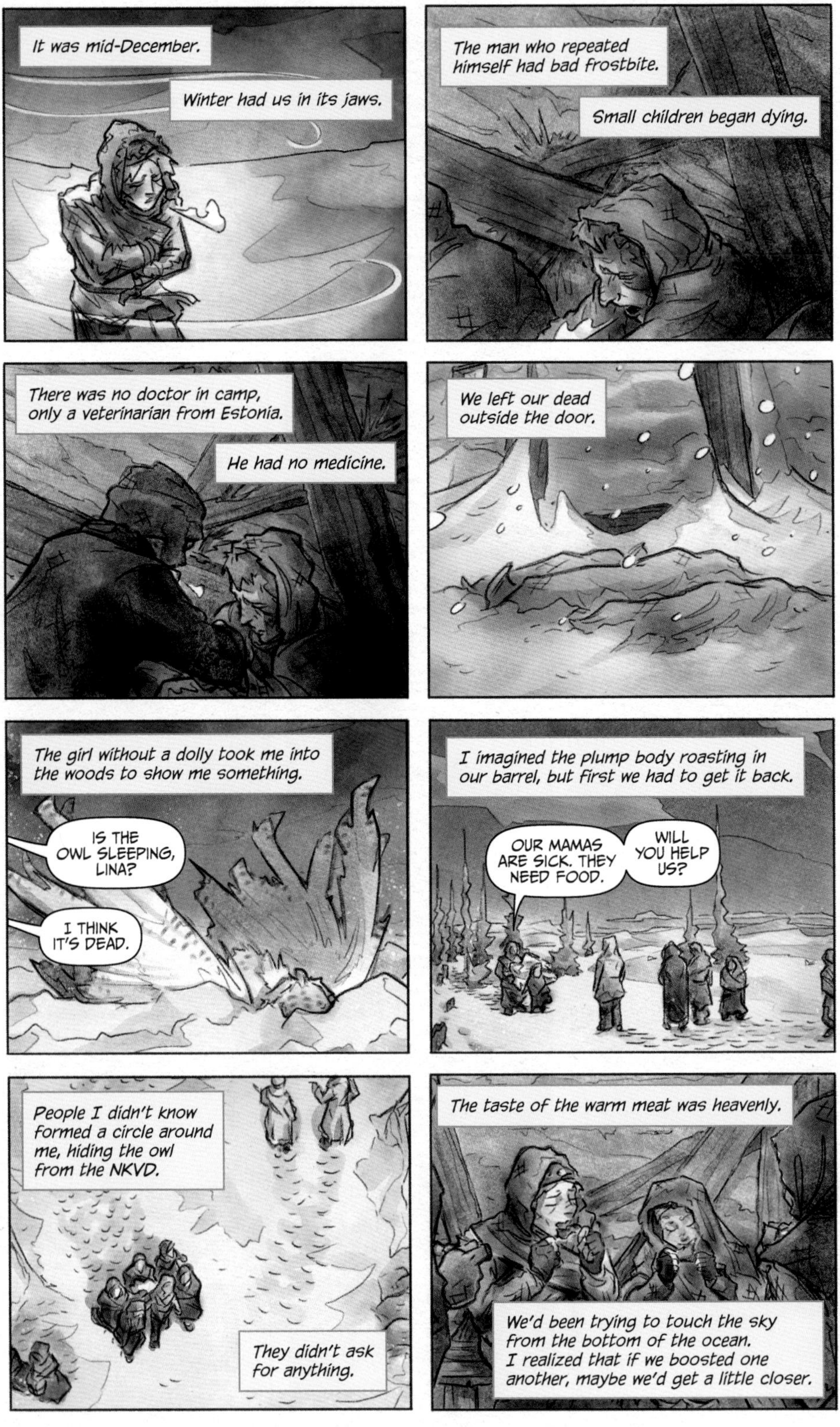
It was mid-December.
Winter had us in its jaws.
The man who repeated himself had bad frostbite.
Small children began dying.
There was no doctor in camp, only a veterinarian from Estonia.
He had no medicine.
We left our dead outside the door.
The girl without a dolly took me into the woods to show me something.
IS THE OWL SLEEPING, LINA?
I THINK IT'S DEAD.
I imagined the plump body roasting in our barrel, but first we had to get it back.
OUR MAMAS ARE SICK. THEY NEED FOOD.
WILL YOU HELP US?
People I didn't know formed a circle around me, hiding the owl from the NKVD.
They didn't ask for anything.
The taste of the warm meat was heavenly.
We'd been trying to touch the sky from the bottom of the ocean.
I realized that if we boosted one another, maybe we'd get a little closer.

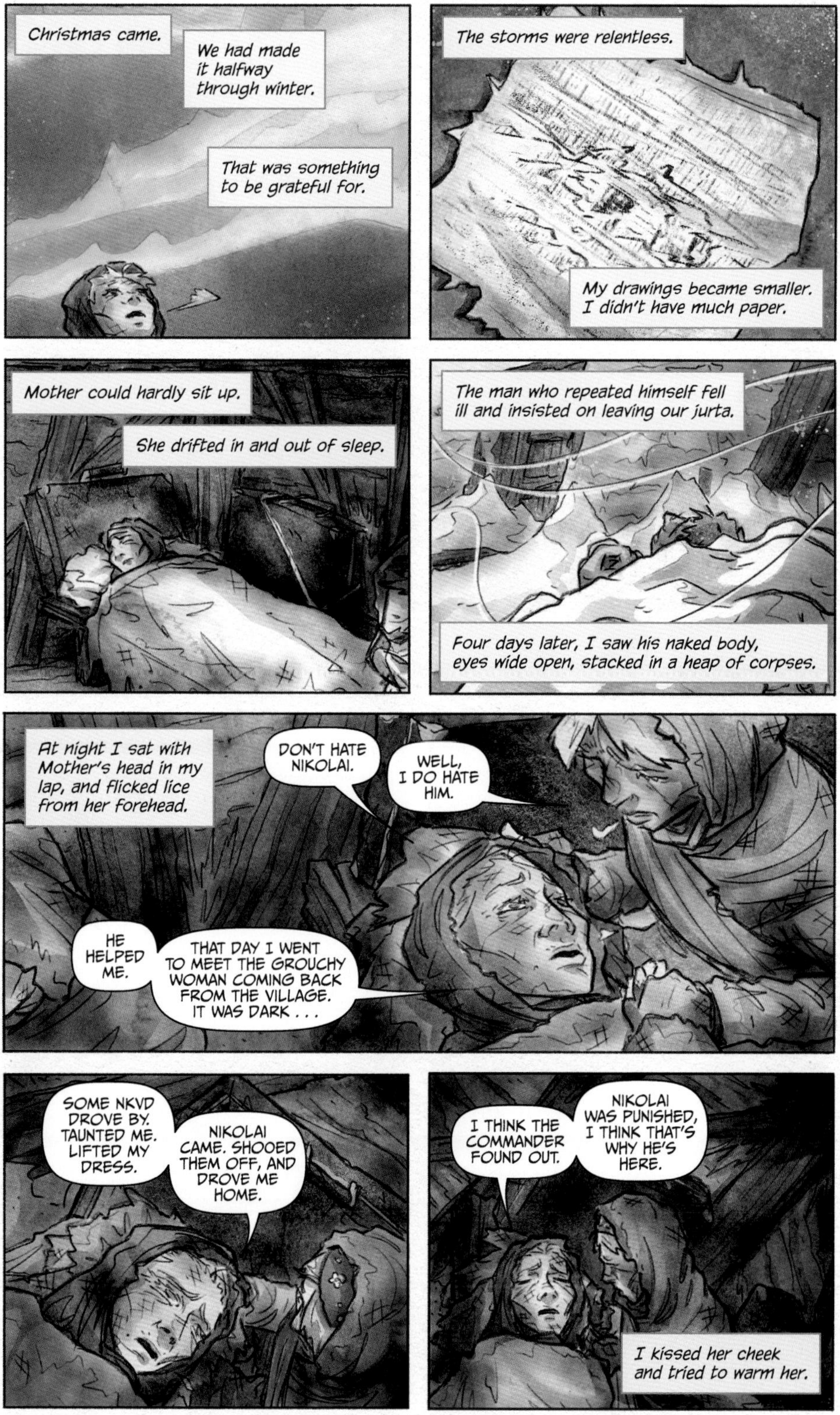

Christmas came.
We had made it halfway through winter.
That was something to be grateful for.
The storms were relentless.
My drawings became smaller. I didn't have much paper.
Mother could hardly sit up.
She drifted in and out of sleep.
The man who repeated himself fell ill and insisted on leaving our jurta.
Four days later, I saw his naked body, eyes wide open, stacked in a heap of corpses.
At night I sat with Mother's head in my lap, and flicked lice from her forehead.
DON'T HATE NIKOLAI.
WELL, I DO HATE HIM.
HE HELPED ME.
THAT DAY I WENT TO MEET THE GROUCHY WOMAN COMING BACK FROM THE VILLAGE. IT WAS DARK . . .
SOME NKVD DROVE BY. TAUNTED ME. LIFTED MY DRESS.
NIKOLAI CAME. SHOOED THEM OFF, AND DROVE ME HOME.
I THINK THE COMMANDER FOUND OUT.
NIKOLAI WAS PUNISHED, I THINK THAT'S WHY HE'S HERE.
I kissed her cheek and tried to warm her.

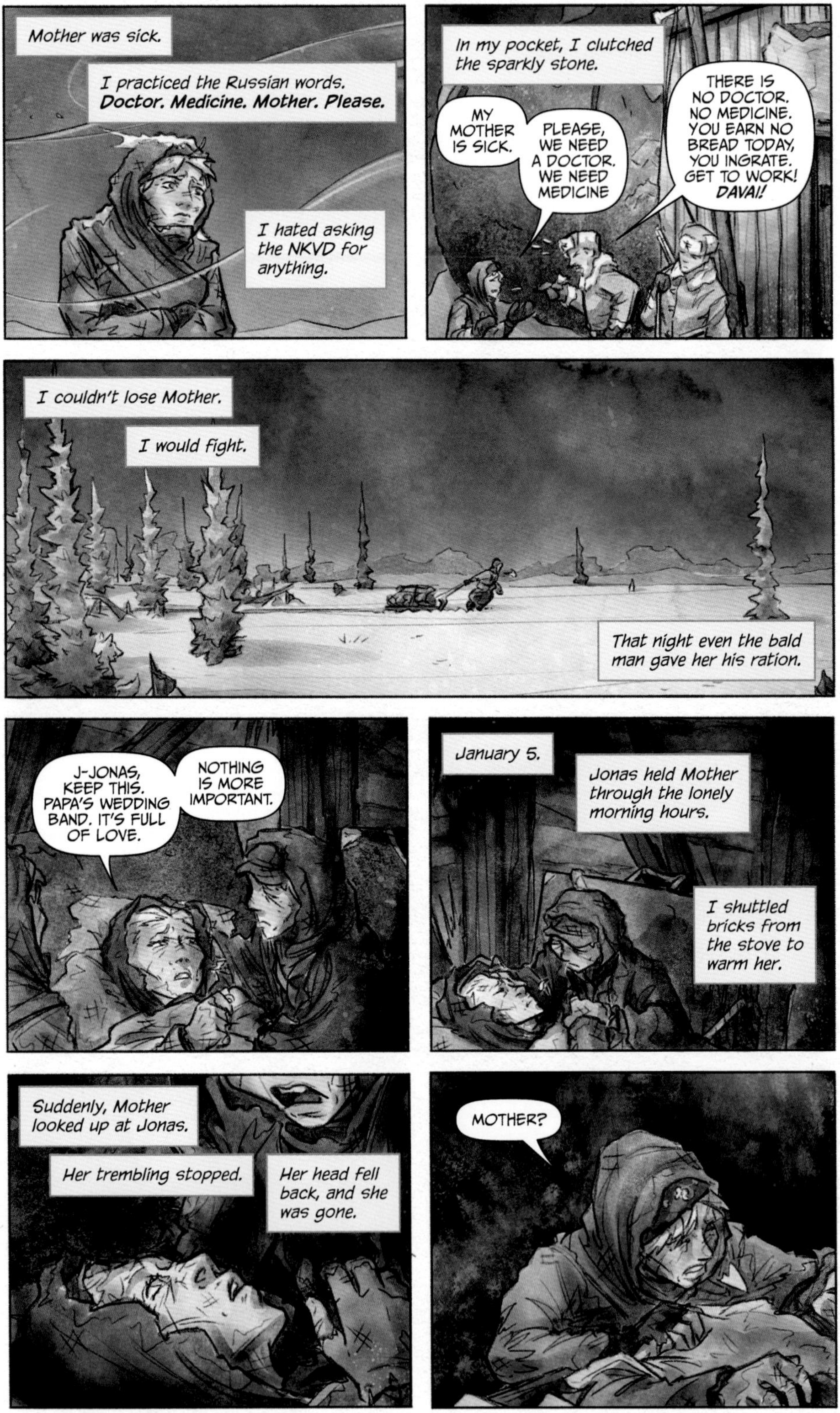
Mother was sick.
I practiced the Russian words. **Doctor. Medicine. Mother. Please.**
I hated asking the NKVD for anything.
In my pocket, I clutched the sparkly stone.
MY MOTHER IS SICK.
PLEASE, WE NEED A DOCTOR. WE NEED MEDICINE
THERE IS NO DOCTOR. NO MEDICINE. YOU EARN NO BREAD TODAY, YOU INGRATE. GET TO WORK! ***DAVAI!***
I couldn't lose Mother.
I would fight.
That night even the bald man gave her his ration.
J-JONAS, KEEP THIS. PAPA'S WEDDING BAND. IT'S FULL OF LOVE.
NOTHING IS MORE IMPORTANT.
January 5.
Jonas held Mother through the lonely morning hours.
I shuttled bricks from the stove to warm her.
Suddenly, Mother looked up at Jonas.
Her trembling stopped.
Her head fell back, and she was gone.
MOTHER?

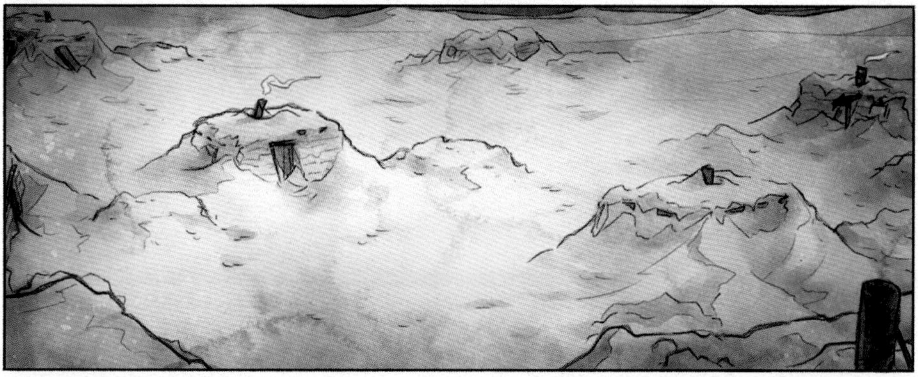

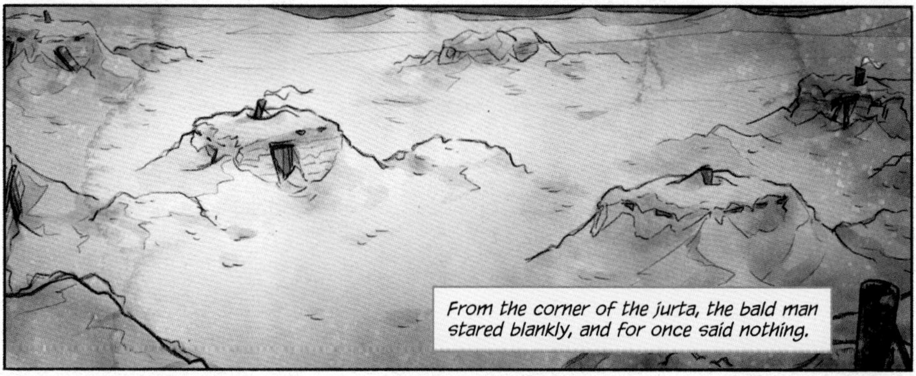
From the corner of the jurta, the bald man stared blankly, and for once said nothing.

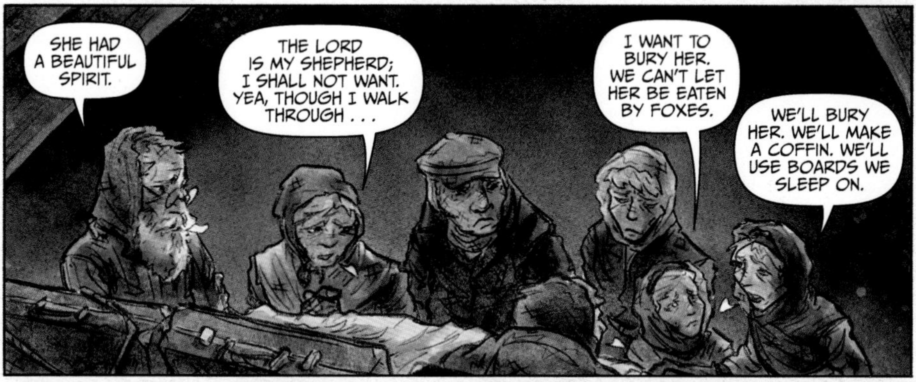
SHE HAD A BEAUTIFUL SPIRIT.
THE LORD IS MY SHEPHERD; I SHALL NOT WANT. YEA, THOUGH I WALK THROUGH . . .
I WANT TO BURY HER. WE CAN'T LET HER BE EATEN BY FOXES.
WE'LL BURY HER. WE'LL MAKE A COFFIN. WE'LL USE BOARDS WE SLEEP ON.

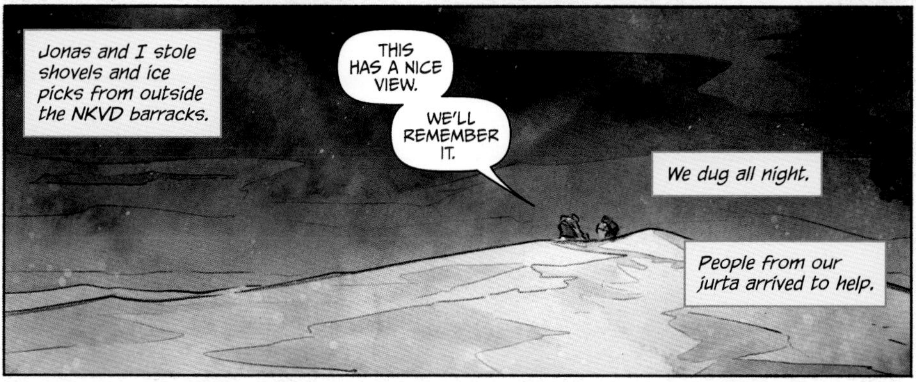
Jonas and I stole shovels and ice picks from outside the NKVD barracks.
THIS HAS A NICE VIEW.
WE'LL REMEMBER IT.
We dug all night.
People from our jurta arrived to help.

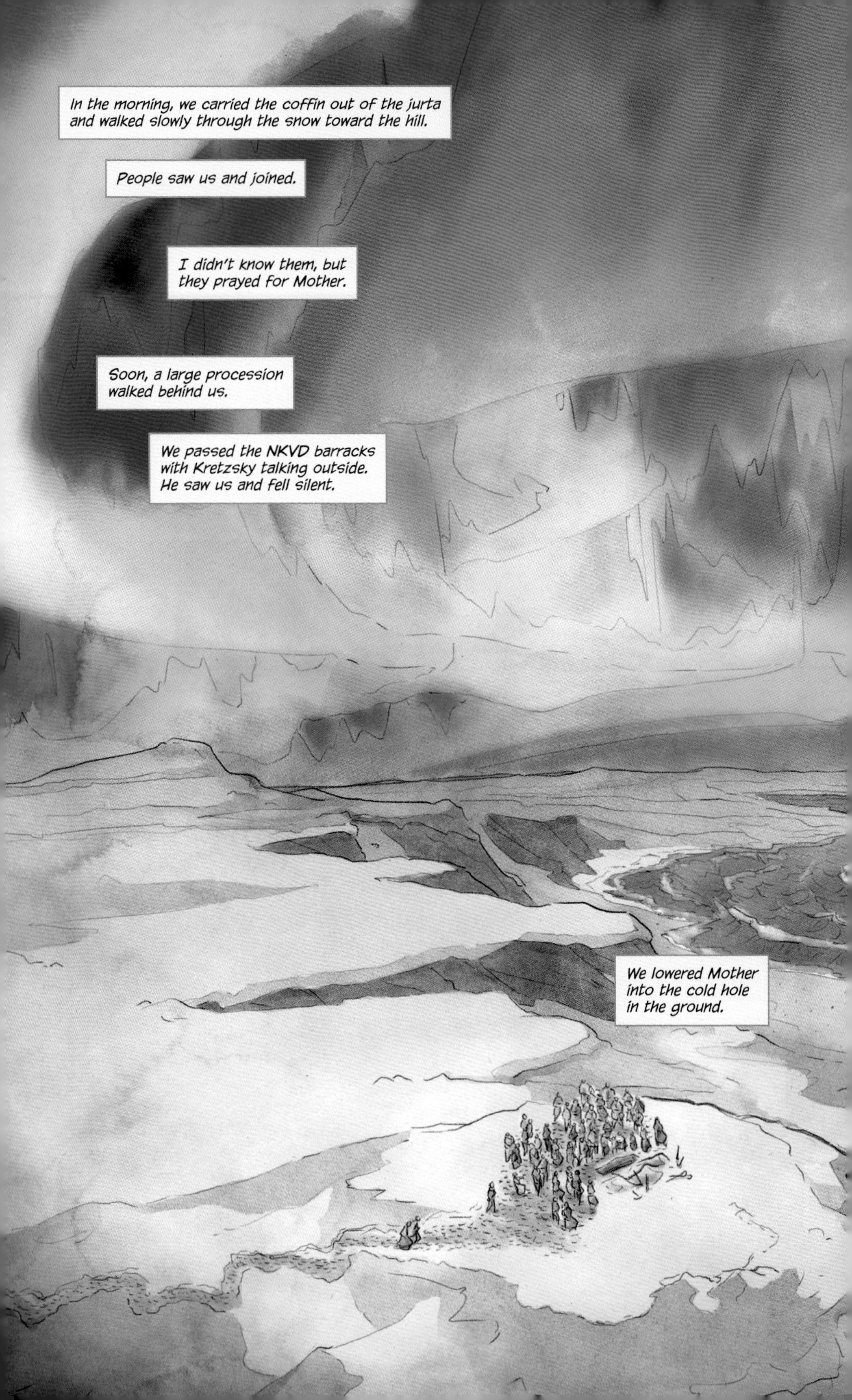
In the morning, we carried the coffin out of the jurta and walked slowly through the snow toward the hill.
People saw us and joined.
I didn't know them, but they prayed for Mother.
Soon, a large procession walked behind us.
We passed the NKVD barracks with Kretzsky talking outside. He saw us and fell silent.
We lowered Mother into the cold hole in the ground.

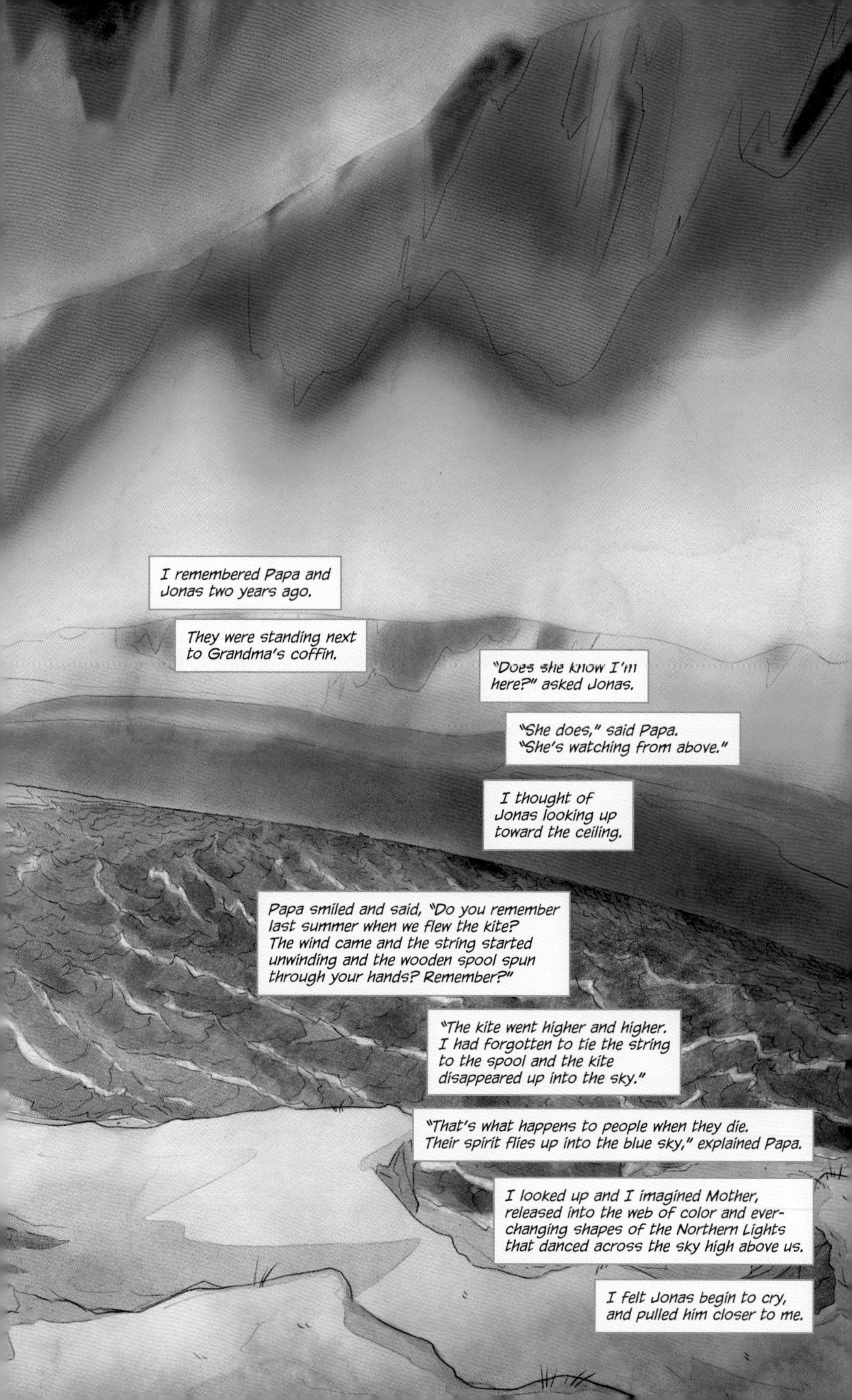

I remembered Papa and Jonas two years ago.
They were standing next to Grandma's coffin.
"Does she know I'm here?" asked Jonas.
"She does," said Papa. "She's watching from above."
I thought of Jonas looking up toward the ceiling.
Papa smiled and said, "Do you remember last summer when we flew the kite? The wind came and the string started unwinding and the wooden spool spun through your hands? Remember?"
"The kite went higher and higher. I had forgotten to tie the string to the spool and the kite disappeared up into the sky."
"That's what happens to people when they die. Their spirit flies up into the blue sky," explained Papa.
I looked up and I imagined Mother, released into the web of color and ever-changing shapes of the Northern Lights that danced across the sky high above us.
I felt Jonas begin to cry, and pulled him closer to me.

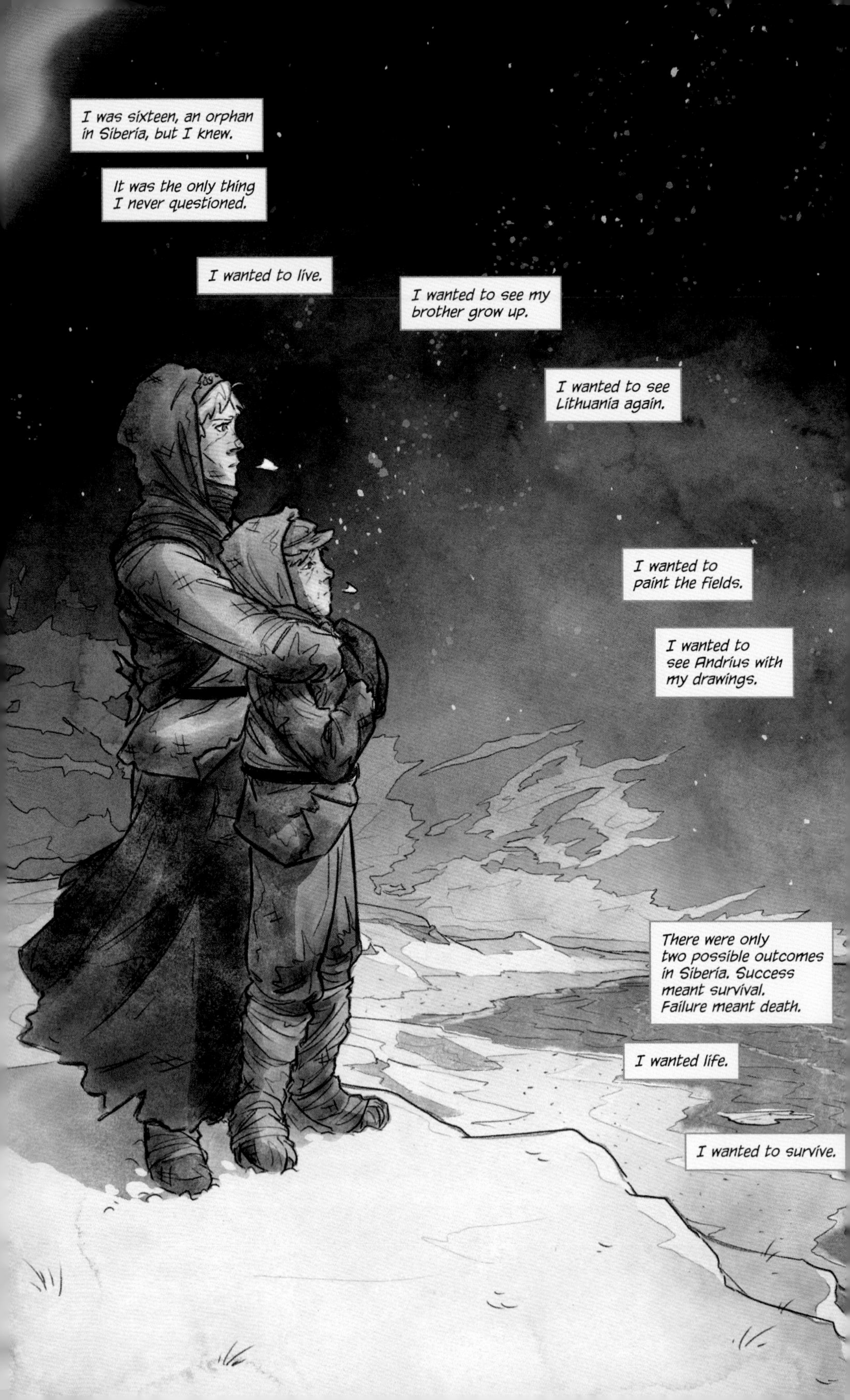
I was sixteen, an orphan in Siberia, but I knew.
It was the only thing I never questioned.
I wanted to live.
I wanted to see my brother grow up.
I wanted to see Lithuania again.
I wanted to paint the fields.
I wanted to see Andrius with my drawings.
There were only two possible outcomes in Siberia. Success meant survival. Failure meant death.
I wanted life.
I wanted to survive.

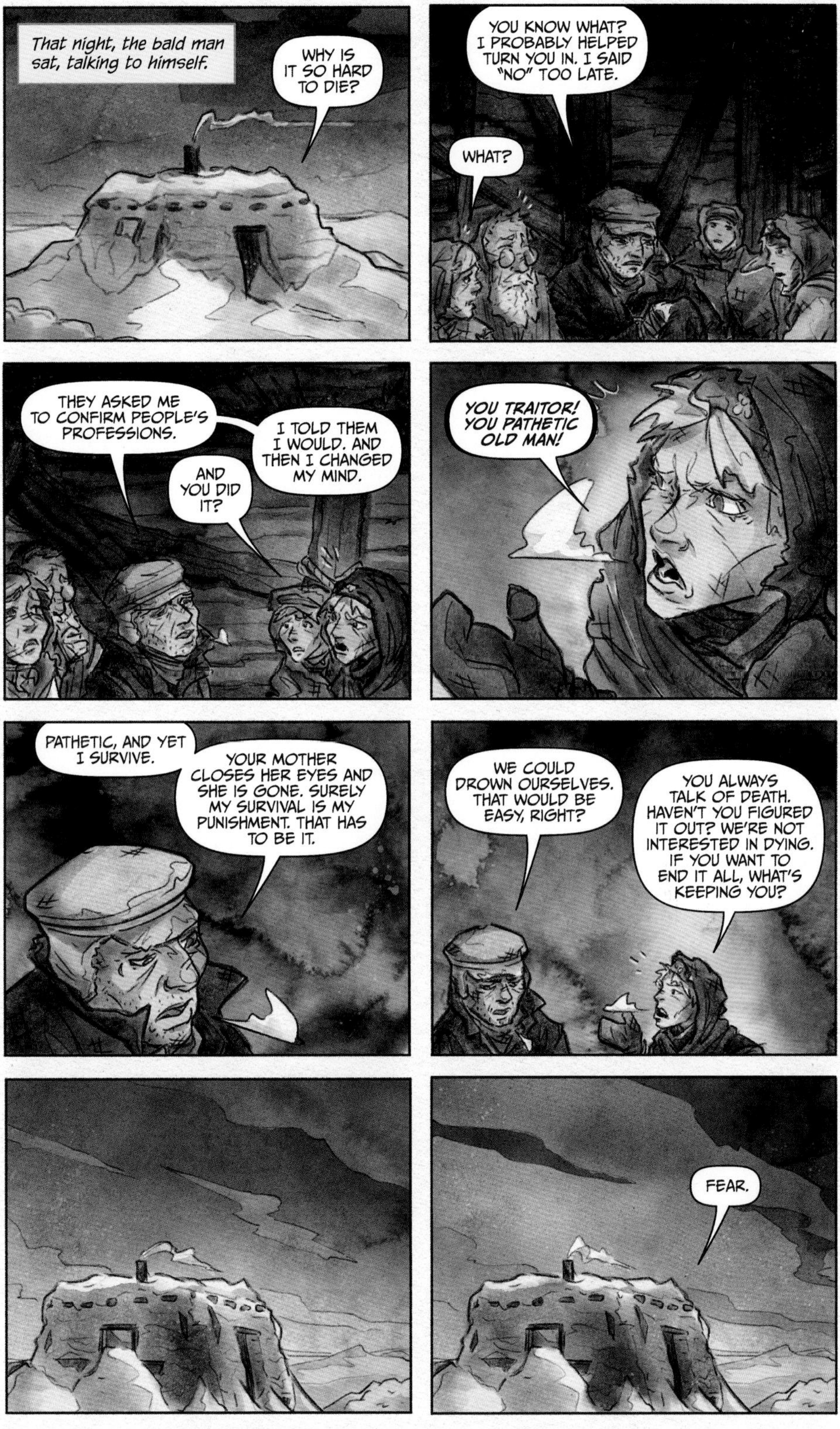

That night, the bald man sat, talking to himself.
WHY IS IT SO HARD TO DIE?
YOU KNOW WHAT? I PROBABLY HELPED TURN YOU IN. I SAID "NO" TOO LATE.
WHAT?
THEY ASKED ME TO CONFIRM PEOPLE'S PROFESSIONS.
I TOLD THEM I WOULD. AND THEN I CHANGED MY MIND.
AND YOU DID IT?
YOU TRAITOR! YOU PATHETIC OLD MAN!
PATHETIC, AND YET I SURVIVE.
YOUR MOTHER CLOSES HER EYES AND SHE IS GONE. SURELY MY SURVIVAL IS MY PUNISHMENT. THAT HAS TO BE IT.
WE COULD DROWN OURSELVES. THAT WOULD BE EASY, RIGHT?
YOU ALWAYS TALK OF DEATH. HAVEN'T YOU FIGURED IT OUT? WE'RE NOT INTERESTED IN DYING. IF YOU WANT TO END IT ALL, WHAT'S KEEPING YOU?
FEAR.

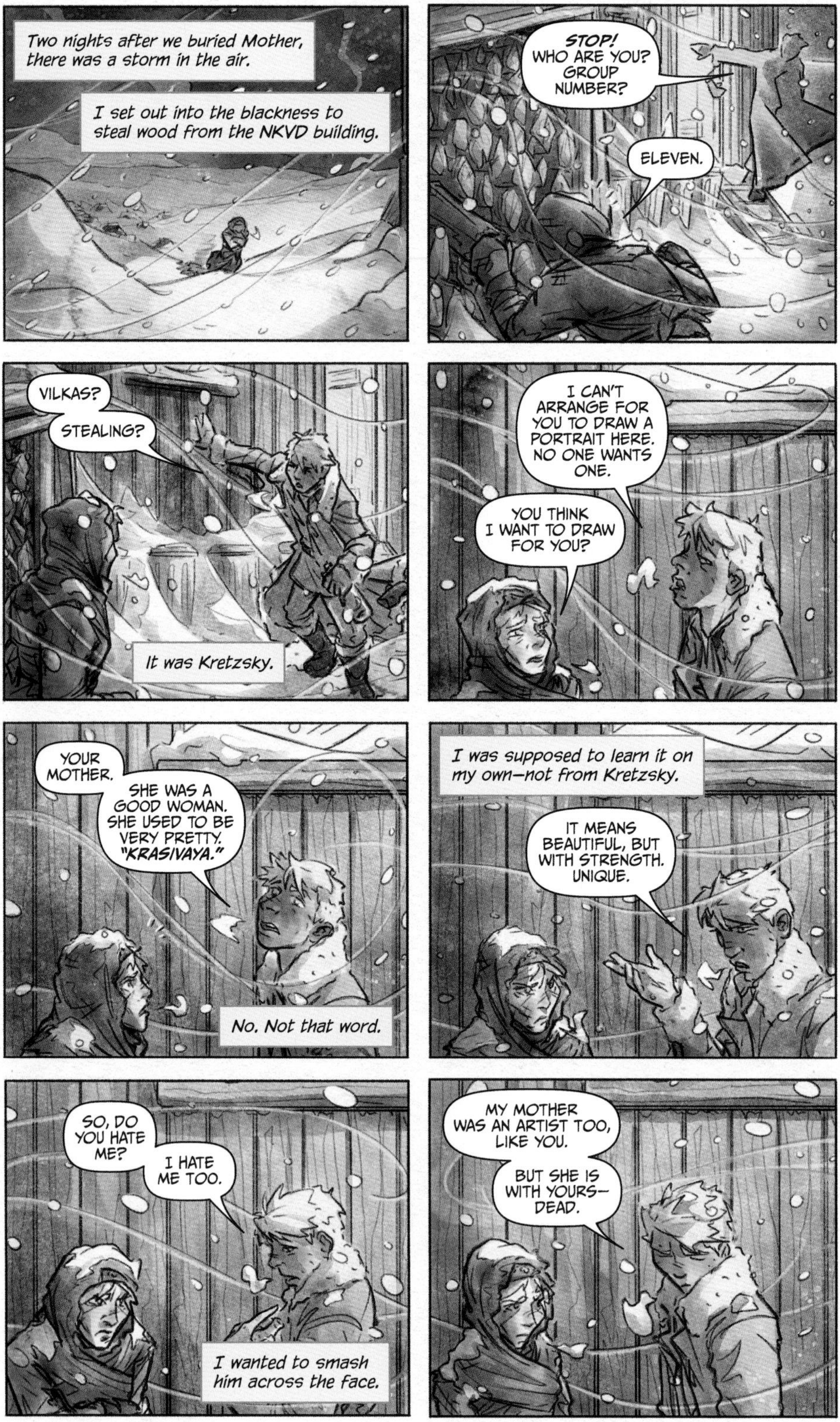
Two nights after we buried Mother, there was a storm in the air.
I set out into the blackness to steal wood from the NKVD building.
STOP! WHO ARE YOU? GROUP NUMBER?
ELEVEN.
VILKAS?
STEALING?
It was Kretzsky.
I CAN'T ARRANGE FOR YOU TO DRAW A PORTRAIT HERE. NO ONE WANTS ONE.
YOU THINK I WANT TO DRAW FOR YOU?
YOUR MOTHER.
SHE WAS A GOOD WOMAN. SHE USED TO BE VERY PRETTY. "KRASIVAYA."
No. Not that word.
I was supposed to learn it on my own—not from Kretzsky.
IT MEANS BEAUTIFUL, BUT WITH STRENGTH. UNIQUE.
SO, DO YOU HATE ME?
I HATE ME TOO.
I wanted to smash him across the face.
MY MOTHER WAS AN ARTIST TOO, LIKE YOU.
BUT SHE IS WITH YOURS—DEAD.

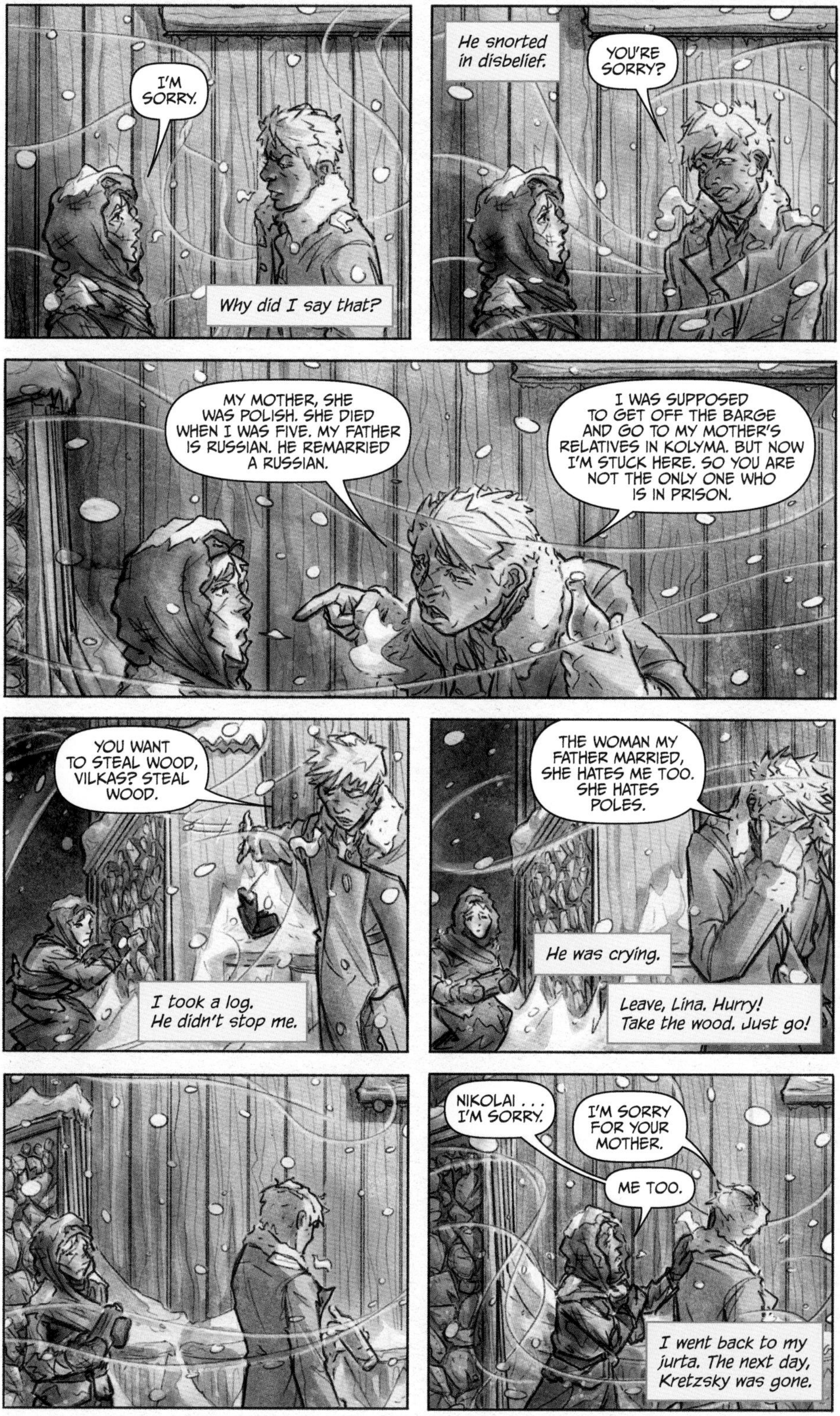
I'M SORRY.
Why did I say that?
He snorted in disbelief.
YOU'RE SORRY?
MY MOTHER, SHE WAS POLISH. SHE DIED WHEN I WAS FIVE. MY FATHER IS RUSSIAN. HE REMARRIED A RUSSIAN.
I WAS SUPPOSED TO GET OFF THE BARGE AND GO TO MY MOTHER'S RELATIVES IN KOLYMA. BUT NOW I'M STUCK HERE. SO YOU ARE NOT THE ONLY ONE WHO IS IN PRISON.
YOU WANT TO STEAL WOOD, VILKAS? STEAL WOOD.
I took a log. He didn't stop me.
THE WOMAN MY FATHER MARRIED, SHE HATES ME TOO. SHE HATES POLES.
He was crying.
Leave, Lina. Hurry! Take the wood. Just go!
NIKOLAI . . . I'M SORRY.
I'M SORRY FOR YOUR MOTHER.
ME TOO.
I went back to my jurta. The next day, Kretzsky was gone.

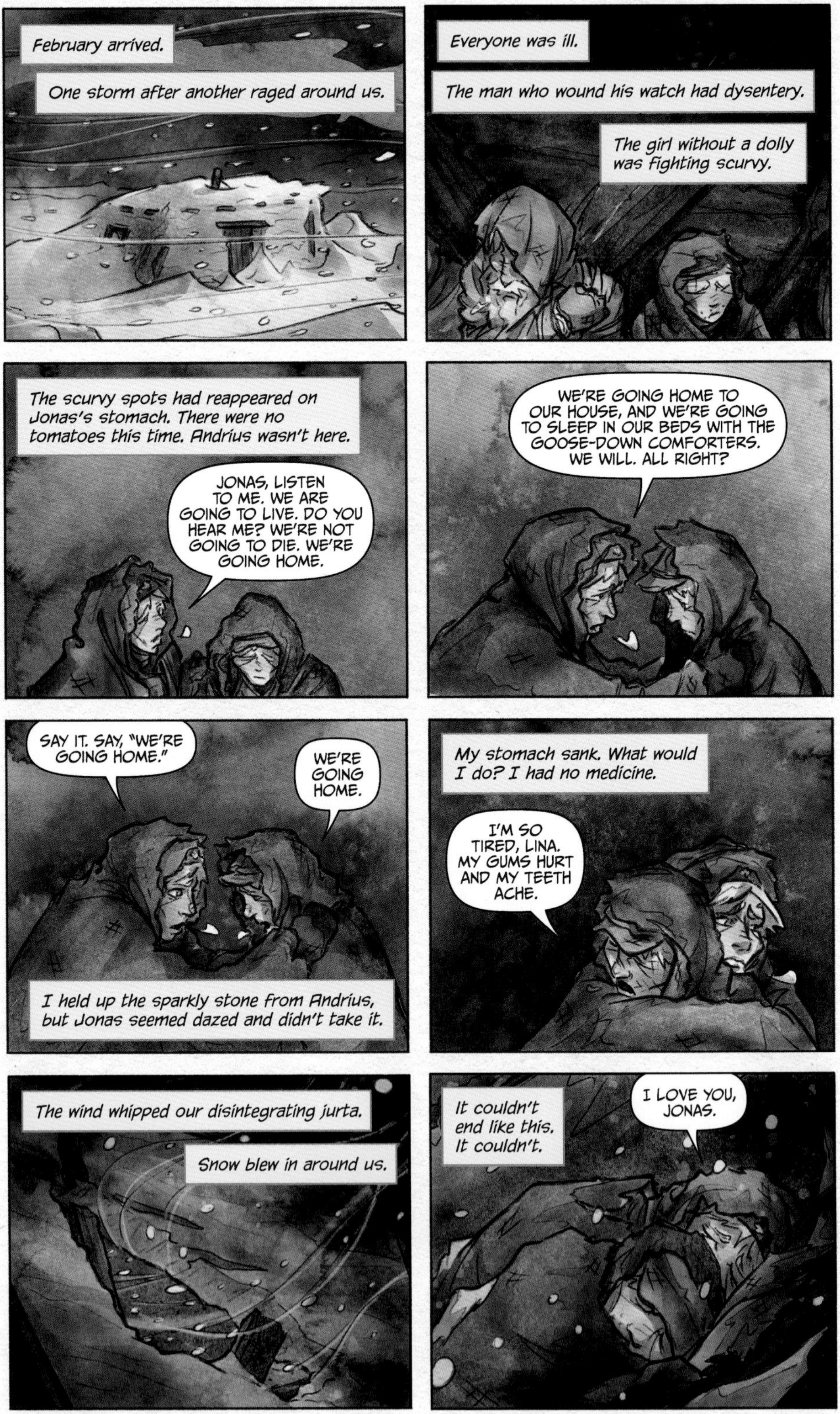

February arrived.
One storm after another raged around us.
Everyone was ill.
The man who wound his watch had dysentery.
The girl without a dolly was fighting scurvy.
The scurvy spots had reappeared on Jonas's stomach. There were no tomatoes this time. Andrius wasn't here.
JONAS, LISTEN TO ME. WE ARE GOING TO LIVE. DO YOU HEAR ME? WE'RE NOT GOING TO DIE. WE'RE GOING HOME.
WE'RE GOING HOME TO OUR HOUSE, AND WE'RE GOING TO SLEEP IN OUR BEDS WITH THE GOOSE-DOWN COMFORTERS. WE WILL. ALL RIGHT?
SAY IT. SAY, "WE'RE GOING HOME."
WE'RE GOING HOME.
I held up the sparkly stone from Andrius, but Jonas seemed dazed and didn't take it.
My stomach sank. What would I do? I had no medicine.
I'M SO TIRED, LINA. MY GUMS HURT AND MY TEETH ACHE.
The wind whipped our disintegrating jurta.
Snow blew in around us.
It couldn't end like this. It couldn't.
I LOVE YOU, JONAS.

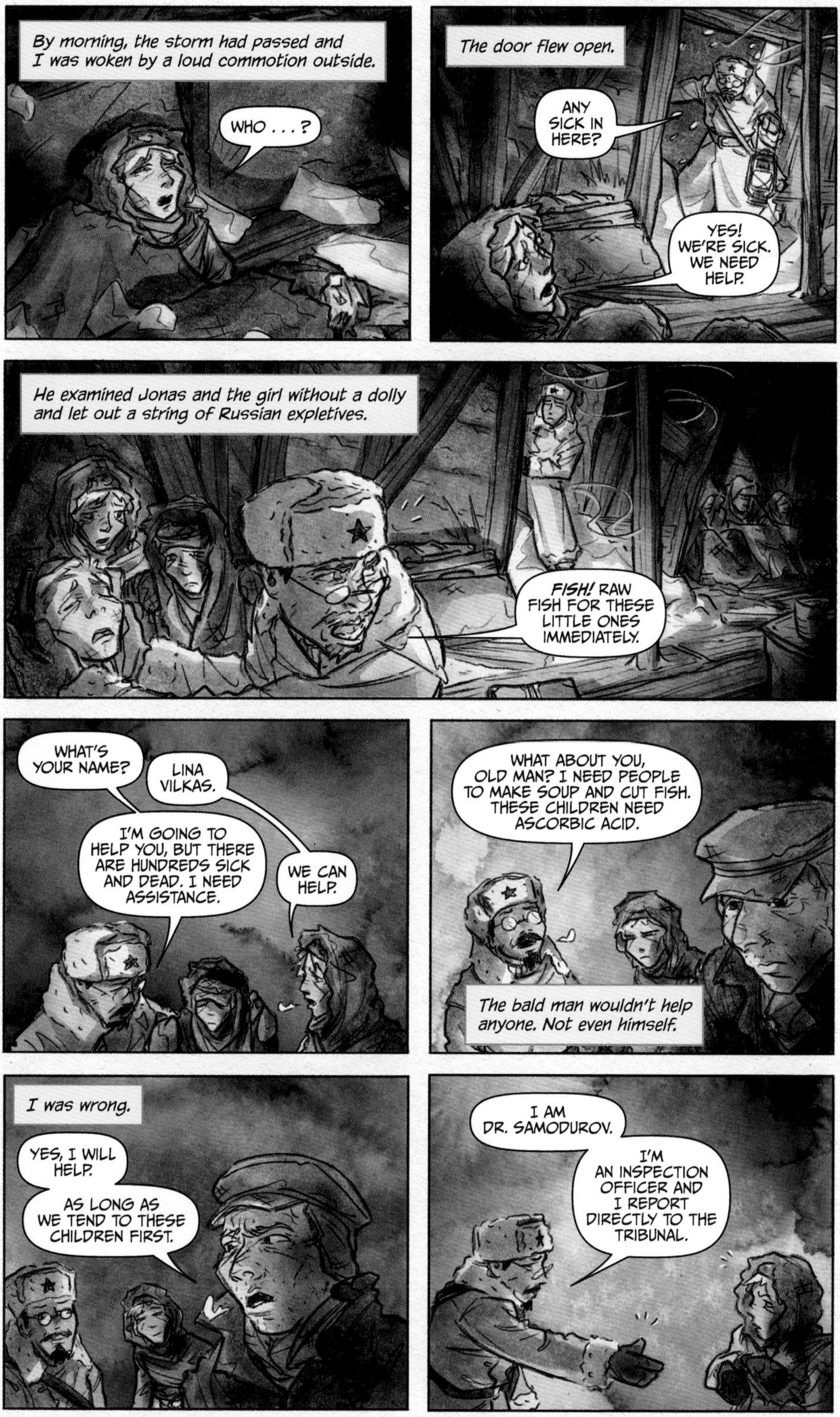
By morning, the storm had passed and I was woken by a loud commotion outside.
WHO . . . ?
The door flew open.
ANY SICK IN HERE?
YES! WE'RE SICK. WE NEED HELP.
He examined Jonas and the girl without a dolly and let out a string of Russian expletives.
FISH! RAW FISH FOR THESE LITTLE ONES IMMEDIATELY.
WHAT'S YOUR NAME?
LINA VILKAS.
I'M GOING TO HELP YOU, BUT THERE ARE HUNDREDS SICK AND DEAD. I NEED ASSISTANCE.
WE CAN HELP.
WHAT ABOUT YOU, OLD MAN? I NEED PEOPLE TO MAKE SOUP AND CUT FISH. THESE CHILDREN NEED ASCORBIC ACID.
The bald man wouldn't help anyone. Not even himself.
I was wrong.
YES, I WILL HELP.
AS LONG AS WE TEND TO THESE CHILDREN FIRST.
I AM DR. SAMODUROV.
I'M AN INSPECTION OFFICER AND I REPORT DIRECTLY TO THE TRIBUNAL.

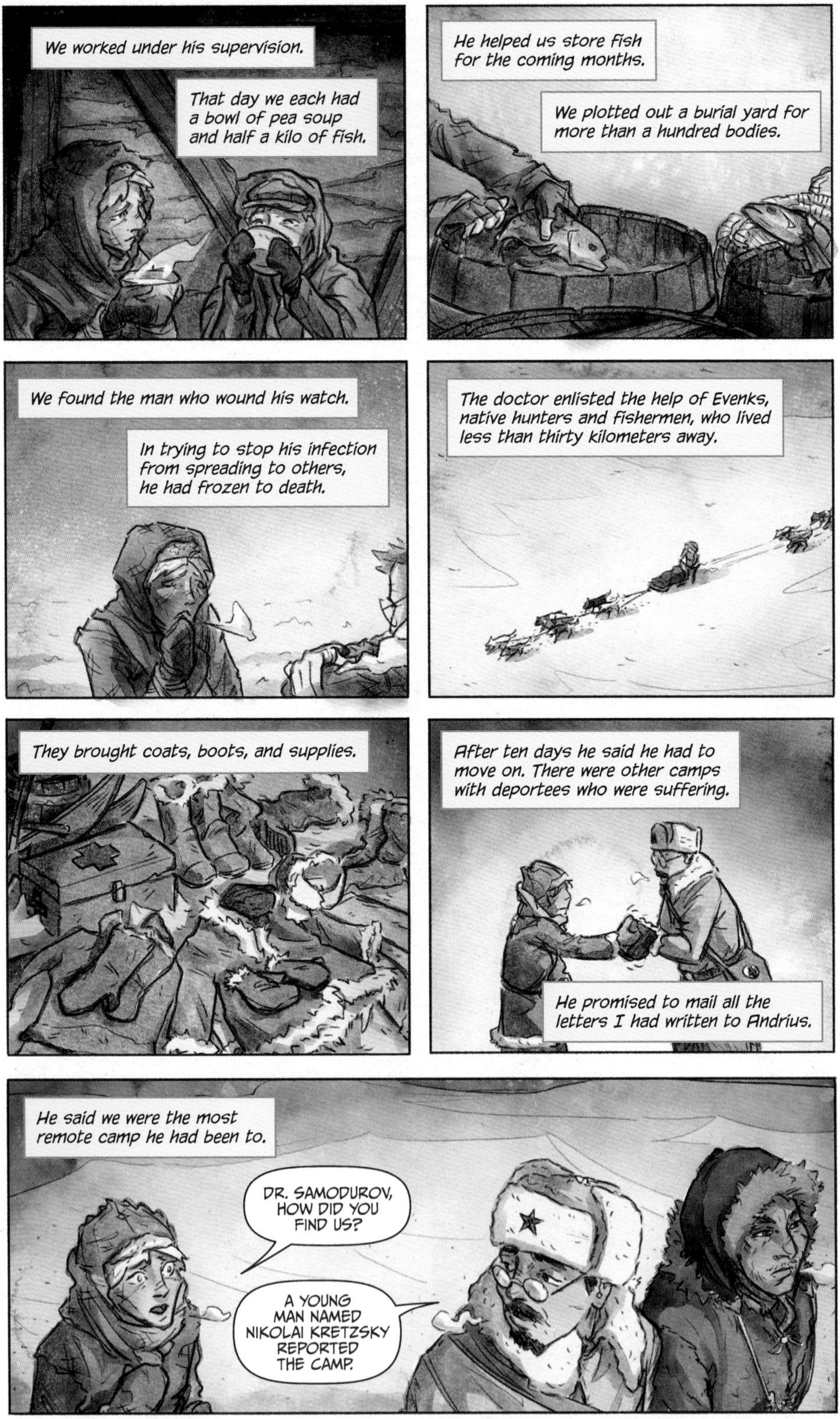

We worked under his supervision.
That day we each had a bowl of pea soup and half a kilo of fish.
He helped us store fish for the coming months.
We plotted out a burial yard for more than a hundred bodies.
We found the man who wound his watch.
In trying to stop his infection from spreading to others, he had frozen to death.
The doctor enlisted the help of Evenks, native hunters and fishermen, who lived less than thirty kilometers away.
They brought coats, boots, and supplies.
After ten days he said he had to move on. There were other camps with deportees who were suffering.
He promised to mail all the letters I had written to Andrius.
He said we were the most remote camp he had been to.
DR. SAMODUROV, HOW DID YOU FIND US?
A YOUNG MAN NAMED NIKOLAI KRETZSKY REPORTED THE CAMP.

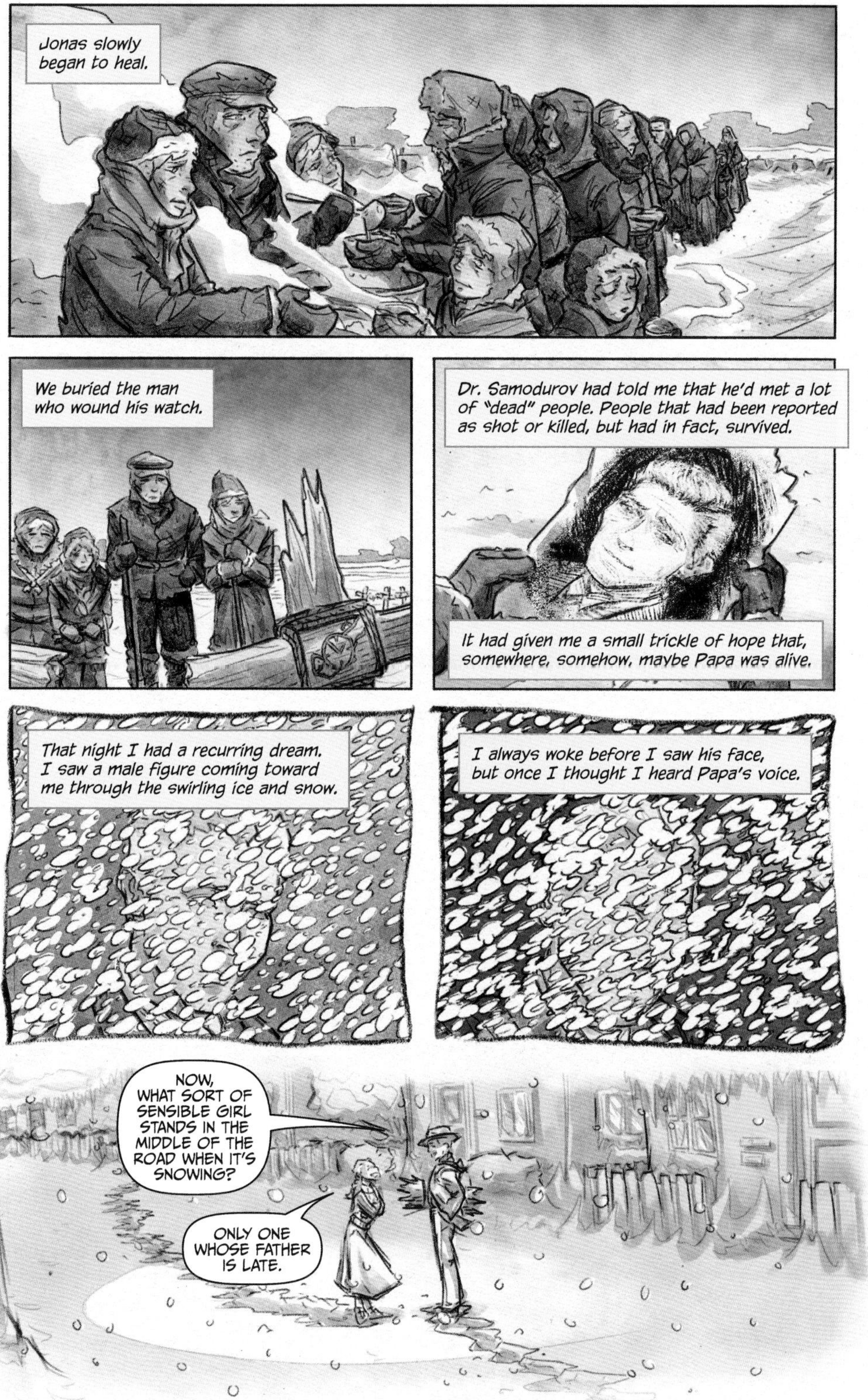
Jonas slowly began to heal.
We buried the man who wound his watch.
Dr. Samodurov had told me that he'd met a lot of "dead" people. People that had been reported as shot or killed, but had in fact, survived.
It had given me a small trickle of hope that, somewhere, somehow, maybe Papa was alive.
That night I had a recurring dream. I saw a male figure coming toward me through the swirling ice and snow.
I always woke before I saw his face, but once I thought I heard Papa's voice.
NOW, WHAT SORT OF SENSIBLE GIRL STANDS IN THE MIDDLE OF THE ROAD WHEN IT'S SNOWING?
ONLY ONE WHOSE FATHER IS LATE.

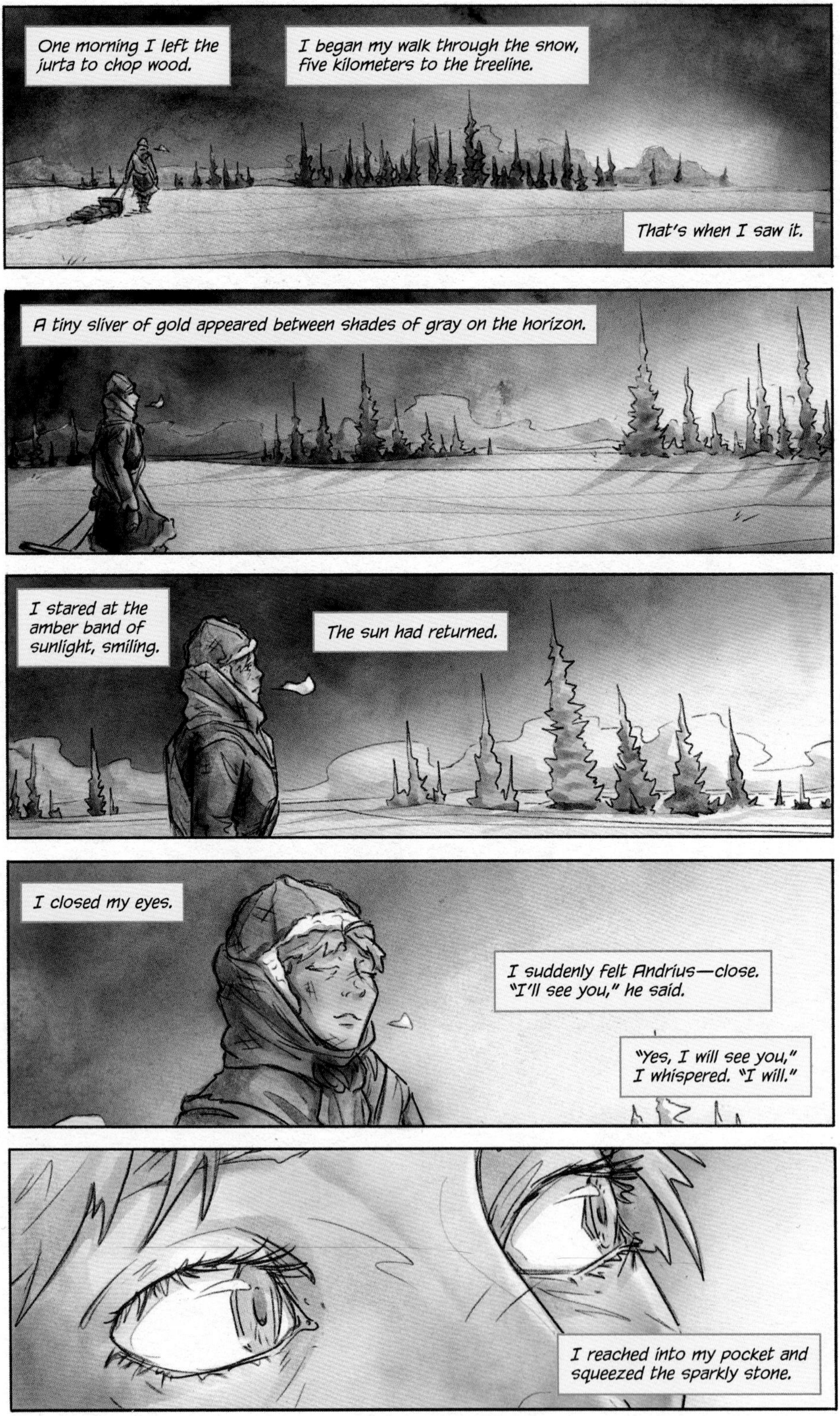
One morning I left the jurta to chop wood.
I began my walk through the snow, five kilometers to the treeline.
That's when I saw it.
A tiny sliver of gold appeared between shades of gray on the horizon.
I stared at the amber band of sunlight, smiling.
The sun had returned.
I closed my eyes.
I suddenly felt Andrius—close. "I'll see you," he said.
"Yes, I will see you," I whispered. "I will."
I reached into my pocket and squeezed the sparkly stone.

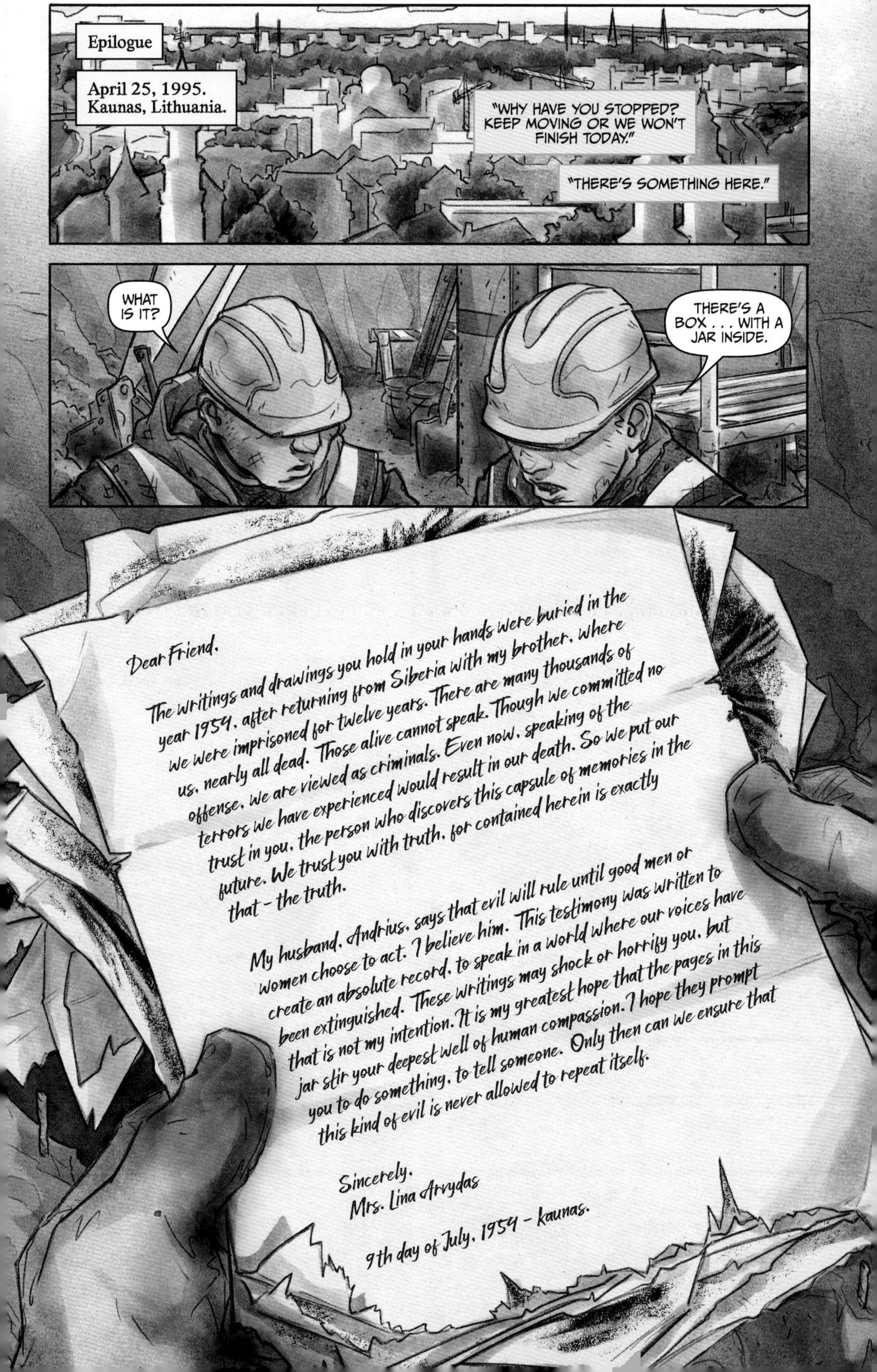
Epilogue
April 25, 1995.
Kaunas, Lithuania.
"WHY HAVE YOU STOPPED? KEEP MOVING OR WE WON'T FINISH TODAY."
"THERE'S SOMETHING HERE."
WHAT IS IT?
THERE'S A BOX . . . WITH A JAR INSIDE.
Dear Friend,
The writings and drawings you hold in your hands were buried in the year 1954, after returning from Siberia with my brother, where we were imprisoned for twelve years. There are many thousands of us, nearly all dead. Those alive cannot speak. Though we committed no offense, we are viewed as criminals. Even now, speaking of the terrors we have experienced would result in our death. So we put our trust in you, the person who discovers this capsule of memories in the future. We trust you with truth, for contained herein is exactly that – the truth.
My husband, Andrius, says that evil will rule until good men or women choose to act. I believe him. This testimony was written to create an absolute record, to speak in a world where our voices have been extinguished. These writings may shock or horrify you, but that is not my intention. It is my greatest hope that the pages in this jar stir your deepest well of human compassion. I hope they prompt you to do something, to tell someone. Only then can we ensure that this kind of evil is never allowed to repeat itself.
Sincerely,
Mrs. Lina Arvydas
9th day of July, 1954 – kaunas.

AUTHOR'S NOTE - RUTA SEPTYS

"In the depth of winter, I finally learned that within me there lay an invincible summer."

- Albert Camus

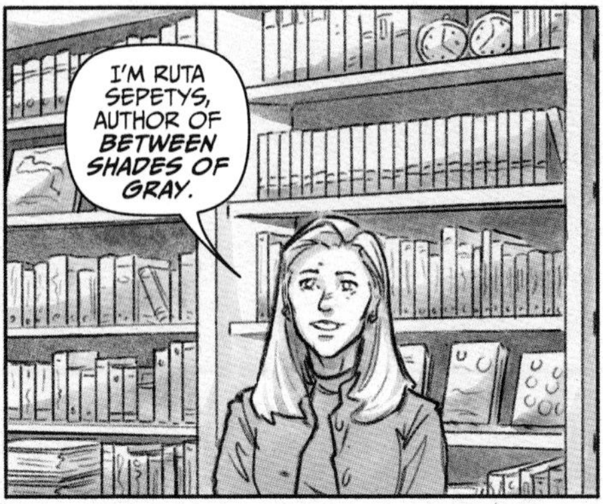
I'M RUTA SEPETYS, AUTHOR OF *BETWEEN SHADES OF GRAY*.

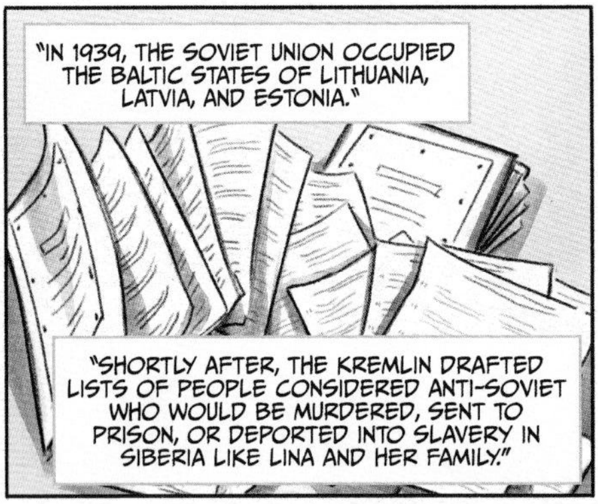
"IN 1939, THE SOVIET UNION OCCUPIED THE BALTIC STATES OF LITHUANIA, LATVIA, AND ESTONIA."
"SHORTLY AFTER, THE KREMLIN DRAFTED LISTS OF PEOPLE CONSIDERED ANTI-SOVIET WHO WOULD BE MURDERED, SENT TO PRISON, OR DEPORTED INTO SLAVERY IN SIBERIA LIKE LINA AND HER FAMILY."

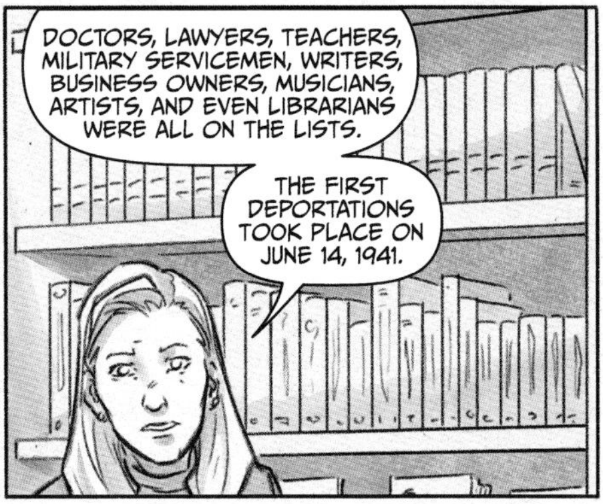
DOCTORS, LAWYERS, TEACHERS, MILITARY SERVICEMEN, WRITERS, BUSINESS OWNERS, MUSICIANS, ARTISTS, AND EVEN LIBRARIANS WERE ALL ON THE LISTS.
THE FIRST DEPORTATIONS TOOK PLACE ON JUNE 14, 1941.

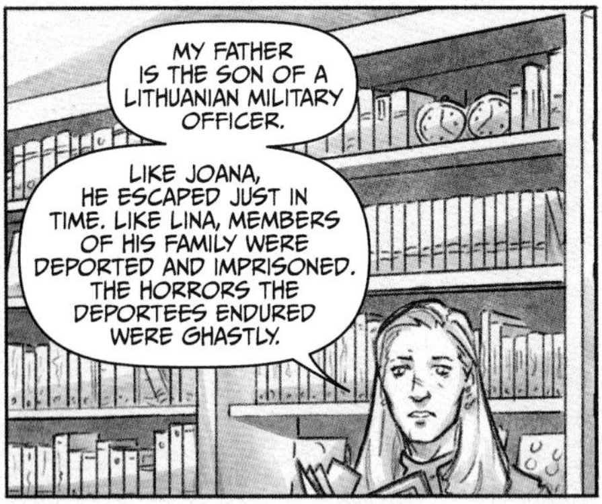
MY FATHER IS THE SON OF A LITHUANIAN MILITARY OFFICER.
LIKE JOANA, HE ESCAPED JUST IN TIME. LIKE LINA, MEMBERS OF HIS FAMILY WERE DEPORTED AND IMPRISONED. THE HORRORS THE DEPORTEES ENDURED WERE GHASTLY.

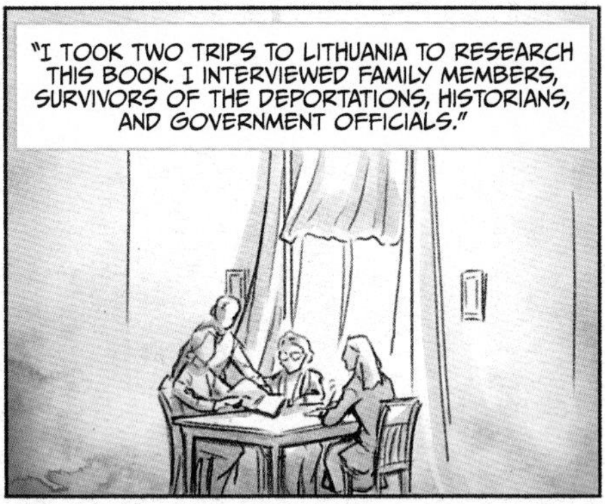
"I TOOK TWO TRIPS TO LITHUANIA TO RESEARCH THIS BOOK. I INTERVIEWED FAMILY MEMBERS, SURVIVORS OF THE DEPORTATIONS, HISTORIANS, AND GOVERNMENT OFFICIALS."

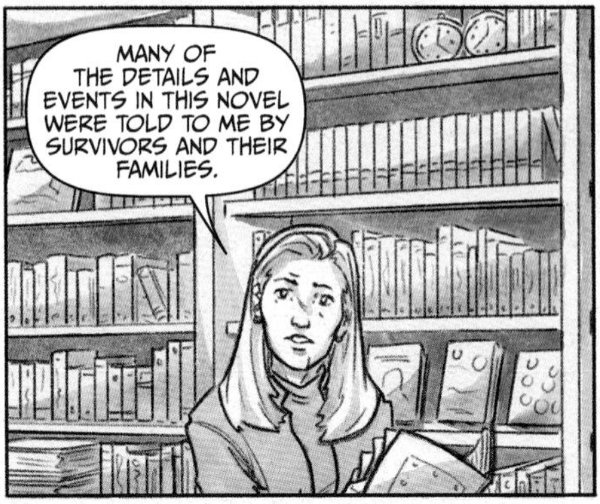
MANY OF THE DETAILS AND EVENTS IN THIS NOVEL WERE TOLD TO ME BY SURVIVORS AND THEIR FAMILIES.

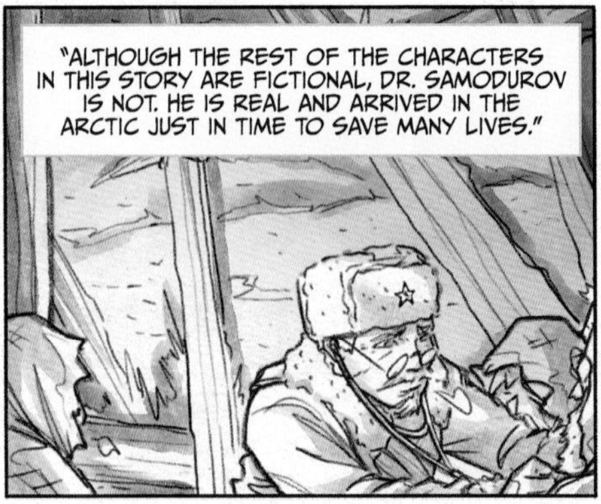
"ALTHOUGH THE REST OF THE CHARACTERS IN THIS STORY ARE FICTIONAL, DR. SAMODUROV IS NOT. HE IS REAL AND ARRIVED IN THE ARCTIC JUST IN TIME TO SAVE MANY LIVES."

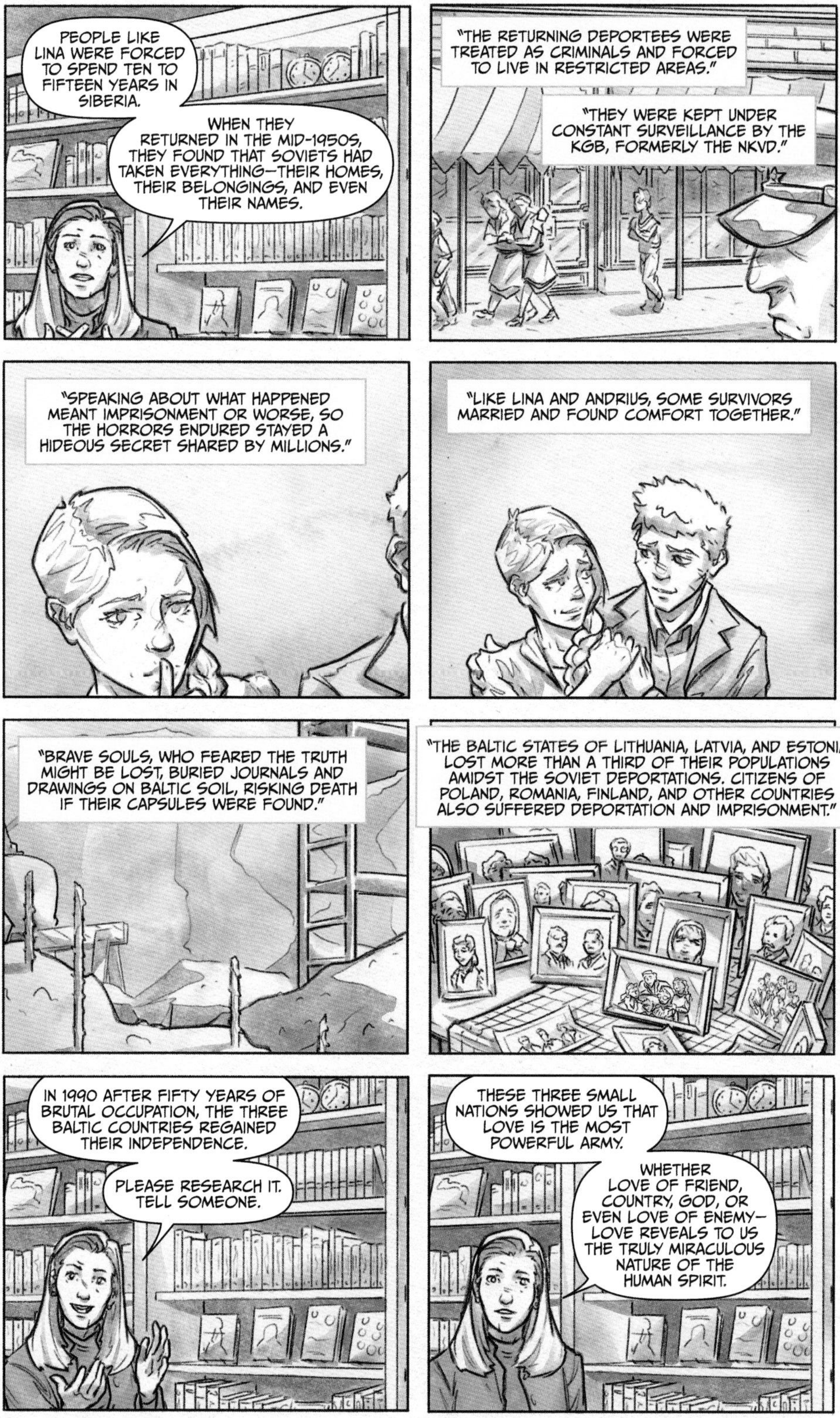
PEOPLE LIKE LINA WERE FORCED TO SPEND TEN TO FIFTEEN YEARS IN SIBERIA.
WHEN THEY RETURNED IN THE MID-1950S, THEY FOUND THAT SOVIETS HAD TAKEN EVERYTHING—THEIR HOMES, THEIR BELONGINGS, AND EVEN THEIR NAMES.
"THE RETURNING DEPORTEES WERE TREATED AS CRIMINALS AND FORCED TO LIVE IN RESTRICTED AREAS."
"THEY WERE KEPT UNDER CONSTANT SURVEILLANCE BY THE KGB, FORMERLY THE NKVD."
"SPEAKING ABOUT WHAT HAPPENED MEANT IMPRISONMENT OR WORSE, SO THE HORRORS ENDURED STAYED A HIDEOUS SECRET SHARED BY MILLIONS."
"LIKE LINA AND ANDRIUS, SOME SURVIVORS MARRIED AND FOUND COMFORT TOGETHER."
"BRAVE SOULS, WHO FEARED THE TRUTH MIGHT BE LOST, BURIED JOURNALS AND DRAWINGS ON BALTIC SOIL, RISKING DEATH IF THEIR CAPSULES WERE FOUND."
"THE BALTIC STATES OF LITHUANIA, LATVIA, AND ESTONIA LOST MORE THAN A THIRD OF THEIR POPULATIONS AMIDST THE SOVIET DEPORTATIONS. CITIZENS OF POLAND, ROMANIA, FINLAND, AND OTHER COUNTRIES ALSO SUFFERED DEPORTATION AND IMPRISONMENT."
IN 1990 AFTER FIFTY YEARS OF BRUTAL OCCUPATION, THE THREE BALTIC COUNTRIES REGAINED THEIR INDEPENDENCE.
PLEASE RESEARCH IT. TELL SOMEONE.
THESE THREE SMALL NATIONS SHOWED US THAT LOVE IS THE MOST POWERFUL ARMY.
WHETHER LOVE OF FRIEND, COUNTRY, GOD, OR EVEN LOVE OF ENEMY—LOVE REVEALS TO US THE TRULY MIRACULOUS NATURE OF THE HUMAN SPIRIT.

ACKNOWLEDGMENTS

I'm so grateful to my editor, Liza Kaplan, who suggested a graphic novel edition, Talia Benamy, and Ellice Lee who assembled such an incredible team. Andrew, Dave, Brann, and Chris—thank you from the bottom of my heart! Steve Malk, Philomel, my husband, and my family make all things possible. To victims of oppression, past and present: We see your strength and courage in the face of repression. We support you in your call for freedom, democracy, and dialogue. You are not forgotten.

—RUTA SEPETYS

With grateful thanks to everyone on the A-Team who created this book. That's Liza; Ellice; Talia; our brilliant artist, Dave; colorist, Brann; and Chris Dickey, aka the World's Greatest Letterer. Special double-page-spread-sized thanks to Ruta for being so lovely to work with and for writing such a brilliant novel in the first place. Thank you all so much. Gratitude and homefront hugs to Viv Francis, Lexie Donkin, and Fisher Donkin. Finally, a doff of the creative cap to Sophie Hicks and Ron Fogelman. Be seeing you.

—ANDREW DONKIN

An unquantifiable thank-you to Brann Livesay, who championed overseeing the colors that breathed life into the linework, and who brought a steadfast focus to this book's art, page by page.

Appreciation goes out to Ruta Sepetys, Andrew Donkin, and Chris Dickey—accomplished veterans in their fields who are all humbling forces to collaborate with.

Notable thanks and immense gratitude to the incredibly talented team whose additional contributions carried the color to where it needed to go—Anthony Miller Jr., Haley Potter, Antonio Scricco, Matthew Hernandez, Christina Rycz, and Tarynn Ortiz.

Thank you to the folks at Philomel and Penguin Young Readers who saw to the assurance that this book would take material form, especially Ellice M. Lee, Liza Kaplan, Monique Sterling, Talia Benamy, and Vicki Olsen. They make the craft of quality book-making look easy, when in fact it can be completely otherwise.

And a particular thanks to my family and my family of friends, whose support on creative ventures like this one means more to me than I can ever truly convey. The multitude of kindnesses you've thrown my way are not lost on me.

Finally, one extra-special shout-out to Floyd, Pat, Tom, and Phil. The influence of your mentorship in visual storytelling is expansive. Your enthusiasm for the craft is unmatched, and inspiring beyond measure. Thank you.

—DAVE KOPKA